continued . . .

"[*The Dragon Master*] provided a quick break from reality that carried me away just for a little while . . . I found it an enjoyable story and a series that I'd like to continue."

—*All About Romance*

"A very entertaining, readable, and superhot story . . . I enjoyed the twists and turns of this one and, as always, appreciate the light humorous touches . . . The story and the relationship proceed at a measured pace with gradually increasing tension. And the tension and sexual interactions between our hero and heroine are red-hot from the first."

—*Queue My Review*

The Black Dragon

"One of my favorite authors. A unique and magical urban paranormal with dragons, witches, and demons. Will keep you enthralled until the very last word!"

—Cheyenne McCray, *New York Times* bestselling author of *The First Sin*

"Tasty and tempting reading! HOT."　　　—*Romantic Times*

"A fabulously delicious read."　　　—*Darque Reviews*

"Begins with a bang and the action never lets up, not for one single, solitary, wonderful moment. I devoured this book in just a few hours . . . So overwhelming that I couldn't even consider putting this book down. The story is unusual, wonderfully original and filled with intriguing characters . . . Dragons, magic, and a fight to save the world—Allyson James has a winning combination that makes *The Black Dragon* a story to remember!"　　　—*Romance Reader at Heart*

"A book destined to leave a smile on your face and dragons in your dreams. Get your copy today."

—*Romance Reviews Today*

"[Allyson James] keeps the sexual tension up to the point of boiling . . . Such an incredible talent."　　　—*TwoLips Reviews*

Dragon Heat

"A new series filled with magic, humor, and excitement. Exciting and passionate, this story is gripping from beginning to end."
—*Romantic Times*

"[A] delightful romantic fantasy . . . A fun tale of life between a mortal and her dragon."
—*The Best Reviews*

"Ms. James's imaginative story is exceptionally intriguing . . . Highly sensual."
—*The Eternal Night*

"This story has a wonderful fairy-tale feel about it. Allyson James does an outstanding job of creating and bringing these mystical creatures to life with characteristics and emotions that you can't help but fall deeply in love with; even the so-called *evil* Black Dragon with his cocky, bad-boy qualities will make the reader hum in pleasure and clamor for his story."
—*TwoLips Reviews*

"A sizzling paranormal romance. Ms. James pens a riveting story that's brimming with action, sinfully sexy characters, and the beautiful gift of love. A magical and thoroughly enchanting read."
—*Darque Reviews*

"A sexy, funny romantic romp . . . A truly mesmerizing read. The chemistry between Caleb and Lisa is searing and the love scenes are wonderfully entertaining."
—*Romance Reader at Heart*

Mortal Temptations

"The balance of intrigue, romance, and unbridled sexual fantasies makes James's story of gods, demigods, and mortals a sizzling page-turner. This book is the start of a series featuring these delicious partners."
—*Romantic Times*

"Hot! Hot! Hot! It doesn't get much hotter than this one . . . If you enjoy stories full of action, both in the bedroom and out, this is one story you will want to read."
—*The Romance Studio*

Stormwalker

Allyson James

BERKLEY SENSATION, NEW YORK

THE BERKLEY PUBLISHING GROUP
Published by the Penguin Group
Penguin Group (USA) Inc.
375 Hudson Street, New York, New York 10014, USA
Penguin Group (Canada), 90 Eglinton Avenue East, Suite 700, Toronto, Ontario M4P 2Y3, Canada
(a division of Pearson Penguin Canada Inc.)
Penguin Books Ltd., 80 Strand, London WC2R 0RL, England
Penguin Group Ireland, 25 St. Stephen's Green, Dublin 2, Ireland (a division of Penguin Books Ltd.)
Penguin Group (Australia), 250 Camberwell Road, Camberwell, Victoria 3124, Australia
(a division of Pearson Australia Group Pty. Ltd.)
Penguin Books India Pvt. Ltd., 11 Community Centre, Panchsheel Park, New Delhi—110 017, India
Penguin Group (NZ), 67 Apollo Drive, Rosedale, North Shore 0632, New Zealand
(a division of Pearson New Zealand Ltd.)
Penguin Books (South Africa) (Pty.) Ltd., 24 Sturdee Avenue, Rosebank, Johannesburg 2196,
South Africa

Penguin Books Ltd., Registered Offices: 80 Strand, London WC2R 0RL, England

This is a work of fiction. Names, characters, places, and incidents either are the product of the author's
imagination or are used fictitiously, and any resemblance to actual persons, living or dead, business
establishments, events, or locales is entirely coincidental. The publisher does not have any control over
and does not assume any responsibility for author or third-party websites or their content.

STORMWALKER

A Berkley Sensation Book / published by arrangement with the author

PRINTING HISTORY
Berkley Sensation mass-market edition / May 2010

Copyright © 2010 by Jennifer Ashley.
Excerpt from *Firewalker* by Allyson James copyright © by Jennifer Ashley.
Cover art by Tony Mauro.
Cover design by George Long.
Interior text design by Kristin del Rosario.

ISBN: 978-0-425-23469-3

BERKLEY® SENSATION
Berkley Sensation Books are published by The Berkley Publishing Group,
a division of Penguin Group (USA) Inc.,
375 Hudson Street, New York, New York 10014.
BERKLEY® SENSATION and the "B" design are trademarks of Penguin Group (USA) Inc.

PRINTED IN THE UNITED STATES OF AMERICA

10 9 8 7 6 5 4 3 2 1

Acknowledgments

Thanks go to my editor, Kate Seaver, for her encourage-ment and guidance throughout this project. I also thank author Glenda Garland for her spot-on critiques and her clearheaded brainstorming. Thanks also go to my husband for his tireless support—for reading early drafts, brain-storming, and proofreading, and for making sure we have food, clean dishes, and, most important, cat food whenever I'm lost in storyland.

For more information on the world of *Stormwalker* and forthcoming books, see the Stormwalker website: www.allysonjames.com/stormwalker.html.

One

It was already dark by the time I zoomed out of the mountains, heading east toward the deserts and the town of Magellan. The elevation dropped, the cool green of pine country fell behind, and the heat returned. Lightning forked far to the south, the approaching storm tingling through my body like a lover's touch.

By the time I reached Winslow and glided through its traffic lights, clouds had blotted out the stars, but still there was no rain. I took the road under the railroad bridge at the same time a freight train rumbled over it, then I headed south to open desert, my Harley throbbing in the quiet.

Fingers of lightning lit the clouds with intense white, and I lapped up the residue like a greedy cat. I'm a Storm-walker, which is my father's people's way of saying I can harness the power of storms for my own use. On a calm day, I can't work much more than simple spells, but put a storm near me, and I can make the wind, lightning, and rain dance to my bidding. I'm good at it. Deadly.

Storm magic drove me crazy and left me more hungover than a three-day bender, but too long between storms had the same result. I hadn't tasted a storm in the two weeks since I'd moved to Magellan to investigate the disappearance of Amy McGuire, the police chief's daughter. I needed a fix.

I took the turnoff that led to Magellan. The smudge of the small town's lights beckoned to me from twenty miles away. The larger glitter of Flat Mesa, the county seat, lay a little north. The red taillights of a pickup bobbed ahead of me as it dipped and rose through the washes. Half of the left light was broken, giving the truck an uneven look. No one else was on the road with us.

A sudden gust of wind threatened to knock me off my bike, and a voice floated on it across the dark desert.

Janet.

I skidded to a halt, heart hammering, and dragged off my helmet. Wind buffeted me, clouds flowing toward me thick and fast.

Daughter. The whisper was feminine, soft, almost loving.

Oh, holy crap.

The other reason I'd come to Magellan was to face my mother and stop her, like I should have stopped her years ago. But I'd been too young then, too scared. The invitation to investigate Amy's disappearance gave me the opportunity to return, and this time, I would fight her. As soon as I figured out how to.

Six years had passed since I'd met my mother in, of all places, a diner in Holbrook, where she'd scared the shit out of me. It was easy to convince myself that I was ready to confront her while safe behind the heavily warded walls of my new hotel, not so easy out here in open desert with the vortexes beckoning to me. Here in the darkness, alone under this vast sky, I had to admit that she still scared the shit out of me.

Come to me.

"Like hell." When I'd met my mother, she'd done her best to make me her willing slave, but I had this problem with free will. I liked it.

Janet.

"Not this time!" I shouted.

The whisper died on the wind as lightning flared. The electricity of it sparkled through my fingers and pinged across my helmet.

The storm magic was earth magic, which I'd inherited from my grandmother, a small Navajo woman who was stronger than she looked. My mother came from Beneath, the same realm that created the skinwalkers, and I'd inherited magic from her too. My mother didn't much like earth magic, because although earth magic had enabled me to be born at all, it also made me strong enough to withstand her.

I put on my helmet, my fingers shaking, and glided onward. A curtain of rain washed over me, its sudden chill welcome. I caught up to the pickup, whoever it was traveling slowly, and I realized that the encounter had taken only a few short moments.

I pulled into the oncoming lane of the two-lane road to pass the truck. Another sheet of lightning ran through the sky, reaching from the mesas to the south and spreading in all directions. It lit the clouds in cold, white radiance, and in that light I saw a giant figure burst from the side of the road, heading directly for me.

I hit my brakes, cranking my bike sideways, trying desperately to avoid the impact. A horrible stench filled the air as the figure missed my front wheel and struck the pickup with a resounding *boom*.

My back tire skidded out from under me on the rain-soaked pavement. At the same time, the pickup rose into the air, almost in slow motion. It rotated once, twice, before it crashed to the pavement, landing on its cab. The pickup screeched forward upside down a few yards, sparks flying into the night, before it lay still like a dead thing.

My bike kept skidding. I missed the truck by inches, was thrown free of the Harley, and landed facedown in a rapidly filling ditch.

I lay unmoving in the wet dirt, the face shield of my helmet cracked. My bike sprawled on its side next to me, front wheel bent, my legs just as bent under me.

No one moved inside the pickup. It was black dark out here; I couldn't even discern the color of the truck. I could still smell the skinwalker, though, lurking in the darkness beyond us. My mother could control the things, who thrived on the energy of the vortexes, and she'd sent this one to discipline me. Not kill me—I knew she didn't want me dead, just obedient. I wouldn't be useful to her if I were dead.

I struggled out of my helmet. My gloves had ripped, and blood slicked my grip. I unfolded myself painfully and climbed to my feet, dragging in aching breaths.

I heard the skinwalker coming back. The legends of my people said that skinwalkers were human sorcerers who dabbled in dark magic, wrapping themselves in skins of dead animals to take on that animal's characteristics. True about the dead animals part, usually after they'd tortured them, but skinwalkers weren't human. They were throwbacks to the previous shell world, the one Beneath, where my mother was a goddess. Skinwalkers were evils, like demons, that should never have made it through to this world with the rest of humanity. But they had, clawing their way out and breeding down the generations.

It charged me. The thing was huge, about eight feet tall, wrapped, as far as I could tell, in the skin of a dead bear. Faster than fast, stinking like the worst charnel house, it picked me up and slammed me down on the road again. I hit and kicked, making no more of a dent than if I'd hit a wall. It put its filthy face close to mine, lips pulling back from yellow teeth.

I screamed. Not that it would help. No one lived out here, and whoever had been in the pickup wasn't getting out.

The storm answered me. Thunder cracked in the distance, and I reached desperately for the lightning. I couldn't create storms or move them; I could only use what nature decided to give me, but if the storm was close enough . . .

Lightning flowed from the black cloud and into my outstretched hands. I exhaled in relief. It wasn't very strong, the storm still too far away, but it would help. I gathered what lightning I could and threw it at the skinwalker. The skinwalker grunted with the impact and danced back a yard or so, but that was about all I could manage. I scrambled to my feet.

Skinwalkers are damn hard to kill. This one was shambling toward me again. I reached for the wind and raised my hands to direct it at the disgusting thing. The skinwalker stumbled. I hit it again and again with wind power, throwing sparks of lightning into the mix.

The skinwalker ran at me again, bent on destruction. I didn't think my mother wanted it to kill me, but did *it* know that?

The creature made it back to the road. Instead of pummeling me, it turned and kicked my bike.

"No!" I shouted. That bike was my baby. This old girl and me had racked up a lot of miles. She symbolized my freedom, my independence, *me*. I grabbed a handful of lightning and blasted the skinwalker. Electricity arced around him, but he still didn't die.

At times like these, I regretted riding away from Mick, my man of wild fire magic. I'd seen Mick burn up a skinwalker without breaking a sweat. Mick had made me crazy with his mixture of bad-boy charm, protectiveness, and elusiveness, but my time with him had also been the best of my life.

Before we'd parted ways, Mick had given me six light spells locked into little silver balls. I had one in my pocket now, the last of the remaining two. The balls, when activated, radiated a white light that drove away every shadow—temporarily. They had no heat, only light, but they were useful in emergencies, against skinwalkers or demons or Nightwalkers, creatures that shunned the light.

The electricity ebbed, the storm diminishing. The skinwalker came at me, a murderous look in its red eyes.

The situation definitely qualified as an emergency. I dug into my pocket, digging out the spell that was about the size of a ball bearing. It didn't take much magic to activate them, which meant I could use them whether I had a handy storm or not.

The skinwalker loomed over me, huge fists ready to crush me. I lifted the spell ball, but before I could call it to life, the skinwalker gave a sudden cry of anguish. A blue nimbus sprang up to surround it, one not created by me. The skinwalker fought it, trying to beat its way out, while I stood with my palm outstretched, watching in astonishment.

The skinwalker ran off into the darkness, still surrounded with glowing blue, until it was lost to sight. I blew out my breath in sudden relief and returned the spell ball to my pocket.

The stench receded, a sure sign the thing had gone. Had Mama called off her pet? Or had some other entity interfered? I didn't know, and at the moment, I didn't care.

I limped toward the pickup. The next burst of lightning revealed a dusty red truck that looked familiar, and my heart sank as I read the words on the now upside-down door. "Fremont Hansen, Install and Fix-It."

"Shit," I whispered. Fremont was the plumber I'd hired to help me restore the derelict hotel I'd bought on the outskirts of Magellan. He was a friendly guy with a receding hairline and innocent brown eyes, who claimed to have a little magical ability of his own. "I can fix anything," he'd boasted, wriggling his fingers.

I closed my bloody hand around my cell phone, but the fall had smashed it. Plastic shards stuck to my fingers, and the battery dangled from useless wires.

I tossed the phone aside and crouched on the road next to the pickup's cab. Blood coated the inside of the driver's window, and I saw a head pressed against it.

"Fremont." I tried the door, but I couldn't budge it. I hobbled around to the other side of the truck, my leg hurting like hell. The passenger window was open. I saw no gleaming pebbles of glass, so the window must have already been open before the wreck. The man lay in the blackness inside, upside down, neck bent unnaturally.

I fumbled in the debris inside the truck and found no cell phone, and the frame was too crimped for me to open the glove compartment. I withdrew, my nose wrinkling with the stench of death.

Another flash of lightning lit the sky, farther to the east, the storm moving on. The lightning died, and red and blue lights took its place, accompanied by the wail of a siren. I sat down, exhausted, my back against the pickup, as a vehicle came charging toward me, headlights blinding.

An SUV with "Hopi County Sheriff's Department" painted on its side stopped a few feet from me, its tires sliding a little on the wet pavement. The door popped open, and booted feet hit the asphalt, followed by sharply creased khaki pants. The boots were polished to a sheen, strange for a man who worked in the dusty desert all day.

Nash Jones, sheriff of tiny Hopi County, squatted down next to me, regarding me with eyes ice gray in the glare of his headlights. Blearily I heard another truck pull up and more boots crunch on dirt and pavement.

"Janet Begay." Nash's voice was flat and hard. He didn't like me. When I first arrived in Magellan, I'd tried to talk to him about Amy McGuire, and he'd shut me down before I'd done more than introduce myself. Amy McGuire had been his fiancée. Jones had hated me before he'd even met me.

He turned on a pinpoint flashlight and trained the light right into my eyes. "You all right?"

"I'm alive," I croaked.

"You ran into him with your motorcycle." His voice held no sympathy. "The impact flipped the truck. Am I right?"

"Something hit him. Not me."

He didn't believe me. "Can you get up? Do you need the paramedics?"

"I think I'm okay."

Nash didn't believe that either. A woman in a black coverall came over at his signal, and she helped me stand. Nash abandoned me while the woman got me to the back of a paramedics truck and cleaned the blood off my hands. She checked me over, took my blood pressure, felt my limbs for breaks, asked me if I wanted to go to the hospital. I said no but asked her for a lift into town, my motorcycle wheel bent like it was. She agreed but said she had to wait for the sheriff's okay.

I felt hollow inside. Fremont was dead in that truck. Dead because a skinwalker sent by my evil goddess mother had missed me and hit him.

Nash Jones and his deputies surveyed the accident and started cutting the body out of the truck. I sat there sick and miserable. The storm was dying, leaving me drained and sick as usual. I really wanted some coffee. Or a stiff drink. I was a lightweight drunk, so I never drank much, but tonight I'd make an exception.

Nash returned and beckoned with a curt gesture. "Begay. Come with me."

Probably the only reason he didn't manhandle me was because the paramedics woman might get mad at him. Nash Jones had made it clear as soon as I arrived in Magellan that he resented the hell out of my presence and the fact that Chief McGuire had asked me here. Nash had never been officially charged regarding Amy's disappearance, but he'd been questioned as a suspect, and the talk on the street was that no one knew for sure. The things Chief McGuire had told me about Sheriff Jones were . . . interesting.

Nash didn't touch me, but he made me hobble in front of him to his SUV. He opened the back door. "Get in."

"Why? The nice lady with the blood pressure cuff is giving me a ride home."

"I'm taking you to the sheriff's office. For reckless driving, possible manslaughter."

"You are kidding, aren't you?"

"I don't kid."

Jones could glare. He had gray eyes that could turn on you with the intensity of a supernova, black hair cut in the military style he'd brought back from his army time in Iraq, and a hard, handsome face. I'd seen women in Magellan and Flat Mesa turn their heads to watch him go by, his looks marred only by a scar on his upper lip.

"There's something out there," I said. "It hit Fremont's truck, hard enough to flip it. It ran off, but the storm's dying, and it could come back anytime. It can tear this SUV apart like a paper bag if it wants to. Skinwalkers are frigging strong."

He answered me with a flat stare. Nash Jones was an Unbeliever, one of those people who didn't buy the fact that Magellan was built near a mystical confluence of vortexes, where the paranormal was normal. He'd grown up here but derided those who made money from the tourists who flocked to Hopi County in pursuit of the supernatural.

"Get in before I throw your ass in."

"Were you like this in the army? Not believing anyone who warned you of danger?"

"There I was with trained men. You're a Navajo girl from a sheep farm. Get in the damn truck."

"It killed Fremont, easy as anything." I was close to hysterical tears. I liked gossipy, quirky Fremont.

"It's not Fremont."

I looked at him in shock. "What?"

"It's his assistant. Charlie Jones."

I'd seen Charlie helping Fremont work on my hotel's plumbing, a quiet, kind of scruffy kid in his late teens who'd kept to himself. I'd known his first name was Charlie, but that was about it.

"Jones?" I repeated.

"My fourth cousin."

"Oh, Nash, I'm sorry. I'm so sorry."

Nash gripped me under the elbow and all but threw me into the backseat. "Stay there."

He slammed the door and clicked a remote, and the locks engaged. As I suspected, the windows wouldn't roll down for the prisoner in the back, and a black grill separated back from front, with another one blocking me from the storage space to the rear. I decided to be thankful that Nash hadn't handcuffed me.

I slumped down in the seat, but I knew I couldn't hide. If the skinwalker wanted to find me again, it would. I didn't sense it nearby, though. The flashing emergency lights and activity might be keeping it away. Skinwalkers didn't like light, noise, crowds. That didn't mean it wouldn't rise out of the desert and attack again when Nash drove me away.

I also worried about my bike. Would Nash leave it by the side of the road like a mangled toy? I could imagine him doing that, sending impound to retrieve it when he felt like it.

I didn't have much in the way of possessions, feeling freer without them, but that Harley was important to me. I'd ridden her across this country and down into Mexico, first on my own, then with Mick, then alone again, when I'd finally left him five years ago.

The bike represented my means of escape. No matter how many roots I put down or how much trouble I got into, I could always throw a change of clothes into my saddle-bags, swing my leg over my Harley, and disappear into the night.

I saw the poor thing in the flicker of police flares, the wheel bent, the handlebars sticking up forlornly. It was a machine, a piece of metal, I told myself, but it was like looking at the twisted body of my own child.

When Nash finally opened the driver's door, I smelled no stench of skinwalker on the night. I inhaled, tasting the ozone tingle of the storm. I toyed with the idea of snatching the lightning's power and zapping Nash with it, but that would make me no better than the skinwalker. Hurting for the fun of it. I shuddered.

"Should I consider myself under arrest?" I asked.

Nash slammed the door and put on his seat belt. "Being taken in for questioning."

"My bike?"

"Deputies are impounding it. It's evidence."

"Damn you, Jones. I didn't run into that truck."

"Save it." He put the SUV in gear and pulled out past the flipped pickup as the deputies lifted my Harley and tossed it carelessly into the back of their truck.

Nash didn't turn on his emergency lights, but he gunned the SUV and roared down the highway. Ten miles along, the road ended in a T-intersection, another narrow highway heading north to Flat Mesa, the other south to Magellan. My hotel stood here, at the Crossroads, a dark, forlorn square against the darker sky. The Crossroads Bar, which shared a parking lot with the hotel, was lit and swarming with people.

I gazed longingly at the hotel, picturing my bedroom in the back with its waiting bed and bathroom, even if the water didn't work yet. That hotel was my haven, my defiance if you like.

Nash turned left, passing the hotel without stopping, and drove north toward Flat Mesa.

Two

"I thought you brought me here for questioning."

Nash Jones kept his hard grip on my arm as he stopped outside a cell in the Hopi County Sheriff's Department. He'd had his deputy give me a breathalyzer test and seemed irritated that I wasn't drunk. Said deputy then patted me down while Nash watched. They took away all my personal items, and Nash dragged me off to lock me up.

There were four cells in the jail, empty except for the first one, which held a man drunk on the floor. Nash took me to the very end of the block and slid the bars open on the last cell. Inside was a bunk with a thin mattress and a toilet. Lovely. Nash shoved me inside and closed the grate.

"You forgot to strip-search me," I said.

Nash gave me a cold stare. "Don't push it."

"Don't I get to call a lawyer?"

"Tomorrow. Tonight you'll cool down, and tomorrow

you'll tell me all about the accident that resulted in Charlie Jones's death."

"No time like the present."

"Tomorrow," he repeated with finality.

Bastard. He *could* question me now, but then I might be able to convince him I was innocent, and he'd have to let me go. He'd feel so much better knowing I was sweating overnight in a jail cell.

No one knew where I was, not Fremont, or Chief McGuire, or my friend Jamison Kee, who'd been responsible for me coming to Magellan at all. Jamison had recommended me to Chief McGuire as an investigator of the weird when McGuire turned to unconventional means to find his daughter. McGuire would eventually get word of my detainment, but probably not until morning. I didn't think Nash would call him, because the accident had taken place on county land, Nash's jurisdiction. I'd come to learn in the short time I'd lived in Magellan that Nash took his jurisdiction seriously.

I felt awful about his cousin Charlie. Among my people cousins could be as close as brothers and sisters, and the loss of one family member sent ripples of grief down the line. Nash was certainly going to blame me, and it was true that if I hadn't been out there, Charlie wouldn't have died.

Nash walked away, his footsteps loud in the silence. I lay down on the mattress and pulled my knees up, my feet flat on the bed. My leg felt better, so I hadn't sprained or broken it, just temporarily wrenched it. My muttered healing spells helped a little, but I didn't have enough magic left to make the pain go completely away.

Nash had taken everything: my broken cell phone, the chaps I wore over my jeans, my wallet and keys, the silver ball spell. I didn't worry about him activating the spell, because only people with magic could do that, and Nash had no aura of magic around him, thank the gods. The spell would remain safely unused, but it was anyone's guess as to whether he'd let me have it back.

I closed my eyes.

I must have fallen into instant sleep, because suddenly I was floating above the desert, seeing everything as though through a flying creature's eyes. Below me was the gleam of Flat Mesa, larger than the circle of light that was Magellan. Between the two towns lay the Crossroads Hotel, dark, and the bar, loud and full of light. To the east of the Crossroads, beyond the empty railroad bed that cut through the land like an artery, lay dark desert.

Except it wasn't entirely dark. Swirls of mist moved through it, glowing an unhealthy white. The air was heavy, warm with the smell of rain, but the wind out of the retreating clouds was freezing cold.

The tightly whirling mists marked the vortexes. Vortexes are places in which mystical energy gathers, combining the magics of earth, air, fire, and water into one concentrated space. Some people claim that standing among the vortexes makes them feel better, more alive. Witches seek them to enhance spells, and mystics like to draw in vortex energy to build up their own. Some New Agers even believe that they hold cosmic energies that aliens use to locate places to land, but that's complete nonsense.

Few people know what the vortexes really are, but I do. They're gateways. Sealed gateways, but openings nonetheless, to Beneath.

Beneath is the world below this from which humans once emerged, eons ago. There'd been still another world below that one, and so on. Some storytellers say that the world we inhabit now is the last and best of them; some think there is another, better one beyond this, which we will reach when we figure out how to get to it.

Gods had led the way from Beneath to this world, pushing up through the vortexes and bringing people with them to populate it. Those gods had sealed the way behind them before some of the crueler entities could emerge. The ones who hadn't made it out, like my mother, were very, very angry.

The vortexes were sealed now, but skinwalkers and other demons collected around them because there they could feed on the tiny residue of power from Beneath. Gods like my mother could direct skinwalkers using that magic.

I could sense her out there now, trying to reach me, the white mists swirling to ensnare me.

Janet.

"Leave me alone!" I screamed.

Be with me.

"No!"

A long, vicious growl filled the air, and I jumped awake to an overpowering stench and something hitting the roof full force.

I was off the bunk and at the bars before the second blow landed, yelling at the top of my lungs. The building shook. Thunder boomed, a second storm racing through the narrow fingers of canyons to the town huddled under the night.

"What the hell is the matter with you?" Nash Jones stopped in front of my cell, his face suffused with anger.

"We got struck," his deputy told me from behind him. "But don't worry. This building is solid stone." He sniffed. "What's that smell?"

"It wasn't a lightning strike," I said. "We're being attacked."

Nash scowled. "Not the skinwalker story again."

"Hey, skinwalkers are real," the deputy said. "At least around here."

"As you were, Lopez. Don't encourage her."

"Listen to me," I said. "It will tear down this building to get to me, and it won't care who it kills on the way. Are there rooms behind me?"

Lopez nodded, ignoring Nash's glare. "Old cell block. Unused. Locked off."

"Open it up. Flood it with light. They don't like light. Flood it or he'll bring the building down around us."

Lopez looked alarmed, but Nash's face was like granite. "Anyone ever tell you that you're a lunatic, Begay?"

"Sure, all the time. Doesn't mean I'm wrong."

Something boomed against the outer wall beside me, and Nash's gaze flicked to it. I smelled the skinwalker; I sensed it and its rage. Nash acted like he smelled and sensed nothing. Maybe being an Unbeliever made him oblivious.

"Lopez, check out the cell block," he ordered.

Lopez looked worried, but he squared his shoulders. "Yes, sir."

"Don't check it out alone," I said quickly.

Nash gave me a withering look. "Lopez is a big boy. He's not afraid of the dark, and neither am I."

"You should be," I said.

Nash walked away. Lopez gave me another scared glance and went after him. I heard Nash tell the guy at the desk outside that they needed to get into the old cell block.

I paced while they talked, taking their time. The stench didn't fade. At length, Nash came back to my cell, this time without Lopez. I held on to the bars, flakes of rust staining my skin.

"We couldn't get it open," Nash said. "The door's rusted shut."

"Put me somewhere else, then, somewhere with lots of light."

"You're drunk."

"Your breathalyzer said I wasn't. I'm not drunk, I'm not high, and I'm not kidding." I gave up and leaned my forehead on the bars. "It doesn't matter. It will just track me."

"Will you shut up about the damned skinwalker?"

"Don't you believe in the legends of your own lands?"

"No." Nash said it with a force.

Never argue with an Unbeliever, my friend Jamison, a Navajo shaman, artist, and shape-shifter, had told me when I first arrived in Magellan. He'd said it with a wry smile that spoke of experience.

"Fine," I said. "Go away, then."

I closed my eyes. If Nash couldn't do anything about the skinwalker, it would be up to me. I didn't like tapping the full power of a storm, because it tended to leave me sick and immobile for days. What I'd done out there at the wreck had been very little, and the storm hadn't been full strength.

The kind of lightning I felt playing around outside now was lethal. Clouds from the west had collided with those from the south, swelling over the desert plateau to form one dense, thick entity. If I tapped this storm, it would be heady, exhilarating, and I'd dance in it with a fiery joy. I'd pay the price, but I'd breathe pure pleasure first.

"No more noise," Nash was saying.

"Sweet dreams to you too."

Nash walked away without another word. He reached the end of the cell block and went out, the gate clanging behind him. The drunk in the first cell, who'd been whimpering to himself, wound down, and then everything got quiet.

I lay back down on the mattress and clasped my hands loosely over my chest, my shirt already soaked with sweat. The skinwalker's stench filled the cell, and I gagged on it.

Trying to ignore the smell, I closed my eyes and reached for the storm.

Power whipped through my fingers as I curled myself through the molecules of water and wind, the storm exciting and deadly, difficult to control.

I opened my arms to embrace it. An ache started between my legs and throbbed through my belly like the best kind of sex. I arched back, the feeling welling, until a groan escaped my mouth. I became the storm, channeled it, and power crackled through my fingertips.

Yes.

The warm air from the desert spiraled to meet the ice-cold air of the storm front. Winds whirled together, hot and cold, and thunder boomed. No windows let me see the lightning, but I knew the bolts stalked through the dry grasses surrounding Flat Mesa and the county jail. I unclenched my hands and let the storm unleash its fury.

Hail pounded the roof. Wind tore at the building, shrieking and howling, and the lights inside flickered. My body rippled, my hips rocking as the storm entered me. The ecstasy was raw. The danger was raw too, which wound me up even more.

"Come *on*," I whispered, drenched in sweat.

I wished Mick were here, adding his fire magic to my power. He'd be lying next to me, laughing, hard with desire, unashamed of his reaction to me and my magic. Damn, I wanted him here. I missed him.

I lifted my hands. White light spilled out of my palms and mouth as I reached for the lightning. Power met power, and I pulled the storm down on the building.

An explosion split my ears, then the jail plunged into darkness. I heard Lopez in the outer room give a yip of panic. The wall beside me shuddered, and stones fell to the lot below.

One more.

Lightning poured up the dark corridor to my cell. I smiled in welcome.

I heard a snarl and a screech, then screaming, as the skinwalker buckled before the storm. The stench flared up, unbearable, and he started bashing the wall double time.

The building shook and shuddered. A hole opened in the cell's outer wall, blasted by my power on this side, the skinwalker on the other. His stench rolled in, and I saw him, the same skinwalker who'd accosted me in the desert, eight feet tall and mad as hell.

He came for me. I rose to meet him, power arcing around me. The storm I'd handled on the highway had been weak and miles away; this one was right on top of me. He now faced a Stormwalker at full strength. I laughed and let him have it.

The skinwalker screamed as lightning struck his body. He convulsed with it, the forces of my magic and the one my mother had infused him with tearing him apart. His hot blood sprayed over me, his scream dying to a gurgle, and he slowly crumpled into a heap of stinking flesh.

I directed a final bolt into him. The skinwalker burst into flames. He clawed at himself as he burned, collapsing into a pile of ash on the wet pavement of the parking lot. Rain and wind dispersed the ash, and his stench vanished, leaving behind the clean scent of dust and mud, rain and lightning.

I let out my breath. My arms ached, my belly clenched, and I wanted to vomit. The storm tore away from me, the clouds continuing northward to dump much-needed rain on the desert.

I heard Nash's footsteps and voice, Nash assuming the building had been struck and coming to check on me. He found me huddled in the middle of the floor, making no attempt to crawl out through the hole and run for freedom. The power still gripped me, though the heart of it had receded, leaving me sick and weak. Besides, I figured that if I ran, Nash would just shoot me.

Nash banged open the cell door, hauled me to my feet, half dragged me to the next cell, and tossed me inside. I fell onto the bunk, too exhausted even to swear at him. I wiped away my tired tears and found my fingertips covered with blood.

Three

"Janet Begay."

Nash Jones read from a folder he'd opened flat on the table. I sat across from him, leaning on the scarred surface, arms cradling my head. My eyes were closed, but I couldn't quite shut out the daylight that poured through a high window and stabbed into my brain.

I'd spent the rest of the night heaving out my guts into the waiting toilet in my cell. Now my head pounded, and my eyes were dry. The drunk had looked much better than I had when the on-duty deputy came to escort me to an interrogation room.

"Born in Many Farms," Nash droned. "Father a Navajo, mother—no record. Her name?"

"I don't know."

That was true. My mother didn't have a name. The woman she'd possessed to seduce my poor, kindly father, who wouldn't hurt a fly, must have had a name, but she'd refused to tell it. The name on my birth certificate said "Jane Doe." I'd never lived that down. Among my people, not knowing your mother's family or clan was a handicap. To my grandmother, it was anathema.

"Graduated from high school in spite of frequent disciplinary problems," Nash went on. "Attended NAU for a while."

"None of this is a crime," I said. I'd enjoyed my time studying art at NAU, far enough from home to feel independent but in the shadow of mountains still sacred to the Navajo.

Nash ignored me. "Arrested twice for being disorderly— once in a bar in Flagstaff, once in Albuquerque." He flipped over a page. "Caught shoplifting, in Gallup this time."

"A bottle of Tylenol when I was ten." I made myself lift my head and instantly regretted it. "For my grandmother. I thought that had been wiped off my record." I knew now what I hadn't known then, that when we'd been attacked on that dark road from Window Rock, my mother had instigated it. My grandmother and father had fought what I'd thought were gang boys who attacked us when we stopped on a lonely stretch of road. The demons had eventually run off, but my grandmother, though physically unhurt, had been in excruciating pain. Headache from magic, I realized now. When we'd stopped for gas in Gallup, I'd swiped a small bottle of Tylenol from the convenience store inside. I'd been caught, of course, and the police called. My grandmother had been furious and made me give the store owner a cringing apology. He'd been touched by my tear-streaked contrition, far more than my grandmother had, and hadn't pressed charges. My grandmother, on the other hand, had whacked me across the backside and never let me hear the end of it.

"I talked to the tribal police this morning," Nash said. "They know many things about you, not all of it official.

You were a troublemaker, they said, even burned down a school building. I'm surprised you're not in prison."

I laid my head down, willed my roiling stomach to calm. "The sins of a frustrated youth. I'm a grown-up now."

Nash closed the folder and looked at me with his cold gray eyes. A person might think that Nash Jones was as hard as he was because of the tragedy of his missing girlfriend. But Fremont, my font of county gossip, told me that Nash had never been a sweet man. Getting shipped out to Iraq hadn't improved things, and he'd been in a building in Baghdad when several bombs went off inside it. The building had collapsed on him and his squad, and no one had made it out but him.

This morning, he'd obviously slept, showered, shaved, and dressed in clean clothes, every crease in his uniform sharp. The perfect sheriff, was Nash. Like he'd studied it in a book, trying to pin down the character he was supposed to play. It was as though he knew what he was supposed to do and went through the motions, but some part of him just couldn't make it work.

I was still sweaty and gritty from the wreck and my subsequent night in jail. The faucet in my cell had given up only a trickle of water, barely enough to rinse my face. The water had been clean for washing out my mouth, but its metallic taste left me feeling like I'd gargled acid.

Result: Nash was clean and rested, while I looked and felt like shit.

"Who called in the accident?" I asked groggily.

"What?"

"My cell phone broke, and there was no one on the road. How did you know there'd been an accident? Or are you clairvoyant?"

He gave me an Unbeliever scowl. "That drifter who calls himself Coyote. He saw."

I'd never met the guy. "Maybe he can corroborate my story."

"He was walking from Magellan and saw the flipped truck. He didn't witness the accident itself."

Damn. "Why didn't he stick around?"

"He never does. But I'll find him and question him."

I was certain he would. Nash Jones was a thorough guy.

He reached into a shallow box next to him, took out the silver spell ball, and rolled it onto the folder. "What is this for?"

I glanced at it. "It's a ball bearing."

"No it isn't. It's too light. I asked you, what is it for? What's it part of?"

"Something off my motorcycle."

"Try again."

"All right. None of your business."

Nash turned the ball around and around in his fingers. "Is it part of a weapon? Or a way to transport drugs?"

My head pounded. "You have drugs on the brain. All right, it's part of a weapon—a mystical, magical weapon. Give it here, and I'll show you."

The way I felt, I doubted I could ignite a match, but wouldn't it be fun to activate the light spell and give him a scare? Of course, if I saw that much light right now, I might personally die, but it wouldn't hurt anyone else.

"I'll just hang on to it."

As Nash started to set it down, a needlelike spark arced between his thumb and the ball. I held my breath, but nothing happened. Nash didn't notice the spark, but the pulse of the spell beat at the inside of my skull.

Nash dropped the spell ball back into the box, then leaned toward me like a sergeant dressing down a raw recruit. "Listen to me, Begay. I know you fed McGuire a load of crap, playing on his grief, telling him you can find his daughter with your psychic abilities. But let me tell you, if you try to scam any more money out of him with your bullshit, I will kick your ass all the way back to the reservation and make sure you stay on it for the rest of your life. Got it?"

I didn't make the mistake of raising my head again, leaving it on the cool tabletop. But he pissed me off. I hated white people who called the Navajo Nation "the reservation," and I was just as free as he was to come and go as I pleased. "I don't charge to investigate anything; I'm doing it as a favor. And it's not illegal to renovate a hotel or ask questions about a missing woman. I told Chief McGuire I couldn't guarantee that I'd find his daughter. I only told him I'd try."

"Reckless endangerment *is* illegal. A man is dead after you ran your motorcycle into the back of his truck."

"I didn't hit him, I keep telling you. Check the skid marks."

"My deputies are out there right now, trust me. If they find one thing that doesn't add up, I'll bust your ass so hard you'll never get up again. You'll pay and pay for killing my cousin."

I forced my head off the table. "You are one angry man, you know that? I'm sorry about your cousin, I really am, but I never touched his truck. It's not my fault your girlfriend disappeared. I'd think you'd at least let me try to find her, that you'd want to *help* me try to find her."

"I'm not McGuire, and I don't want to hear your false promises about your woo-woo investigating. Amy's dead. I know that."

"How do you know?"

His stare burned all the way to the back of my skull. "I just know."

Nash Jones had been both suspect number one and the biggest pain in the ass to the investigation when Amy first went missing. Chief McGuire had never actually said that,

but I could interpret. Nash admitted to having episodes of
PTSD since returning from Iraq, and even to having one
the day Amy vanished. He'd apparently gotten into his car
and driven all the way to Albuquerque and had a meal, not
remembering any of it. But even with this, McGuire con-
cluded that Nash Jones truly had no idea what happened
to Amy.

The police file on Amy was pretty sparse. Nice girl,
lived alone in a decent neighborhood, sang in the church
choir, volunteered at the library, enjoyed gardening. No
enemies—everyone professed to liking Amy. Last seen at
ten in the morning on a Saturday, one year ago, watering
her plants. No report of an unfamiliar vehicle in the neighborhood, no report of strangers. Amy had lived at the end
of a road with no outlet, and her neighbors had not noted
anyone going in or out that day.

McGuire had asked the state DPS special investigations
unit to step in, since both he and Jones had close ties to
the missing woman. Every single conventional method
of tracking down Amy had been utilized. After a year of
nothing, the McGuires decided to try unconventional meth-
ods, namely me. I'd had success solving seemingly inex-
plicable crimes such as one I'd done in Flagstaff, where
a murdered man's shade had pointed me to evidence that
told me his business partner killed him. The McGuires had
invited me to Magellan to determine whether something
magical hadn't carried off their daughter. People believed
such things in Magellan, and I knew that where my mother
was concerned, anything was possible.

"Why the hotel?" Nash asked.

"What?" I looked up at him. Nash had his arms folded
on the table, which made his biceps bulge in his uniform
shirt.

"You came to Magellan because Chief McGuire thinks
you're psychic. Why buy the hotel?"

I shrugged, which hurt. "Why not?"

"It's been derelict for fifty years."

I couldn't explain that the place had called to me. When I'd looked at the empty three-story square building, its windows broken and dark, something in it had spoken to me. The hotel reminded me of myself, sitting off to the side, alone and unwanted. It was also the perfect base of operations from which I could conduct my investigation and a fortified stronghold to keep my mother from simply sending along her skinwalkers to drag me to her.

"I thought the people of Magellan might like me better if I was doing something besides asking questions," I said. "Anyway, I'm giving jobs to a lot of locals."

"Where did you get the money?"

"That's really none of your business."

"Everything in Hopi County is my business."

I was getting that idea. "I take photographs and sell them. In art galleries, from California to Santa Fe. They're popular."

"I've seen them."

From the grim line to Nash's mouth, I surmised that he either disapproved of my talent or flat-out didn't like the pictures—studies of landscape or portraits of Native Americans living their lives. Probably both.

"So I won't give you one for Christmas," I said. "When can I go home?"

"When my deputies are finished with the accident scene. Then we'll go see the magistrate."

"I want a lawyer."

"The public defender will meet you before we go to the courthouse."

I rested my forehead on the table. "How did you get to be sheriff when you have PTSD?"

I knew I shouldn't have asked such a dangerous question, but I didn't have the energy to care.

"Because I do the job better than anyone else," Nash answered. I believed him, somehow. "I haven't had an episode in a year."

"Not since Amy."

As soon as the words came out of my mouth, I knew I'd just blown any chance of getting out of here today. I peeled open my eyes and looked up, wincing when I saw Nash's gray ones.

"You give up this so-called investigation and go home," he said in a hard voice, "or I'll bust you for fraud and expose you for the con artist you are."

I started to answer that I had the right to live in any town I wanted to, but my stomach decided just then to punish me for the night of storm magic. I pressed my arm over my abdomen, but it didn't help.

I staggered to my feet and made it to the trash can in the corner before my morning coffee and a gob of bile came up.

"Damn it, Begay—"

Nash's diatribe was cut off by a deputy outside saying quickly and worriedly, "You can't go in there."

The door banged open, and a man shouldered his way in, shoving aside the deputy who tried to get in his way. He was six-feet-six of solid muscle in jeans, a black T-shirt, and motorcycle boots, had a silver earring dangling from one ear, and dragon tattoos snaking down both arms. His hair was black, the wild curls of it just contained in a ponytail. He had the bluest eyes I'd ever seen, and I vividly recalled staring into them the night I lost my virginity.

My mouth formed the name, "Mick," at the same time Nash rose to his feet and aimed his nine-millimeter right at Mick's head.

"Stop."

Nash might as well have tried to stop a freight train. Mick came on.

"I said, *stop*."

Nash's voice was ice-hard. He might have scared the hell out of insurgents in Iraq, but he didn't know Mick. Mick ignored him, and Nash fired.

The sound exploded in my head. I screamed. The bullet hit Mick in the shoulder, and he grunted with the impact, but it barely slowed him down. He made it to me and scooped me up.

"Hey, baby," he said, grinning. "Miss me?"

Four

The deputy leapt out of the way as Mick ran out of the room, carrying me over his shoulder. I raised my head in time to see Nash aim his gun, then lower it again, face thunderous. He couldn't be sure of not hitting me, and I was getting the idea that Nash was the kind who'd follow the rules to the core. He'd never allow a prisoner to be hurt in his custody.

Banging against Mick's hip, upside down, wasn't helping my unsteady stomach. I clapped my hand to my mouth, trying to keep from spewing.

In the parking lot Mick set me gently on my feet and took my face between his hands. He gave me his cocky smile, the one that said he looked at life and saw nothing he couldn't handle, no matter how dangerous. The world might be full of badasses who tried to kill him, but Mick knew he could out-badass them any day.

"Can you hold it together for me, sweetheart?"

If Mick had been anyone else, I'd be screaming at him to get to a hospital, worried to death about the gunshot wound. But I'd seen Mick laugh under an onslaught of deadly sorcerer's magic, had seen him grab fire with both hands and eat it. I had a hard time believing a mundane piece of lead in the shoulder would do much more than irritate him.

"You all right?" he asked me again.

I nodded. My stomach was still roiling, but he made me want to feel better. "What the hell are you doing here?" I asked between shallow breaths.

"I told you, Janet. When you need me, all you have to do is call. Anytime."

"I didn't call you."

"Sure about that?" He caressed my cheek with the backs of his fingers. "We need to go. Can you ride?"

Did I have a choice? I could either let Mick take me out of there or run back to the nice cell Nash Jones was giving me rent-free. I nodded again, and Mick helped me onto the back of his bike, a big Harley for a big man. He started it up, the throbbing too loud for my aching skull.

Questions and emotions whirled through my brain, but all I could do was wrap my arms around Mick's waist and hold on as he pulled into the street. I looked back to see Nash and his deputies watching from the parking lot, the officers with mouths open, Nash's face dark with fury. I couldn't resist raising my hand in farewell as we rode away.

I was about ready to fall off the bike by the time we pulled into the deserted parking lot between my hotel and the Crossroads Bar. The sun was overhead, the May morning hot. Everything was quiet, no one in sight. I wondered briefly if they'd all stayed home because of the accident and me being in jail, then I remembered it was Sunday. No one would have come to work on the place today, anyway.

Good thing. I couldn't have dealt with all their questions or the hostile looks of my Latina electrician, who didn't like me for some reason. I especially didn't want to face Fremont. I needed to sort out my thoughts before I talked to him, plus I had to figure out what to do with Mick.

Mick carried me inside and laid me on my bed. He hadn't changed since I'd last seen him, more than five years ago. I mean he hadn't changed *at all*. He was wearing different clothes, but that was about it. His face was still as granite hard, his black hair as unruly, his eyes as amazingly blue. His eyes could turn completely black when he was enraged or ready to fight, and I'd never seen Mick lose a fight. I'd never figured out exactly what he was—very magical, and definitely not fully human—but other than that, I didn't know. He could shoot fire from his hands and cast spells, but he wasn't a full sorcerer, as far as I knew. He wasn't a Changer, not a Nightwalker, not a demon—I didn't think.

Mick tugged off my boots one-handed, cradling his other arm against his chest. Blood from his T-shirt stained his neck.

"You're not all right," I told him.

I shook so hard I could barely speak. What did you say to a lover you hadn't seen in five years? *How have you been? What are you doing back in my life? Why now?*

"Neither are you," he said.

My cropped top bared my midriff, and Mick put his large hand on my belly. His hand was warm, and I wanted to rise to it.

"You sucked down a lot of power from that storm," he said. "I felt it from miles away. I've never seen you use that much power."

He moved his palm, and the residue of storm magic flowed toward his hand. Sparks crackled across his fingertips, warming me inside.

"I've learned a lot since I saw you last. Why are you here?"

Mick leaned to me. His blue, blue eyes were darkening to black, the irises widening to fill the whites. "I came to rescue my girl."

He leaned closer, nearly nuzzling me. He'd always done that, like an animal identifying its mate by scent. Mick was the most tactile person I'd ever met; he'd wanted to touch, smell, taste every inch of me. I who'd grown up learning to respect other people's personal space had found it unnerving at first. Once used to it, I'd liked it, and decided that Mick could invade my personal space when he wanted to. No one else, only Mick.

I liked it now. Even though our breakup had been volatile, I wanted to lift myself to meet his lips, to drag him down into my embrace. I wanted to hold his body against mine and find out whether he still liked sex to be wild and wicked and need safety words.

"I'm not leaving you alone, Janet," he said softly. "Not this time."

A drop of scarlet blood fell on my cheek. I half sat up, pushing him away. "You can't help me when you're bleeding like crazy."

Mick sat on the bed and peeled off his shirt. His entire right side was coated with blood, scarlet clots covering the dragon tattoo. In spite of the care he took of his right arm, he acted as though he felt no pain. He clasped my hand in his, raised my fingers to his lips. "Help me heal?"

I wanted to. My thoughts shot back to the nights we'd go to ground after a fight, when we'd wash each other's bodies and heal each other with magic. The heady spells had led to kisses, and hands stroking, arousing, and then to sex. Most activity with Mick had led to sex.

The bullet had gone deep into Mick's shoulder, high enough to miss the lung, but it left a ragged, bloody hole. Anyone else would be in agony, but Mick shrugged it off like he would a mosquito bite. He kissed my fingers, rose from the bed, and headed for my bathroom.

"There's no water in there," I called after him. "That's what I was doing in Flagstaff, finding more plumbing parts."

My words were cut off by a *whoosh* from the pipes. Air exploded through the taps to be replaced by the steady trickle of water. I sat up, surprised. Maybe Fremont had finished while I was gone?

"It's clean," Mick announced. I heard splashing, and Mick returned with a handful of wet towels. He sat down on the bed again and handed me a clean one. "Hold that on the wound."

I folded the towel into a thick wad and pressed it to the hole in his shoulder. Blood seeped out, quickly staining the cloth red.

Mick grunted. "Shots like this are always a bitch."

He closed his eyes. Mick didn't need rituals or chants or accoutrements to work his healing magic; he simply got very quiet and forced his body to fix itself.

Under my touch, his skin started to warm. More than warm, his skin grew hot, sweat beading up and spilling down his arm. Mick tilted his head back, jaw clenched, cords standing out on his neck. I held the towel so tightly against him I could feel his muscles moving beneath it, changing shape, rearranging themselves.

I put my other arm around him, my hand right over his heart. His skin was hot to the touch, almost fiery.

He growled. I pressed my body against his hot back, keeping the towel tight to the wound. His power crawled through me, meeting the last vestiges of my own. Mick gripped my hand over his heart, tighter, tighter, until my fingers ached. I sucked in a breath, feeling our natures entwining.

Something tugged Mick's shoulder. I held the towel beneath the wound as the bullet wriggled its way out of Mick's flesh and dropped onto the bloody cloth. Mick dragged my other hand to his lips and kissed the palm. I watched the hole in Mick's flesh close over itself, until the wound was nothing but an angry mark and a black bruise.

Mick turned to me, his eyes dark. "We work some wicked magic together, don't we, sweetheart?"

"We did," I said.

"It was always good," he whispered as he slid his hand behind my neck. "The best." He kissed me, a brief but intense brush of lips, followed by another, and another. His arm went behind my back, pulling me to his sweat-slicked chest.

His mouth was hot with promise, his hands knowing exactly how to arouse. He had me straddling his lap, my legs wrapped around him, while he rolled with me down into the mattress.

I brought my hands up and pressed them flat against his chest. "Mick."

He gave me an innocent "what?" look, but he still smiled at me. My heart turned over. Gods, the man had a sexy smile. "I missed you so much, baby."

"I missed you too." I touched his face, fingertips caressing. "But you can't stay." My voice didn't hold much conviction, but I meant it.

"Sweetheart, if you're here to face your mama and the vortexes from Beneath, you're going to need all the help you can get. You know that. Don't lie to me and tell me you don't."

"Maybe, but I don't need to feel guilty because I got you hurt." As powerful as Mick was, I knew that if my mother wanted to get to me enough, Mick would be blown out like a spent match.

"You've gotten a lot stronger." Mick traced my cheek. "The way you took down that skinwalker was beautiful."

"It was a good storm."

"But you controlled it with the skill of a master. When I first met you, your power was all over the place."

That was true. I'd met Mick when I was twenty-one, and by then I'd at least learned to contain my storm power and not hurt people arbitrarily with it. But I hadn't yet honed the ability to handle it well or channel it where I needed to. What Mick had taught me in the six months I was with him doubled my ability, and I'd worked on it diligently since.

"Explain to me how you knew I was here, in Magellan," I said. "And stuck in the sheriff's office."

"Let's just say I always know where you are. I came to finish off the skinwalker for you, but like I said, you got him, and you got him good. I thought the sheriff would let you go in the morning, but you didn't come out. When I felt one of my spells go off, I decided I needed to get you out of there."

I thought of Nash rolling the silver ball between his fingers. "It didn't go off. It sparked when Nash touched it, but that's all. He's not magical."

Mick lifted his brows. "You sure? I felt the pressure."

"Believe me, I would have noticed incandescent light searing through my brain. The spell didn't go off. It must have been something else."

"Maybe." He kissed the tip of my nose and finally got off me, making me feel cold and bereft. I heard him running water in the bathroom, and he returned with more clean, damp towels. He seated himself on the bed again and started wiping my face. The cool water felt delicious on my hot, dirty skin. "You warded this place."

It wasn't a question. The day I moved in, I'd gone to Paradox, the local New Age store, and bought smudge sticks, incense, candles, stones, and oil, and spent the evening chanting spells and marking wards everywhere.

"Wards, spells, offerings to the gods," I said. "Anything I could think of."

Mick ran his gaze over the symbols I'd drawn. They were invisible to the human eye, but I knew Mick saw them. "They could stand strengthening."

From the look he gave me, I knew how he wanted to strengthen them. Mick had once taught me the fine art of Tantric.

"Not now," I said. "You just had a bullet in you. You need to finish healing."

"It's not that bad. Your sheriff is a lousy shot."

"He wasn't trying to kill you, just stop you." I knew that in my heart. Nash might be an asshole, but he wasn't a killer. I'd met enough killers to know one when I saw one.

Mick didn't look convinced. He finished wiping my face and started on my hands.

"Not that I don't appreciate you helping me out," I said. "But you know you've only made it worse for me if Jones decides to charge me. I'm sure he'll recommend holding me without bail and somehow get the trial scheduled for two years from now."

"He won't charge you. He'd have already done it if he had clear evidence, and he won't get any."

I wondered how he could be so sure. Nash Jones followed the book, but would his deputies be able to tell what had happened out there on that highway? I was the sole witness. Maybe. Who was this drifter who'd seen the flipped truck? *Calls himself Coyote,* Nash had said. What would he say?

"I'd still love to know how you knew I was in trouble," I said.

"You know I'm not going to tell you." Mick's voice was reasonable, his arrogant refusal to answer my questions raising familiar anger in me.

"Mick . . ."

"Forget it. There are some things you aren't meant to know."

Remembered exasperation returned. During our brief relationship, Mick had been adamant about not wanting me to go anywhere on my own, but he'd disappear when he damn well pleased and refuse to tell me where *he* went. He'd driven me insane. I'd been torn between loving how treasured I felt with him and wanting the freedom to live my life.

Mick had argued with me for days when I told him I wanted to go, threatened to chain me up or put stasis spells on me before I finally wore him down. And now, in a place where the danger from my mother was its greatest—here he was.

"You know, one reason I took off was because I got tired of being treated like a child," I said.

"You *were* a child, Janet. Twenty-one and a legal adult, certain you could take on the world."

"I've been on my own since then and can take care of myself just fine."

"Because you ran in the right direction—away from here. This place will kill you, and you know it." He leaned to me again, his smile gone, his eyes serious. "I don't want to see you die. Call me selfish. That's why I'm here, and that's why I'm staying."

"Staying in Magellan?" I asked, trying to sound casual.

"In your hotel. With you."

"Excuse me." I tried to push myself into a sitting position, but I could only manage a slump against the headboard. "My hotel, Mick. Mine. Guests will pay for a room or be personally invited by me. *After* I get the damn thing finished."

He wouldn't budge, his body heat like a blanket. "I let you go before, because you weren't heading to danger. This time, if I don't stay with you, you'll be dead, and that's all there is to that."

He was challenging me. When I was younger, I let him lead me. Now I knew what I had to do.

"It is dangerous here, yes," I said. "Dangerous for *you*. I don't need to be worried about you on top of everything else."

"So don't worry. You run your hotel, and I'll watch your back. You need someone watching—tonight is proof of that."

"All right, maybe." I admitted that for all his mysteriousness, Mick was a good person to have on my side. "Why are you still so damned protective of me?"

"You have to ask?"

"I do."

Mick came closer still, until his face hung an inch from mine. "If you have to ask, then you wouldn't believe my answer." He drew away and continued wiping my hands.

"You are still an arrogant pain in the ass."

Mick flashed his teeth in a brilliant smile. Gods, he was gorgeous. His smile warmed the room and made me remember how precious he'd made me feel. *Stay with me and nothing will ever hurt you,* he'd say.

Had I been wise or foolish to stay? Or to leave?

He finished with the towels and kissed the tips of my fingers. "You sleep now. I'll stand guard."

"Are you sure you're all right? Your shoulder still looks awful."

"I'll take care of it." The man who'd been my first, last,

and only love smiled and touched my forehead. "Sleep, Janet."

Maybe he infused the command with magic, because the world went black, and I slept hard. I slept through the rest of the afternoon and on into morning, a dark, thankfully dreamless slumber. When I woke again, I felt better, the sun was rising, and Mick was gone.

Five

I wondered briefly whether I'd dreamed Mick. Maybe I'd passed out in Nash's office, and Lopez or someone had gotten me home and to bed. Not that I could see Nash being that kind to me.

I found bloody towels in the bathroom when I hobbled into it, and Mick's torn T-shirt tossed into my hamper of dirty clothes. He was no dream.

I also hoped I hadn't dreamed the running water. Nope, it streamed out of the taps, gloriously hot. I peeled off my shirt and stood in my bra while I washed my face and hands. I turned on the cold water to rinse out my mouth and brush my teeth. Toothpaste had never tasted so good. I drank a few mouthfuls from the faucet, realizing I hadn't eaten or drunk since leaving for Flagstaff two evenings ago.

I dried my face, lowered the towel, and saw a man staring at me through my bathroom window.

I screamed. The man was a big Native American, mus-

cled like Mick, but he wasn't Mick. He didn't smell of
skinwalker—I caught a scent of sage and wild grasses.

The man ducked away at my scream, and I rushed to
the window. I saw nothing outside but a coyote trotting off
toward the empty railroad bed behind the hotel. No sign of
any human except the prints of bare feet in the dust outside
the window. Human feet, large and masculine.

My eyes narrowed as I watched the spot where the coyote disappeared. I'd seen the same coyote hanging around
the hotel since I'd moved in. They were scavengers, ready
to eat anything humans threw away, or their pet dogs or
cats if the animals strayed too far from home.

I went into the bedroom and opened the window. The
early-morning air was cool, and I breathed in the beauty
of it. I saw no sign of the coyote, just blue sky blossoming
on the eastern horizon. But in the interesting life of Janet
Begay, things were never as simple as they seemed.

"Peeping Tom!" I shouted into the desert. Far off, I
heard a *yip* that sounded suspiciously like laughter, and
then silence.

I fixed a sheet over the curtainless window and
took a shower. Because my hotel stood alone two miles
north of Magellan, and my bedroom and bathroom faced
the back, away from the road and the bar, I'd not felt the
need to bother with curtains or blinds. I preferred sleeping
where I could wake up and see stars and moon, and the
privacy out here was nice. I'd forgotten that there were more
things in my world to worry about than nosy neighbors.

I dressed in clean clothes and walked out the back door
to scatter a handful of corn to the rising sun. I had a lot to
do today—I planned to go over the Amy McGuire case
again and see if anything new jumped out at me. I'd gotten a list of her friends from her mother, young women

who hadn't been asked to give statements for the police file, but they might tell me something useful about where Amy might go, who she might meet. I wanted most of all to question Nash Jones about her, but he was thin ice I had to tread on carefully.

Even so, I took time to perform my ritual greeting of the morning. I'd done this with my grandmother every day of my young life, and I'd retained the habit into adulthood. I hadn't always been able to do the ritual during my life on the road, but I'd decided that while I was here, I'd make sure that I gave thanks to the gods for the dawn. I needed all the earth magic I could get out here by the vortexes, and it never hurts to keep the gods happy. Today, no one watched me but a big crow perched on top of a juniper at the edge of the parking lot. It peered at me with a stern black eye, and I got the feeling that it approved of what I did.

I had no idea where Mick was. His bike was gone, but I knew he wouldn't have left me unless it was safe to. Even the times he'd disappeared when we lived together, he'd made certain that I was in a safe place, or got to a safe place, to hole up until he got back. Protective, yes, but also suffocating.

The hotel's electricity wasn't on yet, but I'd bought some nonperishables for a makeshift breakfast. The kitchen, like the rest of the hotel, was an empty shell, wires hanging out of holes in the walls like so much spaghetti.

I ate my cold toaster pastries while reading Amy's file, and then workers started showing up. Maya Medina, my electrician, got out of her sleek red pickup, wearing her white coverall, her glorious black hair tucked under a cap. She was the only female electrician in town, and from what I'd seen, she was damn good. Not that she acknowledged any praise I gave her. Maya was unfriendly to me to the point of enmity. I had no idea why, but at least she showed up and worked.

Behind her came carpenters, tile layers, roofers, and glaziers, mostly locals from Magellan, with a few Hopi men down from Second Mesa. They needed the work, and there was a lot to be done here.

To my surprise, Fremont Hansen pulled in not long after the others. I was standing by the front entrance, a huge old-Spanish door I'd picked up at an auction in Santa Fe, watching the workers come in. Fremont gave me a sorrowful look, set down his toolbox, and hugged me.

Usually I don't like to hug, and never without permission, but I sensed that Fremont needed the contact. I squeezed him back.

Fremont pulled away, his hands still on my shoulders. He was a little taller than me, slim, in his late thirties, with receding brown hair and friendly hazel eyes. "I'm glad you're all right, Janet."

"Just a few bruises." My leg still hurt, and my back was sore as hell from both sleeping in the jail cell and the motionless night I'd spent on my own bed, but I'd live. The healing magic that had leaked into me from Mick, plus the sleep, had done the trick. "Fremont, I'm really, really sorry."

"It wasn't your fault." Fremont gave my shoulders another pat, then released me. "It should have been me driving that truck, you know, not Charlie. He was running an errand for me." He shook his head. "Poor Charlie. He messed in some bad stuff, and he paid the price."

"Bad stuff? You mean drugs?"

"Black magic. Dangerous, if you don't know what you're doing."

Fremont spoke with authority, but I knew damn well that Fremont, for all his boasting, didn't have much magical ability. He wouldn't be able to handle anything darker than light gray. He was assuming that something Charlie had done had caused the accident, and I didn't correct him.

I didn't think he'd believe my explanation, and the less he knew, the safer he'd be.

Fremont picked up his toolbox and squared his shoulders, like a man ready to battle demons but not looking forward to it.

"Take the day off," I said. "The plumbing will still be here tomorrow."

"Nah. I'd just sit home and brood. Working keeps my mind off things. Besides, I want to get the water in your bathroom hooked up."

"You did," I said in surprise. "It's working."

Fremont gave me a puzzled look and strode through the lobby and down the back hall to my private suite. I followed him into the bathroom, where he cranked on both faucets at the sink. Nothing came out, not even air. The sink bowl looked dusty and unused.

"It was probably just some residue," he said. "I hope you didn't drink it."

I didn't answer. I'd showered, used the toilet, and brushed my teeth in plumbing ecstasy. Mick had showered too, obviously, from the pile of damp towels he'd left.

I made myself shrug. "You're probably right."

Fremont turned on his big flashlight and sank down under the sink. I left him to it, not sure what to think. That was the trouble with Mick. I spent a lot of time pushing him away, but when he was around, things had a way of working out for me. He'd give me that devilish smile, and I'd start feeling warm and comforted, and the impossible became possible.

But could I justify keeping him around because he gave me hot water and a good night's sleep? I didn't know what Mick was, but I was pretty sure facing a goddess from Beneath wouldn't be good for him.

Plus, the fact that Mick looked exactly the same unnerved me. I'd never asked him how old he was, assuming around thirty when I'd met him. But even five years affected people, didn't it? They gained or lost weight, changed how they cut their hair, got more lines in their faces. Very few stayed *exactly* the same. But Mick had.

The workers started clanking and banging, power tools whirring. No one needed me underfoot, so I left the hotel and made my way to the empty railroad bed behind it.

The big black crow flapped past me as I climbed the four-foot bank that used to carry trains from Winslow and the main line to the mountain towns of Heber-Overgaard and Show Low. The railroad had been abandoned early in the twentieth century, the ties and rails eventually disappearing, leaving the forlorn bed a reddish streak across the desert. My hotel had once been the railroad hotel, thriving in the 1890s, closed and forgotten, reopened in the thirties for a time, then again in the sixties, and finally completely abandoned. I'd bought an almost empty shell and was piecing it back together.

The crow landed in a gnarled juniper that clung to the bank of a wash. The desert to the east of my hotel was deceptively flat. The earth bore a reddish tint, like rust seeping through the dirt, and clumps of wild grass and thorny plants carpeted the ground. Occasional clusters of trees signaled where arroyos, washes, and narrow canyons sliced through the seemingly featureless desert. These washes served as runoff channels for the mountains. In rainless months, the washes were bone-dry; after a storm, they filled with torrents of water that destroyed everything in their way.

In and among these washes lay the vortexes. They were most prevalent to the south and east, where the land rose to a stunted ridgeline. Long, flat boulders studded the hill—some of the rocks had been eroded from beneath, giving them the look of anvils made for giants.

I gazed that way for a long time, my body still, listening.

I heard nothing but the wind in the grass, the quick slither of a hidden lizard or snake, the trickle of water in the sandy wash below, a leftover from last night's deluge. The crow ruffled her feathers against the wind, and far down the railroad bed, the spindly legged coyote trotted leisurely from the wash to the shade of another tree.

The sky arched blue overhead, not a cloud in sight. No storms to torment me, but then again, no magic to defend myself with either. She was out there somewhere, waiting for me.

As I stood there with sun pounding down on the top of my head, I remembered my first and only encounter with my mother. I'd just bought myself the Harley, a sweet little Sportster now in the impound lot of Nash Jones's jail. There I was, no longer a student living in cramped student housing in Flagstaff, no longer running home between terms to listen to my grandmother berate me.

I'd had the grandiose dream of riding up and down the country, taking photos, first of Diné lands, and then of the traditional lands of all tribes everywhere. I had visions of myself showing the collection at a gallery, selling them as a series, perhaps getting them published in a book.

My dream lasted as far as Holbrook, a town only twenty miles from the Navajo Nation. I pulled in for lunch, my camera at my side, in case I decided to do a study of roadside diners. I'd just given my order to the bored-looking waitress when a woman, pale even for a white person, slid into the booth across from me.

She had blond hair and light green eyes, a blouse and jeans on her slim form, and wore much silver jewelry. I had no idea who she was.

"Hello, Janet," she said in a low voice. "I'm your mother."

I laughed. I was Navajo through and through, and she

was so very white. "Sorry, lady. You're mixing me up with someone else."

Her answering smile was wide, her teeth perfect. "No mistake, love. I am your true mother."

I laughed again. "You're way too young to be my mother, and besides, my mother died in a hospital in Albuquerque when I was born."

She kept trying to look me full in the eyes, which I had been brought up to consider rude. My evasive eye flicks weren't dissuading her.

"Oh, you're mine all right, Janet Begay. What a beautiful young woman you turned out to be." She touched my wrist, her fingertips so chill I swore I felt my blood congeal. "And so strong. You'll do very well for me."

I snatched my hand away, not hiding my shiver. "You're crazy, lady."

She leaned a little to me, her perfect breasts resting on the table. "The storms, they get under your skin, don't they?"

I stared at her in sudden alarm. No one knew about the madness the storms stirred inside me. When I'd first manifested the power, at age eleven, I hadn't been able to control it at all. I'd nearly destroyed my father's house before I'd run away into the desert, pulling the lightning with me. Later I'd burned down one of the prefab buildings at my school, fortunately with no one in it at the time. I'd learned to stay away from other people when storms approached, which meant ditching school and running away. But better to get suspended than to let people die because I couldn't handle my own power. Learning control had been a slow and painful process, and even then, at age twenty-one, I still struggled with it.

"What are you talking about?" I managed.

Again the cold smile. "I gave you magic too, Janet. If you don't fight it, if you let it come, it won't hurt you anymore."

I had no idea what she meant. I sat, frozen, my heart beating double time.

She traced a light design on the tabletop. "Your biological mother, poor little thing, wasn't strong enough to take both you and the power. I can't stay in people for long, so I had to leave her alone and pregnant. She died having you, but you lived."

"You see?" I croaked. "You've just admitted you weren't her."

Her fingers were drawing runes of power. Nasty things, with little trickles of darkness following them. I reached over and slapped her hand to the table.

The woman smiled. "Ah, you do understand. Your mother was the vessel I chose to bring you into the world. She was weaker than I'd anticipated, unfortunately. Your father was the means." Her green eyes took on a warm gleam. "He was a handsome young man, and oh so virile. Is he still as . . . robust?"

Hearing this woman talk about my father, a quiet, slim Diné, as though he'd been her personal toy made me sick. Quiet, shy Pete Begay, a man who'd learned to say little in his houseful of headstrong women, was beautiful to me, but I wasn't about to share my thoughts with this scary bitch of a woman.

"Stop talking about my father, and get away from me."

She gave me a pitying look. "Poor baby. Did he not tell you that your mother was a magical woman from beyond the sky? That's what he thought I was, and it's more or less true. What you are looking at now is a shell, not my real form. I can only come out when I find a body that can take me, a woman strong enough and young enough to endure my power. This one won't last long, but I can use her long enough for me to talk to my daughter."

Her words trickled beneath my skin, stirring fear so deep I didn't want to look at it.

"I'm twenty-one," I pointed out. "If you truly are my mother, why wait so long to find me?"

"Because my power can only stretch over so much distance, before I have to retreat to Beneath and replenish. Your pokey town on the reservation is too far away, and so was the university you chose. Besides, your grandmother's magic is powerful on her home territory—like mine is, except hers is earthbound. As long as you were tied to your home, I couldn't get to you. But now you have that." She glanced out the window at my gleaming new Harley. "And you can come to me whenever you like."

My heart pounded, fear overlaid with confusion and anger. "What are you talking about? My grandmother has no magic. She hates magic."

"If she told you that, she lied. She's a mage, a shaman, and dangerous to you. You are right to flee her, because she will destroy you."

"My grandmother doesn't like me, but she wouldn't do that." I spoke without conviction, and the woman knew it.

"No, my dear, she is strong. That's why I chose your father, because I knew he'd carry the power to you, even though he has none himself." She leaned to me again. "You feel it, the two natures inside you. You will come to me, and I will teach you. You will be so powerful, so strong, that you'll be able to squash your grandmother like a bug."

I sat in a pool of fear, because I knew she was right about the two natures inside me. I felt them when my storm power manifested, a second power trying to mesh with the first, not quite able to. It made my storm power that much more difficult to control, had made the first shaman my grandmother took me to pronounce me a witch.

"I can make it better, my dear." The woman touched my face, her fingertips like ice. "Be with me."

Something inside me tingled, woke up, yearned to claw its way through me and respond to her touch.

"You feel it, don't you?" she purred. "My daughter. My love. Let me teach you. I can make you powerful beyond your wildest dreams."

I tried to get up, to run, but I was fixed in place, mesmerized. Her eyes were deep green, the green of ferns that choked stagnant ponds.

"You are mine, Janet," she whispered.

The power wanted me to touch her. It wanted me to take her hands and look deep into her eyes, to do whatever she told me to.

I seemed to hear my grandmother's voice from far away, shouting at me in Navajo. *Janet Begay, what do you think you're doing?*

The sound snapped through my mind. The woman gasped and blinked, and my rigid gaze broke. I jerked away, my eyes wide, my face slick with sweat.

I jumped to my feet. "Stop talking about my mother," I said to her in a vicious voice. "And stay away from me."

She sat back, and I fled the diner, ignoring the protests of the waitress who'd been hurrying toward our table with my food. I made it to my bike, shaking with rage—to find the woman standing beside it.

Fear came flooding back. No one could move that fast, except maybe skinwalkers. This woman was evil, pure, powerful evil. And I knew, though I didn't want to give voice to the thought, that her evil was also inside me.

"Get out of my way," I said, my voice shaking.

"We will meet again, Janet. This I promise you. In time, you'll come to me on your own. You won't be able to stop yourself."

She reached for me, but I shoved her aside, swung onto my bike, and rode the hell out of there. I didn't look back, didn't slow down. I gunned it through the small town, drove up the freeway ramp, and opened up the bike, heading out at top speed. If she could only move so far, all I had to do was keep riding and not come back.

I rode so fast that I got stopped for speeding before I hit the state line, but I didn't care. As long as the woman with the strange green eyes didn't follow me, I didn't mind about tickets.

"Begay."

Memories shattered, and I swung around to see Nash Jones climb up the railroad bed, his sheriff's badge winking in the sun. His uniform was as crisp as ever, flat, black sunglasses hiding his eyes. He didn't have his handcuffs out, but that didn't mean he hadn't come to drag me back to jail.

I drew a sharp breath, banishing the gut-chilling thoughts of my mother. "I want a lawyer," I said before he reached the top.

"I'm not here to arrest you." Nash halted a yard from me and trained his sunglasses stare on me. "Your story checked out."

I blinked. "It did?"

He gave me a curt nod. "No paint on your bike, no corresponding dent in the truck. Looks like an animal ran onto the road, a big one, and hit the truck. Might have been a mountain lion or even a bear."

Both animals came down out of the mountains to look for water in the dry months, but mountain lions were shy and avoided humans whenever possible. Bears, though less worried about humans, weren't stupid enough to charge a truck moving at fifty miles per hour. But I clamped down on my argument. Jones the Unbeliever wasn't going to buy my skinwalker claim, and if he wanted to think an animal had done this, fine.

"You came here to apologize?" I asked. "For wrongly arresting me?"

He didn't look one bit sorry. "No. I was doing my job."

"Aren't you afraid that I'll complain to my tribal government about a white sheriff harassing a Navajo?"

"Not really. They know you."

He had a point. "So why are you here?"

"To return your personal belongings and tell you your bike has been taken to the garage in Flat Mesa."

That meant I wouldn't be riding around Magellan today, talking to Amy's friends. I didn't like to think of my bike in the shop, broken and alone. I'd have to get up there somehow and make sure the mechanic knew what he was doing.

"I also came to see if your boyfriend was all right," Nash went on. "I can't find where he's checked into any hospital."

I was surprised he cared enough to look. "Mick will be all right," I answered "He's good at looking out for himself."

"I won't charge him, if that's what you're worried about. Just tell him that when I say stop, I really mean it." He paused. "How is he?"

I had to shrug. "I don't know. He took off." When Jones just looked at me, I fumbled for more explanation but couldn't find one. It bothered me that once again, I had no idea where Mick went or what he did when he wasn't with me. He hadn't changed in that respect either.

"What's his name?" Nash asked.

"Mick."

"Mick what?"

I didn't know, another thing that bugged me. I gave him the name I invented a long time ago. "Burns." It was my little joke. Mick did like to play with fire.

"Where's he from?"

"I don't know, actually. I met him in Nevada, about five and a half years ago."

"And you still don't know where he's from?"

"I was never nosy enough to ask. Navajos stay out of other people's business." That wasn't strictly true, especially in the case of my grandmother, but he didn't need to know that.

"I like to find out where people in my county have come from and what they plan to do here."

"I haven't seen Mick in a long time. Why don't you ask him?"

Nash trained his stare on me for a while, before he said, "When he gets back, tell him to come talk to me."

"Is that an order?"

"It's a request."

I shuffled my feet, stirring the gravel with the toes of my boots. "If I see him again, I'll pass it along."

"Good."

"What do you—" I began, then I broke off and raised my hands as Nash abruptly drew his pistol. "Whoa. Don't worry. I'll tell him."

Nash wasn't looking at me. He raised the gun and pointed it at the coyote that had wandered toward us while we talked and now sat on his haunches, watching us.

"Don't," I said quickly. "It's just a mangy coyote. Leave it alone."

Nash fired. I clapped my hands over my ears as the *boom* of the pistol tried to deafen me. The bullet hit the ground about five feet in front of the coyote, spewing an arc of dirt and gravel. The coyote scrambled back a few paces, an annoyed look in its eyes. Nash fired twice more, and the coyote, with a final sneer of disgust, turned and slunk down the wash.

My ears rang. "What did you do that for?" It was never

a good idea to idly shoot at animals. One might be a god in disguise, and you should never piss off the gods.

"Coyotes are vermin. They carry rabies."

"You couldn't wave your arms and shout at it?"

"I got my point across." Nash shoved the pistol back into his holster. "Tell your boyfriend that if he doesn't come see me, I'll find him."

"You don't want to mess with Mick, Sheriff."

"Want to tell me why?"

I hesitated. "He doesn't exactly follow anyone's rules."

"In my county, he follows mine." Nash gave me a severe look. "I expect you to follow them too."

"Of course you do. It's been fun talking to you, Jones, but it's getting hot, and if you don't mind, I'd like to go back inside."

Nash stood back, making me an "after you" motion. I scrambled down the railroad bed and heard Nash's quiet footfalls behind me.

Without speaking, we walked the twenty yards to the hotel and the activity there. Nash had parked his sheriff's SUV a little way from the workers' trucks, the vehicle sparkling and gleaming in the sun. He probably had it washed and waxed every morning.

I stopped, and Nash almost ran into the back of me. He looked over my shoulder at what I saw and started to swear.

The coyote that Nash had driven off was shooting a stream of yellow piss onto his SUV's front tire. I pressed my hand over my mouth, trying not to laugh, while Nash continued to swear. He ran at the coyote, waving his arms and shouting this time.

I heard peals of laughter from the direction of the hotel. Maya Medina had emerged, and she stood straight, hands on hips, watching the coyote and laughing hard. Her dark eyes flashed, and ringlets of black hair straggled from her cap. She was truly a beautiful young woman, and now she laughed as though she hadn't seen anything this funny in a long time.

The coyote finished his business and sauntered back out into the desert. Maya signaled to me, wiping her eyes. "Hey, I need to show you something. In the basement."

Maya never addressed me by name, if she could help it. She also seemed to delight in telling me the problems that I was having with the electrical system, which had been installed during the renovation attempt in the 1960s. I had no idea why Maya disliked me. It might be nothing more than resentment of a stranger in her small town, or her not liking me renovating the hotel, or she might not like Diné women. People got hostile for the strangest reasons.

"What is it?"

"Something I found." Maya glanced thoughtfully at Nash. "You might want to look too, Sheriff Jones." The last two words were inflected with scorn.

Oh, gods, what? More wiring that had to be completely replaced? Was the building so hopelessly beyond code that Nash would declare it a disaster area and make me move out?

Nash kept his face straight as he walked to us, but the thin scar above his lip was jumping. Maya wouldn't look at him but turned and went back inside. I followed, with Nash coming behind.

The dry-rotted door to the basement was off its hinges now, and the opening gaped like a black hole in the bricks. My leg hurt a little again as I navigated down the slippery stone stairs to the basement with its seven-foot ceiling. A new water heater gleamed in the corner, waiting for electricity and plumbing.

As Maya led me across the room, beneath the lobby, my shoulder blades began to itch. Nash breathed heavily behind me, but none of us said a word.

Maya lifted her flashlight and played it on a wall until she found what she was looking for. She'd knocked away some of the old paneling to trace wiring running down from the kitchen. She trained her light on a square she'd pulled away, and I gasped. Jones said another swear word.

There, grinning at us from behind the wall, was the face of a half-decayed corpse.

Six

The three of us stared at the skull in stunned silence. From the fine bones and the gleam of gold jewelry around the neck, I assumed it was a woman, although I wasn't expert enough to know. She'd been dead for some time, the skin still on the bones, some hair still attached to her head.

Without taking his eyes from the corpse, Nash picked up the crowbar Maya had left against the wall, wedged it against the panel, and ripped away more of the rotted wood.

The entire body stood there, half-skeletal, with part of a shirt and shorts that she'd been wearing, and sneakers. It was bizarre, the dry decay of the rest of her, but the sneakers still pretty much whole. Her clothes looked not so much decomposed as torn—insects and animals that had made their homes here had chewed them for food or to line nests.

I'd done a spell when I moved in that asked the animal life to leave—much more effective than an exterminator—because the place had been infested with mice, snakes, spiders, and scorpions. An empty building provided fine shelter for desert critters. The animals and insects had chewed the woman too, of course, which made it all the more gruesome.

I put my hands on my hips and tried to control the instinctive panic that lodged in my throat. I hated death and places of death. Traditionally among my people, when someone died inside a hogan, the entire building was abandoned. Easier to build anew than to live with the ghosts. My father and grandmother had a horror of hospitals, because people went to die there. When my grandmother had gone in to have her gall bladder out ten years ago, we'd had a hell of a time convincing her to stay overnight. She still hadn't forgiven me, or my father, for that.

"Holy shit," said a new voice. Fremont came across the basement floor, the beam of his flashlight bobbing. "That's not Amy McGuire, is it?"

He voiced what the three of us hadn't dared. A woman, dead for months, walled up in a place that had been abandoned for years. Even if the hotel had been searched when Amy disappeared, no one had thought to remove the paneling down here until Maya had started working on the electricity.

"It's not her," Nash snapped.

The three of us jerked our attention to him. He stood with crowbar in hand, the glow of the flashlights making his uniform look gray. His face was just as gray.

"You sure?" Fremont adjusted his cap. "She's missing, and here's a dead woman about her size."

Nash's eyes glittered menacingly. I had the fleeting vision of him taking each of us out with the crowbar, walling us up behind the paneling to keep Amy company.

"I want everyone out of here," he said. "Upstairs, and don't come back down. Maya, don't go anywhere. I'll need a statement from you. You too, Begay."

"It's my hotel," I said. "I'm not leaving."

"Good." He gestured with the crowbar. "Out."

Maya gave him a look of undisguised fury before she nearly ran up the stairs, a string of muttered Spanish floating down after her. Fremont, the gentleman, politely waited for me to go ahead of him. I heard Nash click on his radio.

I swung back. "Don't call McGuire," I said quickly. "Don't let him see this."

I imagined what it would be like for my own father to view the remains of a woman who might be me, not knowing for sure whether the pile of bones and flesh was his daughter.

"It's not Amy," Nash replied, words clipped.

"Doesn't matter. It *could* be her. Don't make him have to identify her."

Nash regarded me for a long time. I don't know what went on behind those eyes of his, but finally he nodded. "I'll call Salas."

Salas was the assistant chief of police in Magellan. I didn't know much about him, and I didn't know whether he could keep this quiet, at least until the woman was identified. But if I could spare kindly Chief McGuire any agony, I would.

"Go upstairs and stay there," Nash repeated. "Tell your workers to stop what they're doing. This is now a crime scene."

Terrific. I went up after Fremont. He moved to the carpenters to break the news to them, but Maya wasn't in the lobby. I suppressed a growl of exasperation as I went to look for her. If she took off, Nash would probably blame me.

I found Maya outside, standing in the shade of the building, arms folded, staring across the parking lot to the desert beyond. I leaned against the door frame, inhaling the clean morning air, trying to wash away the crawly sensation of death.

I'd been here two weeks and not sensed or seen the woman's ghost down there, nor had my protective spells signaled me that something was wrong. Why not? Maybe the spells knew that the dead woman wasn't a danger? She wasn't a demon or similar evil; she was a poor, sad person locked away in the dark, killed and abandoned.

Lack of a ghost either meant that she was at peace, which didn't tally with her being buried behind a wall, or it meant she hadn't died here. I'd felt no residue of violence in the building, not even the emptiness of death.

Fremont came outside and joined us in contemplation of the desert. "Do you think she was walled up alive?" he asked, half in horror, half in fascination.

Maya looked over at him, her bleak look replaced with impatience. "I doubt it. The paneling was dry-rotted and easy to pull apart. Even a weak person could have kicked it out. It doesn't look like she was tied up or anything, as far as I can tell."

"You looked?" Fremont asked.

"Of course I did. Don't tell me you're not curious."

Of the three of us, Maya seemed the most contained; in fact, she looked angry. Maybe she used anger to cover her true feelings, but Maya always looked angry, so how could I tell?

"When you bought this hotel, didn't you notice that there was a body in the basement?" she asked me.

I stuck my hands in my pockets. "The building inspector didn't mention it in his report."

"Very funny."

"Do you think Nash is right?" Fremont asked. "That it's not Amy?"

Maya shrugged. She was good at shrugging, managing

to put a day's worth of insolence in a quick rise and fall of shoulders. "How should I know? I'm not an expert on dead bodies." She eyed me. "Can't you tell with your mystical senses? Or Navajo medicine magic, or whatever?"

"I take it you're an Unbeliever?"

Maya laughed, the laughter edged with anger. "Damn right. There's nothing in this town but frauds and con artists. There aren't any vortexes; there isn't any 'mystical energy' crap. It's all a big, fat, tourist-trap lie, and you're not doing anything but encouraging it."

Her vehemence puzzled me. I'd never extolled the mystical virtues of Magellan, never joined in the group sing-alongs Heather Hansen led at the vortexes on nights of the full moon. "So, definitely an Unbeliever," I said.

"You got it."

Fremont shook his head. "You don't see what's under your nose, Maya Medina."

"You're just as bad," she snapped at him. "Telling everyone you're a magician. You can't even fix Janet's plumbing."

"I'm working on it. The system is ancient."

"So go work on it, then."

Fremont gave me a look that said, "Humor her; she's a little nuts," and went back inside.

Maya and I stood in uncompanionable silence a few moments, while sirens sprang up in the distance, Salas answering Jones's call from the far side of Magellan.

"I think she was killed elsewhere," I said, thinking out loud. "And someone brought her and put her behind the wall."

"Well, it wasn't me."

"Any reason it should have been?"

"*Dios*, you're nosy. All right, if I don't tell you, someone else will. I hated Amy McGuire. Hated her skinny, blond, goody-two-shoes ass, and I wasn't sorry when she disappeared."

I hadn't mentioned Amy specifically, but Maya gave me a defiant look, as though she expected me to be shocked or appalled. I was neither. I wasn't here to pass judgment on what people thought about Amy; I was here to figure out what had happened to her.

"Anyone share your views?" I asked. "Enough to want to make her vanish? Or kill her and wall her up in my basement?"

"Are you kidding? Everyone loved Amy McGuire. She was prom queen and sang in her church choir and was in the honor society. She went to U of A on a big scholarship. God knows why she moved back here."

"To get married to Sheriff Jones?"

"They got engaged *after* she came back from college." Maya's mouth flattened. "Everyone loved Amy, Nash Jones most of all."

She didn't bother to hide her rage. Here we were at a murder scene, the victim possibly a woman she'd hated, and Maya was venting about her. The surge of anger when she mentioned Nash didn't escape me either, nor had the way she'd laughed when the coyote had emptied his bladder on Nash's tire. Interesting.

The sirens grew louder. A car marked "Magellan Police" turned onto the lot, dust spiraling into the blue sky behind it. I left Maya and went to greet Assistant Chief Salas and a younger uniformed cop who got out of the car. I led them through the lobby, past my curious workers, who showed no sign of leaving, and to the basement door. I clattered down after Salas. Nash was still standing near the wall, his body rigid, his gaze fixed on the corpse.

"Jones," Salas said, approaching him. "You okay, man?"

Nash jerked, glared at Salas, and then strode across the floor, boots clicking in the sudden silence, past me up the stairs, and out.

*   *   *

By the time I got back outside, Maya was gone, and Nash was in his SUV, pulling out of the parking lot, a cloud of dust in his wake. Once on the highway he turned on his red and blue lights and headed north toward Flat Mesa. I wondered if Nash had talked to Maya, but I noticed that Maya's truck had gone as well.

The crow I'd seen earlier sailed to the tree at the northeast corner of the lot and perched there. The coyote came out from behind the hotel about the same time. He stopped in the shade of the tree and sat down, tongue lolling.

"Better watch it, smart ass," I said to him. "The sheriff is trigger happy. Next time he might not stop at scaring you away."

The coyote's yellow eyes held scorn. I was pretty sure that even were Nash a dead shot, the bullet would do nothing to this one.

"The question is, who sent you?" If it was my mother, then the coyote and the crow were my enemies. If Mick, my friends, or at least, they'd be told to help me. If my grandmother, it was an open field. I never knew with my grandmother.

Neither answered. Very helpful. The could be just animals, but I doubted it. Wild animals tended to avoid people, wise creatures.

My speculations were cut short by the arrival of the medical examiner's van. Two men went inside with a stretcher. People from town started showing up to ask what was going on. Fremont appeared from the hotel and decided to be spokesman, telling the tale over and over. Instead of this irritating me, I was grateful to him for drawing attention from me.

Not long later, Salas came out of the hotel and walked to me. Salas seemed like a competent guy, a calmer version of

Jones. "I don't think it's Amy," he said to me. "This woman was older, the ME says, maybe in her forties or early fifties. I'll call the chief, let him know."

I nodded. "Sheriff Jones didn't think it was her either."

Salas gave me a look, but he turned away to make his call without commenting.

The stretcher came up out of the basement at that point, and I watched in silence as the body was loaded into the medical examiner's van. The medics climbed into the front, and the coyote and I watched the van drive away toward Flat Mesa.

Another woman, another disappearance. And my mother hovering out there by the vortexes, waiting to possess people so she could move about in this world and interact with others, just as she had the day I'd met her in Holbrook. I remembered how she'd told me that the "shell" she inhabited was weak, just like my biological mother's had been. The woman who'd borne me had died. I didn't think this woman's death was a coincidence, and I swore I'd stop my mother before she could cause any more damage.

Good.

I swung around at the voice, but I saw no one except the coyote. When I caught his eyes, he looked innocent and determinedly scratched at a flea.

Seven

The Crossroads Bar had opened before Salas finished inside. My workers had already been told to go, and they'd packed up trucks and vans and driven away. Salas came up from the basement at about five o'clock, followed by the uniform. I'd retreated inside as the day grew hot. The hotel had been built long before air-conditioning had been invented, but the walls were thick enough to keep out the heat of the day.

"You have somewhere to stay?" Salas asked me when he emerged.

"Yes. Here."

"It's a crime scene."

"The basement is. My bedroom isn't."

"I'm sorry, Janet. We need to go over the entire place, try to find out if the woman was brought here or killed here."

"I've been renovating." I gestured at the freshly plastered walls, the newly tiled floor and staircase. "Any evidence is on the county dump."

Even with my aversion to staying in a place where death had happened, I had no intention of abandoning my hotel. The place was becoming a part of me, something I couldn't walk away from. The problems I kept encountering made it more challenging, but I wasn't about to give up. I wouldn't give my mother the satisfaction.

Salas conceded. "All right, but you see anything out of place, anything weird, you call me," he said. "Me, not Jones or the chief."

"Got it."

Salas was neutral on the subject of Amy, or at least not as closely connected as the other two, as far as the police file told me. Of course, the reports hadn't mentioned Maya's fierce hatred of the girl either. But Maya hadn't been a witness and hadn't been questioned, and so had made no statement.

Salas left, and I was finally alone. The uniform had covered the gaping hole of my basement door with crisscrossed police tape, the yellow stark against the darkness. Death oozed from the opening even though the woman had been removed. Another cleansing spell was in order, I decided, but I was too tired and unnerved to do it now.

I found that Nash had stashed my belongings behind the old reception desk—wallet and keys, belt, what little money I'd been carrying, receipt for the supplies I'd ordered in Flagstaff—everything there except the spell ball. Nash hadn't returned that.

I wanted to get out and find food, since I hadn't eaten all day, but without my Harley, I was stuck. I could always walk the two miles into Magellan and eat at the diner, but everyone there would want to talk about the dead woman, and I'd be bombarded with questions. Barry, who owned the Crossroads Bar, could probably give me something to snack on, but same problem about the questions. I scrounged through my pantry and ate some pretzels, not really hungry for much else.

Restless, I climbed the staircase that rose to a gallery, which ran in a U-shape around the second floor. The guest rooms, half-finished, opened out to it.

The staircase to the third floor lay at the end of the gallery, beyond a locked door. I'd decided that the rooms up here would be private, including an office for me. In the biggest room on the low-ceilinged third floor, I'd found an old-fashioned rolltop desk that I'd refinish and a gigantic mirror that had once hung over the bar in the saloon. The mirror was in good shape, solid frame, glass still whole. Some of the silver had started to flake off, but I'd send it somewhere to get re-silvered and then hang it in the saloon again.

The third floor was only a partial floor, and a door led from the big room to the flat roof. I'd swept off the roof when I first moved in, creating a place where I could sit and watch the stars come out. It was peaceful up here, away from noise and people.

Tonight the sky was clear, but lightning flickered on the northeastern horizon. Stars pricked out and a half moon hovered in the sky.

I heard Mick's motorcycle throbbing below, then cut off into silence. Not long later, he strolled out onto the roof.

He'd found a holeless shirt somewhere and a clean pair of jeans, but other than that, he looked the same as he had yesterday. I rose to meet him, and in total silence, he gathered me in and held me close.

It felt good to lean on his rock-solid chest and rest my head against his shoulder. He ran his hands down my back, lips brushing my hair.

"I heard," he said. "You all right, baby?"

Lightning struck so far away that I didn't hear a rumble, but I jumped. "No."

Mick slid his palm to the small of my back. "Want me to make you feel better?"

I did. I truly did. I craved him, and this storm, if it rolled in, was going to hurt me. I hadn't had enough time to recover from the gigantic one two nights ago.

"What about you?" I asked. "Are you all right?" I touched his shoulder where the gunshot wound had been, but I found no indentation from the bullet or any bump of scar.

"Yep. All better."

I wanted to ask where he'd gone and how he'd so completely healed himself. And why, if he claimed he'd come to protect me, he hadn't been here when the body was found. I knew he wouldn't tell me any of these things, so I didn't bother with the questions.

"How did you know about the woman?" I asked instead.

"Everyone in town knows. I stopped for gas, and three people asked me if I'd heard about the dead woman buried in the Navajo woman's hotel."

I tried to laugh. "I'm getting a reputation."

"You're shaking. Have you eaten anything?" I shrugged, trying to downplay, but Mick gave me a severe look. "I'm taking you to get some food," he said.

"Not the diner. I don't want to talk to people right now."

"No, not the diner." He laced his fingers through mine. "Come on."

Mick took me out of the hotel, boosted me onto his bike, and rode with me up to Winslow. The storm grew closer as we went, sliding down the freeway toward us as we dined at a fast-food restaurant. I needed this: normal, generic surroundings with normal, generic people.

The storm moved south as we rode back to the hotel, the smell of rain on bare earth fresh and pungent. I stopped myself from reaching for the lightning, not wanting the storm's crazy magic tonight. The storm had other ideas, and I fended it off with effort, sweat breaking out on my brow.

We reached the hotel. While I locked up, Mick went into my bedroom and took candles and sage sticks from the top drawer of my dresser. Without argument, I helped him set the candles out and light them. We moved through the hotel with smudge sticks, wafting fragrant smoke everywhere. The storm kept trying to find me, and I gritted my teeth while I chanted spells and Mick silently traced runes over doors and windows. I could feel my magic and his seeping into the walls, connecting with the spells I had laid before, erasing the spidery fingers of darkness that came from the basement.

We finished in the middle of the lobby. Mick dropped both smudge sticks into a ceramic bowl, then he took me by the elbows and pulled me against him.

I felt the tension in him, the magic that spiraled through his body. Lightning sizzled in my fingers as Mick leaned down to kiss my lips.

"You taste as good as ever," he murmured. "Want me to draw it off?"

I knew what *that* would lead to. "Why did you really come here?"

"I told you, to protect you." In the candlelight, Mick's black hair shone with a glossy hue. When he let it out, it went everywhere, curls so crazy they almost had a life of their own.

"You said yourself you were impressed with how I handled that skinwalker," I said. "You know I'm much stronger now."

"You are. But there are things much worse than skin-walkers out there. Very bad things are coming, Janet, and you know it. You need me."

I couldn't deny that Magellan was a dangerous place for me. "I don't want you to get hurt. Least of all because of me."

Mick ran the backs of his fingers across my cheek. "Let me? For old time's sake?"

The hotel lit with lightning, and the answering *boom* came the next second. Electricity crackled along my skin, wanting me to grab it, to throw it at something, to *destroy*.

Silently, I nodded. Mick smiled his old, devilish smile. "Come on, then. Give me your best shot."

I closed my eyes. Magic danced through me, released at last, channeling out through my fingers and straight into Mick. He took a deep, shuddering breath. "Oh, that's good."

My body squeezed in delight. Being caught in a storm was like the best foreplay, and here I was with a strong, virile man who wanted me. I moved my lightning-encased hands to his face and pulled him down for a long kiss.

Magic flowed from my mouth to his. I hadn't seen this man in five years, and yet his kiss, the way he swept his tongue into mine, felt so familiar, so right. I *needed* him to do this.

Mick ran his hands over my body, and I tugged up his T-shirt. Beneath, his skin was smooth and hot, hard with muscle. The shoulder where he'd been shot was whole and unblemished; even the bruise had disappeared.

My own shirt ended up on the floor, and we were kissing, kissing. Magic floated between and around us, touching the spells we'd begun and flaring them to life.

Mick had taught me all about Tantric, the use of sex and sexual pleasure to build up magical power and then channel it. I remembered the first night we'd tried it, a week after I'd met him, remembered every press of his fingers on my skin, the slide of his body against mine, every thrust of his hips. He'd tied my hands to the headboard so I couldn't touch him, which had driven me crazy, as he'd known it would. My frustration, coupled with the things he'd done to me, made the final release, when it came, incredibly intense.

Mick carried me into the bedroom and laid me on the bed. I feasted my eyes on him while he got rid of his pants and boots and underwear. His chest and arms were replete with muscle, and his abs were flat, the indentation of his navel a shadow. He had strong thighs, and his long, thick penis, now hard, stuck straight out.

The sight of him stirred the primal female in me. No more worry about what he was, why he was here, where he'd been. I wanted that beautiful male body on mine, urges as old as time wiping out my questions and my common sense.

The electricity eased away as he kissed me, a slow, deliberate kiss that explained how he wanted to proceed. He kissed down my throat, lingering at the hollow, then down to my breasts. Each kiss was unhurried, and each caress made my body hum, my blood warm.

By the time he'd undressed me, he'd drawn off the worst of the storm magic, and I felt damn good. And needy. Mick pinned my hands above my head, his mouth on mine as he entered me. Magic drifted through the room, the marks on the walls we'd traced starting to glow.

I lifted my legs and wrapped them around his hips. He was big, filling me. The sensations were so familiar, as though we'd lain together only last night, not five long years ago. As though we'd never been apart.

Mick had skill and finesse. He built us toward release until we were both ready to peak, then he eased off, cooling the sensations.

"Damn you," I growled.

"It's the way it works, sweetheart."

"I know. You don't have to like it so much."

Mick's laughter was low, wicked. "Believe me, this is torture. I want to do you hard and not stop until we're done. It's all I can do to hold back."

"Sure," I said. He was so full of shit. "Let me torture you some more, then."

I made him regret that he'd taught me so much about sex, and that I'd been such an eager pupil. His smiles died as I arched to him, and soon he was growling at *me*, trying to slow his thrusts and make it last.

Magic swirled through the room like dancing comets. We built again and again, Mick taking us down before we reached the peak every time. My body felt open and hot, I was dripping with sweat, and my thoughts narrowed to nothing but the crazed need inside me.

Mick's body lit with sudden, incandescent light, and for one instant, I thought I saw a monster with us in the bedroom, something so huge it would burst the walls. Its skin glistened black, and its eyes were like midnight but with red fire in their depths.

I screamed, and the vision vanished. There was only Mick making love to me.

He kissed my swollen lips. "Now," he whispered.

I screamed again, this time in ecstasy. Mick's shout answered me. Pent-up magic shot out of us, the room burst into light, and the spell runes burned as red as the fire in the monster-creature's eyes.

Mick and I went on climaxing, hours of buildup peaking into one amazing, drawn-out release. I twisted under him, and he thrust into me, holding me hard. Finally, after a long time of drowning, I gave out and collapsed, panting. I knew I'd never be able to move again.

Mick fell beside me, laughing. The glowing runes vanished into the walls; the magic absorbed into the building.

"Gods, I missed you, Janet," Mick said, voice raw. He kissed my face, my hair. "I missed you so damned much. Don't ever leave me again, all right?"

I was too tired to answer, too tired to argue, but I couldn't deny that I'd missed him too. I wished with all my heart that we were two simple, boring humans, with nothing complicated between us.

For now I felt safe, the magic in here strong.

He circled my wrist with his finger and thumb, his pupils widening until his eyes were nearly black. "You are so beautiful." He rubbed my wrist, then kissed it. "I don't think you ever believed me when I told you how beautiful you were."

"Mmm, I thought you said that just to get into my pants."

"I did want to get into your pants." Mick licked my wrist, his hot breath stirring need. "I still do. I love every part of you." He released my wrist and plied his tongue to my abdomen, my navel, and down to the curls between my thighs.

I groaned. "Mick, I can't. I'm too tired for more."

Mick had always enjoyed proving me wrong. He licked and kissed me for a while, then he rolled me on top of him, moving me to straddle him. He was already hard, and it was easy to slide right onto him.

My eyes closed, need I'd thought gone for the night returning with amazing strength. Mick cupped my breasts as I rode him, and I smiled down at him, enjoying the pleasure he so freely offered.

Much later, after we'd both fallen asleep, exhausted and sated, I woke to blissful silence. Mick slept next to me, moonlight bathing his naked body. In addition to the stylized dragons that ran down his arms, a tattoo hugged Mick's waist and hips like a chain, a point of it dipping to the cleave of his buttocks. The ink was stark black in the moonlight, and the eyes in the dragon tattoos seemed to glitter as though they watched me.

I slid out of bed and went to the window. The night was beautiful, shadows sharp, the moonlight shining hard on the empty desert. Something moved under the juniper at the edge of my property, but I neither smelled the stench of skinwalker nor felt the terror they exuded.

I shrugged on a long shirt, slid my feet into shoes, and went out the back door.

The coyote lay under the tree, paws out, tongue curling with his fast breath. He watched me approach, then glanced at the bare patch of ground next to him. *Come. Sit.*

I sank down, bunching my shirt under my butt to cushion the hard ground. We sat quietly for a few moments; then I said, "So tell me. Who sent you to me and what do you want?"

Eight

The air shimmered and resolved into a very large, very naked man with long black hair. He had a Native American face, though I couldn't tell what tribe he belonged to. I knew a Hopi from a Havasupai from an Apache, and all those from tribes not Southwestern, but I couldn't place him.

"Questions, questions. Always the questions." His voice was gravelly, similar to Mick's, though his body was more raw, more brutish.

"A coyote changes into a man and watches me through my window," I said. "It makes me inquisitive."

"You have a cute ass."

"Thanks," I said dryly. "Why are you so interested in looking at it?"

"You have to ask?" His grin was almost evil.

"Who are you?"

He kept smiling but watched me with eyes dark as smoke. "You know the answer to that."

A drifter, Nash had called him, one who hung around the Crossroads Bar with the biker gangs. "You're Coyote as in Coyote the god?"

"That's what they call me."

"My grandmother calls you a pain in the ass and blames everything that goes wrong on you."

"Your grandmother is quite a woman."

I somehow didn't have trouble believing that Coyote knew my grandmother, or at least who she was. I pictured her, a small Diné woman who refused to wear anything but her long skirts, chasing a yelping coyote with a broom.

"So what do you want?" I asked. "Besides an eyeful of me?"

"Oh, that. I'm here to stop you."

"Stop me from doing what? Finding Amy McGuire?"

Coyote gazed off into the desert, to a bright star on the horizon. "You know better than that. You're a harbinger, Janet Begay. A cute harbinger, but a harbinger nonetheless." His voice lost its edge of humor. "This is a good world. I like it. I won't let you destroy it."

I gave him a startled look. "Do you think I would? Or even could?"

"I don't think you'd intend to." Coyote's tone was grim.

I scrubbed my hands through my hair. "I don't *intend* anything."

"I know. That's why I haven't broken your neck and left your bones for the vultures. But people will get hurt. They already have. If you give in to what's inside you, if you let her win, I'll crush you. Nothing your big, bad boyfriend will be able to do about it either."

"I'd never hurt anyone," I repeated stubbornly. "I'm more worried about what you'll do to me, or to Mick."

Coyote grinned. "Me and Mick, we've tangled in the past."

Mick had never mentioned this interesting fact. "Why

do I feel like the only one out of the loop? Who *is* Mick? Why did you 'tangle' with him?"

"He'll have to tell you that himself. He'll try to stop you, like I will, but maybe without harming you. Me, I might not be so picky."

"Stop me from what?"

"Being who you are."

I heaved an exasperated sigh. "Save me from cryptic god-speak. Do you think I chose to be who I am? To be illegitimate and ridiculed and all but shunned by my own people?"

Coyote shook his head, his hard face almost sympathetic. "People like us don't choose our paths. Those choices are made for us, long before we exist. Do you think I *want* to be an all-powerful, fine-assed god all the ladies love? It's a lot of work."

"Be serious. I tried to run away from this place, but I always knew I'd come back here. I have to. I have to face her. I have to stop her."

"About time too. I've been poking around this town for years waiting for you."

I blinked. "You knew I'd be coming to Magellan?"

"I knew that, eventually, you wouldn't be able to stay away. I'm glad it finally happened. Do you know how boring this town can be? Why couldn't you be pulled to the vortexes around Las Vegas?"

"They're not the same." I didn't know to what realm the vortexes around the foot of the Sierra Nevadas led, and I didn't really want to know. The ones here were scary enough for me.

"No, but I like Las Vegas," Coyote said. "Lots to do there."

I stared at him in sickening suspicion. "You didn't make Amy disappear, did you? So I'd come out here?"

"I had nothing to do with that. And no, I don't know what happened to Amy. I was away at the time."

"Thanks. You're a lot of help."

"I'm not here to help. Well, not help *you*, anyway."

I closed my hands to fists. "I'm not your enemy."

"Yes, you are, little girl. By the way, you never said thank you for the other night."

"The other night?"

"The skinwalker. You didn't have enough storm to take him on, though it was fun to watch you try."

I remembered the blue nimbus around the skinwalker and how the creature had screamed as it ran off. "That was you?"

"The same."

"You couldn't have killed it for me? It came back for more while I lay alone in a jail cell."

"I was too far away." Coyote looked chagrined. "Did the best I could. Besides, you got him in the end. I was impressed by your technique."

"That's what Mick said. Next time, I wish one of you would *help* instead of standing back and being impressed."

"You were doing so well on your own." He sounded like a teacher praising a student. "You should get back to your man of fire before he wakes up. You know, you two have a lot of stamina. I thought you'd never stop."

I jumped to my feet. "That's it. Tomorrow, I'm getting blackout curtains."

"Hey, don't ruin my fun. Before our showdown, you and me could have some good times."

I ignored him. I'd heard plenty of stories growing up about Coyote's sexual appetites, which often got him into trouble. I'd laughed at them then, but it was less funny now that one of those stories could involve me.

As I strode back toward the hotel, Coyote's voice floated after me. "You two want some threesome action, I'll be there."

I gave him the finger. I heard his laughter, loud and clear, which turned into coyote yowls before I ducked back inside.

When I woke the next morning, the sun was well up, and my bed held an indentation where Mick had been. I didn't need to check outside to see that his motorcycle was no longer parked against the back of the building to know that Mick was gone. The place screamed of Mick's absence, as though his aura had become part of the walls and now they missed him.

I grew angry—at Mick and at myself. He'd taken to walking in and out of my life again, and I was letting him. Worse, I'd gone and had sex with him. It had been great sex, mind-blowing sex, after I thought I'd given up sex for good. I'd never let myself sleep with human males, because I feared I'd hurt them, even now that I could better control my storm power. Mick was the only person with whom I'd ever been able to let myself go, and he knew that, damn him.

I'd wanted to talk to him about my encounter with Coyote, ask him what Coyote had meant that he and Mick had tangled. Mick was strong, but Coyote was a god. Then again, Mick was still alive, leading me to wonder who'd won whatever fight had been between them.

I went into the bathroom and tried the faucet on the off chance, and sure enough, hot water shot out of the pipes. Fremont hadn't been able to finish yesterday because of the police, so Mick must have provided this for me again. Maybe Mick should go into the plumbing business.

After I finished showering and eating a dry cookie

breakfast, Nash Jones showed up, just to get my day off to a good start.

When I unlocked the front door for him, Nash went immediately to the basement to see whether I'd disturbed the tape.

"Disappointed?" I asked him, when he found it untouched.

"You have a problem with respect, Begay."

"You rub me the wrong way, Sheriff."

"Your boyfriend came to see me this morning," he said.

I had told Mick last night while we ate in Winslow that Sheriff Jones wanted to see him. Mick had shrugged like he didn't care.

I'd have loved to know what they talked about, but Nash didn't enlighten me. "The woman in your basement was called Sherry Beaumont."

I looked at him in surprise. "You know her name already? That was fast."

"She was listed as a missing person about a year ago. Dental records were e-mailed to the medical examiner this morning and confirmed. Name mean anything to you?"

"No. Should it?"

"She was from Ventura, a tourist. The man who owns Crossroads Bar—Barry—he's from Los Angeles, isn't he?"

I thought of Barry, the lanky bartender I'd made friends with on arriving in Magellan, figuring I needed to be a good neighbor. He let me use the shower in the tiny bathroom behind the bar since I didn't have any water—at least none that Mick hadn't magicked up. Barry didn't talk much, and I didn't pry.

"Los Angeles is a big place," I said. "So is California."

"She was married but separated. Her husband said she'd come out here to see the vortexes."

The vortexes. My blood chilled. "How was she killed?"

"There were no signs of trauma on her body, none of a

struggle. She wasn't visibly hurt. She could have died of heat stroke or severe dehydration. Tourists do that."

They did. People came out here from friendlier climates, not realizing how potentially deadly the desert was. One of Jamison Kee's brothers led tours through Canyon de Chelly, a spectacular place but lethal if you weren't careful and knowledgeable. He'd told me tales of lost hikers who'd fall into crevices and not be found, people wandering off by themselves without water in one-hundred-degree-plus temperatures. "This land might be beautiful and even nurturing," he'd say. "But it will kill you in a heartbeat."

"The medical examiner thinks she passed out from heat exhaustion or sunstroke and died," Nash said.

"So how did she end up in my basement?"

Nash bent me a look. "That's a good question. The only fingerprints on the paneling were Maya's."

"She was working down there when she found the body," I pointed out.

"Sherry Beaumont was also pregnant."

My eyes widened. "Was she?" That made it even sadder.

"Her husband says the child isn't his."

"That's something you can't blame on me, Sheriff."

"But you have an interesting boyfriend who turned up out of nowhere, and you claim to know nothing about his past."

Damn it. I wanted to spring to Mick's defense, but it was true that I had no idea what he'd been up to for the past five years.

"I did a little research," Nash was saying. "I couldn't find record of a Mick Burns who matched his description. I mean *any* record. He has no credit cards, no bank accounts, no property, nothing. This morning I talked to him for forty-five minutes and came out of the conversation with a big fat zero."

I wanted to laugh. "I lived with him for six months and didn't get any more than that. What made you think you could wear him down in forty-five minutes?"

"People usually talk to me."

"I'll bet." I had heard the story of how Nash, as a deputy when he'd come back from Iraq, had personally hauled to jail five big-city gang members who'd tried to hide out in Magellan. The hardened youths had been wetting their pants to get away from him in the end, according to Fremont. But then, they hadn't been Mick. I'd always marveled at how gentle Mick could be with me, when his natural state seemed to be so hard-edged.

I wished Nash would stop looking at me like that. He was making me wonder all kinds of crazy things, like why Mick had chosen to return the day before a woman was found buried in my basement. And why, if he was so protective of me, had he let the skinwalker nearly kill me?

"I don't think Mick did this," I said.

"Maybe he didn't. But I want to know more about him."

I wanted to say, *You and me both.* "Can my workers continue in here?" I asked. "I can't afford to just let this place go."

Nash looked around at the half-plastered walls, the studs still exposed between lobby and saloon, and gave me a reluctant nod. "Forensics say they're done in the rest of the hotel. But stay out of the basement."

"Where my water heater is," I said. "Thanks a lot."

Fremont arrived, ending our conversation. He at least assumed work would be progressing.

Today, Fremont looked less buoyant, and his face was wan, as though he'd aged ten years overnight. "You all right?" I asked him.

He gave me the nod of a man determined to bury himself in his work. "I'm fine. I didn't get your bathroom hooked up yesterday. I want to finish."

"Sheriff Jones won't let us in the basement."

Fremont shot Nash a dark look. "I don't need to get to the basement."

I'd never seen Fremont this unhappy before. I felt a large twinge of guilt. After all, the skinwalker had been targeting me; Charlie had just been in the wrong place at the wrong time. "Fremont, I've decided to buy you a new truck; you won't have to wait for the insurance. I'll just get it for you. Want to go looking for one today?"

"I don't care about the damn truck." Fremont growled. "It wasn't your fault, Janet. A skinwalker did this. That's what Coyote is saying."

Nash's voice went hard. "Coyote is a crazy man who should watch his mouth."

"Skinwalkers are real," Fremont said. "Janet knows it. Everyone around here knows it. I want to go after the son of a bitch."

"Don't you dare." I could imagine Fremont stalking through the desert at night armed with a flashlight and pipe wrench. He might have a tiny bit of magical power, but nowhere near anything strong enough to fight a monster who dealt in death. "Anyway, the one that killed Charlie is dead."

"How do you know that?"

"Lightning strike. He attacked the jailhouse when I was there. The lightning burned him up."

Fremont gave me a skeptical look. "How do you know it was the same one?"

"I know."

"Listen to you." Maya in her white coveralls had come in while we talked. She set down her toolbox and settled her cap over her dark hair, her brown eyes filled with scorn. I noticed she didn't look at Nash. "Skinwalkers, my ass. She's lying to you, Fremont. She hit your truck and flipped it."

"Shut up, Medina," Fremont snapped. "You don't talk

about skinwalkers like they don't exist. They can hear you. They'll come for you."

Maya shook her head in disgust. "*Dios mío*, get me out of this fucking town."

"Don't let the screen door hit you," Fremont said.

"Maya." Nash's voice was sharp, stentorian. From the look Maya gave him, I had the feeling she had an even bigger problem with respect for him than I did. "I want to talk to you."

Maya picked up the toolbox with a jerk. "I'm busy. Appliances should be coming today."

Jones's eyes flashed in fury as Maya stalked off to the kitchen. I could see that he didn't want to run after her, but he also didn't want her to get away with blowing him off. Mouth set, he walked to the kitchen, anger in every line of his body.

More men came to work, and the routine began, my hotel filling with the comforting sounds of construction. The workers talked among themselves, speculating about Sherry Beaumont and her death, but mostly, they just worked. Nash must have finished with Maya, because I saw him move past the lobby windows and drive off in his SUV.

Nash's questions about Mick unnerved me. I knew Mick wasn't human, but plenty of nonhuman creatures inhabited this world incognito. My friend Jamison was a Changer who could turn into a mountain lion, but no one knew that but me, his family, his wife, Naomi, and his young stepdaughter, Julie. Witches are real—maybe not the New Agers who came to Magellan by the busload, but true Wiccans who follow the earth-goddess religion and have more power than people give them credit for. Nightwalkers, bloodsuckers that fiction calls "vampires," exist as well, indistinguishable from humans though they are thankfully rare. Then there are gods like Coyote who can look like anything they want.

I didn't think Mick was a god, he wasn't a Wiccan witch,

and since he went out during the day and didn't crave blood, that ruled out Nightwalker. His aura was Changer-like, but if he were a Changer, I thought he'd have revealed his animal form to me by now.

Yes, his dragon tattoos sometimes seemed to move, sometimes to watch me, but dragons didn't exist—they were legend. The dragons might symbolize the streams of fire that came out of Mick's hands, or they might mean he belonged to some cult that symbolized their god with a dragon. Not that I'd ever seen Mick worshipping anything.

What irritated me most of all was that he wouldn't just tell me. If Mick had nothing to hide, what was the harm?

The only thing I knew was that Mick, whose last name was not Burns, was very dangerous, more dangerous than most things out there. I'd known that from the very first night I met him.

Nine

"I called the cops, girl. Do you understand me?"

I had a broken pool cue in my hands. I had no idea where I'd picked it up or why, but I hefted it as I faced the men in the middle of the bar.

I'd just wanted a beer. One cold beer to refresh myself after a battle with dark forces—was that too much for a girl to ask?

Apparently so. Lightning flickered outside in the Mojave Desert, near a town too far north of Las Vegas to be entertaining. These people had no idea what had been crawling around out there, waiting for lone travelers on the empty highway, no idea how hard I'd fought to kill the creatures.

Ingrates.

I'd finished with the demons and ridden toward the lights, exhausted and sick, storm magic pounding through me. Thirsty, I'd found a bar in a town with one intersection. The faint neon signs outside advertised brand-name beers and "the loosest slots in town." By the look of things, they were the only slots in town. A beer to wet my throat, I'd thought, maybe a bit of food if I could keep it down.

So what did I get? A seedy-looking asshole hitting on me.

I don't think he'd bathed in a week. He had lank brown hair and a scruffy goatee, and he reeked of stale cigarette smoke, packs of it.

"Come to visit, Indian girl?" Great pickup line. "Maybe I can provide some accommodation."

I tried to be nice. Really I did. "Sorry," I said. "I'm just passing through."

He stroked my hair, and I jerked away. I wasn't *that* nice. The man scowled. "Now, Tommy don't like to take no for an answer."

I assumed that he was Tommy. I hated men who referred to themselves in the third person. "Well, he'll have to take it tonight."

I think it would have been all right if Tommy's friends hadn't laughed at him. But they did laugh, and he got embarrassed and mad.

He closed his hand around my neck, proving stronger than his gangly limbs had led me to believe.

The bartender said, "Easy, Tommy," but Tommy was drunk and didn't care.

He yanked me backward off the stool, hand on my neck like a vise. His armpit was far too close to my face, and I gagged on his BO as he shook me.

"You listen to me, bitch . . ."

I let him have it. Storm magic still raced through my system from the battle in the desert, and I didn't have to try very hard to tap it. But it hurt—bad. This was going to kill me one day.

I slammed my hand into Tommy's face, and he arched back with a wordless scream. I gave one push, and his body flew across several tables and tumbled with them to the ground. Tommy's head hit the floor, and he lay still.

"Shit," someone said. The room went deathly quiet. I could hear a *drip*, *drip*, *drip* from one of the taps at the bar that hadn't shut off right.

Tommy wasn't dead; I'd given him enough only to knock him out. Whatever these people thought, I didn't kill humans.

I think I would have been all right, even then, if they'd let me walk out. I'd get on my bike and ride away, leaving their town far behind. They'd never see me again.

Tommy's friends looked at one another. They were as scruffy as he was, one large with a huge beer belly. Beer Belly lifted a pool cue from the nearest table, and his friends did the same.

"Take it outside," the bartender said. "I don't need my place wrecked."

They ignored him, and I didn't bother to wait for them to strike. I was crazed, sick, and scared, not of them, but of the magic inside me. Tonight, in the desert, as I battled the demons, I'd seen for the first time what I really could do with my powers if I wanted to.

It had terrified me. The storm had wrapped itself around me with glee, and it wouldn't let me go. I'd killed so many demons, and the others had fled in terror. The triumph that had welled in my throat had made me sick.

And now these losers came at me with intent to take me down. I fought back like a crazy woman. I wasn't skilled in any kind of martial art, but punching and ducking seemed instinctive. I coupled my rage with the power eating me raw and threw it at them. Bodies flew, but they were so drunk and so angry that they got back up again and kept coming. *Idiots*.

One of them tried to hit me with a pool cue. I sliced it in half and grabbed it out of his hands. I guess that's how

I ended up with it. By now all the people in the bar were on their feet. Some tried to scramble outside; others, men and women alike, dove in to teach the Indian chick that she'd better not come to a white town and try to push them around.

"I called the cops, girl," the bartender yelled. "Do you understand me?"

I didn't care. Let them come. I could level this place, kill everyone in it. I could destroy the whole town, turn the cop cars that came after me into fireballs. No one would be able to stop me. I'd hate myself later, and probably die from the forces inside me, but at the moment, my adrenaline and fury made me want to destroy the bar and the malicious people in it. I drew all my power to one bright, hot point.

Arms closed around me like steel bands and lifted me off my feet. I screamed as the air was crushed from my lungs by a tall, brute-like man who hulked well over six feet. I flailed with the broken cue, but with a twist of my wrist, he wrenched the cue away and tossed it to the floor.

I kicked and fought, but there was no budging the guy. I threw my power at him, but nothing happened—it stuck inside me; it was tearing me apart. I screamed, only to find a hand over my mouth. Biting didn't help.

The impossibly strong man dragged me outside. The crowd from the bar followed; more waited outside. Who knew so many people lived in this wide spot in the road? A few of Tommy's friends laughed, panting from the fight, as they watched the big man carry me away.

"Put her in her place, Mick." "Kick the bitch's ass." "Show her what women are for."

I didn't much care what they said; I cared that I couldn't fight this man. He was far stronger than I was, even with my body full of magic. I should have been able to throw him twenty feet, far enough for me to make it to my bike and get the hell out of here, but nothing I tried made a dent.

The man called Mick dragged me across the highway to a fleabag motel—me flailing all the way and him not caring. He was going to rape me; I knew it. Cold fear ate through me. I'd never had sex before, and now this man planned to force it on me, and it was going to hurt.

I moaned and struggled. He kicked open a door and dragged me inside, all the way to the bed, which he threw me on.

While he turned to slam and lock the door, I bounded to my feet and ran at him. He wrapped his hand around my throat and pushed me back, firmly, not brutally, but hard enough that I couldn't resist. I found myself flat on the mattress again.

Mick had a hard face, a nose that had been broken once, incredible blue eyes, and black hair that curled all over the place. He was huge, like a wrestler, broad shoulders, thick wrists, tattoos down his arms. He could snap me like a twig.

I kicked him. "Bastard."

He held me down, his body crushing mine. The only good thing in the situation was that he didn't stink. In any other circumstance I might think he smelled nice, like mountain air.

"Do it," he said in a rumbling bass. "Blast me."

"What?"

"I feel the power in you. It's crawling through you, dying for a way out. It will burst you like a balloon if you hold it too hard. Come on, girl. Give me your best shot."

He had to be crazy. The fact that he could sense and understand my power made me sick with fear. He shouldn't be able to; no one should.

He *wanted* me to smack him with it? What kind of lunatic was he?

"You'll die," I said.

"Do I look like a wuss? Hit me."

Because I lay there like an idiot, he hit *me*. An open-handed slap, right across my face.

My rage boiled over. I screamed at him the filthiest, foulest things I could think of and poured into my fist all of the power I'd wanted to unleash on the bar.

As I punched him, white light snaked out of my hand, whipped around him, picked him up, and flung him across the room. He hit the wall, cracking the Sheetrock, plaster raining around him. He was on his feet in an instant, arms outstretched as I threw all of my power at him.

Snakes of lightning circled his body like he was being electrocuted, and he shouted words I didn't understand. I knew I could have run. He was a long way from the door, and my power was besting him. I could be out of there, back across the street for my bike and away.

But I lay there and watched, mouth open, while my magic slowly killed him.

And then—it didn't kill him. Little by little he absorbed the white light that shook his body; then the last tendrils of power slithered up into his mouth, and he swallowed.

Then he laughed. A big, loud laugh of someone who'd just enjoyed the hell out of himself. He let out a whoop, his eyes sparkling like diamonds. "Baby, that was *good*."

I kept staring at him from the bed, my jaw probably on my chest. He looked fine. Not fried, not baked, not a heap of steaming flesh on the floor.

"Stormwalker," he said, grinning. "I thought so when I saw you. You were insane with power, and I knew you'd just ridden that storm. What were you fighting out there?"

I remained on the bed, shocked senseless, staring up at the man who'd just taken a blast of my power and lived.

"Demons. I guess." My teeth chattered.

"Some of my best friends are demons. But don't worry. I think I know what you mean."

"You do?"

"Things from Beneath. Don't look so surprised. Not everyone on this side is ignorant."

"Who are you?" I choked out. "*What* are you?"

"They call me Mick. Who are you?"

"Janet Begay." I was pretty sure.

"Very nice to meet you, Janet. Do you feel better?"

I got off the bed and realized, once standing, that yes, I did feel better. Walking a storm left me sick and drained. I'd collapse once the storm dispersed, queasy, fatigued, and sore, with a migraine pounding behind my eyeballs. A fight like tonight's, when I'd drawn from the storm again and again, should have left me groaning in bed for days.

Now I felt like I'd just woken from a good night's sleep.

"What did you do?" I demanded. "How did you do that? You should be dead."

"You wouldn't have killed me." He grinned. "You're too nice."

"Bet me."

He shrugged. I noticed then that I liked his muscles. They stretched out his shirt in a good way, the fabric molding to each one. When he moved, it was like a beautiful song.

"You look hungry, Janet," he said. My stomach growled in answer, betraying me. "I know a place in Vegas where the food is good, and they like me there. Think you can make it that far if you ride with me?"

"I don't want to leave my bike. Not here."

"Not to the mercy of those assholes? Don't worry. I'll get a friend to run it down."

"A demon friend?"

He chuckled, a warm, toe-curling sound. "Everyday average human being, I promise. He owes me a favor."

I did feel good. And hungry. And energized. A nice ride with the air in my face would clear my brain.

Janet didn't do wild things like ride off with biker guys to Las Vegas. Such things would be daring and risky, and I'd learned to be cautious. But I felt daring all of a sudden.

"All right," I said.

It wasn't that easy. The cops had shown up, and Mick had to talk fast to keep them from arresting me. The guy called Tommy and his friends were nowhere in sight, but the bar owner pointed me out as the troublemaker. Mick slid his arm around me, told the cops he'd take care of everything, and unbelievably, they backed down.

"Did you glam them?" I asked Mick as he took my hand and led me to my bike.

"Not glam. Sweet reason. If you feel well enough to ride on your own, you can follow me."

I chose to ride on my own. Yes, I could have cut left when he went right, ditching him and riding away before he could find me. But I didn't. I followed him to a restaurant on the outskirts of Las Vegas, where everyone did seem to know him. I hungrily ate what the waitress put in front of me, and Mick and I talked and talked.

Never in my life had I talked to anyone who truly listened. There had been no one—not my father, who really didn't have time or energy to listen to a babbling girl; definitely not my grandmother; not my aunts, cousins, or kids at school—to whom I could talk. I opened up to Mick like I'd never opened up before, telling him the story of my life. I left bits out, like about my mother and her awful revelation to me six months before this, but everything else—growing up on the Navajo Nation, discovering my storm powers, hitting the road after college, my growing collection of photos from my travels, my hopes, fears, dreams. No holding back.

Mick talked too, although not until much later did I re-

alize that though I told him everything, he told me almost
nothing about himself.

After we'd eaten, I followed him to a hotel that was
ten times nicer than the fleabag where I'd attacked him.
Mick booked an expensive room and then took me to it and
kissed me while he undressed me.

He touched me in ways I'd never been touched before,
his strong hands stroking my breasts, my hips, my buttocks. He tasted me and taught me how to taste him, then
he taught me everything I needed to know about going to
bed with a man.

My time with him that night was wicked and glorious.
He went slow, didn't laugh at my ignorance, and never let
it hurt.

I woke early the next morning to find him sitting on the
edge of the bed in nothing but his jeans, my open wallet in
his hands.

I sat up with a gasp, my bubble of happiness bursting.
"What the hell do you think you're doing?"

"Going through your wallet," Mick answered calmly.
There wasn't much in it but my spare change, my driver's
license, and a photo of my father in a formal velvet shirt and
silver clasp on his string tie. He rarely wore those things,
but never let anyone photograph him if he wasn't dressed
up. I had nothing else, no credit cards or bank cards, not
even a library card.

"How far did you expect to get on this?" Mick held up
the five and three ones he'd plucked from inside.

I shrugged as though money didn't interest me. "Back
home."

"To Many Farms? That's a long ride. I don't think so."
Mick slid a roll of cash out of his pocket and held it out to
me. "This might help."

I stared at the money, first in shock, then in anger. I

grabbed the wad and shoved it at his face. "You sleaze. I should make you eat this. I'm not a hooker."

He stared at me in surprise, then lifted his hands away, not touching me or the cash. "You'll need gas if you're going to ride with me. Consider it a loan if you're too proud for a handout."

I immediately felt stupid and dropped the money on the bed. "Who says I want to ride with you?"

"I'd like you to." Mick gave me his most charming smile. "I'd be honored if you did."

I met his gentle kiss with my own, and then the kiss turned hot. It was a long time before we got up for breakfast.

I stayed with Mick for six months. He taught me amazing things about magic, about fixing up my Harley, about sex. I was more intimate with him than I'd been with anyone in my entire life, but though he was both tender and wicked, I never learned any more about him than I had the first night.

Then he started disappearing. He'd leave for days at a time while I waited for him in some little town with nothing to do. Or he'd leave me a note telling me to meet him in another town in a few days. And I'd do it.

I finally left him on my birthday. I'd followed his directions to meet him at a motel in Louisiana, arriving to find that he'd booked a room, scattered it with rose petals, and left a bottle of champagne and a cake that read "Happy Birthday, Janet" in pink lettering on the table. I found a bottle of bubble bath sitting beside the large tub in the bathroom, the lip of the tub surrounded by candles. I sat in the room alone for an hour, looking at the cake, until I heard his motorcycle.

I got up and put my clothes back into my one bag and put on my coat. I was zipping the bag when Mick opened the door, clad in a leather jacket against January cold. He leaned on the frame and watched me, then came all the way inside and shut the door.

"What are you doing?" he asked.

"Leaving."

He gave me his warm Mick smile. "Why? You don't like cake?"

"How did you know it was my birthday?"

"You told me. Didn't you?"

"No, I didn't. I never talk about my birthday, for obvious reasons."

Mick shrugged, his leather jacket creaking. "It's on your driver's license. I guess I remembered from that."

"From going through my wallet the night we met."

Mick's eyes started going dark. "I wanted to surprise you."

I knew that. He'd wanted this to be a treat for me, which was nice of him. He'd decided we should celebrate a day I'd never celebrated. He wanted to make it special.

I wanted to throw the cake in his face. "So when is your birthday?" I asked him.

He just looked at me, absently brushing back a stray curl that had escaped his ponytail. "You know, I'm not sure."

"Everyone knows their birthday. And if they don't, they make one up. What does it say on your driver's license?"

"Does it matter?"

"You don't have a license, do you? We've been riding around for six months, and you've never been asked to show it. Even when we get stopped, somehow, you manage it that they never ask you for yours."

He shrugged. "I like to keep my private life private."

"From everyone, including me. Where do you go, Mick? Why do you expect me to be waiting for you when you disappear?"

"Knowing you're waiting gives me a reason to hurry back," he said in a soft voice.

"You didn't answer the other question."

"It's nothing you need to know about." His voice was still quiet. Mick never yelled at me.

I picked up my bag. "That's one of the reasons I'm out of here. If you're boinking someone on the side, fine. We're not married. I have no hold on you. Just be honest enough with me to tell me."

"Janet, love, there is no other woman for me but you."

"Very romantic. I'm tired of sitting on my butt waiting for you to get around to me. I'd like to move on with my life."

"Not without me."

"Then stay with me. Can you do that? Can you stay with me without running off at the drop of a hat?"

Mick scrubbed his hand through his hair, the evasive look he wore when he didn't want to talk about something appearing. "No."

"Then I'm going."

I started for the door. His strong hand slammed across it, stopping me. "No, Janet. I can't let you leave unprotected."

I gave him a withering look. "Spare me."

"You know damn well you can't control your powers. Every time there's a storm, you're dangerous—to others and to yourself. Plus there are bad things out there, bad things that will squish your little Stormwalker body in a heartbeat. You can't face them yet. You need me."

"Get out of my way."

"No."

I glared at him. "What are you going to do? Force me to stay?"

He could. He was bigger than me, stronger, more powerful. He'd proved that he could take any magic I threw at him and laugh it off. I should have been terrified of him, but I was too angry to be afraid. I'd fallen in love with him, but he treated me like a naïve schoolgirl, he didn't trust me, and I'd had enough.

"Get out of my way," I repeated.

"Don't be stupid."

"I've already been stupid. I *am* stupid. I'm stupid enough to ride around with a guy who has no last name, no birthday, no driver's license, and who won't tell me who he is, what he is, where he comes from, or where he goes. I don't know what kind of sorcerer you are, or what kind of glam you've put on me, but I'm finished with it."

"I haven't glammed you. You stay with me because you want to."

"And now I don't want to."

His arm remained across the door, solid as granite. "It's not that simple."

"Yes, it is. I want to go. Alone."

"No matter what I might think? No matter what I might feel for you?"

"If you feel something for me, you'll stop making me live like your woman, at your beck and call. Sorry, Mick. I don't answer to anyone."

"I can't protect you if you run off." He sounded frustrated.

"And I can't protect *you* when you disappear," I said. "There are things after me that would tear through you to get to me. Whenever you're gone, how do I know that they haven't found you? How do I know you'll be back?"

"Do you mean your mother in the vortexes? From what you've told me, she doesn't have a range much farther than about forty miles. We're safe if we leave that part of the country alone."

If that was true, then why the hell was he so worried about protecting me? "Fine. I've heard that Cape Cod is pretty. And I've always wanted to see New York City."

"I'll show you New York, if that's what you want. I'll rent a penthouse, and we'll do it right."

"I don't want to do it on your money. I have my own money."

"Will you stop worrying about that? I have lots of money. I like taking care of you."

"I'm not your call girl."

"I know that, damn it. I take care of you because I love you."

Gods, he broke my heart. I dropped the bag, tears filling my eyes. The birthday setup had confirmed for me that he had all the power in this relationship, but I was sensitive enough to know that he didn't see it that way.

"You did all this for me, tonight," I said, "because you thought it would make me happy."

"Yes, why else would I?"

He'd pictured me gushing with joy, pouring him champagne, pulling him to the bathroom so we could make love in the tub. He'd done this to please me.

"Mick." I put my hands to my face, wiping away tears, then I went to him and put my arms around him. "Thank you. Pink icing is my favorite."

Mick laughed then, a baritone rumble, and he scooped me to him. His kiss opened my mouth, his tongue hot against mine, and he completed my heartbreak.

I stayed with him three more days. We argued every day from the moment we woke until the moment we slept, until Mick finally put me on my bike, gave me the light spells, and kissed me good-bye with tears running down his face. I turned my back on him, wiping away my own tears, and headed north to New England. I hadn't seen him from that day to the moment he broke into Nash's office and carried me out.

* * *

A shrill scream jerked me from my memories. I spun around, but the carpenters were banging away, none giving any sign that he'd heard the scream. I ran into the kitchen, where Maya was hooking up a six-burner range and Fremont was unscrewing a protesting pipe.

"Are you all right?"

Both of them looked up in surprise. "Fine," Fremont said. Maya didn't bother to answer.

Another shriek pierced the hotel, and I slapped my hands over my ears. "Can't you hear that?"

Maya looked at me as though I'd lost my mind. Fremont pushed back his hat, rubbed his head. "I hear a buzzing from somewhere, but it's not very loud. In the pipes maybe?"

This wasn't squeaky pipes, these were screams of agony. Maya went back to her wires. "Maybe it's the ghost of Sherry Beaumont."

Fremont went white. "Don't say that."

"You'll believe anything," Maya said. "Maybe it's one of your skinwalkers."

"It's not a skinwalker," I said. They didn't come out during daylight, and they just killed you; they didn't bother scaring you first.

"Stay here," I told them. Fremont and Maya exchanged glances before Maya rolled her eyes and turned back to her work.

I raced back into the lobby and upstairs. The power saws and drills and nail guns should have drowned out the noise, but I heard it loud and clear. The screams beat inside my skull, like someone going insane and taking me with them.

The noise didn't come from any of the guest rooms. I ran past them, slammed open the door to the attic, and charged up the stairs, panting when I reached the top. I entered the largest room, the one with the desk and the mirror. No one was there. Nothing smelled of death, or life either, for that matter. The air felt no different than it had last night when I'd come through here on my way to the roof.

The screams escalated, raking like nails on glass. I pressed my hands to my head. "Stop!" I shouted.

The screams ended as though someone had thrown a switch. All was silent, except for the coo of the doves that nested under the eaves.

"Well, aren't you cranky," a voice said from the vicinity of my knees. It was a low, husky male voice that held the lilt of a drag queen. "Like maybe you didn't get enough sleep last night." The voice laughed. "Oh, wait, you didn't. You were screwing that incredible hunk and releasing all that beautiful sex magic. It was . . . so *stimulating*."

"Who are you?" I asked the air.

"Darling, don't you know? And you call yourself a witch."

I had a good idea now what was going on, but these particular magical beings were tricky and had to be handled with care.

"I don't call myself a witch," I said. "What do you call yourself?"

"I don't call myself anything. You can call me what you want to, darling."

I crouched in front of the mirror and looked into it. The glass reflected my shocked face and wide dark eyes. My hair was coming out of the ponytail I'd tucked it into, and my cropped top was dusty from the construction downstairs. The mirror reflected nothing but me and the room behind me. No face, no mists, nothing.

"You don't look so good, girlfriend," the voice observed. "Mirror, mirror, on the wall. Who's the fairest one of all? In this room, that would be *me*, sweet chick."

I closed my eyes. Perfect. This was all I needed.

"Gods help me," I said. "You're a magic mirror."

Ten

"Well, state the obvious, sugar," the mirror said.

I wasn't sure whether to rejoice or run like hell. Magic mirrors were problematical devices. I'd met a witch in Oklahoma who'd had a magic mirror, a thing worse than a foul-mouthed parrot. At least parrots slept. Magic mirrors never shut up.

On the other hand, they could be immensely powerful, if you could handle them. They'd watch out for you, protect your home, let you communicate through distant magic mirrors and sometimes even ordinary mirrors. They stored knowledge for centuries and remembered everything they saw with computerlike precision. If one broke, the pieces could be used separately or the whole thing melted down and re-formed without losing the magic. The mirror's personality might change, but the essential magic wouldn't fade.

They also didn't have to be mirrors as we think of

them—any reflective surface could hold the magic. In fact, I knew that some of the large polished copper disks found in archaeological sites in Rome, Britain, and the American Southwest had been magic mirrors.

Magic mirrors were extremely rare. Witches scoured the world for them, because a sorcerer with a magic mirror could easily double or triple his or her power. But only if the sorcerer could handle the mirror, which could be touchy and rude at best, psychotic at worst.

I wondered how it had come to be hanging in the saloon downstairs, but perhaps whoever had brought it in hadn't realized it was magical. Or maybe they had—this was Magellan.

Mirrors could communicate only with the magic-touched; normal human beings couldn't use them and couldn't hear them. However, a mirror could, if it was very talented, make nonmagical humans hear faint, unexplainable sounds. Some haunted houses were simply magic mirrors having fun. I wondered whether I'd stumbled onto the reason the Cross-roads Hotel had kept closing; maybe the magic mirror had scared people off.

I studied it with mixed feelings. On the one hand, it could be a powerful weapon in my arsenal against my battle with my mother. On the other, I now had to deal with a magic mirror.

"I've been living here two weeks," I said. "I've gone through the place with spells twice. Why didn't I know I had a magic mirror?"

"I'd gone dormant, darling. So many years, so long alone. And then, last night, all that *sex* you had with that gorgeous man. Your manic Tantric woke me up. Activated me. Oh, it was *wonderful*. I thought I'd need a cigarette."

"Terrific."

"Next time, hang me in your bedroom and let me watch."

I got to my feet. "Not in a million years."

"Sweetie-pie, you are so *mean*."

"How did you get here?" I asked it.

"On a train. A long, long, long, long time ago. Back when men were men. Movie stars used to come out here to get away from it all. That Dougie Fairbanks was, ooooo, so handsome."

"Who made you?"

The voice quieted. "Now, that, I don't want to talk about."

Only a very powerful sorcerer could create a magic mirror. The technique, the energy, the magic all had to be precise, and it took a long time, years even. I'd never be able to make one because my power came and went. The magic had to be concentrated and sustained for a great length of time.

That sorcerer, if he or she was still alive, could claim the mirror anytime he or she wanted. Once created, the mirror belonged to its maker. However, in the absence of that sorcerer, the mirror belonged to whatever powerful mage could tap it and wake its magic. Which, in this instance, meant me and Mick.

"Who was the woman in the basement?" I asked it.

"Woman?" The mirror sounded blank.

"The one my electrician found behind the wall yesterday morning. Do you know who she was?"

"Oh, that woman. No. I've been asleep, I told you, until last night. Until all that wonderful, *glorious* sex."

"Thank you, you've been a lot of help."

"I didn't see anything. Believe me, if I had, I'd tell you all about it. Or better still, send that man of yours up here. I'll tell him anything *he* wants to know."

It was true that if a mirror went dormant, which it could after years of nonuse, it became nothing more than a piece of glass to comb your hair in front of. If the mirror had been dark when the murder occurred, it would not have recorded the act or even who'd gone in and out of the building that day. Just as well, I thought. I couldn't imagine myself trying to explain to Nash Jones that the sole witness to the woman's murder had been a magic mirror.

"You're in touch with the building," I said. "Didn't you feel her down there?"

"No, sugar. I didn't notice. The dead are of absolutely no use to me."

"Your compassion runs deep."

"I'm a mirror, honey. I reflect; I don't feel. But I do have interests. Tell me about your lickable boyfriend. Is his ass as firm as it looks?"

I rose, grabbed drop cloths that lay in the corner, and flung them over the mirror. The mirror gave a muffled shriek. "Oh, sweetie, don't do that. I'll be good. I know what your Micky is, you know. I can see his true nature."

I lifted the edge of the cloth. "All right, what is he?"

"I felt his magic last night." It drew a long, happy breath. "Is he powerful, or what?"

"Tell me," I said in a hard voice.

"Trust me, darling, it's something you wouldn't, wouldn't like."

I knelt down, peering into its depths. "I order you to tell me. I awakened you, and you belong to me."

"Funny thing about sex magic, sweetie. It takes two. Or more. More is so much fun. I belong to you, but I also belong to the lovely Micky. I know he doesn't want you to know what he is, so I can't tell you. My lips are sealed."

"Not even if I threaten to pound you into shards?"

"No, not even then." It hesitated. "You wouldn't *really* do that, would you?"

"I haven't decided."

In truth, I already knew I wouldn't destroy the mirror, no matter how tempting it was to drive it to the dump and leave it there. A magic mirror was too powerful a talisman to ignore, and I needed all the help I could get.

"I can give you clues if you want, honey," the mirror said. "Like, what's black and red and hot all over?"

"If you mean he's a demon, he's not." At least, I didn't think so. I remembered the black creature with red eyes I'd glimpsed when we made love, but I had no idea whether that was Mick's true form or whether it had been a manifestation of the magic we'd been driving away. "I already guessed that one."

"I'm not going to answer. Not straight questions."

I stood up. "Here's a riddle for you. What happens to mirrors who don't shut up?"

"I give up, darling. What?"

I bent to it. "They get melted back into sand."

"Oh." It sounded nervous. "Really?"

"Yes, really. So what's it going to be?"

There was a silence. "Well, if you put it like that . . ."

"Good." I rose and dropped the cloth over it.

It shrieked. "Oh, that is *so* not fair."

I ignored it and left the room. As I headed back downstairs, the mirror called to me, pleaded to me, shouted to me, and finally lapsed into swearing. Because I'd been born with strong, latent magic, I'd always be able to hear it.

Lucky me.

That afternoon, I told everyone to take off early so those who wanted to could attend Charlie's funeral. I rode with an unusually quiet Fremont to Flat Mesa, where the funeral was being held at the county's one cemetery. Almost the whole town was there, Flat Mesa being full of Joneses. Magellan was the home of Hansens, Medinas, Lopezes, and McGuires; likewise Flat Mesa's phone directory listed a ton of Joneses, Morrisons, and Salases.

Nash Jones turned up in his sharp-pressed uniform. He gazed at me with cold eyes but didn't try to approach me, which was fine with me. Fremont, looking grief-stricken, introduced me to Charlie Jones's mother.

"Fremont says you blame yourself." Charlie's mom was about fifty, with short gray hair, a slightly overweight body, and brown eyes filled with tears. "But I know it wasn't your fault, dear. A skinwalker did this. Oh, yes, I know they're real, though some people disagree." Her look at Nash left me no doubt to whom she was referring.

Her graciousness made me feel even worse. "I'm truly sorry, Mrs. Jones."

"I'm glad you were there; that he wasn't alone in his last moment." She caught tears with a tissue. "The vortexes around here draw evil magic as well as good. I wish the New Agers would understand that."

Yes, they would be safer if they did. I stayed for the brief but sad service, drifting away to leave Charlie's immediate family and close friends to say good-bye to him. I walked a few blocks to the mechanic shop, found out my bike was a long way from being finished but that at least the mechanic was well qualified to work on Harleys. We talked bikes for a few minutes, before I walked another block to a rental car agency. I drove back to Magellan in a bright red SUV, the windows down, feeling claustrophobic as I always did in an enclosed vehicle. I preferred the openness my Harley provided.

As I neared Magellan, watching the sun sink toward the pile of mountains far to the west, the temptation to keep going was incredible. I could drive away from the vortexes, my mother, Amy's disappearance, Mick, Nash Jones, and a host of other problems, and keep going.

Which was what I'd done my entire life. I'd made the vow this time to stop and face my problems. I wanted to help the McGuires, and I needed to stop running from what

I was. I sighed, slowed the SUV, and pulled into the parking lot of my hotel. Mick's bike was there, and I wished with everything I had that I wasn't so happy to see it.

Mick wasn't in the hotel, but at the Crossroads Bar. I joined him there. We talked a little, and his eyes lit with interest when I told him about the mirror.

Everyone from town was talking about the woman walled up in my basement as well as Charlie's death and funeral. They gave me speculative looks—weird things had started happening since the Navajo woman had come to town to investigate Amy McGuire's disappearance. It couldn't be coincidence. I hated that they were right.

I watched Barry tending bar and talking to his regulars, mostly bikers who liked this back-road haven. If Barry heard the whispers in the room about him and Sherry Beaumont being from the same metropolis, he made no indication.

Mick was his usual charming self. He talked with the bikers and kept his arm around me, radiating protectiveness and possessiveness. Without saying a word, he made it clear that I belonged to him and that anyone who touched me would be toast.

I'd loved that about him when we'd first met. No one had ever protected me like Mick had. I'd always been certain that, no matter what happened, Mick would take care of me. Trusting him with my whole being had been so easy, so comforting. I remembered sitting across from him at the restaurant in Las Vegas, letting myself be lulled by his deep voice and beautiful blue eyes. I'd wanted to fall in love with him, and I'd done it.

Now I was thinking about things that had bothered me from the beginning. How had Mick happened to be on hand to rescue me that night north of Las Vegas—the only being I'd ever met who could draw off my power? And how had he known that I was here in Magellan, when I hadn't communicated with him for five years? And why had Coyote said to me, *He'll try to stop you?*

Damn it, stop me doing what? I suddenly didn't want Mick's arm around me. I told him I had to use the ladies', and when he released me, I walked out the front door instead.

Mick caught up to me before I even reached the hotel. He said nothing, only held the carved front door open for me and locked it behind us.

"I needed some air," I said defensively. "The smoke was thick in there."

"So was the bullshit." Mick started for the stairs. "I want a look at this magic mirror."

"It's annoying."

"They all are. I've never had one under my control before."

"I also think it's flaming."

Mick laughed. "It's a mirror. They don't have sexual orientation."

"This one does."

When we reached the third-floor room, Mick pulled the drop cloths from the mirror and crouched to peer into it.

"Well, hel-*lo*, firewalker," the mirror said. "Nice view, honey. Spread those knees a little wider."

Mick didn't even flinch. "A pretty strong one," he said to me.

"You've seen a lot of them?" I asked.

"About a dozen, I think. They're good, solid earth magic. Made of silicon and silver, elements that have been part of the earth for eons."

I bent down. The mirror reflected us side by side, a muscle-bound man and his slim, Navajo girlfriend. "Why do they have to be so mouthy?" I asked.

"They know they're powerful, but also helpless," Mick said. "The mage who owns one controls it completely."

"Oh, I wouldn't say that," the mirror purred.

"Now we own it, according to it," I said, leaning closer.

"Mmm," the mirror said. "Nice cleavage."

I straightened up in a hurry. "I thought you preferred men."

"I swing both ways, honey. I'm an equal opportunity mirror."

Mick laughed. He left the drop cloths off, to the mirror's delight, took my hand, and led me out onto the roof.

I greeted the cool desert night in relief. I really did need air. The stars were out in abundance, but far to the east, heat lightning flickered.

I sat down with my back against the wall, liking how the cool of the stone leeched through my shirt. Mick folded himself next to me, brawny arms around his knees. We lapsed into silence. The night was beautiful, the cool bite to the air pleasant after the warm day.

"You're quiet tonight," Mick said. "Something happen at the funeral that upset you?"

"No. It was just a funeral."

Mick didn't pursue it. One thing I'd liked about him from the start was that he never would make me talk when I didn't want to, unlike my grandmother, who demanded to know every single thing going on inside my head. Tonight, however, his casual attitude irritated me. I wanted Mick to be easy to love or easy to hate. Gray areas are a bitch to navigate.

"I know you don't want me here," he said. It was a flat statement, not a question. "But I'm not leaving."

"I wasn't looking for an argument."

"I'm not giving you one."

His quiet stoicism brought my anger to the surface.

"I'll tell you what's wrong, Mick," I snapped. "I'm tired of people asking me things about you, and me not having any answers."

Mick's brows went up. "People like Nash Jones?"

"For one."

"You let me take care of Jones."

"He's not stupid. He'll keep poking and prying. Not like me. I just let you have sex with me and welcomed you back with open arms."

I felt his stare through the darkness. "I'm not expecting us to pick up where we left off."

"Well, I'm acting like I do," I said. "I'm the stupid one. I don't know who I'm more mad at—you or me."

"I came back to help you," Mick said. "You need help, and I was worried about you."

"I don't want to talk about it." I folded my arms, breathing hard. I didn't like arguing with Mick, because our arguments always ended one of two ways—me storming off or Mick persuading me into bed. Arguing with him solved nothing.

Lightning flared again at the edge of the horizon, and an answering flicker shone in the darkness much closer to us. The blackness of the desert was absolute out here, Magellan's lights too few to penetrate the night. North of us lay the small smudge of Flat Mesa, but east was one big empty nothing.

"Janet, go back inside," Mick said, coming alert.

I stood up. The tiny star of the flashlight barely pricked the darkness. "Oh, gods, I bet it's Fremont. He was upset today, and he told me he wanted to go after the skinwalker that killed Charlie."

"That skinwalker is dead. You got it."

"So I told him. I don't think he believed me."

"Is he stupid?" Mick asked. "Even if he doesn't find a skinwalker, there are plenty of things out there to hurt him."

Rattlesnakes. Mountain lions. Even javelinas, if he pissed one off. The big porkers were having babies, it would be easy to stumble into a nest, and Mama Javelina wouldn't be happy.

The desert floor was also pockmarked with holes made by rodents and snakes—easy to twist an ankle in one and lie there helplessly, waiting for the sun. On top of that, there were things out there no human could handle, and I wasn't talking only about skinwalkers.

"Go inside," Mick repeated. "I'll find him and bring him back."

"Not alone, you won't."

"I'll move faster on my own."

His blue eyes glittered in a way I didn't like. But as angry as I was at Mick right now, I also didn't want him running into something dangerous and dying.

"That's my territory out there, whether I like it or not," I said. "I have to face it sometime."

"Not when there's no storm. That one's too far away."

"Fine. Come and protect me. But I'm going."

Mick wasn't happy, but he stopped wasting time with words and followed me off the roof. We went downstairs, and Mick grabbed a couple big lantern flashlights I kept in my bedroom before we left the hotel.

I saw no sign of Coyote as we crested the railroad bed and stopped to get our bearings. A trickster god would be helpful about now, but of course one was never around when I needed one.

For a few minutes I saw nothing—no flashlight, no movement. Then Mick pointed far to our right, and I spotted the pinpoint of light moving in the emptiness.

Mick took the lead, his long stride breaking a path and eating up distance. I kept my flashlight beam directed alongside his, trying not to trip over loose rocks or stare into my own light. Night-blinding myself wouldn't help, and Mick was right—I was essentially powerless without a nearby storm.

Mick dropped down a wash, navigating between brush that clung to the banks. I heard the quick slither of snakes, the reptiles fleeing our light, and lizards skittering over pebbles. We climbed up the other side of the wash, startling a group of rabbits who'd tried to freeze into invisibility.

Ahead of me, Mick stopped. I followed suit, in silence, and listened. Not a breath of wind moved the air.

Mick snapped off his flashlight and motioned for me to do the same. He navigated the uneven ground with ease, making me feel clumsy and ineffectual. He must possess incredible night vision, another thing I hadn't known about him.

Mick's stride quickened. I let him go ahead, knowing that if I ran after him, I'd only fall on my butt and slow him down. Mick was sure-footed as a mountain lion, bounding from rock to rock, jogging up a ridge laced with rock that made footing treacherous. I followed more slowly, quickening my pace when I heard someone yell.

When I caught up to Mick, he'd stopped near an anvil-shaped boulder, its silhouette weird against the night sky. Mick had a man pinned against the rock, and I turned on my flashlight to reveal a white-faced, red-eyed Fremont.

"What the hell are you doing out here?" I asked in exasperation.

Fremont's eyes glittered. "I'm going to get one of the bastards even if it kills me."

"It *will* kill you," I said. "A skinwalker will rip you apart before you can blink."

"I don't care. I'll take it with me. It should have been me that died, not Charlie."

"No one should have died," I said in a firm voice. "If you want to blame someone, blame me. The skinwalker was going for me and missed."

Fremont shook his head. "You're a cute girl, Janet, but it wanted *me*. It's been stalking me for a while, because of this." He wriggled his fingers. "It wants my powers. Charlie was driving my truck because . . ." His voice broke. "I wanted to head home early. I had a date. But I got a call that a part I'd been waiting for, for another job, had come in up in Winslow. Charlie offered to run and get it for me, so I wouldn't be late for my date, and I let him."

I think the most surprising revelation in that confession was that Fremont had had a date. He'd never talked about interest in any particular woman. "That's not your fault," I said. "You couldn't have predicted that Charlie would be in the wrong place at the wrong time."

"I should have run my own errand, or waited until the next day. I was in a hurry and nervous. And Charlie died." He hefted a metal pipe in a shaky hand. "So I'm going to get the son of a bitch."

"I told you. I already got him. He died in the storm when he chased me to Flat Mesa."

"I have to do *some*thing. I'm a mage. I can fight it."

Mick gave him a shake. "Your magic could barely light a candle. You keep wandering around out here and the sheriff will be hunting for *your* body."

"I'm not going back until I get a skinwalker."

I winced as he said the word again. Fremont hadn't been wrong when he'd told Maya that talking about skinwalkers could call them. We'd been fairly safe from them in broad daylight at the warded hotel, but out here in the dark, in their territory, we were vulnerable. The lightning was still too far away for me to touch, and Mick carried no weapons.

In a sudden move, I wrenched the pipe from Fremont's hand and knocked his flashlight to the ground. Fremont yelped and grabbed for the pipe, but Mick easily held him back.

"If you're going to be disarmed that quickly, you have no business being out here," I said. "Are you going to fight me for this?" I hefted the pipe.

"No. You're a girl."

I laughed and swung the pipe against the stone. A chunk of sandstone broke away and fell to the ground. "What if I were a skinwalker? They can take human guise, did you know that? If they're very powerful, they can steal a human's skin and their essence."

Fremont's eyes bulged. "You're not. You're Janet."

"Yes, but is that what you want? For a thing to kill you, wrap itself in your skin, and pass itself off as you? Who else do you think would get hurt besides Charlie?"

Fremont stopped. Being familiar with vengeance myself, I knew that pointing out to Fremont that he couldn't possibly fight the things wouldn't change his mind. But if he thought that his actions might hurt more people he cared about, maybe that would move him. It sometimes worked with me, making me a good little girl. Mostly.

Mick came alert, whipping around and peering down the ridge into the darkness to the east. "Janet," he said softly.

I smelled it in the next heartbeat. A rotting, fetid smell, a cross between backed-up sewers and weeks-old corpses.

"What the hell?" Fremont whispered. "What is that?"

"What you came to hunt." I pressed the pipe back into his hands. "Hit anything that comes near you, except me."

"Where will you be?"

"Right next to you."

"Janet," Mick repeated, his voice still controlled.

I stepped to Mick's side and looked down the hill. The desert floor at our feet, which a few minutes ago had been so silent and peaceful under the stars, seemed to move. Things were crawling out of the wash we'd crossed and making for the slope on which we stood. The little animals we'd disturbed had fled in absolute terror.

"I think we're on a hive," Mick said. He glanced once at me, and in the darkness, his eyes looked solid black all the way across.

"A hive?" Fremont gave me a wild look. "What does that mean?"

Mick answered, his voice quiet. "It means, we are so fucked."

Eleven

Fear pooled in my stomach. I reached for the lightning on the horizon, but it was still too far away for me to feel anything but the barest flicker. *Damn.*

We were cut off. Behind the boulders at our backs was open desert, the undulating ground treacherous in the dark. The homey lights of Magellan winked in the opposite direction, relative safety mocking us. Between us and the town, a horde of skinwalkers.

"How many?" I asked Mick in a low voice.

"A couple dozen I think." He turned to look at me, and there was no doubt this time. The whites of his eyes were gone, as were the blues of his irises. I found myself staring into voids of black. "I'm going to cut a path for you," he said. "Take Fremont and get back to the hotel. Flood the place with light, and stay there."

"What about you?"

"I'll fight them. You can't."

"A couple dozen? By yourself? Are you crazy?"

He glanced at the horizon, and I felt his magic building like I'd never felt it before. "And how are you going to help me?"

I knew Mick was powerful. I *knew* that. I'd seen him in action. But how could he stand against two dozen skinwalkers, not to mention who controlled them?

I was angry at him for keeping secrets from me, but that didn't mean I wanted to see him go down under a horde of crazed demons in animal skins. Then again, without a storm, I didn't know what I could do to help.

Damn Fremont and damn the skinwalker that had wrecked his truck and killed Charlie. Damn my mother for sending the things after me; damn me for coming back to Magellan at all. I could be holed up with Mick somewhere cozy, my blind trust in him undamaged, avoiding who I was with the precision of long practice. But no, I'd decided to confront my demons and find out more about myself. Illusions were being stripped from me one by one, the fog I'd lived in all my life burning away. And I found I hated the light.

Mick handed me his flashlight and stripped off his T-shirt. Starlight gleamed on his tight body, his black tattoos stark on his skin. He lifted his hands, giving me a view of his back muscles rippling to his low waistband. The tattoo around his hips took on a red outline, as though fire burned him from within.

Mick shouted something—a word or words, or just guttural sounds, I couldn't tell. The sky lit up like a torch. Under the sheet of fire, I saw the skinwalkers, at least twenty of them, seven feet tall with blazing eyes and white flesh. A few of them had shifted to animal form—a mountain lion, a coyote, a bear. The animals looked wrong, more like zombified creatures than true shifters. The stench that rolled off them made my eyes water.

Fremont gaped in terror. I think his revenge fantasy consisted of him whacking a rather spindly skinwalker on the head and having said skinwalker fall dead at his feet. The reality put panic on his face.

Mick's magical fire stymied the skinwalkers a little, but not as much as I'd hoped. The skinwalkers were on their own territory and they'd banded together—unusually—and they came on.

Mick drew the fire along the skinwalkers' left flank, and as one they moved away from the light, clearing a sort of path toward the hotel. "Go!" Mick shouted at me. "Now!"

I seized Fremont and dragged him down the rocky slope, leaving the man I loved to stand alone against a mess of demons. I wanted to cry and scream and rage, but I kept it together and ran with Fremont toward relative safety, the twin flashlights I held cutting a swath through the blackness.

Hiking without a track was dangerous, and the terror of leaving Mick behind clawed at me. I had the benefit of knowing the skinwalkers *probably* wouldn't kill me, because my mother wanted me, but they'd have no compunction about killing Mick.

Fremont screamed as our lights gleamed on the faceted reflection of a big cat's eyes. A mountain lion bounded toward us, running flat out. I pulled Fremont behind a low boulder, which didn't hide us, but it might make the cat break its stride before it ran into us.

The mountain lion never stopped. It leapt over us, boulder and all, giving me a glimpse of the thick fur of its belly. I smelled no skinwalker stench, only pure night air. The cat's spirit shimmered with a faint silver light.

Fremont raised his pipe, but I caught his arm. "It's not one of them." *It's Jamison Kee,* I wanted to say, but I wasn't sure how happy Jamison would be if I told the font of Magellan gossip that he was a Changer. Jamison landed and ran on, the air of his wake brushing my skin.

Another animal hurtled toward us out of the darkness, this one a coyote, a big one, growling. A blue light surrounded it, and it ran on rapid feet.

"About time you showed up," I said as it streamed past. The only answer I got was a tail flicking upward, looking for all the world like he'd flipped me off.

"Are they on our side?" Fremont asked shakily.

"The mountain lion is. The coyote is on his own side. But they'll help Mick."

"Janet, I'm sorry. I made it all worse, didn't I?"

"Mick is a big boy, and he has help now." I laid Mick's flashlight, still lit, on top of the boulder and took Fremont's arm. "Come on, let's get you inside."

I let Fremont into the hotel and told him to lock the doors and stay put. Fremont, still white-faced, tried to get me to stay with him, but I declined. Mick was out there fighting, and even with Coyote and Jamison helping him, I had no way of knowing whether they would prevail.

I also had no way of knowing what Coyote would do with Mick once they were alone. *We've tangled in the past,* Coyote had said. I didn't know what "tangled" meant, but I didn't like it.

I rummaged in the drawer of my nightstand until my fingers closed on the smooth round ball that was the last of Mick's spells. I stuffed that into my pocket, took up the metal pipe Fremont had laid down, and went outside, retracing the path toward the boulder on which I'd placed Mick's flashlight. Fire raged in the darkness, flames licking the night.

I hurried through the wash, stumbling on loose rocks. Swearing under my breath, I trudged out the other side and scrambled on toward the light I'd left to guide me.

Janet.

The word whispered on the breeze, and I froze. Oh, damn her.

I stood on the top of a hill, looking down the slope. At the bottom was another wash, a black streak in the middle of shadows. A pale light slid against the ground, marking for me and any magical person who might see it, a vortex.

They're closed, I reminded myself. *Closed for eternity.* "This is as far as I'm coming."

Be with me, she whispered.

My skin prickled. For all my bravado, I was terrified, and I bet she knew it. I swore I could feel her gloat.

"If you sent the skinwalkers to scare away my friends, you don't know my friends," I said clearly.

They are not your friends. They want to destroy you.

"Why should they?"

Because you are powerful, more powerful than they will ever be. They fear you.

"I don't think so."

Low laughter. *They pretend. They know you are the key.*

I had a sudden vision of myself standing at the bottom of this hill, lightning streaming from my hands. It filled the crack of the wash and the earth buckled, heaving upward, opening . . .

"No!" I shouted. "Never."

When the time is right, you will open the door.

"Stay away from me!" I screamed.

The wind picked up, but it was natural wind, cold air pushing from the desert floor and meeting pressure from the mountains. I stood there for a long time, starlight and the half moon playing on the ground, leaves of bushes outlined in black.

I stood still until I heard an owl swoop past me and the squeak of some hapless creature as it struck. I said a prayer for the mouse, grabbed Mick's flashlight from the boulder where I'd left it, and made for the flames at the top of the ridge. Cold penetrated my bones, and I felt exhausted. I wanted a cup of hot coffee, a shower, and a bed, no more skinwalkers, vortexes, or evil goddesses calling my name.

But I couldn't leave Mick and the others to fight the skinwalkers alone. I hurried on, willing the distant storm to come in, but I knew it wouldn't listen to me. Storms have minds of their own.

The glowing nimbus surrounding the coyote flared in the darkness. The skinwalkers retreated from him, but Jamison, the mountain lion, didn't have that defense. Mick fought next to him, my boyfriend stark naked, fire streaking from his hands.

Coyote fought easily, but more demons kept coming at him, drawing his attention from the other two. Mick fried one, and Jamison tore out another's throat. That creature should have died, but it reared up, Jamison's jaws still closed on it. It shook Jamison like a cat shaking a mouse, until I feared the mountain lion's head would snap. I hefted my piece of pipe and ran toward the skinwalker, beaning it on the back of the skull.

Mick turned. His eyes were no longer black but orange red, as though flames danced inside them. He conjured a fist-sized fireball and threw it at the skinwalker that had attacked Jamison. The skinwalker screamed as it burned alive, the stench gagging me.

Jamison and Mick immediately turned to deal with more. The damned things kept coming, as though the earth belched them out. If my mother wanted to eliminate the strongest help I'd have, she was doing a good job of it.

I reached for the lightning again, but still it eluded me. Ducking behind Mick for protection, I wormed my hand into my pocket, drew out the silver ball, and tossed it into the air.

"Burn!" I shouted.

The ball exploded into light. The flare of a thousand fires

burned the sky, and by the incandescent glow, I saw at least a hundred skinwalkers in that little valley. They flinched and screamed, but they didn't flee.

Coyote gave a howl of glee and launched himself into the middle of them. Jamison retreated, panting, his muzzle covered with blood. Mick walked forward, fire dancing in his hands, the dragon tattoos seeming to slither around his arms.

Mick threw fire right and left. The noise, the smell, the smoke made tears stream from my eyes. A skinwalker got behind Mick, ready to take him down. I lifted my trusty pipe and hit the thing behind the knees. I'd hoped to make it fall, but the skinwalker swung on me. I tried a round-house kick, but he caught my ankle and threw me onto my back. I rolled to my feet before he could jump on top of me, not wanting to be in a clinch with a skinwalker.

I ducked, came up under him, and smashed the pipe into what passed for his elbow. He howled and punched me. I felt my face open, blood drip down my skin. The skin-walker hit me again, and I landed on the ground again, my head banging into the dry earth. The skinwalker came at me, drawing back a thick-booted foot, preparing to kick the hell out of my ribs. I tried to roll away, but my bruised body moved slowly. His kick came down.

Before his foot reached me, the skinwalker exploded into fire. As I watched, wide-eyed, his body disintegrated, held firmly by two hands that glowed with flame. The skin-walker faded to a stream of ash, and then Mick was grin-ning at me through the falling powder.

"Sorry I took so long," he said.

I hesitated to touch the hand he held out to me, the one that had been outlined in flames a second ago. Mick grabbed me and hauled me to my feet, his palm surpris-ingly cool.

Jamison had returned to human form, a tall, nude, well-muscled Navajo, breathing hard and wiping sweat and soot from his face. Coyote leapt over the smoking remains of the skinwalkers, changing to human form as he landed.

Jamison, more modest than the other two, morphed back into the broad-shouldered mountain lion as I neared them. Neither Mick nor Coyote seemed worried about their lack of clothing, standing casually naked in the middle of the desert night, the light from the spell gleaming on their sweaty skin.

"*Ya'at'eeh*, Janet," Coyote said. "Nice light spell."

"Mick gave it to me," I answered, trying to catch my breath.

"Impressive."

Mick shrugged modestly. "Light magic concentrated into a transportable object. Simple to make but takes several hours of intense focus. I'm surprised you kept them," he said to me.

"Why wouldn't I have?"

The look he gave me was warm, too warm. I had the feeling that if Coyote and Jamison hadn't been there, Mick would have carried me off to a comfortable boulder and showed me how touched he was that I'd kept the spells.

"Good fight," Coyote said. He cracked his knuckles and laughed.

Around us, little fires sparkled where the skinwalkers had burned, the smoke oily and disgusting. Too much for me. I hobbled a little way away and retched into the dirt.

Mick's large hands came to rest on my shoulders. "You okay, sweetheart?"

"No. I am very certainly not okay."

Mick turned me around to him, his skin smelling of sweat and smoke. I was suddenly angry with him, and Coyote, and even Jamison, for standing around complimenting one another and feeling good about the fight. "Damn it, this is dangerous. My mother seriously wants to kill you."

"I know that, sweetheart. But I'm not leaving you to her mercy. I told you that."

"How do you think I'd feel if you stayed to get killed for me?" I demanded. "Do you think I'd get a warm glow and sing ballads about how brave you were? No, I'd be sick with it. I'd rather know you were elsewhere. Safe."

"Leaving you alone?"

"Coyote can protect me."

Mick glanced at the god-man who gazed out over the dying fires, hands on hips. Jamison, still in his mountain lion form, stood at Coyote's side.

"Coyote can't be trusted," Mick said. "He does what he wants, and if you had to die, he wouldn't care."

"Not really true," Coyote remarked without turning around. "I'd care."

"You're powerful," I said to Mick. "But not powerful enough."

"She's right, you know," Coyote put in.

"I don't give a rat's ass," Mick said. "And I don't give a rat's ass what you say, Janet. If you're staying near the vortexes, I'm staying. Got that?"

I was too tired to argue anymore, at least not tonight. I flicked on my flashlight, my heart burning. "Tell Jamison to go home and be safe. I'm heading back to the hotel."

I walked away, not waiting for Mick, not saying good-bye to the others.

As I reached the railroad bed, I heard sirens, Magellan's two fire engines hurrying to discover what was burning out in the desert. What they'd make of the remains of the skin-walkers, or whether Coyote would make certain they found nothing, I didn't know.

Mick caught up to me before I reached the hotel, dressed again, his T-shirt damp and dusty. He took my flashlight, threaded his fingers through mine, and led me inside.

Twelve

Fremont had fallen asleep on top of my bed. Mick showered, I woke Fremont, and he called a friend to come and pick him up. Once he was gone, I raided the kitchen, finding an unopened package of cookies. Fights to the death always made me hungry.

I stuffed down about a dozen double-chocolate-chunk cookies before I got tired of them and dumped the rest into a plastic container in the pantry. Mick was pulling on a clean pair of jeans as I walked back into the bedroom. His wet hair left beads of water on his shoulders, a look that I found sexy as hell.

I suddenly wanted more than anything to get on Mick's Harley with him and tell him to take us wherever the road led. We'd done that before, riding all day, making love all night, sleeping in some hotel in the sunshine until we got hungry enough to get up and find food.

I wanted to taste that life again.

"Fremont get a ride home all right?" Mick asked me.

"Yeah, he'll be fine. I think we cured him of going after skinwalkers."

"Good." Mick's eyes were blue again, not the solid black or fiery red they'd been during the fight.

The way he looked at me brought back every reason I'd fallen in love with him. I was sweaty from running, had reddish dust creasing my skin, and my hair was tangled. I probably had chocolate on my lips too. And still he looked at me as though he wanted to devour me.

"I'm not leaving you, Janet," he said softly.

I didn't want him to. I selfishly wanted him to stay and make me feel safe, protected, wanted.

"I'm too tired to argue about it." I rubbed my hand through my hair, feeling it dusty too. "We can argue some more in the morning. I need a shower."

Mick caught me before I'd taken two steps. He cradled my face in his hands, thumbs softening on my skin. "You are so beautiful, Janet. I don't think you understand how beautiful you are to me."

My heart beat faster. I was exhausted and angry, afraid and unhappy. My mother wanted me, and she wanted to kill my friends to get to me. But right now, with Mick in front of me, I just wanted to bury myself in him and forget.

I smoothed my palms down his wet back, sliding fingers beneath his waistband, following the tattoo around his waist. "I don't mind you telling me," I whispered.

He smiled, lips curving sinfully, then our mouths met.

I let him ease my shirt off over my head, open my tiny lace bra. He flicked his thumbs across my areolas, making them rise to points, then he leaned down and took a nipple gently between his teeth.

I wanted to make him feel good. He'd fought hard out there, done everything he could to protect me, killed a skinwalker with his bare hands for me. I popped the button of his waistband and slid my body down his leg.

I crouched there in my dusty jeans and boots, naked from the waist up. He hadn't put on underwear after his shower, leaving his arousal for me readily obvious and accessible.

Mick made a raw noise as I took him in my mouth. I loved the familiar way he tasted, loved the gentle tug of his hand fisting my hair, loved the heat of his skin.

I moved my tongue over his shaft, gratified when he shifted in response. His skin smelled like soap and warm water, a scent I could bury myself in. I reached between his legs and gently cupped his balls, finding his scrotum firm and tight. His hand in my hair moved in answer.

"Janet," he murmured. "I promise you, I never stopped loving you."

I didn't know how to respond to that. He'd break my heart again if I let him, and I was in danger of letting him. I answered by speeding up my feasting on him, and he groaned.

I stayed down on him until he couldn't stand it anymore, and then Mick lifted me, took me to the bed, and made love to me like a wild thing.

In the morning, Maya didn't show up. Neither did Fremont. Fremont I understood, and I hoped he was resting. Maya being AWOL irritated me. I needed my electricity finished so I could get my appliances and hot water up and running.

What I did get was a bunch of painters sent by the decorator, who started painting the finished walls. Nice, bright colors, none of the "Southwestern" pastels the interior designer had tried to push on me. I wanted yellows, red oranges, blues, greens—bright colors that warmed and soothed at the same time.

Mick had been gone from the bed when I woke up and seemed to find plenty to do so that we didn't have a chance to talk alone. I didn't mind, not really wanting to continue arguing with him.

The painters and carpenters pretty much took over, so I told Mick I had a couple errands to run in town and got out of the way. Taking my rented SUV, I dropped in on Fremont to make sure he was all right. He was exhausted and a little groggy, and he didn't want to talk about the night before. I asked if there was anything I could do for him, and he said no. He looked so sad and tired that, after making him coffee, the best I could do was leave him alone.

Next I went to the decorators to talk about furniture. I chose pieces designed for comfort and decided to use my own framed photographs as artwork. I could commission other Native American artists like Jamison to create artworks for the hotel as well, which I could also offer for sale to the tourists. I liked the idea of providing a way for people who needed the funds to get through the freezing winters the high desert could throw at us. Even these days many Diné had to rely on wood-burning stoves as their only source of heat.

The problem with my decision was that I'd sent all my photos not in galleries and gift stores back home to Many Farms for storage. I'd either have to ask someone to drive them down to me, or I'd have to fetch them myself. The thought of walking into the long, low house outside Many Farms made me cringe. Home. Why did I fear it so much?

Next I went to the little phone store outlet and got a replacement for the cell phone that had gotten smashed in the accident. They let me keep my phone number, and I got a phone with more functions for the same price, so at least that worked out.

After that I headed for Paradox, which was somewhat busy today. Tourist season hadn't officially begun, but visitors had already started arriving in Magellan in search of magic. Several gray-haired women in light-colored clothing wandered through the aisles, staring in curiosity at the packs of tarot cards and displays of crystals, while a woman wearing a pendant of the triple moon of the Goddess calmly filled her shopping basket.

I discussed spells with Heather Hansen, the owner, a witch with a solid grasp of magic and the ethics of it as well. We talked about protection spells and spells to enhance aura reading as I bought more smudge sticks and candles.

Next in my rounds was Hansen's Garden Center, run by Jamison and Naomi. Naomi, busy in the greenhouse, greeted me with a smile and told me Jamison was in his art studio.

The hogan-like studio in Naomi's backyard was new, the old one having been destroyed last Christmas during a battle with a skinwalker. Inside Jamison was chipping away at a black stone, but he put aside his tools to greet me. Naomi's ten-year-old daughter, Julie, had been watching Jamison with great concentration, but she broke off and waved to me when she saw me come in.

"Jamison's teaching me to sculpt," she said out loud and in sign language. Julie had been born deaf, but had learned to speak as well as sign.

"What I'm allowed to," Jamison amended. "Nothing involving sharp tools, or Naomi would take my head off."

I smiled with Julie, then the three of us chatted for a few minutes about comfortable, mundane things, while Julie taught me a few signs. The little girl thought me backward because I'd never learned sign language, so she made sure to teach me something new whenever she saw me. In return I taught her a couple of Diné words, which she learned with quick precision.

By tacit agreement, neither I nor Jamison mentioned the

fight last night in front of Julie. I asked Jamison if I could commission some of his art for my hotel, and told him of my plan to feature the art of local Native Americans. He liked the idea and said he'd work on something special.

That pleased me. Jamison was a well-known sculptor, and his works commanded high prices. Having his art in my lobby could be a nice draw. The highest compliment I'd ever received was when Jamison attended a showing of my photos in a gallery in Flagstaff. The art patrons had gaped to see such a famous artist at a novice's exhibit, but once Jamison had given my artwork his nod of approval, people lined up to buy my pictures. I'd made a nice pile of cash on that show and gained the confidence to try more.

After we'd run through our art discussion, Jamison sent Julie off to help Naomi. Perceptive Julie rolled her eyes and left the studio. She knew we'd talk about the exciting stuff once she was gone.

"How is Naomi dealing with you being a Changer?" I asked as we watched Julie stride toward the Garden Center. "She thought she was getting a good-looking Diné and ended up with a mountain lion."

Jamison laughed. He had a warm smile, black hair pulled into a braid, beautiful dark eyes, and a deep, smooth voice. I'd known Jamison since high school, when he'd been kind to me, a scared, messed-up teenage girl. Jamison had some shaman powers, and he'd helped me learn how to control my storm magic. Not only that, but I'd discovered a friend with a warm heart. I'd have fallen in love with him myself, but I was too terrified of hurting people to pursue relationships. Not that Jamison had ever suggested we go out or be more than friends. I wasn't his soul mate. I'd been happy for him when he met and moved in with Naomi, eventually marrying her. Jamison deserved the love Naomi lavished on him.

"She's fine with it." Jamison's smile made me envious.

He and Naomi had a love and a trust that had been tested and stood firm.

I stuck my hands in my pockets, hesitant about broaching the next subject. "Jamison, how did Mick fight the skinwalkers?"

Jamison picked up a cloth and started polishing the black rock he'd been working on. "With some damn good fire magic. I've never seen anything like it."

"Did he change into anything? He stripped off, so I wondered . . ."

Jamison shook his head. "I think he just didn't want to burn up his clothes and have nothing to walk home in."

I sighed. "It's embarrassing, Jamison. I sleep with the guy, and I don't even know what he is."

"I think he's some kind of firewalker, as far as I can tell."

The mirror had called Mick a firewalker, but I'd never heard the term. "So, what is that? Do firewalkers look like dragons?" Dragons might not be real, but that didn't mean a demon or something couldn't resemble them.

"I met a firewalker in Mexico, a human, not a shape-shifter. They can tap into fire for their own purposes, bend it to their will, the same way you can with lightning and wind. Mick is similar, but not the same. The firewalker I knew couldn't conjure fire from nothing. With Mick, it was like the fire was inside him."

"I'm not an Unbeliever," I said, frustrated. "Why won't he tell me?"

"Now, *that* is a relationship issue. Which means you two have to work it out for yourselves."

"Thanks a lot, Jamison."

"It's wisdom I've learned the hard way. Don't keep secrets from Mick and then wait for him to be honest with you. You either trust him with all you've got, or you walk away."

I touched a mountain lion carved from red sandstone that stood prominently in the middle of the room. It was unfinished—the lion's head and shoulders flowed toward me out of jagged red orange rock.

"This is beautiful. Would you let me display it at the hotel?"

"No."

The answer was immediate and without thought. "I'll make you something else," Jamison said when I looked at him in surprise. "The lion—it's special to me and Naomi."

I stroked the animal's smooth forehead. "I can see that it's special." I could feel so too. Its aura was one of strength and wildness and, at the same time, peace. "I'm sure whatever you come up with for me will be beautiful."

I kept running my fingers over the sandstone as I gathered my courage to broach the next subject. "By the way, if you're going to Chinle anytime soon, would you mind driving on up to my dad's to pick up the photographs I have stored there? I want to display them in the hotel when it's done. I'd pay for your gas and tell them you're coming so they can get them ready for you."

Jamison picked up his chisel and turned to his black stone. "No."

"It's just that you go home so often, Many Farms isn't far from you, and I can't leave the hotel . . ."

I trailed off as Jamison looked at me, his brown eyes intelligent. "You have to go back sometime, Janet. Face your ghosts. Believe me, it's worth it."

I wondered what Jamison's ghosts had been and if he could possibly understand about mine. He looked at me awhile longer before he turned to his stone and gently chipped a bit from it.

I swallowed, thanked him again for agreeing to do a sculpture for me, and left before I started whimpering.

* * *

Instead of driving back to my hotel, I drove to Amy McGuire's house and parked in front.

Amy lived at the end of a cul-de-sac, in a small white house with a short driveway in front. The back of Amy's house faced the empty railroad bed, which ran north-south on the eastern edge of town. Magellan folk now used the railroad bed as a handy place to walk their dogs, jog, and hike from one end of town to the other. Beyond that the desert stretched to a low ridge, the sky above it vast and blue.

The McGuires still owned this house; they had not wanted to rent it out or sell it after Amy vanished. All her stuff was still in it, locked away, waiting for her return. I'd investigated the house during my first week in Magellan, even spending the night to listen to it, but it had told me nothing.

Amy had planted flowers to either side of the driveway, but they'd long since died and no one had bothered to pull them out. They lay like dried straw in the unwatered beds, food for the birds.

As I walked up the driveway, a large crow flapped toward me and perched on the chain-link fence. It cocked its head and watched me, as if waiting to see what I'd do. I still had the key to the house Chief McGuire had given me, and I unlocked the door and went inside.

The small house had a short hallway just inside the door, which led to the living room on the right and two bedrooms on the left. Straight ahead was the kitchen, small and functional.

Amy had photos all over her living room—of herself and her parents, of herself in the middle of her blue-robed church choir, of herself with her arm around Nash Jones. The few pictures with her and Nash never showed him smiling. They were candid photos—in them he contemplated a

cup of coffee, or was listening to someone else, or looking at something beyond Amy. None of them showed him
looking at her, smiling at her, paying any attention to her.

I took out the smudge stick I'd bought from Heather
Hansen, propped it in a coffee cup, lit the stick, and let the
sage smoke fill the room. I closed my eyes, breathing in
the scent, letting my mind and body become attuned to the
house and the faint noises inside and out. I heard the crow
hopping along the fence, and I knew without opening my
eyes that it had moved so it could watch me through the
living room window.

The aura of the house wrapped around my senses. It was
clean and soft, a little lonely, but patient, waiting. I sensed
no violence, no despair, no struggle. Just Amy living day
after day through her routines, her choir practice, the prep-
arations for her coming wedding.

I sighed and opened my eyes. I hadn't really expected
the house to tell me anything more than it already had. I let
the sage stick continue to burn while I stepped out into the
yard. I felt nothing there either, just the inky aura of the
crow as she stared at me. I don't know how I knew that
the crow was female—I just did.

"Do you know what happened?" I asked it.

The crow regarded me silently, black eye shining.

"I know." I sighed. "It's something I have to work out
for myself. But if supernatural beings are going to hang
around me, they could at least help."

The crow sidestepped in its ungainly way, then it took
off, soaring on outstretched wings into the very blue sky. Its
hoarse caw drifted back to me, sounding for all the world
like an admonishment.

If my mother had anything to do with Amy's death—
for example, if Amy had died because my mother had possessed her in order to have form in this world—I'd expect

to find more signs of darkness in Amy's house and in the nearby desert. Her body might have been found after all this time, as dried out and spent as Sherry Beaumont's walled up in my basement. I had grave suspicions that my mother had possessed Sherry Beaumont, and Sherry had died of it, though how the woman had ended up in my basement I still had no clue.

I let myself out of Amy's back gate, trudged over the railroad bed, and set off across the desert, angling north and east toward the place we'd battled the skinwalkers.

Under the bright light of day, with a few white clouds hanging far to the south, the land was starkly beautiful, the miasma of last night's fear gone. A few hikers wandered in the distance or on the railroad bed, likely following maps to the vortexes they'd picked up at Paradox.

The trail I took and the vortex I found wasn't on any map. A mile or so from Amy's house, I stood at the top of the little rise where I'd heard my mother last night and looked down to the narrow wash between gentle slopes. Sunshine burned the earth orange red, the grasses green. It was mid-May, and wildflowers were out in a profusion of red, blue, yellow, purple.

A nonmagical person walking here would see a pretty scene, nothing more. A vortex didn't actually *look* like anything to the mundane eye; it was more a feeling, a prickling sensation, a warmth that didn't come from the blazing sun.

The sensations pounded me like a dozen shovels on the top of my head. I walked down the hill to the heart of the vortex, where I'd been afraid to go last night, and put my hands on a boulder that jutted out of the ground.

The vibrations from it nearly jarred me off my feet. This was an entrance, all right. Closed and sealed, but if it opened . . . Well, I had no idea *exactly* what would happen, but I imagined it wouldn't be good.

A click of rocks above me announced a presence, but I didn't turn around. I knew who it was even before he stopped behind me like menace manifest.

"Why were you and your boyfriend starting fires out here last night?" he demanded.

I took my hands from the rock, rubbed them on my pants, and walked past him up the hill. Nash Jones fell into step behind me, for once not in his sheriff's togs but in shorts, T-shirt, and hiking boots. He had well-muscled legs, strong and tanned, and his sunglasses were firmly in place.

"Day off?" I asked him when we reached the top of the hill. "I didn't know you took them."

"The fire department came out to investigate," he said, ignoring my question. "And called me. Why do you keep giving me excuses to arrest you?"

"I didn't start any fires, Sheriff. Besides, they were out before the fire department arrived."

The flat black of his sunglasses was unnerving. I hated not being able to see a person's eyes. "I asked what were you doing out here," he said.

"What are you doing out here now? Hiking is a popular pastime in Magellan."

"In the middle of the night?"

"It's pretty under the stars."

"Don't mess with me, Begay."

"Don't mess with *me*, Jones. You are so out of your league I can't believe it."

The scar pulled at his upper lip. "It's my fiancée who's missing. I don't need an outsider telling me I'm out of my league."

"Why do you think she's dead?"

"What?"

"You told me when you interrogated me in your jail that you thought Amy was dead. The case file said you had a

PTSD blackout that day." I hesitated, but I needed to ask. "Are you afraid you killed her?"

I doubt I would have asked so bluntly if Nash had been carrying his gun. I figured, in his civvies, maybe he couldn't hurt me as much. Maybe.

"That's none of your damned business."

"So, are you?"

Nash opened his mouth to roar at me. Then he stopped and flinched, as though some pain twisted his gut. "I don't know."

"For the record, I don't think you did."

My statement, if anything, made him even madder. "What the hell do you know about it?"

"Because I don't think Amy's dead. I was just at her place, reading it again. There's no sign of a struggle, no blood, nothing. And no ghosts."

"There aren't any effing ghosts."

"Houses have an aura just like people do," I said patiently. "They retain an imprint of those who live there, of the emotions the house witnesses. Violence and death leave a vivid mark. A friend of mine, a Navajo, once toured Auschwitz. He said the aura there was so black and sticky that it was like walking through tar. He couldn't stand it and had to leave. And he has only a little bit of shaman magic."

"Your point?"

"Amy's place has no aura of violence, death, or fear. I felt nothing there but her quiet life, day in, day out. Which could mean she left on her own, her choice."

"Her car never left her house, and no one came to pick her up," Nash said in a tight voice, repeating what I had read in the files.

"That anyone saw," I said. "She could have gone when no one was looking out their windows. Even the nosiest neighbor has to go to the bathroom sometime."

"Then she must have walked somewhere," Nash said.

"No one walking the railroad bed that day saw her. Plus, I've hiked through the desert out here several times and sensed no trace of her, psychic or physical."

"Then how do you account for this?" Nash pulled out his wallet and extracted a photo. "I found this in this very spot a year ago. In a place you were compelled to come to last night and again today."

He held the photo in front of my face. It was Amy, wearing a dark blue strapless gown, her hair pulled up and styled in golden ringlets. She smiled, eyes sparkling, lips red and smooth. The photo was stained and creased, one fold across Amy's face like a knife cut. It had also been savagely torn in half, obliterating the man who'd had his arm around Amy's waist.

Thirteen

I reached for the photo, and Nash handed it to me with reluctance. I got nothing from the physical picture, no aura, no presence of magic. It could be that the tingling sensation of the nearby vortex erased what I might have felt, but somehow, I didn't think so. I hadn't seen a twin of this picture in Amy's house, nor had it been mentioned in the police file.

"Is this you in it?" I asked. Strong, tanned fingers that could have been Nash's curled on Amy's waist.

He shook his head. "We weren't together then. It's from a formal dance when she was down at U of A."

Amy's escort had been effectively erased from the photo. Had Amy done that? Or Nash in a fit of jealousy? Or my deranged mother?

"Who was the guy?"

"My brother, Kurt."

I looked at Nash in surprise. "Your brother?"

"Kurt dated Amy in high school and college. They broke up, and he got married and moved to North Carolina. Three years ago now."

Kurt Jones hadn't figured in any of the reports McGuire had let me read. Maybe because the brother had already married and gone, and therefore was not a suspect? "What did he have to say about Amy's disappearance?"

Nash snatched the picture back. "Kurt hadn't left home in months; he hadn't seen her. He had nothing to do with it."

"And he was fine with you getting engaged to her?"

"Why the hell wouldn't he be? He fell in love with someone else and is happily married. His wife has a daughter on the way. Kurt and Amy both moved on."

"Kind of an odd match, you and Amy."

Nash stuffed the picture back into his wallet. "She was good to me."

But were you good to her? Had Amy started dating one brother because she was still hung up on the other? Or had it been a clean break as Nash so emphatically stated? And who had torn Kurt out of the photograph?

I didn't voice my questions, because this was the most Nash had opened up to me about Amy, and I didn't want to ruin it. Maybe being out of uniform softened him a little. I looked at the grim set to his mouth. Only a little.

"Why didn't you give the picture to McGuire?" I asked him. "It might be evidence."

"I know. That's why I kept it."

"You're a confusing man, Sheriff. Why shouldn't the chief of police have the evidence?"

"Because McGuire is too upset to run a proper investigation. He always has been. He confirmed it by asking you to come here. I don't care if this is Magellan, it's not good procedure to bring in a psychic."

"Police departments do it all the time," I countered. "Especially on missing-persons cases."

"The last resort of the desperate. Investigators should find answers based on logic, facts, and a knowledge of human nature."

I wondered how much Nash understood human nature. He didn't seem understanding of any point of view but his own.

"Are you saying *you* aren't too upset to investigate? You were going to marry her."

"McGuire and I both conceded conflict of interest. We asked for it to be investigated under state jurisdiction."

"Then why are you still investigating on your own?"

"Because no one else has turned up a damn thing," he said. "I'm not too upset to do my job."

"A building fell on you out in Iraq. That could mess up anyone."

"It's what happens in war." Nash spoke with his jaw so tight, I thought it might snap.

I had a sudden vision of Nash's face under an army helmet paling as explosions ripped around him. I saw plaster rain down, his arms coming up to stave off the falling beams. I smelled the dust, the smoke, heard noise so loud it drowned out his shouting and the screams of the others.

I shuddered, and the vision vanished. I found myself back in the desert, the sun beating down on me, the wildflowers pungent. I knew the vision had been a real one. Psychic distress didn't cling only to buildings; it clung to people too.

As I turned away, trying to catch my breath, my foot struck something tangled in the weeds at the base of a rock. I leaned down and parted the grasses.

Nash was right behind me. "What is it?"

"Bones." I looked down at the stained brown remains. "Animal. Rabbit, I think."

"Yes, I can see that. What about it?"

"More over here."

I moved dirt on the slope down to the vortex to reveal three more carcasses—birds. I heard a flap of wings and looked up to see the big crow land on a nearby scrubby piñon pine. She looked down at the bones in disapproval.

"What the hell is this?" Nash stood with hands on his hips. "Some kind of freak Native American ritual?"

"I didn't do this. These bones have been here for a long time. Some of them for years."

"It's an ecosystem. Birds and rabbits are eaten by coyotes, owls, and snakes."

I stepped away from the vortex, feeling cold. The animals had simply died here; I knew that, caught in the evil energy of the place.

"Don't come out here again," I said. "Not alone, and definitely not at night. Never, in fact."

"Funny, I was going to say the same thing to you."

I rubbed the back of my neck where the tingling was worst. "Can you feel that? I barely have any power right now, and it's driving me crazy."

"No."

"Is that true, or are you just determined to be an Unbeliever?"

"I don't feel a damn thing, and you don't either."

"The fact that you don't believe in magic doesn't mean it doesn't exist, Jones."

"Cut the crap. I get it all day long from losers who claim that magic put the stolen TV in their car or the meth in their pocket."

I put my hands on my hips. "You know, you and Maya should get together. When she talks, she sounds just like you."

Nash went crimson from neck to forehead. He opened his mouth like he wanted to swear at me, then he closed it again.

Had I struck a nerve? I thought of the deep anger in

Maya's voice when she'd talked about Nash and Amy after she'd discovered the body in the basement, the flattening of her lips when she spoke Nash's name. I studied Nash with new interest.

He glared back at me. "Mind your own damned business, Begay," was the best he could come up with.

I got back to the hotel to find that the workers had dragged the magic mirror out of the attic and hung it on the freshly painted saloon wall. Mick lingered in the kitchen behind it, watching my refrigerator get installed.

"The mirror?" I asked him.

"I figure we'll have to bring it down sooner or later. It can keep an eye on things."

"I suppose." I didn't look forward to listening to it every time I walked into the saloon.

"The nonmagical won't hear it, and the nearly magical will enjoy thinking the place is haunted."

Ever-practical Mick. The sinful smile he sent my way felt nice after being glared at by Nash.

I drew Mick a little way from the others and said, "I'm going to have to go up to Many Farms so I can bring back my photographs. Come with me?"

He was silent for a long time, and my heart began to pound. "Do you really think I should?" he asked in a quiet voice.

"Why not?"

He grinned, the corners of his eyes crinkling. "I'm the big, bad biker you rode off into the sunset with. What's this grandmother of yours going to say to that?"

"My grandmother is five feet tall and seventy years old. What is she going to do to you?"

"I don't want to find out."

"Come on, Mick. Don't make me go up there alone."

Mick regarded me a moment. "You have to go, Janet. You know that, right?"

"Face my ghosts? That's what Jamison said."

"Jamison's smart. He knows all about facing ghosts."

"What about you? What ghosts have you had to face? Are you afraid of *your* grandmother?"

"My family is dead. There's no one left to face."

I stopped, shocked. "You never told me that. What happened?"

"It was a long time ago. Too long ago to matter now."

"Mick." I caressed his arm, fingers brushing the black lines of his tattoos. Saying *I'm sorry* felt ineffectual. I'd whined to him constantly about my overbearing grandmother and how I'd never been accepted into my own family—*the unfortunate incident,* I'd heard my grandmother refer to me as once. I hadn't realized Mick had been all alone.

On impulse I asked, "How old are you?"

Mick's smile deepened, making his hard face fine and handsome. "Two hundred and fifty-three."

While I gaped, he kissed my parted lips and walked out of the kitchen.

I dithered. I had plenty to do the next day as more and more people tramped through the hotel, banging, painting, plastering, varnishing. I went out and interviewed some of Amy's friends, who told me pretty much the same thing Maya had, only they'd liked Amy. She was kind and generous, they said, pleasant to all, thrilled to be marrying Nash. A young woman with all the blessings of life. They shared Nash's opinion that Amy was dead, because she had no reason to leave town of her own accord. She'd had everything in the world going for her.

They weren't much help. I needed something more,

some sign that Amy was upset, was worried about something, had enemies. But she seemed to have been the perfect girl, and everyone but Maya had loved her.

By the time I returned to the hotel the new bar was being installed in the saloon, a polished thing with brass around it. I'd projected the first of June as my opening date, which meant I had to get busy and hire employees.

I'd never done anything as scary as hire people before, and the stack of applications I'd already received daunted me. Did I really have time for a trip home?

I watched Mick as I summoned the courage to go. He looked the same as always—which meant wicked smile, warm blue eyes, snappy comebacks.

Whatever Mick was, he was amazing in bed. Last night, when we'd found ourselves all alone, the hotel quiet, he'd had me on my hands and knees, his body enclosing mine, making love to me as though he'd never stop.

My feelings about him confused the hell out of me. Even though he hid everything about himself from me, Mick had been the first person who'd ever listened to me, talked to me, treated me like I wasn't some kind of misfit freak. Even Jamison had been a little standoffish until he'd become a Changer and understood what it was to be a magical person. But Mick had always seen *me*, the real Janet, and had liked her.

The next morning, I knew I needed to quit sniveling and go. I packed a duffel bag and headed out to my SUV to find Mick there, leaning on his bike next to it.

"Ready?" he asked.

"You're coming with me?" I asked in sudden hope.

"I told you, I don't want to let you out of my sight. Coyote said he'd look after the place while you're gone."

That idea made me pause, but I was too happy that Mick would be coming with me to argue. I kissed him and got into my SUV while he mounted his bike. The coyote watched from the shade of the juniper as I left the parking lot and pointed my rental north out of Magellan, heading toward Navajoland. I hadn't been home in nearly six years. That wasn't in any way long enough for me.

I didn't question why Mick rode his bike instead of in the SUV with me. First, he hated enclosed vehicles even more than I did. Second, if things got uncomfortable, for him or for me, he could easily take off and not leave me stranded. Third, the empty passenger seat gave me more room to haul my photographs.

The hundred-and-fifty-mile drive to Many Farms took me into another world. I reached Holbrook and joined the freeway and then turned off again on the 191 and rode north onto the Navajo Nation. Home. The familiar beauty of the place caught in my throat as flat lands became desert hills and then sharp cliffs beside which the highway snaked. The sun shone hot and hard, the land starkly beautiful, the sky soaring and blue.

I passed Chinle, where Jamison had grown up. Chinle was the gateway to Canyon de Chelly, a crevice in the land with cliff dwellings and the phenomenal rock formations. People came from all over the world to look at its wonders.

North of Chinle I followed the road until I reached the small community of Many Farms. Many Farms was just that, a small cluster of farms irrigated from the waters of the nearby lake. My family lived on a small plot of land just north of the town, with a range where we ran about twenty head of sheep. My grandmother did some weaving, but mostly she and my father sold the wool to other weavers. Cliffs hugged the horizon, places I'd explored and climbed as a kid.

I pulled to a stop in front of a long, low, tan-colored

house that sat alone at the end of a road, and Mick pulled in behind me. When I'd been a kid, children's toys had littered the yard along with the old car my father had always said he'd get going again but never had.

The car was gone, sold for scrap one year when we needed the money. Most of the kids' toys were gone too, though one or two new ones had appeared—my cousin Cindy had two little boys now. A brown dog lay in the shade under the porch overhang, watching me without much concern.

I parked next to the pickup I'd bought my father after I'd started selling my photographs. My dad hadn't liked taking gifts from his daughter, but on the other hand, his bone-rattling truck had ceased to work, so he'd swallowed his pride and invited me to try it out with him.

I drew a breath and hopped out of my rental. Mick stopped his bike, the throbbing dying away to stillness.

Homecoming is always problematic. Either things are exactly as you remember when you'd hoped they'd changed, or what you remembered most fondly has vanished. Homecoming was especially problematic for me, because I'd grown up constantly trying to please my grandmother and my father's three disapproving sisters, until I'd simply given up and left.

"Anyone home?" Mick asked me.

"I'm sure they're around somewhere."

Mick gave me a smile, not getting off his bike. "You should go on in, Janet."

"Aren't you coming with me?" I heard the panic in my voice.

"I think the first step is one you should take alone. I'll be right out here if you need me."

He was right, but I didn't feel better. Not allowing myself to dawdle or even think about what I was about to do, I squared my shoulders, walked up to the porch, and opened the front door.

Fourteen

An empty living room greeted me. The house was small, nothing more than a living room, kitchen, and three bedrooms, all spare and painfully clean. My grandmother liked bright colors and no clutter. My dad considered himself lucky to have a chair in the corner where he could read his newspapers.

I made my way down the narrow hall, noting the silence. One side of the hall was lined with small windows that looked out to the front yard. The other side of the hall held doors leading to my grandmother's room, my father's, and last, mine.

When I opened the door to my bedroom, I found the window blind up and my single bed covered with pictures. More framed photos were stacked against the wall. I'd alerted my father that I'd be coming, but I couldn't tell whether he'd put these in here for me or stored them like this the whole time.

I heard a step behind me. I wasn't alarmed, because I recognized it.

My grandmother stood watching me from the end of the hall. Seventy now, she'd lost her former plumpness but stood plenty straight, her hair still black. She never admitted to dyeing it, but I was pretty sure my cousin Cindy did it for her. Her eyes behind her glasses were dark brown, with enough of an almond shape that some people mistook her for Asian. Not many, because Grandmother rarely left the Navajo Nation.

"Six years without bothering to come home," she said. She spoke the Diné language—Grandmother never spoke English if she could help it. "And now you turn up just to pick up your photographs."

"I know." What could I say to that? I felt myself wilting under her sharp stare, me the all-powerful Stormwalker. "I'm sorry."

"That biker. Who is he?"

I tried a smile that didn't last. "His name's Mick."

"What is he? His aura is fiery."

I shrugged. "Ask him."

She gave me a disapproving look. "You need to come with me, Janet. There's something I want to show you."

I closed the door to my bedroom. "Where's Dad?"

"On the land."

Which meant communing with the sheep. Dad had a favorite spot in a cool niche of rock, where he'd watch our flock wander. He could sit there for hours. Grandmother always warned him he'd get heatstroke, but he never did. Considering that my dad spent most of his time in a house full of loud-voiced, opinionated women, I couldn't blame him for finding a haven. The silence out there was immense.

Without waiting to see whether I'd follow, Grandmother walked out of the house and started for my SUV.

"Where are we going?" I asked as I hurried after her.

"I'll show you. But you have to drive. I'm too old."

I knew Grandmother could see just fine and was fit enough to drive a car, but she preferred other people to do things for her.

Mick was leaning against his motorcycle. "Want me to come with you?"

Grandmother stepped up to him. She was barely five feet tall, and Mick was six-foot-six, but she tapped a thin finger to his chest without fear. "This is none of your business, Fire Man," she said in perfect English. "I'll talk to you later."

Mick grinned, eyes impish. "Yes, ma'am."

"Now, be useful and open that door for me."

She stood back while Mick opened the passenger door of the SUV, but she hopped into the seat on her own. I got in the driver's side and started it up, throwing an apologetic glance to Mick as he closed the door.

"Where to?" I asked Grandmother.

"East."

Very helpful. Mick patted my grandmother's door and waved us off. I pulled out of our lot and down the dirt road toward town.

On the other side of Many Farms, Grandmother directed me to the road toward Rough Rock. We rode in silence, the only vehicle on the road. After my long drive from Magellan I'd been looking forward to a shower and a rest, but here I was obediently heading out into the desert with no water but what was in a half-empty sports bottle, hoping my grandmother knew where she was going.

I started thinking she'd have me drive all the way to Kayenta when my Grandmother said sharply, "Here. Turn."

She pointed at a dirt side road, and I obediently pulled onto the track. At the end of the narrow and very bumpy washboard road, a hogan rested in a fold of land, shaded by a gnarled tree.

"Here?"

Grandmother nodded. I stopped the SUV, and Grandmother hopped out.

"Who are we here to see?"

She didn't answer me; she walked to the hogan and opened its door. Inside, it was mercifully shady, but stuffy and hot.

"I brought you here to see this," Grandmother said. "This is where Harold Yazzie died two weeks ago."

I had no idea who Harold Yazzie was. Yazzie was a common Diné surname, but I didn't know anyone called Harold. What amazed me more than her bringing me to the hogan of a man I hadn't known was that she'd let herself come this close to a place where death had walked. "Who was he?" I asked.

"I'd never met him. His daughter came to me when he was dying, asked if I'd sit with him. He wanted to tell me something."

The air was still, no birds calling outside. They too must know a death had taken place here.

"Tell you what?"

"That he'd fathered a child. A girl. About thirty years ago."

"What girl?" I asked, baffled.

"She died at birth."

"Oh. That's sad."

"The mother died too when she gave birth. Harold told me this on his deathbed. He kept the secret for thirty years."

My grandmother studied me with clear eyes. The only indication she felt the heat was a faint beading of perspiration on her cheeks.

"Why would he keep it a secret?" I asked, not following.

"Because the woman who died was white and not his wife." Grandmother's voice held significance. "Harold was already married when he met this other woman. Harold's legal wife is still alive and living with her grandchildren in Window Rock. She doesn't know about his affair and baby—no one knows. Harold sent for me and told me, no one else."

"Why did he tell you? If he didn't even know you?"

"*Think*, Janet. You're smart. A woman, not Harold's wife, had a child and died, thirty years ago. She was a white woman, he said, and she seduced him, dazzled him. He got a bastard child on her, a girl, and he didn't know what to do. But both mother and child died, so the decision was taken from him. Harold heard about how Pete Begay had got a woman pregnant who died and left you to him. And he knew. The woman who seduced Harold was a sorceress, just like your mother."

She was beautiful, Janet. My father's voice rang in my head, voicing the words he'd said so many times to me. *Like a goddess. She begged me with her last breath to take care of you, to make sure you never came to harm.*

The realization hit me like a blow between the eyes. I slid down the rough wall of the hogan, my legs folding up under me.

A man, a mysterious and beautiful woman, a girl child, the woman dead. My father had never told anyone about his affair with my mother until he'd brought me home right after my birth.

"Gods," I whispered. "Oh, gods."

I'd known that my mother possessed women in order to move around what little she could on this earth, just as she'd possessed the blond woman who talked to me in Holbrook, and maybe had possessed Sherry Beaumont, and possibly even Amy McGuire. She couldn't roam far, she'd told me, and when the body weakened, my mother had to return to the vortexes and slip back through the cracks.

I'd assumed she entered human women simply to be ambulatory and able to communicate, that her encounter with my father had been a chance thing. Now my grandmother's story revealed a more sinister truth. My goddess mother had always been trying to make a child—a child she could use, control, manipulate. A child who would be her liaison and minion in the world above. A child like me. *You are the key,* she'd said.

She'd tried it with Harold Yazzie. When that baby had died, she'd found another man to seduce. My father. This time, the child had lived and thrived. Me.

"Why?" I asked with dry lips. "Why did I survive when Harold Yazzie's child died?"

"The women on my side of the family have powerful magic in them. My mother was very strong, like you. Your aunts barely have any magic and neither do your cousins. But you inherited it through me."

My eyes were burning. "How did you know? About my mother? How did you know what she was?"

"A goddess from Beneath? Because I'm not stupid. Young people think the old are fools, but I remember when your father brought you home with his story of the woman he'd been seeing in secret. You stank of her sorcery. And then power manifested in you stronger than I've ever seen it. The two magics—the Stormwalker power and the Beneath power—war with each other inside you. If you hadn't been strong—if I hadn't made you so strong—the struggle would have killed you by now."

"It is killing me." Tears slid down my cheeks. "I don't know how to stop it."

"You can't stop it. You can only control it."

I dashed away tears with the back of my hand. "Why didn't you tell me? Why didn't you explain that you knew everything?"

"I didn't know, not for certain. Not until Harold Yazzie told me his story. Your true mother needs a child, one she can control. Tell me why."

I rubbed my aching forehead. "I'm not sure. She's said things to me, that I'm a key of some kind. A key to the vortexes."

"Well, you can't let her have her way. She obviously doesn't mind using and killing people to get what she wants. You make sure you don't let her use you."

"Easier said than done, Grandmother. I've met her—or at least, a glimmer of her. She's very powerful."

"As I say, there are strong magics on my side of the family. Maybe not as potent as hers, but good, earth-grounded magic. That Mick creature, he has great earth magics, though his have an evil taint. Watch him."

"You only just met him."

"I know enough. I haven't decided whether I like him yet, but he can keep your magic from killing you and keep your mother from using you. Or at least he'll try."

I couldn't take much more of this. My heart was breaking into little pieces.

"Gods, the woman in my basement." I didn't explain what I meant, because Grandmother had seemed to know all about Sherry Beaumont when I'd called to announce I was coming home. The gossip network out here was wide.

"She was pregnant," I said, remembering what Nash had told me. "She was pregnant with a baby, not her husband's. And she died."

My mother must have been using Sherry to make another baby, I realized. I'd proved to be rebellious and willful, so my mother had tried again to get a child, maybe one who'd grow up to be obedient this time.

Another thought trickled through my fear, dismay, and anger.

Who had been the father?

Fifteen

By the time Grandmother and I returned to the house, my father and Mick were inside, sitting in the living room in companionable silence. Both rose when we came in.

My father, Pete Begay, was not a demonstrative man. He had an ageless face and dark hair, a slim body, and quiet ways. After I'd met my mother, I'd grown angry with him for letting her use him, and for not putting her out of his mind and getting on with his life, for not marrying someone else. I hadn't seen him from the day I fled her to this.

I decided now, watching him with new understanding, just how strong a man he was. He'd loved my mother with a deep, quiet love that he'd then transferred to me. I saw that now when he came to greet me.

"*Ya'at'eeh*, Janet."

"*Ya'at'eeh*, Dad. How's everything going?"

He shrugged, which was his way of dismissing his early mornings, backbreaking work, nursing sick sheep, keeping watch over the lambs, being on the lookout for coyotes. "Your grandmother told you about Harold Yazzie?"

I felt cold. "You know?"

He nodded. Mick watched, not understanding, but he kept silent.

I didn't want my father to know. I didn't want him to realize he'd been one in a string of my mother's lovers, men she'd essentially used as sperm donors. I wanted him to be innocent of the fact that she hadn't loved him. "Dad . . ."

"We will speak of it later." He started down the hall for my room, returning with an armful of photographs.

I knew that when my father didn't want to talk about a thing, we didn't talk about it. He'd inherited his stubborn streak from my grandmother, all right, though his manifested in taciturnity.

After we'd stacked the first load in the SUV, I returned to the house to find Mick pinned against a wall by my grandmother. The man who could have incinerated her with the flick of a finger was looking down at her, nonplussed, like a huge dog might regard a kitten that knew it had the upper hand.

"I don't care if you have big earth magic or how strong you think you are," Grandmother was saying. "I'll hunt you down. Do you understand me?"

"Grandmother," I said in alarm.

Mick gazed down at her in quiet seriousness. "I do."

"Those tattoos." Grandmother tapped a dragon tail that snaked out of Mick's sleeve. "That's just showing off."

"It's a fault I have. I like to show off."

"I can see that."

Grandmother poked him in the chest, then turned her back on him and walked away. "Janet, you will spend the night. Mick can sleep in your truck."

"I'm not letting Mick sleep outside," I said in protest.

"Well, you're not sharing a bed under my roof." She

started banging open cupboards in the kitchen. "Now, leave me be. I have to cook dinner."

Grinning, Mick ducked out of the house to help my father with the pictures. I hurried out after him. "I'm sorry," I said.

"Don't be. She's trying to take care of you."

"You're a guest."

"She's a matriarch. She's telling me she dominates here, and I respect that." He gave me another grin. "I like her."

He swung away to help my father load more pictures, and I knew then I'd lose all the arguments for the rest of the day.

After our dinner of stew with fresh vegetables, which I hadn't realize how much I'd missed, my father pushed back his chair.

"Come out with me, Janet." He walked outside without waiting for my answer.

I hated to leave Mick alone with my grandmother, but he threw me a look that told me I should go. He started clearing the plates off the table, and Grandmother turned her entire attention on him, fearing he'd break everything. I left Mick to it and went out to where my father rested against his truck.

Without words, we got in, and he drove north and east. About five miles on, he turned down a dirt road that wound toward a mesa rising from the desert floor. He stopped and turned off the engine, and we sat still, watching the moon sail over the mountain.

My dad and I had come out here to watch almost every full moon rise when I was a child. A lump formed in my throat. I'd been so eager to run away from my life here and the hard times with my family that I'd also abandoned the good things.

As usual, Dad and I didn't talk. We drank in the beauty, the bright moon, a little fuller than half, the blue and purple shadows of the mountain, the fading twilight, the carpet of stars that emerged overhead.

"Why did you come back here?" My father's voice was quiet, smooth like the night.

I looked at him in surprise. "To get the pictures. And to see you."

He didn't answer me directly. He watched the night a few moments, then he said, "This Magellan place, this hotel. Is that your home now?"

"I don't know." I hadn't decided. Once I figured out what I could do against my mother, if anything, I wondered whether I'd want to stay in Magellan or go.

"They're not your own kind there. Your own people."

"Who is my own kind, Dad?" I asked, frustrated. "I don't have any people. I rode all over the country looking for somewhere to belong, and I never found it. At least out there in the world, I can help people. Here, I'm nothing."

My heart felt hollow. All my life my grandmother and aunts had viewed me as a constant reminder of my father's failure, of him allowing himself to be bamboozled by a femme fatale. The kids at school had known I was illegitimate, that I had no mother, that I had no idea who she was. I'd been rejected by my own people.

My father glanced over at me, eyes shining in the moonlight. "You will always be strong, and free, Janet, as long as you remember that you are Navajo, of the earth."

"I wish I had your faith in me."

"Mick, he will help you. Don't send him away. Swallow your pride. You need him."

So Mick had managed to get my father on his side. Mick had an uncanny knack for making everyone trust him.

"Why don't you hate her?" I asked my father. "She used you, she tried to kill you, and you always talk about her as though you were still in love with her." I couldn't stand it any longer, and I let my anger bubble free. "She tried to kill us outside of Gallup that time. I know it was her now. She sent skinwalkers, and Grandmother drove them off with her magic."

My father shook his head. "She wasn't trying to kill you. She wanted to take you away from me. I was foolish then, taking you too close to her realms. She'd tried to kill me before that, the night I'd driven to Albuquerque to fetch you."

"You never told me that."

"I was driving back, and I had to stop for gas. All of a sudden, she was there, coming at me with a knife. She tried to kidnap you."

"What did you do?"

He shrugged. "I fought her off, and I drove very fast, up into Navajoland. That's all. I knew that if I got you home, I could protect you." My father smiled. "You didn't like being protected."

I'd never minded *him* being protective, but with Grandmother it had been stifling. "You let me leave home."

"You were riding away from her realms entirely, and I knew that the storm power would serve you well."

"How can you talk about all this so calmly? She's still doing it. If you know about Harold Yazzie, you'll know she's still trying to create another daughter, maybe one who's more easily controlled than I am. I hate that Grandmother told you."

He smiled, with another shrug. "It explains why a goddess was interested in an awkward Diné boy like me."

Tears sprang to my eyes. "You're not awkward. You're wonderful. You're the best man in the world, and I hate her for what she did to you."

"Well, I don't."

I slammed back into the seat. "Shit, Dad. Why the hell not?"

My father laid one strong hand on my knee. "Because she gave me you."

I stared at him in shock. Dad just kept smiling at me, and then I burst into tears.

When we returned to the house, it was to discover that Mick had taken his bike and disappeared into the night, likely to find a more comfortable place to sleep than my SUV. He called me as I was getting ready for bed, telling me that he knew I was safe at my father's house and that he had something he needed to take care of. He didn't bother telling me what, of course. He said he'd meet me back at the hotel, wished me sweet dreams, and hung up.

I got into bed, but I remained awake long into the night. Lying in this bed again dredged up too many bad memories, and my grandmother's revelation about my mother haunted me. Had she succeeded in breeding more children, more daughters? Were there other Janets out there? The thought chilled me.

I started back for Magellan after breakfast. Two of my aunts dropped by as I helped my grandmother tidy up before I left. They told me what they thought of me opening a hotel in a white town (mixed opinions, from admiration to portents that I wouldn't last a week), that they'd visit the place, expecting a (free) bed, and when Grandmother described Mick's blue eyes and tattoos, they warned me against my obviously deviant boyfriend. "He's a bad seed, Janet," my aunt Alice said. "A man like that will bring you nothing but grief."

I noticed my father slipping away from the babbling of women, murmuring something about animals that no one paid attention to. I extricated myself, got into my SUV, and breathed a sigh of relief as I headed south.

I reached the Crossroads Hotel after lunch, went inside, and found people working but no Mick. His bike wasn't out front either. Fremont was there looking a little better. He greeted me almost like his old chipper self, though he still seemed tired.

"Where's Maya?" I asked him.

"Who knows? That young lady, she does her own thing."

I ground my teeth. Maya had taken to showing up or not as she felt like it in the last few days. My appliance installation wasn't finished, and I still didn't have working lights on the first floor. It wasn't as though Magellan was loaded with qualified electricians. I needed Maya.

Fremont helped me carry the pictures inside, and we put them in my bedroom for safekeeping. He admired the orange and pink glory that was a slot canyon—a narrow slit that curved into mysterious shadow.

After we stashed the pictures, I hopped back into the SUV and headed for town.

I'd learned my way around by now, remembering what was on each curve of the highway. Hansen's Garden Center lay just beyond the one-screen movie theater and the small grocery store. Paradox nestled in the next curve, next to the diner and the gas station, which was plastered with posters offering a $12 lube and oil change.

Residential streets curved from the business-filled corners, running back into the desert. Amy's home lay at the end of the last turnoff in the town, and Maya Medina's small house sat closer to the intersection on the same road.

A few houses back here had landscaped yards, probably courtesy of Hansen's Garden Center, with big mesquites, cottonwoods, and junipers to bring much-needed shade. Clumps of cactus and desert grass highlighted open ground, and some residents had dug out gardens for scarlet geraniums and purple petunias that they kept watered. Wildflowers grew in profusion along the road and into yards—yellows, reds, purples, and dark blues.

In this glory of color, Maya's small house with painted clapboard siding looked fresh and neat. Her truck was the only thing in her pristine carport.

I parked, slamming the door hard to let her know I was coming. I'd been taught growing up that it was rude to startle someone with a surprise visit, to rush to a front door and start banging on it. Better to give the person inside time to ready themselves or let them come out and invite the guest inside. On the other hand, Maya was stiffing me work, and she could put up with a little rudeness.

When I stepped up to the small, square porch, I noticed that the front door wasn't closed all the way. At home I'd not think this strange, but even in a small town like Magellan people kept their doors closed and locked.

Maya's living room window was perfectly positioned to overlook the road. Easy for her to see who drove in and out of this neighborhood all day. The day Amy disappeared, Maya had been home, but she'd told Chief McGuire she hadn't seen a soul that day.

Cold formed in the pit of my stomach. Maybe she had seen something in truth and lied for her own reasons. Maybe the person she'd seen had some kind of hold on her. And then I'd come to Magellan, poking around and asking questions. And Maya had come to work at my hotel . . .

I quickly pushed open the door and stepped inside. I saw an empty living room with a nice set of upholstered furniture and a flat-screen television, a kitchen behind a breakfast bar, and a small dining room. All were tidy but empty.

A narrow hall led to more rooms in the back, and a fan wafted cool air through the house. I hesitated, wondering whether to announce myself. Then I heard Maya cry out.

Pulling out my cell phone, I barreled into the back and shoved open the nearest door. I stopped in astonishment, my grip on the phone going slack.

Maya, stark naked, her dark skin a lovely contrast to the white sheets, was on the bed, straddling an equally naked Sheriff Jones. I stopped in my tracks, struck by how beautiful they were together. Maya's black hair spilled to her hips as she tilted her head back, enjoying what Nash did to her. Nash's skin shone like burnished bronze, gleaming with sweat, his brown fingers splayed on Maya's thighs. He gazed up at her, his gray eyes dark with sexual excitement.

I'd moved my thumb from my phone and turned to leave them in peace when Nash spotted me. Maya looked over her shoulder, saw me, and screamed.

I hurried down the hall, but Maya came flying out of the bedroom and thwacked me with a pillow. I stumbled, and my shoulder caught the corner of the wall.

Maya swore at me in a string of Spanish. I wasn't fluent in Spanish, but I'd lived in the Southwest long enough to pick up a few phrases, especially the rude ones, like *Indian skank*. Rich, considering Maya had been the one bouncing up and down on top of Nash.

I regained my balance in time to fend off another attack with the pillow. Jones, every inch a law enforcement officer—and I do mean *every* inch—caught Maya around the waist and dragged her back.

"Get the hell out of here," he roared at me.

I didn't bother explaining I'd been trying to. I rushed out of the house and slammed the door, gaining my truck before I realized that my feet had covered the distance.

I sat down heavily and blew out my breath. Maya's front door was firmly closed this time, probably locked by now. Why had it been open in the first place? Had they been so frenzied they hadn't bothered to check the door?

I started to laugh. I leaned on the steering wheel and laughed until tears trickled from the corners of my eyes. It felt good to have something to laugh about. I was laughing at myself as much as at them, for blundering in and spoiling their moment.

No wonder Nash had turned so red when I suggested that he and Maya get together. No wonder Maya always grew angry and uncomfortable when she talked about Nash. The tension between them was thick enough to cut. Small wonder it had burst out like this. It couldn't have been going on long, or Fremont would have been sure to tell me.

I wiped my eyes, started up the SUV, and pulled out of the driveway. I didn't see Jones's sheriff's SUV or even an anonymous car near Maya's house. He obviously didn't want anyone to know he'd stopped at Maya's, and I had probably just blown his cover.

Chuckling, I turned onto the highway to drive back through town. I was still minus an electrician, but at the same time, finding Nash and Maya in flagrante had cheered me up.

Halfway between Magellan and the hotel, red and blue lights flashed in my rearview mirror, and the sheriff of Hopi County, presumably with his clothes on this time, pulled me over.

Sixteen

I waited with hands on the wheel for Nash to reach my SUV and lean on the open window. "Hello, Officer," I said, smiling. "Is there a problem?"

Nash's hands tightened on the sill. "Don't you say one damn word about what you saw, Begay, do you hear me? Maya doesn't need any kind of talk about her."

I suppressed my laughter at his discomfort. Poor Jones. He had no idea how to handle something so personal. "Don't worry about me, Sheriff. It's none of my business."

"Maya and I used to go out," he said, as though needing to explain. "Before Amy. I've been worried about Maya since she found the body in your basement. I stopped by to talk to her about it, and things . . ." He trailed off.

"Just happened?" I shrugged. "That's natural, especially if there was something between you before."

"Keep it to yourself, all right?"

"I hadn't planned to say anything at all. Like I said, it's

none of my business." I looked at him in curiosity. "Why
do you want to keep it such a secret, anyway? I don't think
anyone would blame you."

Nash took his hands from the windowsill, and when he
spoke his voice was hard. "It's not that simple."

"Why not? I think even Chief McGuire would understand that you were trying to move on with your life."

"I'm not moving on. Not like this."

"That's something you need to work out with Maya." I
straightened up, reaching for the gearshift. "I won't say a
word, if you don't want me to. I like Maya; I wouldn't want
to see her get hurt. But she does need to get her butt back
to my hotel and finish my electricity. Will you tell her that
if you talk to her again?"

Nash straightened up without answering, his frown in
place. I put the SUV in gear, and pulled away, spinning my
tires a little bit, just to annoy him. When I looked back, I
saw him glaring and patting dust off his perfectly creased
trousers. I laughed again, and drove on.

My good mood lasted all the way to the hotel. Inside,
the workers were carrying on, but Mick hadn't returned.
My irritation surged. Again, he was insisting that he keep
tabs on me without telling me anything in return.

I went to the saloon and whispered to the mirror, "Do
you know where Mick is?"

"Search me, darling. No, really, I'd love it if you'd
search me."

"If he's in trouble, you tell me, all right?"

"I might if you give me the right incentive. Like wriggling those pants off your sweet little buns. Or going down
on your honey-bunny where I can watch."

I gave it a withering glance. "Forget it."

"Don't be such a sourpuss. By the way, sweetie, have

you thought about doing something with your hair? That 'ready-for-fighting' ponytail does nothing for you."

Fremont wandered into the saloon and gave the room a puzzled look. "Do you hear a noise in here? Like a buzzing sound?"

I glared at the mirror. "It's nothing important."

The mirror gave me a raspberry, and Fremont frowned at the room. "Did you find Maya?" he asked.

I coughed into my hand. "She was busy. By the way, I never knew that she and Jones used to be together."

"I didn't tell you that?" Fremont sounded surprised he'd forgotten to pass on an important piece of Magellan gossip. "Yeah, they were pretty hot—this was before he shipped out to Iraq." Fremont rested his toolbox on the bar, taking on the interested look he got when relating some juicy tidbit. "He picked up with Maya again when he got back, but it wasn't long before they had a bad fight. A knock-down, drag-out, screaming fight—right before he decided to run for sheriff. Actually, I think that was one thing they fought about. People said you could hear them yelling all the way from her house to the diner. Finally Jones storms off, and the next thing you know, he's going out with Amy."

"Kind of sudden," I said.

"Amy was good for him. She calmed him down. She smiled at him and held his hand like a real girlfriend. Maya was a firecracker, always riling him up. Amy was more like cool water. Jones was head over heels in love." Fremont lifted his box. "Then Amy up and disappeared. Poor thing. It's been hard on her folks. And Jones."

"I know."

"I think if they can all just find out what happened, they can put it to rest. Closure, people call it."

"Maybe."

Fremont looked sad, as though he too searched for closure on something.

The workers banged away until about five and then cleared out in a hurry, as they always did at quitting time. Mick still hadn't returned, and I didn't want to call him to ask where he was, as much as I wanted to know. I thought about Coyote's warning about Mick, and my grandmother's as well. *He has great earth magics, though his have an evil taint. Watch him.*

I took myself to the Crossroads Bar, ready for a cold one. White clouds tinged with gray were spilling down from the south. The pressure built into a tingle up under my skin, and I started to itch.

"Just a beer," I told Barry as I slipped onto a barstool. "Where is everyone tonight?" The room was half-empty, unusual for five-thirty in Magellan.

Barry drew a draft into a chilled mug and plopped it in front of me. "People are saying I killed that woman from California." He rested his hands on the bar top, his expression frustrated. "But I never met her. I'm from San Bernardino; she was from Ventura. Might as well be different planets."

"If it's any consolation, I don't think you did it."

"Tell that to my customers."

I sipped my beer, which was generic and weak. "I'd think a grisly murder would be a draw. You could point out my hotel as the scene of the crime. Tourists would flock to you."

"Tourists, sure. But a lot of guys who come here aren't comfortable with the police wandering around investigating. If you know what I mean."

I glanced at the bikers lounging at tables and the bar, or playing pool in the back. No, they probably didn't want Sheriff Jones walking through here, his eagle eyes on everything they did.

"I'm trying to get it cleared up."

Barry thumped another mug under the tap and pulled

the handle. "I'm sorry, but what do you think you can do? You're not a cop. People are saying you're a psychic, but I haven't seen you do anything psychic."

"Because I'm not psychic." *I sense auras and talk to magic mirrors, yes. Predict the future or see the past, no.*

"Then what can you do?"

I didn't answer, because I didn't know. I'd come here to stop my mother from hurting others, and I had no idea how to go about it. My grandmother's revelations told me that my mother had been hurting people for a long time—why did I think I could do anything about it?

However, I knew one lady I was going to put up against a wall and have a long chat with. Maya Medina lived on Amy's street. She'd been home the day Amy disappeared. She admitted to me that she'd hated Amy, and now I find out that Jones had dumped Maya and taken up with Amy without breaking stride. Yes, I definitely wanted to talk to Maya.

"Hey, sugar." A bulky man squashed onto the barstool next to me, taking the beer Barry had finished pouring. Barry moved down to refill more drinks, leaving me alone.

The man stank. Body odor, I thought, but then the tingle inside me grew to an all-out burn. He had brown hair and dark eyes, a nose that had been broken, wide lips that looked swollen.

"I notice your boyfriend isn't here," he said.

"Not yet."

He leaned a little toward me, his nostrils widening as he took in my scent. His aura was smoky, and I knew what he was.

Nightwalker.

"What he don't know won't hurt him, right?" the man was saying.

Not all Nightwalkers were blood-crazed beings who sucked people dry and left a trail of bodies in their wake.

I'd met one or two who were calm and civilized. They stayed inside during daylight hours, drank animal blood, and made sure no one saw them do it. Nightwalkers were rare and usually solitary, and knew that to stay alive, they needed to pass for humans and suppress their bloodlust.

But there were plenty of Nightwalkers who didn't care. They reveled in their strength and their ability to mesmerize their victims, sometimes feeding off them for months before they finally let them die. They lived recklessly and adhered to one philosophy: "Kill or be killed."

It took me all of two seconds to decide that this Nightwalker was in the "kill or be killed" camp. He sensed my blood beating beneath my skin, and he wanted to sample it.

"Listen," I said. "You don't want to mess with me." The storm was moving in, my body firing up in response.

He touched my cheek, his fingertip ice-cold. "Your mama sent me to bring you to her. But she doesn't care what I do to you first." The finger moved down my face, his eyes dark, seductive, hypnotic.

I had a sudden vision of myself, half-drained and weak as hell, being carried to the vortexes, the white mists swirling around me in glee, sucking me down. My mother's voice . . . *Ah, daughter. At last.*

Thunder rumbled, and the vision splintered. I drew a breath, touching the comfort of the storm. Its insanity I could deal with. I smiled. "No, I mean, you *really* don't want to mess with me."

The Nightwalker seized my wrist, fingers clamping to the bone. "If you know what's good for you, you'll get on your knees and make me very, very happy. Then we'll take a walk in the desert."

The hell we would. I lifted my hand, fingers tingling. "Don't say I didn't warn you."

Before he could react, I jammed my hand over his face. The Nightwalker yelped as a net of electricity snaked out

of my fingers and whipped itself around his head. He tried
to jerk away, but I held him in a solid grip.

I leaned toward him, speaking in a low voice. "Listen,
Nightwalker, and listen good. I haven't killed you, because
I don't want to explain to Barry why one of his customers
disintegrated to a bloody pulp on his barstool. So I'm going
to let you walk out. You go tell my mother you were stupid
enough to try to capture a Stormwalker while her power
was rising. Think about what she'll do when you explain
that to her."

The Nightwalker jerked back, rage on his face. I released
him. My fingers had burned a netlike pattern into his skin,
and he stank of burned blood.

"Bitch!" he snarled. He pulled a gun from his motorcycle vest and pointed it at my head. "You're dead."

Someone shouted. Drinkers around me hit the floor or
pulled out their own pieces. My temples were pounding,
the storm happy to play with me. I pushed aside the pain
and reached for wind, which I channeled to the barrel of
the semiautomatic. The pistol's opening squashed flat as
though crushed by an anvil. The Nightwalker stared at it,
his mouth a round O.

"Not tonight, dickhead," I said.

The Nightwalker's lips pulled back from his fangs. He
went for me at the same time Barry brought a shotgun out
from behind the bar and cocked it. "Get out."

Nightwalkers aren't quite the same as vampires in the
movies. Blowing a Nightwalker's head off is just as effective as stabbing it with a wooden stake or decapitating it
with a sword. If Barry shot him, this one would be as dead
as if he were really human.

The Nightwalker looked at Barry, closed his mouth, and
shoved away from the bar. "Fucking Stormwalker. In the
end, you'll be dead. I'll dance on your grave."

"Not during daylight," I said.

He snarled and strode out the open door as more thunder rumbled. But by the flare of the next lightning strike, I saw that the Nightwalker had disappeared.

I decided not to linger. Some of the bikers were laughing, but others eyed me in anger. I dropped a ten on the bar for Barry and went back to the hotel, where the glowing wards on the walls comforted me. The Nightwalker wouldn't be able to cross them.

The encounter worried me, though. Why my mother had sent a minion to capture me while a storm rose, I didn't know, but she must have had a reason. A storm had been rising when the skinwalker had attacked the night I'd been riding back from Flagstaff. Why not when it was calm and I couldn't fight? Why not the night she'd sent the skinwalkers after Mick?

I had no idea, and my head hurt too much to try to figure it out.

Even with my worry, I dropped off quickly, tired from the day. The storm changed direction and drifted away, the better for me to sleep. My headache receded as it left.

In the dead of night, the magic mirror started screaming. I sat up straight as the windows of my lobby came crashing in.

Seventeen

I was up and into my jeans before the rest of the front windows broke. I slammed on my motorcycle boots and slithered out the bedroom window as a horde of bikers hammered down my beautifully carved front door.

The Nightwalker couldn't cross the wards by himself, no. But if he recruited humans to batter my doors and windows and rounded up a sorcerer and a few skinwalkers to combat my marks, he could get inside to kill me. Or simply let humans or skinwalkers do the job for him. My best bet was to run.

Where to go? Down the railroad bed into town? I could get to Jamison and Naomi, hole up in their house while the police sailed in and took care of the humans.

I had my cell phone out as I scrambled up the empty railroad bed, but headlights pinned me when I reached the top, motorcycles rolling toward me from either direction. A

couple more waited to the east of the empty track, and still
more got between me and the hotel.

Another storm rumbled against the mountains to the
south, too far away for me to use against so many. They had
guns, different makes and calibers gleaming in the moonlight. Even my storm powers at full couldn't stop bullets
from penetrating my flesh.

I clutched my cell phone, determined to at least punch
9-1-1, but the thing shattered in my hand as a gunshot rang
out. Bits of plastic cut my fingers, my hand stinging as
what was left of the phone was ripped from it.

The motorcycles closed in. These guys weren't teasing
me, and I smelled the stink of skinwalker in their midst.
Nightwalkers could mesmerize and control skinwalkers if
they wanted to, and I knew damn well who was controlling
the Nightwalker. She might not want me dead, but I was
pretty sure she didn't mind if I got battered while her pet
Nightwalker dragged me to her.

I leapt from the railroad bed and made for a gap between the motorcycles, running like hell for the hotel.
Hands reached to grab me, but I was fast and tricky. A few
punches and kicks, a spring over the back of a bike, and I
was sprinting for the hotel again. Bullets bit the dirt at my
heels until someone in the gang ordered them to stop. They
needed me alive.

I had an idea, the only one left. Mick's light magic spells
were gone, the storm was still too far away to help me,
Mick was elsewhere, and I didn't see Coyote around. I was
out of options.

I pounded into the hotel with motorcycles on my heels. As
I thought they would, the human gang drove right through
my smashed front door and into the lobby, where a few
skinwalkers and the Nightwalker awaited me. Up on the balcony, a guy who looked like an ordinary biker had his eyes
closed, chanting and chanting, his voice already hoarse.

The Nightwalker grabbed me. The damned thing was strong. I jabbed my fingers into his night-black eyes, and he snarled, lips pulling back to bare his fangs. His face was crisscrossed with little red lines where my electricity net had burned him.

I punched him between the eyes, avoiding his mouth. Once a Nightwalker latches its teeth into any part of your body, that's it. They don't let go until they suck you dry.

The Nightwalker danced back long enough for me to get past him to the saloon. I hauled myself up onto the shiny new bar, put my hands on the magic mirror, and screamed, "Find Mick!"

It gasped. "Oh, my *God*! Sugar, look out!"

I hit the bar as a shotgun opened fire. The mirror broke, a hole in the center radiating spiderweb cracks in slow motion. The mirror started shrieking, but it didn't die. Magic mirrors were notoriously difficult to destroy.

Hands reached for me, skinwalker stench making me want to vomit. I fought, kicked, bit as humans grappled with me, punched me, and tore my clothes. I was weirdly grateful to the maniacal bikers from the bar who wanted to teach me a lesson—while they pummeled me, the skinwalkers couldn't grab me and rip me down the middle. Only a matter of time, though.

The humans not holding me shot up everything in sight. The newly plastered walls, the varnished paneling, the bar, the tin ceiling. Thank the gods I hadn't hung my pictures yet—they were still stacked in the back of my bedroom closet.

Someone lifted me by the shirt, and I found myself facing the Nightwalker.

"You know what I'm going to do to you, right?" He leaned close to me, bathing me in breath reeking of blood and booze. "I'm going to fuck you until you can't see straight, then I'm going to pass you around to my new friends. And then I'm going to drink you, just enough to make you weak as hell when I drag you to the vortex and throw you to her."

I reached out for the building storm, sighing with relief when tiny sparks laced through my fingers. The sparks were too weak to do much more than sting, but the Nightwalker jumped and swore.

Then he hit me. My head snapped back, my vision blurred, and I tasted blood.

Damn it, where was Mick? Or Coyote? Unreliable trickster gods. If I survived this, I'd kill him. Mick too.

And then Coyote was there, in the doorway, his coyote form glowing with light. Mick was beside him, fire in his hands.

I'd never known coyotes could snarl like that. I'd heard a grizzly bear growl once, but that animal had nothing on Coyote's fang-bearing fury. The grips on me slackened, except for the Nightwalker's. Coyote leapt, and pistols opened fire.

The Wild West wasn't dead. Except instead of gunslingers and posses, I had bikers and skinwalkers on one side, an enraged coyote-god and a man who wielded fire on the other.

I rolled off the bar and hit the floor behind it. The Nightwalker came with me, his mouth open wide, ready to fasten on my neck, my face, my arm. Never mind about arteries or the jugular, Nightwalkers didn't much care where they bit as long as they got blood.

Lightning danced in my hands. It wasn't easy stilling my mind to channel power with the Nightwalker going crazy on top of me, but the storm was coming closer, giving me strength.

The mirror couldn't do anything but yell. "You get off her, do you hear me? Hit him, honey, *hit* him!"

"I *am* hitting him," I shouted back.

Hitting, kicking, punching, sizzling, fighting for my life. I had the feeling the Nightwalker had stopped caring about keeping me alive. If this one went into a feeding frenzy, my dear mother would be minus a daughter.

I screamed as the Nightwalker's teeth closed on my shoulder and bit down hard.

The storm flowed to me, as though answering my distress. The pain in my shoulder was agonizing, my heart fluttering as the Nightwalker swiftly sucked blood out of my body. A lightning bolt struck outside the broken windows, and I grabbed it.

White-hot fire sparkled in my hands. I laughed, even though my shoulder burned, and I shot every bit of power I had at the Nightwalker.

The Nightwalker's mouth popped from my flesh like a cork from a bottle. He screamed as I climbed to my feet, pushing him into the air with the white light around my fists. I lifted him all the way to the ceiling while he shrieked and cursed at me, his fangs dripping blood. My blood.

I got him against the ornate tin ceiling that had been original to the hotel. Then I surrounded him with lightning and let nature take its course. The ceiling danced with electricity, and the Nightwalker fried.

His death was swift. The Nightwalker screamed as gobs of his blood and gore rained down on me. I couldn't duck out of the way with my lightning power still smoking him, and blood soaked my skin, my nightshirt, and my jeans. The Nightwalker's screams died out as he burned away, until only ash fell on my upturned face.

"You *go*, girlfriend!" the mirror shouted. I turned to it, my reflection splintered across its cracked surface. One hundred crazed Janets looked out at me, each coated with blood, each surrounded by white light.

I swung around as a skinwalker came up behind me,

the huge, brutish thing ready to pound me to nothing. It smelled like a slaughterhouse, its yellow eyes wild with rage.

I killed it with one strike of lightning. The storm was on top of me, and I was unstoppable. Coyote and Mick were fighting like crazy, Coyote leaping and diving, tearing into skinwalkers as he had the other night. Fire danced out of Mick's hands, his eyes once again lit like flames. They avoided killing the humans, I noticed, but the skinwalkers were toast.

Mick flamed a skinwalker and looked around for more. Coyote barreled into the sorcerer who'd come running into the saloon, his aura weakened by the fight with our wards. I saw them go down, and then two of the bikers brought up sawed-off shotguns and emptied them into Mick.

I screamed. Mick fell against a wall, hands pressed to his stomach, his fingers turning crimson as blood poured from the wound. He'd shrugged off the bullet Nash had put in his shoulder, but that had been a flesh wound, no vital organs involved. This was a blast in the gut by guns made to bring down bears.

Mick slid down the wall in slow motion, a thick streak of blood smearing the new paint. I screamed again. Coyote landed on top of one of the shooters, sending his shotgun spinning. I flung the other guy aside with lightning.

I felt the Beneath magic wake up inside me and answer my storm magic, the first time I'd ever been able to sense it as an entirely separate entity. I wanted to tap it, to draw from sorcery of that other world to destroy everything in my path.

Outside, sirens began to wail. I sprinted to Mick, slipped on his blood, and landed on my knees beside him.

"Mick!" I gasped.

He lay motionless, and in the darkness I couldn't tell

whether he breathed. I wanted to gather him into my arms, hold him, but the way power crackled through my fingers I didn't dare touch him. Though Mick usually absorbed my magic, who knew what the magic of Beneath would do to him? "Mick, damn it, please don't die on me."

"Everyone on the floor." The voice of Nash Jones thundered through the room. Red and blue lights swept through the broken windows, staining the walls, floor, mirror, and faces crimson and sapphire. "Weapons down, hands on your heads. I want to see everyone in this room kissing tile."

Nash walked in, his pistol rock steady, his eyes as cold as ice. Deputies and uniformed Magellan police followed him. The skinwalkers were all dead, fried by me, Mick's fire, or Coyote's wrath. The remaining bikers hit the floor, knowing when they'd lost, except one who stayed upright and took a shot at Nash.

Nash plugged him. The guy gurgled as he fell, and the others went still. Silence reigned, broken only by thunder.

I hugged my knees and rocked back and forth, crying. Coyote came to me, human now but naked. He crouched down, gently pushed me out of the way, and reached for Mick.

Nash and his officers started going through the room, taking weapons, cuffing wrists, hauling men up and out. Mick's eyes flicked open. No longer blue, the voids of darkness sought not me, but Coyote.

"Take me out of here," Mick rasped.

Coyote lifted Mick as if he weighed nothing and slung the large man across his shoulders.

Nash pointed his pistol at Coyote. "I said, stand down. Get on the floor."

Coyote ignored him. "Nash, no!" I shouted.

Not listening to me, Nash tightened his finger on the

trigger. I threw every bit of lightning I had at him, no holding back.

The impact lifted Nash and flung him into the wall.
Plaster broke around him, and my electricity lashed him in
place like a cocoon. Nash fired, but his shot hit the ceiling,
the tin ringing like a kettledrum.

Lopez and another deputy tried to get me on the ground,
but I could no longer stop the magic. The storm was right
on top of the hotel, answering the storm inside me. I tossed
both deputies aside like they were straw and ran outside.

Coyote was carrying Mick's body into the darkness, toward the railroad bed and away from the paramedics truck
that was open and ready.

"Wait!" I shouted.

I sprinted after them, but Coyote moved fast. Weeping
and stumbling, I scrambled up the side of the railroad bed
as Coyote laid Mick's body on top of it.

I raced for Mick, but Coyote grabbed me around the
waist and hauled me back. I hit Coyote with my lightning,
but for all his reaction I might have thrown a swarm of
gnats at him.

"Stop it," Coyote said, voice firm. "This needs to happen."

The air around Mick darkened into a dense, inky cloud,
and in a few seconds, I couldn't even see him. I cried out and
again tried to go to him, but Coyote pulled me away along
the railroad bed, my boot heels catching on clumps of dried
grass.

"Begay!" Nash came striding toward us, lights from the
police vehicles gleaming on his drawn pistol. "I said, stand
down."

I gaped at him in amazement. I must have seared him
with a couple thousand volts, but here he was, marching
toward us as though he'd risen fresh from a good night's
sleep. He didn't look hurt or burned or even winded. I

must have made myself pull the punch, I thought, my mind dazed, but I sure hadn't done it on purpose.

"On the ground, Begay. Coyote, you too."

He came on, his face set, leaving me no doubt he'd fire on me if I didn't obey. I dropped to the railroad bed, embracing the scent of cool red earth and grasses. Coyote ignored Nash and remained standing, watching the weird darkness engulf Mick.

Nash's boots stopped right by my face, and he rested one foot on my back. The lightning inside me shot upward through his leg. Nash didn't even flinch.

Cool metal touched my wrists, and I heard a faint *click* as the handcuffs expertly locked. Electricity snaked around the metal and fed back into my skin, and I groaned.

"Stop the light show, Janet," Nash snapped. "It's over."

"I can't," I moaned.

The darkness around Mick swelled and swelled, and then suddenly shot out like tentacles in all directions. A wave of heat rolled out of the blackness, smelling of fire and ash.

"I'd stand back," Coyote said in a mild voice.

The ground shuddered. I yelped, unable to do anything flat on my stomach with my hands behind me.

Nash grabbed me, lifting me up, dragging me off the railroad bed as the black cloud exploded into shards. We hit the ground at the bottom of the little slope, rocks cutting into my knees.

From the shards rose—a creature. It was black and gigantic, like a beast from the deepest part of hell. Huge, leathery wings shot out of a long, sinuous body and flapped once, blasting me with furnace-hot air. The air didn't smell bad—it reminded me of the heat of an intense fire, clean, hot, tinged with fragrant smoke.

"What the fuck?" Nash's words echoed my thoughts.

The creature's wedge-shaped head rotated on its neck as

it looked down at me, its huge black eyes cut with orange red slits. It gleamed black from its head to the barbed tail that snaked out behind it, but its hide glistened faintly red, as though fire surged just under its skin.

I'd seen it before, I remembered. A split second only, when my bedroom had been lit with frantic magic, and I'd seen a flash of the monster that now hovered above me. I'd thought it a hallucination or a by-product of the magic Mick and I worked, but now I realized that in that moment I'd seen the aura of what Mick really was.

They weren't supposed to exist. They were legends only. Weren't they?

The creature roared and swooped down on us. Nash and I both hit the dirt, but Coyote stood straight and grinned up at it. "Feeling better, my friend?"

The beast sailed to us again and opened its mouth, a row of sword-edged teeth passing too close for my comfort. The gleaming scales of its hide and the football field–length tail glided by, and then the monster rose to incredible height, blotting out the stars. I thought it would disappear into the night, but it turned again, angling behind the hotel.

Fire came out of the thing's mouth, a stream of white heat so concentrated it picked out one stray skinwalker fleeing into the desert. The skinwalker screamed, burst into flame, and died to ash.

The creature roared in triumph, and I swore I heard grating laughter in my head. As the giant swooped by me and Nash once more, the lightning inside me arced up to it as though greeting an old friend. The beast opened its mouth and swallowed the forked bolts, then it sped out into the black desert and was gone.

I fell back against Nash, breathing in short gasps, my hands still locked behind me. I wanted both to heave and to curl up in a little ball and never get up again.

"Shit," I rasped.

"You didn't know?" Coyote stopped in front of me, still naked, a god-man with no sense of embarrassment.

Nash's pistol hung slack in his grip, his face shining with sweat. "She didn't know what?"

"That my boyfriend is a—" I coughed to clear my throat. "Holy shit. Mick is a *dragon.*"

Coyote deserted me. That is, he walked off down the railroad bed in spite of Nash growling at him to stay put. The air rippled like a special effect, and when it cleared, Coyote was gone.

"He's a god." I was aching and exhausted, the storm magic still eating through me. I got shakily to my knees, but couldn't dredge up the energy to climb to my feet. "He doesn't listen to anyone."

"A god. Right. And a dragon. What the hell are you—a werewolf?"

"Changers don't run in my family as far as I know. I'm a Stormwalker."

"What's that supposed to be?"

Nash's pistol was on me again. I let lightning flicker across my skin, sparking into the night. "I can call the power of any storm, twist it to my will, as long as it's close enough to me. I can bend the wind, channel lightning, use rain to flood my enemies."

Nash listened to my speech with a skeptical look on his face. "That is the biggest load of bullshit I've ever heard."

"Nash, the Unbeliever. You just saw a dragon, plus I picked you up and threw you across a room with my storm power. I'm sorry about that, by the way. I didn't mean to hurt you—I was upset, because I thought Mick was dead."

"It didn't hurt."

My eyes widened. "No? You put a good-sized hole in my wall."

"Yes, *that* hurt. I'm going to charge you for assaulting a police officer, but your little light show didn't affect me."

"Now who's bullshitting?"

"You might scare drunk bikers with your tricks, but I'm not drunk, and I'm not interested."

I stared at him. I'd convinced myself that something decent in me had prevented my magic from killing him, but thinking about it, now that I knew Mick wasn't dead, just a dragon . . . *Shit.*

I *had* hit Nash with my power full strength. I'd been way too upset for any kind of control, and the lightning I'd sent through Sheriff Jones should have killed him.

"That can't be right," I said, half to myself.

"It is right, and I'm going to testify that it's right, and you're going to do a few years for assault."

I sat back on my heels. "Damn it, I said I was sorry. I'd just seen my boyfriend get shot in the stomach, for the gods' sakes."

"You can say 'sorry' by good behavior while wearing your nice orange overalls."

"You're a shithead, Jones, you know that? And I still don't believe that you didn't feel it."

"I don't care what you believe." Nash holstered his pistol and hauled me to my feet, easy to do because my wrists were still cuffed behind me. "Time to go."

Like hell. I collected more lightning into my bound hands and shot it back to Nash. Because he stood behind me, and because my hands were at about the level of his crotch, he got it there full force. I didn't hold back, and I wasn't nice—I zapped every bit of lightning magic I had right into Nash Jones's balls.

His body jolted, but he didn't let go of me. I gaped over my shoulder at him as my power surrounded his body like arcs in a Frankenstein movie. I gave it to him as hard as

I gave it to Mick, and Nash absorbed every ounce of my power without flinching.

He gazed down at me, his gray white eyes glowing with my magic, and I saw raw need awaken in him. He cupped my neck in his strong hand, pulled me to him, and kissed me.

Eighteen

I knew I should pull away. I should jerk back, get myself free, and kick Nash in the stones. But my body craved the release, and it felt so damn good letting it go, not holding back.

Hell, *Nash* should have pulled away. I was the one in handcuffs, and he'd been in bed that afternoon with Maya. But he really kissed me. His mouth opened mine, his tongue dug deep, and he gripped the back of my neck as though he was afraid to let go.

Humid air licked our bodies. I felt the wild beating of Nash's heart against my chest, the heat of his breath on my skin, the rough scrape of unshaved stubble against my lips. I was hot all over, the power melting my body to his, him hard against me.

My photographer's eye had missed nothing when I'd burst into Maya's bedroom this afternoon. I clearly remembered Nash's arms thick with muscle, his hands strong on Maya's thighs, Maya's beautiful body arching, unashamed of the joy she took in Nash. The memory made me crave sex even more. I wanted what they'd had—a coupling to ease my itch, my confusion, and my heartache. But not with Nash. With Mick.

Neither my thoughts nor Nash stopped us. Mick did.

I heard a light click of rock on rock and opened my eyes to find Mick standing three feet behind us, human once more, wearing jeans and nothing else.

Nash jerked away. His lips were swollen, his hand still locked on my neck. The three of us remained still, frozen in place.

Thunder rumbled but more distant now. The air smelled fresh, of ozone and fire, of the burning crackle of my power.

The look in Mick's eyes took the last of my strength. I collapsed, and Nash, the good cop, had to catch me. When I looked up again, Mick had disappeared.

I wanted to cry, to lie down right here and weep until I had no more tears. Nash growled in his throat, and I felt the handcuffs leave my hands.

"What are you doing?" I asked, too tired to even rub my wrists. "You think I don't need to be restrained anymore?"

"I'm letting you go."

That made me look up in surprise. "What? No more assaulting a police officer? No more destruction of my own property? Or whatever else you were going to charge me with? Disturbing the peace by letting a motorcycle gang drive through my hotel?"

"Just go home, Janet."

"You all right?" I asked him. As much as he confused me at this moment, I also felt responsible for him. He looked tired but in no way harmed by the voltage I'd burned through his body.

"No." Nash's face was lined with dirt, his eyes dead. "You were in my custody. It's the biggest rule. Once the perp is subdued, you don't touch them."

My mouth sagged open, and I started to laugh. The laughter had a hysterical edge.

"You're upset because you broke a *rule*? Never mind that you're busy messing up relationships right and left, never mind that you kissed the hell out of me, never mind that my hotel is a wreck and you had to arrest an entire motorcycle gang. Oh, no, you're upset because you broke procedure."

"It's not funny," Nash growled.

"Yes, it is. Help me up. I can't stand on my own."

Nash hauled me to my feet, none too gently. I started to dust off my pants, then figured it was useless. I was covered with dirt, blood, bits of Nightwalker, plaster from the hotel walls, and shards of glass from the broken windows.

"What relationships?" he asked. "I'll apologize to your boyfriend; he deserves that, but I don't see anyone else out here."

"You're hilarious, Jones. I meant you and Maya."

"I'm not having a relationship with Maya."

"No? What was that I saw this afternoon in her bedroom?"

"Careful, Begay, or I'll put you back in the cuffs, to hell with the rules."

"Why did you dump her?" I folded my arms, lingering. I didn't really want to go back to my destroyed hotel. I didn't want to see everything I'd worked for ruined, didn't want to face the emptiness Mick would leave.

"It was a long time ago and none of your business," Nash said.

"Fremont says Maya kept you riled up and that she argued about you running for sheriff. I think she'd be good for you—someone to challenge you. She'd keep you in your place."

"Damn it, if you don't shut up about Maya, I really will lock your ass up. I said it's none of your business."

"I just hate to see her treated like dirt. She deserves better."

"I thought you didn't like her."

"She's unreliable, sarcastic, and bad-tempered, and we don't get along, but that doesn't mean I don't respect her. She's smart, capable, strong, and can stand up for herself. But what's worrying me a lot more right now is you, and the question of why you're still alive."

"I'm tough."

"No one's that tough. What are you, Jones? A dragon, like Mick?"

The revelation about Mick still wasn't processing. Dragons weren't real. Gods, Changers, skinwalkers, Nightwalkers, sure. Dragons, no. This couldn't be right.

Mick had stood behind us looking completely normal again, the gunshot wounds gone. The look in his eyes had pierced me through the heart, and I wondered if I'd ever see him again.

"I'm cutting you a break, Begay. If I were you, I'd go back inside and start making a list of damages for your insurance company. I have plenty of arrests to process, and a long night of work ahead of me."

Without saying good-bye, Nash pivoted on his heel and strode toward his SUV, now sitting alone in the parking lot. The rest of the cops and ambulances had hauled off my attackers; the curious had returned home. I was sure I'd be front page news of the *Magellan Gazette* tomorrow morning, but for now the townspeople had retreated.

Nash's truck started with a roar, and he peeled out of the dirt lot, tires squealing when they hit the pavement. I stood in the darkness, taking deep breaths of cool air, listening as the night sounds returned. The horizon to the east showed a light gray line, and mockingbirds started to call down in the wash.

I made my numb way back to the hotel, feeling like I had a hole in my chest. It was just a building, I told myself as I walked in through the destroyed front door. Man-made brick piled on brick, temporal, unimportant in the grand scheme of the universe.

But seeing my carved Spanish door smashed to bits, the newly painted walls scarred and broken, the window frames empty of glass, the pretty varnished bar in the saloon wrecked beyond repair, and the magic mirror a broken mess brought tears to my eyes. Blood spattered the walls and floor where the skinwalkers and Nightwalker had died, the vivid streak Mick had left now drying to rusty brown.

I couldn't look anymore. I went upstairs, trying to comfort myself that at least this part of the hotel had survived intact. I wearily climbed the next flight of stairs up through the third floor and to the roof.

The breeze that sprang from the dying storm was cold. I sank down against the wall, my legs folding up in front of me. I ached all over. The magic had exhausted me, and even though Nash had drawn it off—somehow—I didn't feel as cleansed as when Mick did it. Plus I had been knocked around, cut in a hundred places, and bitten by a Nightwalker. I rubbed my shoulder, wincing as I touched the bruised and abraded skin.

I didn't realize I was crying until I had to wipe the water from my face. I needed a tissue, and I didn't have the energy to drag myself downstairs to see if I had any.

I heard the door softly open, the quiet touch of bare feet

on stone. Mick walked past, giving me a view of strong legs in jeans and a few strands of wiry black hair on the tops of his feet.

He folded himself next to me, not touching me, not looking at me. He smelled of sweat and night air, of the scent that was Mick. His hair hung in a wild mess; he hadn't stopped to bind it.

We sat in silence, watching the desert. It was still gray, the light that would make it a colorful wonderland not yet strong enough.

"Dragon," I said after a time. I was still numb, too tired to put any inflection in my voice. "How long has that been going on?"

"Pretty much all my life."

I glanced at him, but he kept his gaze on the horizon. His torso was bare, showing me solid muscle, black hair, and a flat stomach devoid of wounds. In the dim light, I couldn't tell if he even bore scars.

"You healed yourself."

He shrugged, shoulders rippling. "Human weapons won't kill me as long as I'm able to assume my dragon form quickly enough."

I remembered when Nash had shot him in the shoulder, how he'd ignored my pleas for him to go to a hospital. He'd had me help him get the bullet out, then he'd sent me to sleep and disappeared. He must have gone off to turn himself into a dragon to complete the healing.

"I don't see any scales."

He flashed me his smile, but the usual warmth was missing from it. "The human form is completely human."

I touched the inked lines on his arm, his biceps firm under my fingertips. "So these tattoos aren't just for decoration."

"They hold the essence of the dragon."

"Why didn't you tell me?" I tried to sound neutral, not

hurt or petulant. "You know I'm not human, not fully. Didn't you think I'd understand?"

Mick still didn't look at me, the eyes that had seen so much trained on the horizon. "Dragons are of this earth," he said in a colorless voice. "They never existed Beneath. We were created inside volcanoes eons ago, even volcanoes in the depths of the oceans. Dragons are creatures of fire and water, earth and air. We're connected to the land in a way no other creature can be. The earth gave birth to us, not gods. The earth itself shaped us, and it is to the earth alone that we answer."

I'd never heard him sound so serious, so devoid of emotion. "Why the history lesson?"

"Most dragons are extinct now. A few remain in remote parts of the world, or in deep lakes or oceans."

"The Loch Ness Monster?"

"Is a water dragon. I'm a fire dragon—I came from fire and burning rock. That's why fire doesn't hurt me, why I can wield it, and why I can absorb your power. Your storm powers are of the earth. They embody the fire between sky and ground and only make me stronger."

"I figured out a long time ago that my magic enhanced yours. I just didn't understand how."

Mick finally turned his head and looked at me. His eyes had changed from blue to fully black. "The gods trapped Beneath hate the dragons. They crave our power, the greatest earth magic there is, and they hate us for helping gods like Coyote seal the vortexes to keep them in. Those gods still trapped Beneath need to stay there. If they emerge, the last of dragonkind will die—along with so many humans. We've always feared a sorcerer would come with enough Beneath magic to open the vortexes to let out the old gods, a key. That key is you." His eyes burned me. "The dragons sent me to stop you."

I looked away, my heartbeat speeding. "So meeting me at the bar in Nevada wasn't a coincidence."

"I'd been following you, waiting to get close to you. My mission was to take you somewhere alone, and kill you." Mick stopped, and when he spoke again, his voice was tired. "I'm your enemy, Janet. I always have been."

My throat was so tight I could barely swallow. "I don't plan to open the vortexes anytime soon. If the gods of Beneath are anything like my mother, I don't want them up here."

"I know you don't. I realized that once I started talking to you that first night. That's why I let you live."

Coyote had said much the same thing. Ten points to me for being such a softie. I didn't want to destroy the world, so I didn't have to die right away.

"So you took me to bed instead." I didn't have any tears left to cry, but I wanted to weep. It had been so beautiful, the two of us in that hotel room, Mick gently introducing me to the unrestrained joys of sex.

"I fell in love with you," he said.

The blue returned to Mick's eyes, making him look like the Mick I knew. He pushed back a lock of hair that had fallen across his face.

"Is that why we had such a one-sided relationship?" I asked. "Because all those times you disappeared, you couldn't say you were off flying around as a dragon?"

"I convinced the dragon council to let me keep an eye on you and report to them. I had to return at regular intervals and restate the case for keeping you alive. I had to justify letting you live every single time."

My numbness crumbled, and my rage took over. "Damn it, Mick, why didn't you tell me?"

"I was forbidden to. The only reason I let you go off on your own in the end was because you were heading toward

Massachusetts. I had to keep an eye on you, but as long as you didn't return to the vortexes, I could let you think that you were on your own."

The words rained like blows to my gut. "So you've been watching me the entire time."

"Yes."

"Funny, I never saw a dragon hovering outside my window."

He didn't smile. "I'm good at not being seen."

"And when I moved to Magellan, you decided to come back to me."

"The dragons wanted you dead as soon as you came within thirty miles of these vortexes. They would have killed you when you arrived, but I stopped them. They're not happy with me, but they spared you on the condition that if you let loose what's beneath the vortexes, the first to pay is me, with my life. First me, then you."

He regarded me with calm eyes, as though he hadn't just told me he'd used his life as collateral for mine.

"Why would you do that?" I asked, still angry.

"I told you. Because I love you."

I closed my eyes, shutting out the growing light to the east. Everything I knew was overturning and falling, like a pack of cards thrown into the air. One reason I hadn't believed in dragons was because I'd never seen one, never met anyone who'd seen one. They didn't exactly hang out on street corners. I'd encountered skinwalkers, evil sorcerers, demons, Nightwalkers, Changers, and my mother. Never a dragon. Now I was learning that not only was my lover a dragon, but a council of dragons had sent him to kill me. And that the only reason I was still alive was because Mick had decided he liked me.

"If you loved me, why didn't you tell me all this?" I asked. "Why didn't you warn me that your people wanted me dead? Or even what you were?"

"It was part of the price of keeping you alive. You couldn't know."

"And now?"

"I revealed myself trying to protect you—Coyote couldn't get me far enough away before the dragon part of me had to take over. The council already knows, but they haven't yet decided what they'll do."

I pressed my hands to my head, trying to make sense of it all. "Why didn't the dragons try to kill me when I was a kid? Or kill the woman who bore me before she could?"

"Because the dragons didn't know about you until your true mother made contact with you for the first time. When that happened, when they discovered your existence, I was dispatched to waylay you."

"Waylay me. Is that what you call it?" My words tasted bitter. "I gave you my virginity, Mick. Did you know that?"

"I didn't realize until we'd started, but yes, I knew. You were so beautiful, so fragile." Mick's voice softened. "Gods, I was so afraid I'd hurt you."

"You knew damn well I couldn't hurt you, didn't you? You ate my magic like it was a snack. I'm defenseless against you."

"I wouldn't say that."

I was working myself up into a fine rage. "I was lonely and naïve and scared, and you *played* me."

"For the first five minutes." Mick looked straight at me, no evasiveness. "When you faced me down in that little motel room on the highway, I knew that I wanted to be with you, no matter what. I was glad of the excuse to stay with you as much as I could."

Gods, I wanted to cling to that hope. I wanted to believe that he really loved me, that of all the dragons that could have been sent to me, I'd been lucky and got Mick.

"Couldn't you have told me without the dragons knowing?" I asked. "Couldn't you have trusted me? You expected me to trust you."

"I didn't trust myself." He gave a short laugh. "What if what I felt for you was you glamming *me*? What if you'd cleverly turned a dragon to your cause, or what if those from Beneath were manipulating you more than you understood? All I could do was make sure you were all right, that you stayed alive, no matter what."

I leaned my head back against the wall. "This is fucked-up. What do you expect me to say?"

"Nothing. I love you, Janet Begay. Nothing will change that."

My heart lay like a dead thing in my chest. "Even with what you've just told me?"

"Even if you want to stick your tongue down Nash Jones's throat. It killed me to see you kissing him, but I won't stop you if you want to be with him."

I got to my feet, hands balling to fists. "I do not want to *be* with Nash. I don't want to be with anyone. I thought you were dead, Mick. I watched you shot up and bleeding, and I had no idea whether you would survive. I was grieving. It *hurt*. If you had told me before that you were a dragon, that the shots wouldn't kill you, I'd have been spared feeling like someone ripped out my insides when I saw you go down. You expected me to open up to you and give you everything that I was, but you couldn't give me the comfort of telling me the truth. So get the hell out of my life, Mick. I don't need this kind of shit."

"No."

I stared. "What? Did you just say 'no'?"

"I'm not going anywhere. If you stay here alone, your mother will eventually drag you to those vortexes and get you to open them. Or the other dragons will kill you to make sure you never succeed. Either way, I lose you. I can't let that happen. So I'm staying."

"This is *my* hotel," I said, sounding desperate. "You only stay with my permission."

"I'll sleep in one of the guest rooms. You can consider me your bodyguard."

"I don't want to consider you anything. I want to throw you off the roof. Don't you understand?"

Mick stood. "*You* need to understand; I'm not leaving. This is too important to screw up because you and I happen to have gotten our feelings hurt."

I flung open the door, so angry I wanted to tear it from its hinges and throw it at him.

"Fine, I'll stay away from the stupid vortexes. But you stay away from me. I don't want to talk to you; I don't want to see you. And once this is done, I want you out of my life."

I didn't wait for him to agree or argue. I stormed inside and down the stairs. Going to my room seemed too tame, so I kept walking, out through the wrecked lobby door, across the parking lot and then the highway, and out into the desert to the west. Dangerous, yes, but morning was breaking, and nothing short of the gods of Beneath was going to mess with me when I was this angry. I kept walking and the sun rose behind me, breaking through the storm clouds in red and gold glory.

By the time I returned, I was hot, stinking, and thoroughly exhausted. I barely saw the police tape all over the place, or Assistant Chief Salas and other Magellan cops picking over the scene.

The lobby and saloon had been smashed up, shot up, or fired by my magic, Mick's and Coyote's. I saw Fremont drifting out of the kitchen with a resigned look on his face, and I wondered if it too had been wrecked while the main fight went on in the saloon.

I ignored everyone, trudged to the back, and turned on the shower. I had water now without Mick's help, because Fremont had finished hooking up the plumbing, but cold only because the electricity still wasn't on. I didn't care. Cold felt good to my sweaty, overheated body. I didn't so much wash as stand under the stream of water without moving. Finally I halfheartedly passed soap over my skin, then turned off the faucets and leaned against the wall.

I woke up sometime later with my neck aching from bracing my weight. I got out of the shower, dried myself off, and crawled into bed, still wrapped in the towel. I slept for who knew how long, but when I woke, the shadows told me the sun had moved west.

Someone tapped on the door. "Janet? It's me, Fremont. Salas wants to talk to you."

I didn't answer. Talking took too much effort.

"Janet? You all right?" The door creaked, and Fremont peered through a slit, as though terrified he'd catch me doing naked Pilates.

I slid one arm from under the covers and beckoned to him. Fremont took a few steps into the room and stopped, averting his eyes.

"Tell Salas to go away," I said, barely able to form the words.

"He needs your statement about what happened."

I figured. "Tell him I'll talk to him later."

Fremont weighed the decision whether to tell Salas I didn't want to see him or to insist I get up, which might involve me revealing more than my bare arm. Modesty won. "I'll tell him. You rest."

He backed out and closed the door. What I wanted was for all these people to go away and leave me alone. I didn't want to be awake, because then I'd have to think about Mick, and reassess every single thing I'd ever assumed about him, about our relationship, and about how I felt about him. I didn't want to get up, because I'd have to talk to Salas about the fight and the dried blood all over my saloon, and I'd have to make decisions about what to do with the hotel.

Swimming in the back of my mind, just out of reach, was the memory of Nash Jones kissing me. I could still feel the imprint of his lips, the burn of unshaved whiskers against my skin, the taste of his mouth.

Even more troubling was the fact that he'd absorbed my magic without flinching or even feeling it. He didn't believe in my magic, but I'd fed Nash enough to kill him ten times over. And yet he'd lived.

Another part of me hoped that if I lay here quietly, all my problems would go away. As a little girl I'd thought that if I sat still enough and let the world flow around me, everything would get better on its own. I decided to try the trick by staying firmly under the covers in my bed.

I dozed off and on, and when I finally woke up all the way, the window was dark, the hotel out front mercifully silent.

I was stiff and sore, but my resilient body had recovered from the fight. Because Nash had drained off the storm magic, I was relieved of my magic hangover. No storms tonight. I knew even before I looked out the window to see the eastern horizon dark and clear, stars out in profusion.

I showered again, dressed, and wandered to the kitchen. Sure enough the bikers had smashed the new appliances while the Nightwalker had been busy feasting on me behind the bar. My shoulder still ached, even though the bite marks had closed. I had no fear that I'd turn into a Nightwalker, because that took spells and careful, dark magic, not just a hungry Nightwalker getting a blood fix.

My rented SUV stood intact in the parking lot—amazingly. Avoiding even looking at the Crossroads Bar, I got in it and drove into Magellan. The diner next to Paradox was full, but I managed to slide onto a counter stool and tiredly order a burger. When it came, I ate it quickly, surprised at how hungry I was.

I was aware of stares as I ate. The looks were mostly sympathetic, but I still wasn't ready to talk about the incident. I stayed hunched over my burger, not meeting gazes or encouraging conversation.

I felt much better once I finished eating. A big milkshake cleared my brain, and I left to drive two blocks to the brightly lit liquor store. I made my purchase and drove another few blocks to the quiet street I'd driven down yesterday, which now seemed a million years ago.

Maya's living room window glowed with light. I parked and walked to the front door, pressed the doorbell, and waited.

The TV went off in the living room, and after a few seconds, Maya wrenched open the door. She glared at me with red-rimmed eyes, her unbound black hair straggling down her back.

"What do *you* want?" she said.

I held up the bottle of tequila I'd bought at the liquor store. "To share this with you. We can either drink it straight or mix it with ice and lime and pretend we're having margaritas. Either way, we're going to get drunk, and you're going to tell me everything you know about Amy McGuire."

Nineteen

We did use glasses, but we drank it straight. Maya closed the blinds, and we sat on the couch side by side, the bottle and two glasses resting on the coffee table in front of us.

"Amy. I hated the bitch," Maya said after the second glass.

"You told me that before. Because she was perfect?"

"So perfect she made you sick. She had everything—supportive parents, high grades, praise from her church, tons of friends, good looks, you name it."

"She doesn't sound real," I said.

Maya gave me a dark look. "She was real. Some people are just born lucky, you know?"

"I knew someone like that in high school," I said, remembering. "She won beauty contests and ribbons for horseback riding and barrel racing plus scholarships galore. Everyone loved her. But when you got to know her, she was hard as nails. She tricked people into thinking she was sweet. Even her own parents were afraid of her."

Maya shook her head. "Not Amy. She really was nice, all the way through. Went to church every Sunday because she *liked* to. She was a good person. That made it even worse."

"Because it was hard to justify hating her?"

Maya scowled. "Exactly. Now, *you* I can hate, because you really are a bitch. Strutting into town, thinking you're all important because you're renovating the hotel and trying to find Amy. Beautiful Navajo girl in your leather chaps. Nash can't keep his eyes off you."

I raised my brows, hiding a twinge of guilt at the remembered pressure of Nash's mouth on mine. "Funny, when I walked in here yesterday, Nash was in *your* bed, and he didn't look unhappy to be there."

"What were you doing barging into my house anyway?" she demanded.

"I saw your door open, and I got worried. Dead bodies turn up around here and girls go missing. I hadn't seen you in a couple of days."

Maya drained her glass and reached for the bottle. "You wouldn't care if I disappeared. One less problem to worry about."

"Not true. You're a damn good electrician, and I need you. Don't think I give you money because I *like* you. You can out-bitch me any day of the week."

"Fucking Indian."

"Latina ho."

Maya trickled tequila into her glass and took another big swallow. "At least you don't pretend to be my friend and then stab me in the back."

"Is that what Amy did?"

"What do you think? One minute she's telling me how it's only a matter of time before Nash asks me to marry him; the next, I see her holding hands with him at the diner. Nash drove by my house every day on his way to hers, and I got to watch him drive out again the next morning. I lay awake every night, knowing he was down there in bed with her." Tears slid down her cheeks. "I'd call that stabbing me in the back."

"You and Nash broke up before he went out with Amy, right? I heard you two had a big fight."

"What, so now it's my fault?"

"That's not what I said, and you know it. I'm trying to get the facts straight. Nash and you were still together when he came back from Iraq. Then you had a fight and broke up."

"We always had fights. We fought about everything. We stormed out on each other all the time, but one of us always came back. But not this time. He left, and Amy sweet-talked him into staying away."

"I heard that your last fight was because he wanted to run for sheriff."

She didn't ask me how I knew. "Partly. I didn't think he could handle it because of his PTSD."

"Chief McGuire told me he went through stretches when he couldn't remember anything."

Maya nodded, miserable. "That happened a couple of times. He'd do things and not remember them at all. I wanted Nash to see a doctor, and he wouldn't do it, stubborn pain in the ass. He said his problems would go away, and that I was making too much fuss and didn't trust him. But it was killing him." More tears, but she glared through them. "Turns out Nash was right, wasn't he? He didn't need a doctor. He just needed Amy to spread her legs."

I remembered Fremont telling me Amy had been good for Nash, soothing. Maybe Nash had been able to tell Amy what he couldn't tell anyone else, and she'd smiled that prom queen smile and patted his hand. My relationship with Mick had been similar, him encouraging me to tell him everything, smiling at me like he adored me.

"Men are bastards," I said.

"You got that right."

I finished my second glass, noting that my tongue felt warm, my mouth loose. "Have you ever thought about being gay? Maybe giving up men altogether is the answer."

"No." Maya refilled my glass, then hers. "A woman would probably just dump me too. Plus my mother would never speak to me again. She's already pissed at me because I haven't given her any grandchildren."

"Mothers." I drank deeply. "Can screw you up."

"Tell me about it."

"No, tell me about Amy. That day she disappeared. Were you home?"

Maya's gaze went remote. "Yeah, I'd finished a job in Show Low the day before and decided to stay home, doing laundry and stuff. I didn't go out all day." She spoke in a monotone, repeating the exact words that I'd read in the file.

"So you would have been on hand to see who drove in and out," I said, then asked what I'd come here to ask. "Did you see Nash?"

Tears streamed from Maya's eyes. The drink had loosened her a long way, and she sobbed. "*Dios*, Janet, I think he killed her. He killed her and took her body away and dumped her in the desert, and he doesn't remember."

"Did you see him do all that?"

"No. But I saw his car, his own car, not the sheriff's one. He drove down and drove out twenty minutes later, going very fast."

No one else had seen this, according to the files, or at least, no one else had admitted it. "That's not in the report," I said.

"Because I didn't want to tell anyone. I didn't know what to do. If you tell, I'll kill you."

She was crying, shaking all over. I sat still, unthreatened. I'd keep it to myself, because I didn't think Amy was dead. I'd love to know what Nash had been doing at her house, though.

"Think, Maya. Why would Nash hurt Amy if she was so good for him?"

"He might not have meant to. He'd go crazy sometimes—talking to people who weren't there, seeing things."

"What kind of things?"

"Mostly that building that collapsed on him in Baghdad. He'd think he saw the roof coming down, and he'd drag me flat on the floor, no matter where we were. He did it in the diner one day. Then he'd get upset when he realized he'd been hallucinating. And then, the next time I'd see him, he'd act like he'd forgotten all about it."

"So you think he killed Amy, accidentally maybe, while he was having one of his episodes?"

"Maybe he thought she was an insurgent coming to kill him or something. He's strong; he could have strangled her or broken her neck. Like I said, when I saw him that day, he drove out in a hurry."

"No one else saw him?"

Maya shook her head. "So I kept quiet. If he did it, it wasn't his fault."

"Maya, if you thought he killed Amy, why did you jump into bed with him yesterday?"

She wiped her cheeks with the back of her hand. "I couldn't help it. He kept asking me questions about that damned woman in your basement, and I was upset. He started yelling at me about it, and I yelled back at him—I hate it when he treats me like a suspect. All of a sudden his arms are around me, and I'm crying on his shoulder. And then he started kissing me, and . . ." She spread her hands. "You know."

"One thing led to another?"

"Yes. Until you interrupted. Then I threw him out. Maybe I should be grateful to you." Maya scowled. "No, wait. I'm still pissed."

"I don't think Nash killed Amy," I said. "Even accidentally, even during a hallucination."

"No? How the hell do you know?"

"Because I know things. Amy didn't die in her house. There was no sign of a struggle."

"But Nash could have covered that up. He'd know how."

"There was no psychic sign of a struggle either. Nash wouldn't have known how to cover *that* up."

"Oh, please. You're not a psychic."

"No, I'm a Stormwalker. It's different, but I do have the ability to see ghosts or at least specters of violence. Amy's house is clean and peaceful. No one has died there."

"Then where is she?"

"I don't know."

We fell silent while I watched the light dance on what little liquid was left in the bottle.

"This question is going to piss you off," I said slowly. "But I have to ask it." Maya didn't look at me; her eyes were glassy, and I wondered if she'd even be able to answer. "Was Amy pregnant?"

Maya put her hand to her stomach and turned a slight shade of green. "I don't know. She never said anything, but she and Jones were going to get married, and she was so excited . . ." Her face crumpled, and she got off the couch in a hurry. "I'm going to puke. Damn skank, look what you do to me."

Maya got to the bathroom before she started to heave. I sat on the sofa, cradling my glass, trying not to listen.

Poor Maya. How awful it must be for her, thinking the

man she loved had killed the woman she'd hated. I had no doubt that Maya still loved Nash. It must have scared the shit out of her when Nash hadn't come forward to say he'd gone to see Amy that day. That little tidbit had been kept out of every report.

While Maya cleaned herself up in the bathroom, I switched to look at things from Nash's point of view. I had the feeling that Nash thought *Maya* had killed Amy. Maya had never kept her anger at Amy secret, and I was willing to bet Maya hadn't taken the breakup well.

Nash was a shithead. He'd dumped Maya for another woman, got Maya to sleep with him again yesterday, then kissed me the same night. I wished I could put another thousand volts through him, not that the first thousand had done much damage.

Maya staggered back into the room. Her face was gray, but her eyes snapped. "You can get out of my house now."

"I think I'm spending the night. I've drunk too much to drive safely."

She flopped back down on the sofa next to me. "I drank more than you. You did that on purpose. Bitch."

"I'm a lightweight. And if I'm responsible for getting you drunk, I'm staying to make sure you're all right."

"You're not sleeping with me. I heard you when you said you wanted to try being gay."

"I don't think it works like that. I'll sleep on the couch."

"Whatever."

I didn't say anything for a while. She was right; I'd gotten her drunk on purpose, because I figured that was the only way she'd talk to me. I was actually starting to hope that Maya and I might become friends one day. She was complicated and interesting, I was lonely, and she deserved better than to be jerked around by Nash. Also, I knew the difference between someone being belligerent because they were inherently bad and belligerence born of anger and fear. Maya had a lot of anger and fear inside her. If I and tequila could help get it out, so much the better.

"Was Amy religious?" I asked after we'd sat in silence for a while. Outside all was quiet, save for a few coyotes yipping in the distance and a neighborhood dog barking in response. "You said she liked going to church, and she sang in the choir."

"Yeah, she loved church. She wasn't manic about it, but she was all about God loving you, and sunshine and roses." Maya frowned. "Although it's weird, a couple of weeks before she disappeared, she missed one Sunday. That was so unusual that I heard people talking about it, wondering if she was all right."

"What church did she go to? Was she Catholic?"

"Lutheran. In Magellan, you're either Catholic, Lutheran, or LDS. Or you go to church in another town."

"Maybe she did go to church in another town that day."

"I doubt it. She was devoted to Trinity Lutheran. Grew up in it. Although she did ask me once about being Catholic. When I asked if she was thinking about converting, she laughed and said she wanted to know because Nash was Catholic."

"Is he?" Nash didn't strike me as the religious type. "I thought being sheriff was his religion."

"Nash is devoted to his rules and regs," Maya said. "If Nash told Amy he was Catholic, he was feeding her a load of crap. Nash has never gone to church in his life."

"Maybe she'd been trying to get him to the Lutheran church with her, and he was looking for a tactful way out."

"It wouldn't have done him any good. He'd have had to start going when they got married. Amy was the type to drag her husband to church, so their kids could go to Sunday school and sing in the choir, just like her." Maya finished bitterly, "I have to be honest with myself. When Nash decided he needed to get married, of course he'd pick the white-bread, goody-goody girl, not the crazy Latina. It only made sense, especially if he was going to be sheriff."

"Shut up."

"What?" Maya glared at me, color flooding back into her face. "Did you just tell me to shut up?"

"Shut up about Nash not wanting you. Of course he wanted you; he was just mad at you, and Amy slid in when he wasn't paying attention. It's a good thing he *didn't* marry Amy, because she'd have bored him senseless. Nash needs someone who can stand up to him."

"Like you?"

"No, you moron. Like you."

Maya spread her arms. "Do you see him over here? Do you see him running to the door with a bunch of flowers? Amy's been gone a year. He hasn't showed up with a ring and gotten on his knees."

"Because he doesn't know what happened to her, does he? The woman disappeared. He's not going to think, *Oh well, my fiancée's gone; let me go back to Maya like nothing ever happened.* Rules and regs, remember? Nash won't come back to you until he finds out whether Amy is dead or alive, whether she left because she wanted to or against her will. Give him a break."

"Since when are you his best friend?"

"I'm not. But when someone's missing, it's not the same as them dying. You're never sure. That's why the McGuires asked me here, because they want me to give them an answer, whatever it happens to be. Maude McGuire told me that holding on to hope was making her crazy."

Maya's face softened. "The McGuires are nice people. I feel bad for them."

"I do too. Everyone thinks Amy is dead, including you, but it's not the same as knowing she is. So if you know *anything*, anything at all—if Nash has said something that made you wonder—tell me. If I can find Amy, or what happened to her, think how many people can make peace with it. Including you."

Maya fell silent. She reached for the tequila bottle again, then released it without lifting it. "I hadn't thought of it like that."

"I'm begging you, Maya. Help me."

"I can't think of anything right now," Maya said. "I'm too drunk."

"When you can think, call me anytime at all. Day or night." I reached over and squeezed her shoulder, figuring that if I hugged her, she'd either hit me or throw up again. "And come and fix my frigging electricity. All right?"

I did spend the night, and in the morning, Maya let me use her shower before she made breakfast. Neither of us was much in the mood to talk, but we downed coffee, ate Maya's egg burritos, and I shared my bottle of ibuprofen.

"I thought Native Americans were all about natural medicine and chanting and peyote," Maya said as she accepted two tablets.

"Not after a night of tequila."

I was in a little better shape than she was, because I'd had two glasses while she'd downed almost the entire bottle. I really was a lightweight—alcohol put me over the top pretty fast, which was why I only nursed one watery beer whenever I went to the Crossroads.

Maya agreed to come back to work and was less hostile when we said good-bye. I didn't deceive myself into thinking we'd become best friends, but we'd made a start in the right direction.

I drove my rental back to the hotel, noting that work

trucks had already showed up to start repairs. The workers stared at me as I passed, but I ignored them, and I ignored the mess. I even pretended to ignore Mick, who leaned against the counter in the lobby with one of the Hopis, going over the damage. Mick shot me a speculative look, clearly wondering where I'd been, but he didn't try to speak to me.

I went in search of Fremont, knowing I needed someone to oversee the massive repairs here while I followed up the leads I'd gotten from Maya. Before last night, I would have assumed Mick would take charge while I was out, but I no longer wanted him to. Also I wasn't ready to talk to him.

Fremont was flattered to be made foreman, so flattered he didn't even ask why I hadn't given the job to Mick. Before I left again, Maya showed up and went silently to work, wincing a little whenever someone made a loud noise.

I was tired of my rented SUV and wanted my bike back, but I climbed into it again to track down my leads, stopping at the phone place to replace my cell phone—again. I'd lost one in a bike crash and the other had been shot to death in the space of a week. I wondered if I'd set some kind of Magellan record.

Trinity Lutheran was on the main highway, its parking lot holding only two cars on this Tuesday morning. In the office, the secretary gave my midriff-baring top and jeans a disparaging look, but she agreed to tell the minister I wanted to talk to him.

The Lutheran pastor, Reverend Tim, as he asked me to call him, was in his fifties, confessed to a fanatic love of strong coffee, and offered me a cup. He expressed sympathy for the criminal destruction to my hotel and hoped it wouldn't put me off staying in Magellan. We chatted politely about the hotel and how his wife was looking forward to seeing the finished product, then I turned the conversation to Amy.

Reverend Tim confirmed what Maya had told me, that Amy was beloved in Magellan. She'd been attending Trinity Church since birth, had enjoyed Sunday school and the youth choir growing up, moving to the adult choir when she reached high school. Reverend Tim had been greatly surprised when Amy disappeared, and he was certain she hadn't simply run away. The Amy he'd known wouldn't do that.

I asked him a few more pointed questions and liked that he answered them. Reverend Tim seemed genuinely concerned for Amy and said he'd counseled her parents extensively in the past year.

I thanked him, let him convince me to make a donation to the church fund, and went on to my next call.

It was more difficult to make an appointment with the Catholic priest in the church on Fifth Street, but it was agreed I could come back after lunch. I grabbed another meal at the diner, people there still talking about the gang fight at my hotel. I realized that none of them realized there'd been anything supernatural in the attack. They assumed it was a human biker gang out for revenge, confirmed by Barry, who reported the story of the Nightwalker accosting me in the Crossroads Bar, not realizing he was a Nightwalker, of course. Barry had just seen a loser trying to hit on me and pulling a gun when I refused. I let his account stand.

I finished my meal after having to repeat the story of the fight several times, and reassure everyone that Mick was fine. I got more sympathy than I'd expected, and I left the diner realizing that the locals had started accepting me. They were angry at the gang for terrorizing me and happy that Nash had come in and arrested them all. It was a warm feeling.

The Catholic priest, Father Matthews, had gray hair, a plump face, and a big smile. He looked a little like Santa

Claus in a black shirt and clerical collar, and his shrewd blue eyes summed me up in seconds.

"You want to know why Amy McGuire came to see me," he said.

"Did you tell her parents about her visits?" I asked after he invited me to sit down.

"I did after she disappeared. I hoped it might help them find her, but she hadn't confessed a wish to leave home or anything like that. She and I discussed her upcoming marriage, and she asked me why I'd become a priest. She was interested and friendly, easy to talk to. I was stunned when she vanished, and tried to comfort her parents. I doubt she left of her own free will, and I very much fear she's dead. I've prayed for her, lit candles for her, though I don't mention the candles to her parents." He smiled. "Amy and her family are so very Protestant."

I talked to Father Matthews a little while longer. I didn't discover the secret to Amy's disappearance, but I did learn more about Amy the woman, maybe more than her parents and Nash had ever known.

When I rose to leave, I asked, "So why *did* you become a priest?"

Father Matthews stood up with me. "The world worries me, and this was the best way for me to help people withstand it." He shook his head. "I have great faith in God, but sometimes I wonder whether I'm simply hiding here in my church, safe behind prayers and ritual."

Maybe I was hiding too, behind my ritual of restoring the hotel.

Father Matthews shook my hand. "We're always open on Sundays, Janet. It might do you good to stop by."

I grinned. "I believe in the old gods, Father. And what's worse, they believe in me."

He laughed but gave me another shrewd look. "Just think about it."

I made no promises. I drove back to the main street, then north out of town through empty desert to the town of Flat Mesa. I walked into the county sheriff's department, leaned on the counter, smiled at the deputy behind it, and asked to see Sheriff Jones.

Twenty

"I'm busy."

Nash didn't look up from his very neat desk when I walked in. In spite of a stack of file folders and a computer humming away in the corner, everything on the flat surface was squared up, tidy, and dust free, not a scrap of paper or stray paper clip to clutter the space.

When the deputy who'd let me in retreated, I sat down. "Too busy to learn something about Amy?"

Nash looked up at me then, his expression hard. "You leave Maya alone."

I blinked. "Who said anything about Maya?"

"One of my cousins lives across the street from her. He told me you showed up at Maya's house last night and didn't leave until late this morning."

The man had the most accusing stare I'd ever seen. His light gray irises were circled with silver, his pupils inky black and fixed on me.

"Maya and I had a girls' night, which means drinking and bitching about men."

"Maya has enough to deal with without you bothering her," Nash said.

"Do the things she has to deal with include you? I can see why she'd struggle with that." I got up and leaned my fists on his desk. "Did Amy tell you she was having a crisis of faith?"

"What?" Nash looked blank, then angry. "What are you talking about?"

"She'd missed going to her own church a few weeks before she disappeared, an amazing occurrence from what I understand. Did you know about that?"

"Maude McGuire talked a lot with their pastor. I'm sure she knows."

Nash hadn't thought it important, his tone said. His eyes told me he still didn't.

"Amy made an appointment to talk to Father Matthews at St. Peter's," I went on. "Father Matthews wouldn't confide everything they talked about, but he told me she'd asked him whether God abandoned people."

"Abandoned people?"

"I imagine she meant people like her. Something happened to Amy to make her worry that God didn't love her anymore. I wonder what?"

"If you think I know, you're wrong. Amy seemed perfectly happy to me."

I laughed. "Jones, you are so buried in yourself you can't see a foot in front of your face. Why did you want to marry Amy?"

Nash made an impatient noise. "Why do you think?"

"See what I mean? Your response should be 'I loved her.' Instantaneous, no thought, no tossing the question back at me. So either you did love her and are ashamed to admit it, or you didn't love her at all."

"And again we're getting into what is none of your damned business."

I titled my head to study him. "Defensive people only have something to hide. You should know that, with your career in law enforcement."

Nash plopped a file folder onto the desk in front of him. "I really am busy. Please get out of my office."

"Wait." I sat down again, realizing that annoying him would get me nowhere. "This is important. I'm finally learning things that Amy's parents didn't notice or didn't realize were significant. Why *would* Amy be so unhappy she thought God had deserted her? People usually attend church for one of two reasons—either they want to look good to others, or they have true faith. From what people say about Amy, she had true faith."

"I think she did, yes."

"And she was excited about marrying you in her church, had started making the arrangements with the pastor. Suddenly, she's running to Father Matthews and worrying about God not loving her. What happened?"

"I don't know." His voice had an edge to it, a warning.

"Was she pregnant?"

The room went silent. Nash opened his mouth to yell at me, then he closed it and sagged back into his chair. "I don't know."

"Do you think she was?"

Nash's clear eyes held pain. "I'm not sure."

"Which means you think maybe she was. Maybe she got an abortion and was convinced God had turned his back on her for it."

"No." The word rang out, harsh. "She did want to move up the wedding date. She was nervous, but excited. A happy kind of excited. She asked me once whether I wanted kids right away, and I said, fine."

"Very warm of you." I picked my next words carefully,

bracing myself for his reaction. "Is there a chance, any chance at all, that you might not have been the father?"

Nash shook his head. No anger, no defensiveness. "Amy wasn't that way."

"Chief McGuire gave me all her credit card and bank records. I didn't find any transaction for a doctor or clinic where they might have told her she was pregnant, but she might have bought a home pregnancy test."

"Is your theory that she disappeared to have an abortion?" Nash sounded incredulous.

"It's one possibility. She could have had it done in Flagstaff where no one knew her, or better still, Phoenix, and kept it confidential."

"Then why not come home once it was done?" His face changed. "Unless you think it killed her."

"That's always possible. However, if she'd died, I'd think her parents would have been notified—wouldn't she have to give the clinic the name of a person to contact in case of emergency? Even if that person hadn't been her mother or father—a girlfriend, say—I can't imagine that friend *not* telling Amy's parents she was dead."

"Unless she went to some illegal place." Nash's eyes filled with worry, then he shook his head. "But she was happy, Janet. I swear to you. Amy had a sparkle in her eyes, like she was waiting to surprise me with something. If she was pregnant, she wanted the baby."

"She could have lost the child, had a miscarriage. Losing her baby would probably make her think she'd done something to offend God. But then, same thing. There would be a bill for a hospital or a doctor; she'd have had to use her insurance if she had any, or pay for it herself, and hospitals are expensive. But her bank records don't show any large payments or withdrawals, and her credit cards, like I said, list no payments to hospitals or clinics."

"I know. I went through them." Nash's mask came down again. "Your theory is far-fetched."

"There's more to life than bank and credit card records. Amy left Magellan for a reason. You were closest to her, Nash. What was it?"

Nash threw his pen against the wall. The plastic shattered, spraying dots of ink over the white surface. "If I knew that, don't you think I'd have stopped her?" he shouted. "How do you think it's been for me, not knowing whether she decided to leave or was taken away against her will? Not knowing whether she's dead or alive, and I, the powerful sheriff, can't find out which? How do you think I felt when McGuire thought I'd done something to her? I practically had to do backflips to convince the investigators I knew nothing about it. I've been through her damned phone records and credit card bills a hundred times, and there's *nothing* out of the ordinary. So I don't need you to come in here and get in my face that I must have overlooked something."

I let him wind down, my hands in my pockets as I watched him. "You didn't even know she was unhappy enough to make an appointment with a priest," I said. "I'm willing to believe you didn't know much about Amy at all. You were mad at Maya, Amy was nice to you, and you went down the path of least resistance."

"Like hell."

"I also know you're deathly afraid that you killed Amy yourself and covered it up, and don't remember."

"Leave that alone, Janet, or I swear to you I'll drive you back to the reservation and kick your ass out of the car. I might even slow down."

I ignored him. "Or was your true fear that Maya had done something to her?"

I don't think I could have said anything that made him

more angry. Nash's eyes lit with rage. "Maya Medina would never hurt anyone."

"No? She was furious at you and at Amy. You broke Maya's heart. I think you really loved Maya but didn't like how you acted when you were around her. With Amy, everything was calm, peaceful, no inconvenient emotions you had to face."

"You don't know shit."

"You're right. I'm guessing, making stabs in the dark. I *need* to know so I can find Amy. What happened between you and Maya? Why did you run to Amy for comfort?"

I didn't think he'd tell me, but Nash bunched his fists on the desk. "Maya and I would never have worked out. We're too volatile together."

"And you and Amy never fought?"

"No. Never."

"Can I play counselor and say the two of you probably never communicated either?" I was one to talk—the girl who'd had no idea her boyfriend was a dragon. "You never knew what was going on inside Amy. You didn't even know she was worried about her religious life."

"No." It cost Nash to admit that, I could see. He shoved the folder away. "She never told me anything."

But with Maya he'd always known where he stood. I went on. "Can I ask you a question, off the record, as it were?"

He growled. "What now?"

"If I find Amy, if I bring her back home, will you still want to marry her?"

Nash gave me his gray-eyed stare. "If Amy is alive and well, and if she left of her own accord, obviously, she doesn't want to marry *me*."

"That's not what I asked."

Nash clamped down on his emotions, his expression becoming neutral, which meant, for Nash, only mildly pissed off. "The most important thing is to make sure she's all right."

"Yes, I know that." I sat back, let him straighten his folder and take a new pen out of the desk. "Something else you hid from McGuire was the fact that you drove out to see Amy the day she disappeared."

. His cheeks stained red. "Who told you that? Maya?"

"I have my sources." I couldn't bluff him; he knew damn well Maya had given me that tidbit. "I don't think you killed Amy or abducted her, so I'm not going to tell on you. But I'm curious why you went to see her. Was she there when you arrived?"

Nash plucked at the edge of the folder. "I don't know. Before you ask how I couldn't know, I don't remember driving out there at all, the same way I don't remember driving all the way to Albuquerque. I didn't report it, because I didn't remember. Maya confronted me with it later." Mr. Rules and Regs looked ashamed of himself. "I told her not to say anything."

"And she was loyal to you until I poured tequila down her throat. But I think Maya told me because she's worried about you, and I've come along saying I don't believe Amy's dead."

"With no evidence but your premonitions." He sat back. "I was wrong to keep it from McGuire. I feared I'd done something to Amy, but there was no evidence on me, in my car, at her house." He let out a sigh, more misery in his eyes than I'd ever seen. "I lied on my statement, although at the time I didn't remember, and I *still* don't remember. I'll tell McGuire, resign, take my lumps. Are you happy now?"

"Don't be stupid. It's your word against Maya's. No one else saw you; Maya could have fed me the story to cover up for doing something herself."

Nash looked at me in exasperation. "So what are you trying to say?"

"Leave it for now. I'll just tell you that Amy's disappearance wasn't your fault, no matter how worried you are that it was." After my grandmother's revelation about Harold Yazzie and his illegitimate baby, I thought I was close to understanding what had happened. My talk with Father Matthews made me even more certain. "We have more important things to talk about."

Nash's hostility returned. "What things?"

"Like what happened behind my hotel the night before last."

He assumed I meant the kiss. Nash's neck went red. "No, now you need to leave. I have a shitload of work because of your hotel. The bikers we arrested had meth on them, not to mention illegal weapons. I should thank you for helping the sheriff's department make so many good busts."

"Sure, I'll let people drive through my hotel and shoot holes in my boyfriend every night."

"I suggest you consult a good lawyer if you want to sue for damages."

"I don't want to talk about the hotel; I want to talk about me slamming you with every bit of magic I had and not even singeing you. What I did should have killed you."

"Are you confessing to assault or attempted murder?"

"Don't try to be funny."

I reached into my pocket and pulled out a little spell I'd worked up from stuff I'd bought at Paradox: a sage smudge stick with a stone bound to it with wire. The spell should wind a temporary but effective bubble of protection around the person I cast it on. I'd cast similar spells on my father many times, the man who liked to wander the land alone at night. I worried about skinwalkers and spirits and just plain weird people hurting him, so I used to sneak up on him while he napped in his truck or on the sofa and cast the spell.

I lit the smudge stick and slowly waved it in front of Nash while I chanted words in the Diné language.

A silver shimmer issued from the smudge and wound

itself around him, along with the fragrant smoke. The spell hovered in place for a moment or two, quivering like a soap bubble, then it shattered. I jumped as the shards of the spell dove directly into Nash's body.

I stared, openmouthed, holding the sage in cold fingers, and Nash watched me in suspicion. "What are you doing?" he demanded.

"Didn't you feel that?"

"Feel what? All I saw was you waving a weed and chanting in Navajo."

"The spell broke. Exploded is more like it." I searched for the spell's residual aura but felt nothing.

"I have a lot of work to do, Begay. Go away, or I'll have Lopez escort you out."

"I want you to come to my hotel. Say this Friday night? There's someone I want you to talk to." I had no idea whether I'd be able to find who I wanted by then, but this was only Monday. It gave me a little time.

"Who?" he asked.

"I don't want to tell you yet. Will you come?"

Nash flipped open the folder. "I'm too busy."

"Come on, Nash. It's important."

"Maybe." He pointed at the door. "Go."

I snatched up my sage stick and left his office.

I'd never seen a spell burst like that, ever, not even when I faced powerful sorcerers and skinwalkers. They'd thwarted spells but had never smashed one into pieces and sucked it into their bodies. Nash had destroyed the spell without breaking a sweat, and he hadn't even realized he'd done it.

I returned to the hotel and on my new cell phone made a series of calls based on what Father Matthews had told me. It took all frigging day, and no one wanted to tell me what I needed to know. I had to persuade and cajole even to find out I'd gotten the wrong place, and sometimes the person at the other end simply hung up on me. Homeland Security should defend its secrets as well as these people did.

I was about to give up when I made a breakthrough at a place in Tucson. I made an appointment with the reluctant woman at the other end, but she agreed that it was important I come and talk to them. When I finished, my phone rang again, the mechanic up in Flat Mesa informing me that my bike was finally ready. I snapped off the phone and punched the air.

I found Fremont in the saloon refitting PVC pipe behind broken walls. The dent Nash's body had made in one wall was still there, but Mick's blood had mercifully been cleaned from the other. A couple of guys were distastefully mopping up what was left of the Nightwalker behind the bar. My own blood was mixed in with the gore, my bruised shoulder still aching a little from the bite.

The poor magic mirror looked forlorn with its spiderweb cracks radiating from the big hole in the center. I was surprised the glass hadn't fallen from the frame, but magic mirrors were resilient. I had no idea how to repair it, or if it even could be repaired. I'd have to track down the witch I'd known in Oklahoma and ask her.

The damage hadn't shut it up, however. "Hello, sweetie," it said to me. "These cracks make me see dozens of you at the same time. It's *fabulous*."

"Very funny," I told it.

"What's funny?" Fremont asked me. "I'm still hearing that hum in here, but I can't track it down."

"Never mind; it's not important. Will you do me a favor? I need to get my bike and return my rental to Flat Mesa. Will you be my second driver?"

"Sure. Let me finish here . . ."

"Let's lock up and not worry about it. The repair shop closes at five." Another night without my motorcycle suddenly seemed one too many.

Fremont started putting away his tools. "Mick's here. Why don't you have him drive you?"

"He's busy with something." That might even be true.

"Liar, liar," the mirror whispered. I shot it a dirty look.

Fremont took my words at face value. Mr. Gossip of Magellan didn't seem to realize there was anything wrong between me and Mick, which meant Mick had kept our problems to himself. That was fine with me.

Fremont rode with me in the SUV to the bike shop in Flat Mesa. My Harley was there, fixed and gleaming, waiting for me.

It felt so good mounting the bike and starting it up that I could have ridden out and left Fremont and the rental without looking back. I wanted to speed out of town to the winding highways and freedom.

Instead, I made myself wait for Fremont to get into the SUV and follow me sedately to the rental agency.

"Want dinner?" I asked Fremont when I finished turning in the SUV. "Least I can do for taking you out of your way."

Fremont eyed my bike in trepidation, as though it had just dawned on him that I was his ride home. "I can call a friend to pick me up."

I patted the seat. "No, you can't. Mount up. I'm taking you to dinner."

Fremont put his leg over the bike, looking worried. I got on in front of him, started it up, then told him to hang on.

"To what?"

"To me."

Fremont froze. "You're boyfriend's big, Janet. I've seen his muscles."

"He won't touch you, I promise. I won't let him."

"All right, but if he comes after me, I'll . . . I'll scream and run."

I laughed, letting the situation amuse me. It kept me from the empty pain of thinking about Mick.

Fremont clasped my hips in a light hold, but when I glided the bike out of the parking lot, he yelped and threw both arms around my waist. I grinned as I headed down the street, barely topping thirty-five.

Clouds were gathering, not the high, dense clouds of a thunderstorm, but the more uniform gray of rain. Liquid started pattering on us as we rode.

"Well, damn, sugar," said a voice. "Your hunk of a man never told me I'd get wet."

It wasn't Fremont. Fremont was clinging to me, too terrified to make a sound.

"Nice view," the voice drawled. "Tits 'R' Us."

I stared in horror at my right-hand mirror. "Oh, no." I groaned. "Oh, gods, no."

"Oh, yes," the mirror said, and breathed a happy sigh.

Twenty-one

I would kill Mick. Kill him, stuff him, mount his dragon head on the lobby wall.

I knew Mick had done this. Who else would have made sure a piece of broken magic mirror got ground into one of my bike's mirrors? This was Mick's way of keeping his eye on me.

The bastard.

"I *love* this," the mirror said. "I can see right down your shirt."

"Shut *up*," I said.

The mirror laughed, a drawling chuckle. "I always said I wanted to get out more."

I ground my teeth as I drove to the diner at the north end of town. The rain was coming down hard as we parked and hurried inside, me hurrying even faster to get away from the mirror.

The mood in the diner was electric. People in the desert

don't hate rain. The steady stuff, like what started to pour as we ran inside, was rare. Usually we got wild storms with wind, hail, and flash floods, which blew in and out in the space of a few hours. Rain like this was different. Patrons in the diner gazed out at the streaming water with smiles on their faces. The waitress who dropped glasses of water on the table said, "I love this rain. We sure need it."

This particular diner reminded me strongly of the one in Holbrook, where I'd first met my mother. I discovered why when I saw the owner's picture and name on the wall—he owned both of them. I felt a frisson of remembered fear, but Jamison was right about facing ghosts. Besides, I was hungry and happy to get away from the damned mirror.

Fremont and I ordered. As we waited for my burger and his steak, Fremont kept up a steady chatter about goings-on in Magellan. The destruction of my hotel was the most interesting thing that had happened in town lately, but other things had caught Fremont's interest—a tourist shoplifting in Paradox, Sheriff Jones making more than one of the biker gang members cry, a cousin in the vast Hansen clan having a new baby.

I noted that Fremont's gossip never included personal information about himself. He'd never once told me about this date he'd had the night Charlie Jones had died. I wondered if he, like Mick, trained his conversation on trivialities to keep people from learning anything significant about him.

The waitress slid a platter of golden French fries and a burned-black burger in front of me, the white plate punctuated by a crimson puddle of ketchup and a sunflower yellow one of mustard. Worry made me hungry, so I ate in silence while Fremont talked, the rain streamed down, and the humidity rose.

Rain like this didn't bother me as much as did lightning, but the storm still affected me. My skin grew damp, and the urge to draw the water to me grew strong. I resisted, wanting to eat in peace.

A tall man with a tan and sharp eyes stopped beside the booth. Both Fremont and I looked up at him in surprise before he reached down and grabbed Fremont by the neck.

"What are you doing?" I yelped.

"Are you the fucker who was banging my wife?" the man asked Fremont.

His voice was loud in the small diner, and people turned to stare. I started to retort that Fremont would never bang anyone's wife, but Fremont was as red as my ketchup and words died on my lips.

"You might want to leave, honey," the man said to me. "This is between me and your boyfriend."

"He's my *friend*, and I'm not going anywhere." The man wore a light jacket, I'd assumed against the rain, but when he moved I saw the butt of a pistol beneath it.

"It's all right, Janet."

Fremont looked panicky but resigned, but I wasn't about to leave him alone with this guy. "Who the hell are you?" I asked.

The man shook Fremont by the neck. "*He* knows."

"His name is John Beaumont."

"Beaumont?" I repeated in amazement.

"My wife came out here to find herself, she says. Instead she finds this pecker." John Beaumont shook Fremont again. "All of a sudden she disappears and then turns up dead. What did you do to her?"

"Nothing," Fremont panted. "I swear to you. I thought she'd gone back to L.A."

Fremont had sounded more fascinated than devastated when Maya first found the body in the basement. Of course, Sherry hadn't been recognizable, and if Fremont had thought she'd returned to California a year ago, he might not have realized right away who it was. I'd put Fremont's subsequent sadness and loss of buoyancy down to the death of his assistant, Charlie, but I realized now that he'd started to sag after Nash released Sherry's name as that of the dead woman.

"I don't remember you mentioning this to me," I said to Fremont.

"I was afraid to. I had nothing to do with her death, I swear. I really thought she'd gone back home."

"You were the last person she was with," Beaumont said. "And you were screwing her." He moved the jacket so Fremont could see the gun. "Let's go for a walk."

No way was I going to let Fremont leave with him, but if I started screaming that he had a gun, Beaumont might panic and open fire. At the booth across the aisle was a family with a little kid in a high chair. No one in this diner deserved stray bullets ruining their lives.

"Why don't you come outside and talk to me," I said to Beaumont. "You can tell me your troubles."

"Fuck you, bitch. I want *him*."

This was going nowhere fast. I looked at the rain steadily falling, and my fingertips became slick with water.

"Fremont," I said. "Get under the table."

"What?"

The man tightened his grip on Fremont's neck. "He's coming with me."

"Fremont, *now*!"

A giant wave shattered the window and engulfed our table, the remains of our meal, me, and Beaumont. Beaumont shouted obscenities and fell under the onslaught.

Fremont had dived under the table, and the other customers fled their seats as the floodwaters rushed in. I'd put my body between the window and the kid in the high chair, taking the wave and shards of broken glass myself. The cuts stung, rainwater washing the blood away as soon as it flowed.

People were screaming, scrambling away. The stunned father yanked his son out of the high chair and dragged his weeping, babbling wife to the door.

Beaumont scrabbled on the floor, another wave curving over him to pin him down. Water seeped from my body, wanting to join the storm I'd called. I held myself together with effort, grabbed the pistol from Beaumont's jacket, hauled Fremont up, and pushed him toward the door.

"Go!" I ran after him, slipping and sliding on the drenched floor.

We made it to the parking lot. The rain beat down in torrents, the clouds above the diner black as night. The wave of water targeting John Beaumont would hold until I was out of range.

I more or less shoved Fremont onto the bike, stashing the pistol in my saddlebag. I started the bike and gunned it, squealing out onto the highway.

Within twenty minutes, I pulled into the hotel parking lot, which was deserted except for Mick's bike and Fremont's new work truck. The rainstorm had died behind us as wind pushed the clouds west.

Mick walked out of the saloon as Fremont and I came in. A new front door had been fitted, a plain one this time, and Mick locked it behind us. I laid the pistol, a nine-millimeter, on the drop cloth–covered counter in the lobby.

"Mick, will you look after that for me?"

I shouldn't have guns, not with the volatile magic inside me. I'd not even liked the itchy feeling of having the loaded gun in my saddlebag.

"Sure thing." He didn't even ask.

I looked away as Mick left the room. Seeing him at all reopened the hole in my heart.

"I should go," Fremont tried.

I had him up against the counter in a heartbeat. "No, you should stay and tell me everything you know about Sherry Beaumont and how she died."

The light was dim in here because the windows had been boarded up, but in that light I saw Fremont's eyes fill with tears.

"I don't know how she died. I barely knew her at all."

"John Beaumont seems to think you had an affair with her."

I heard Mick come back in, and he leaned on the counter on Fremont's other side. Mick didn't look surprised at my words, but he'd likely been watching us through the mirror on my bike.

"I met her in Flat Mesa," Fremont said. "She said she'd only be here for a couple of weeks, and I knew it would be over when she left. She told me she had a husband and that she was separated from him, but that they might get back together."

I never would have guessed that innocuous Fremont Hansen would have a fling with a married woman, even a separated one, but then I realized I'd only known him a few weeks. Not enough time to discover hidden depths.

"So what happened?" I asked. "Didn't you wonder when she was reported missing?"

"I never knew about that. The last night I saw her, she said she was going back to California. She kissed me good-bye, got in her car, and drove away. I never saw her again. I swear to God."

"Then how did she get back to Magellan, and why?"

"I don't know. I never talked to her again. I assumed she went back to her husband."

I thought I knew what had happened, though it wasn't something I could explain to Fremont. I was pretty certain that my mother had possessed Sherry Beaumont. From the picture printed in Magellan's newspaper after she'd been identified, Sherry had been young, pretty, blond, and athletic, similar to the woman who'd come to me in Holbrook six years ago.

My mother wanted to create more children like me, perhaps producing one more bendable to her will. I figured she'd possessed Sherry and found kindly Fremont, then had Sherry make love to him to impregnate herself. I didn't know at what point my mother had left Sherry alone, probably when the woman was heading back to California. Had Sherry returned to Magellan to try to find out what had happened to her? Had she wandered, looking for the vortex or my mother, until she died of exposure? Or had she been a "weak vessel," as my mother had described the woman who bore me and simply died of the magic inside her? Perhaps Sherry hadn't been strong enough to take it.

"What color were her eyes?" I asked Fremont.

He gave me a faraway smile. "Green. Sort of green gray. Beautiful."

"You didn't realize it was Sherry in the basement when Maya uncovered her?"

Fremont shook his head. "No. I swear I had no idea. How could I have recognized . . ." He broke off and swallowed. "When I heard she'd been identified, I didn't want to tell anyone I'd known her. Salas and Sheriff Jones might have thought I killed her, but I didn't. I didn't even know she was dead."

"So you ran off into the desert looking for skinwalkers. That wasn't just about vengeance for Charlie, was it?"

"I thought maybe a skinwalker had got Sherry too. It was too much. I wanted to kill one of the bastards."

"Did you know that Sherry was pregnant?"

The lines on Fremont's face deepened. "No."

"I'm so sorry," I said.

"Not your fault." Gods, Fremont was trying to comfort *me*, when it was my crazed bitch of a mother out there impregnating and killing women. "I should have said something, should have admitted I knew her. But I swear, I have no clue how she died."

"Or got buried in my basement."

Fremont shook his head. I didn't really believe he'd walled up the body, although Fremont would have been capable of it. He drove a large work truck with an enclosed back and plenty of tools for tearing into walls. The truck that he'd had when Sherry Beaumont died was now scrap, thanks to the skinwalker attack on the highway.

Fremont *could* be a sorcerer, one more skilled than he let on, who'd called a skinwalker to wreck the truck and destroy the evidence, making sure he wasn't driving it at the time. But somehow the scenario didn't feel right for Fremont.

"Go home," I told him. "Lock your doors. I got Beaumont wet, maybe hurt, but I doubt it will stop him."

"Sure thing. You're awesome, Janet. Mick, you should have seen her flood that diner. She's the best sorceress I've ever seen. Maybe you could give me a few pointers?"

"Go home," I repeated.

Fremont gave me a brief hug, throwing a fearful glance at Mick. "Thanks, Janet," he said.

He left finally, his steps heavy. Which left me alone with Mick.

Twenty-two

Was it possible to be indescribably furious with a man and still no-holds-barred attracted to him? I hated that I was still drawn so much to Mick. He was a dragon, yes—a mythical beast I'd never believed in before—but his human shape was fine indeed. No wonder I'd never been able to place what race he was. I'd thought he might be a mix of Asian and white, or Latino and white, although none of those explained his very blue eyes. Did dragons have race? Species maybe?

"I guess you saw everything that happened," I said. "You got the mechanic to grind a piece of the magic mirror to fit my bike, right?"

"A good way to keep an eye on you."

"Including a view of my breasts?"

He gave me a ghost of a grin. "That's not bad either."

His unnerving gaze lingered at the cleavage in question.

I shivered and folded my arms, realizing I was still drenched from the rain and my impromptu flood.

Mick moved past me to my bedroom. I didn't follow, but I couldn't keep myself from studying his backside as he walked. I loved running my hands over that backside when we lay face-to-face, kissing in afterglow.

He was back before I could pull out of the fantasy, his arms full of towels. "You're soaked."

Mick plopped the towels on the counter, shook one out, and then gently wiped my neck and face. He wrapped the towel around my shoulders, holding the ends as he looked at me.

I slid my hands up his warm arms. The storm power still spun inside me, although not as crazily as it would with a full-blown thunderstorm. But I needed to empty myself, to let the power flow away.

I felt the answering flicker of Mick's fire magic. Without a word, he drew my magic into himself, sucking in a breath as the water power flooded from my body to his.

I touched his face, loving the sandpaper feel of his unshaved whiskers. He was my strong Mick, the powerful man who could be so incredibly gentle with me. He watched me, his eyes darkening, lips parting as mine drew near his.

I didn't arch to him consciously—the magic in me sought the answering magic in him, wanting to couple with it, just as it had with Nash in the aftermath of the thunderstorm. I moved my hips, feeling Mick hard and ready for me.

"Stop." Mick's lips brushed mine. "Or I won't want to stop."

Tonight I was cold, worried, frightened, and turned on by our connection. Mick's heartbreaking secrets seemed not so terrible against the other forces working on me.

"I don't mind." I ran my fingers down his chest. "Tonight, I don't mind."

Mick stepped back, breaking the warm contact. "But I do."

"Why?" Did I sound desperate? I felt desperate. I wanted the madness of sex—of wild sex with Mick—to make me forget.

"I won't come to your bed until you truly want me there," Mick said. "Truly want *me*. I think you understand."

I did. He didn't want me to use him, which was exactly what I would be doing. He knew I was still furious with him, damn him, and knew that I asked out of need, not forgiveness.

"I really did love you," I whispered.

Mick studied me with intense blue eyes. "I'm a dragon, Janet, trying to live in a world that no longer believes in dragons. We've learned to be secretive to survive. I thought I'd want to kill you when I first met you, and then I found myself liking you. You had strength, and sass. I decided I'd get to know you, see what you were like inside. That was my mistake."

I swallowed the lump in my throat. "Why would a dragon possibly care what I thought of him?"

"I shouldn't have. But I did. Still do." Mick picked up a dry towel and threw it over his shoulder. "I'll sleep upstairs."

He turned away and walked heavily up the steps, not looking back. The darkness swallowed him. I heard his tread on the balcony, and then a softly closing door.

Tears stung my eyes as I trudged into my bedroom to strip off my sodden clothes. I took a shower, noting with gratitude that the hot water was back, and got into bed, where I tossed and turned, uncomfortable and needy.

My skin itched. I itched on the inside too. My whole body craved sex. So much so that I was tempted to run upstairs and persuade Mick without words that I really, really wanted him.

I suppressed the urge with effort. Nash had kissed me out in the darkness because his hormones had been responding to my magic, nothing more. I'd needed someone to draw off the storm, and sensuality had sparked between us. Nash had reacted without realizing why. I noticed that when I'd talked to him today, he'd been keen to avoid the subject.

Nash was a very good kisser. I thought of him in Maya's bed, the strength in his arms as he'd pushed himself up into her. I'd never been a voyeur, always looking quickly away whenever I saw people so much as kissing in public. So why did I keep seeing Nash's tanned body on Maya's white sheets, Maya's glorious black hair flowing across her latte-colored skin as she made love to him?

Answer: because I was horny, and because they'd looked so beautiful together. If I ever photographed nudes, I'd take a photo just like that and call it "The Beauty of Physical Love."

If photos existed of me and Mick in bed, on the other hand, they would shock even the most avid voyeur. Mick could be . . . creative. When I'd met him, I'd been sexually naïve, knowing the theory but not much more than that. I'd never read adult magazines or watched X-rated movies, having never had much interest in them. I'd embraced what Mick taught me, because he'd made sex fun and exciting, loving. I'd gone through life thinking that everyone used toys and interesting positions and bonds, but now I wondered if Mick just didn't know any other way. Maybe dragons didn't know about the missionary position.

The simplicity of the scene with Maya and Nash made me realize how intimate a man and woman could be. No games, no toys, just two people: face-to-face, open, and vulnerable.

I finally drifted to sleep to erotic dreams, one involving an interesting ménage of me, Mick, Nash, and Coyote—three beautiful men touching, licking, making love to me. Me on Nash as Maya had been, his face twisted in passion as he rose into me. In the dream I turned my head to take

Mick into my mouth, and Coyote was behind me with his arms around me. I could smell sweat and breath, sex and excitement.

I both longed to and hated to wake up. In the morning I dragged myself out of bed and went to greet the dawn, aching, cranky, and still horny.

As I scattered corn, the big coyote came up over the railroad bed and took up his usual place under the juniper. I knew no one had been in bed with me in truth last night—I'd woken with my nightshirt and panties firmly in place—but the look in the coyote's eyes made me blush.

Good dream, he said inside my head, and howled with laughter when I glared at him.

When I told Fremont after breakfast that I was heading for Tucson, Mick turned from talking to some of the workers and said, "I'm coming with you."

I walked outside, slinging a backpack over my shoulder, pretending to ignore him.

"Why?" I asked when I reached my bike. "You have the mirror to keep tabs on me."

"I can come to your rescue faster if I'm already with you."

"Mick . . ."

"It's five hours on open road. There are skinwalkers out there, a man you beat up with a flood looking for you, dragons who don't trust you, and bikers who might be friends of the ones you got arrested. You have a gift for pissing people off."

"Sure, because I ask them to drive through my hotel, shoot my boyfriend, and pull guns on me in restaurants."

Mick gave me a firm look. "You attract trouble, and I'm coming with you."

"Fine." I shoved my backpack into the saddlebags and mounted the bike. I secretly didn't mind Mick's insistence—

I wasn't sure what I'd find in Tucson, and muscle with me couldn't hurt.

I squawked when Mick swung his leg over the back of my bike and settled in behind me. "What are you doing? You have your own ride."

Mick wrapped strong arms around my waist. "It's a long way, I don't want to lose you on the road, and I don't know specifically where you're going."

I gave him a sour look but started the bike. Mick easily balanced his weight with mine as I pulled out, his grip steady but not constricting.

This would kill me. Mick's warm bulk at my back, his strong thighs on either side of mine—damn, it wasn't fair. Was he deliberately trying to drive me insane?

I rode to Winslow, then took the interstates west and south. The back highways were more direct, but they were also narrow roads that wound up and down mountains and dawdled at thirty-five miles per hour through small towns. This time of year the roads would be clogged with ranchers, farmers, tourists, and people in RVs. I was in a hurry, wanting to get down to Tucson and find out what I could. I wanted this to be over.

We rode into the cool altitudes of mountainous Flagstaff, where the ground was black with volcanic rock under thick green pines. I turned south on the 17 and descended back to dry desert, and the air heated steadily. The bright orange red buttes of Sedona appeared far to our right, then dropped behind us as we climbed from Verde Valley to another pass. Over those mountains, then down, down, down, dropping from the rim of the high plateau to the low deserts of the south.

It was frigging hot. In mid-May, the temperatures south of the Mogollon Rim were already in the hundreds and the sun beat on us from a cloudless sky. My bike flew down the miles, sliding between eighteen-wheelers, RVs, cars,

SUVs, pickups. We passed places with the intriguing names of Bumble Bee, Deadman Wash, Bloody Basin, and Big Bug Creek, past hills covered with giant saguaros reaching to the sky, and so on into the ever-spreading sprawl of Phoenix.

The city glittered under the sun, several million people gathered to weather the heat under the blast of air conditioners. The traffic slowed to a crawl as cars began to pour onto the freeway, heading into town.

I stopped for gas at an exit with a large strip mall, the pavement feeding back the heat of the sun. I knew this part of the state would grow much hotter before summer was over; in Magellan, this temperature represented the peak of the year's heat.

We decided to lunch at a Mexican place, where the waitress tried to get us to order the specially priced frozen margaritas. We still had a long drive, and we stuck to water and soft drinks, to her disappointment.

Mick and I ate our burrito combos in silence. We'd often not speak for long stretches when we traveled together, neither of us having need for small talk. But today the silence stretched between us.

Mick never once asked what I hoped to discover in Tucson or where. I would have told him the whole story if he'd asked, but he never did. He was trusting me, for the first time in our bizarre relationship. I wasn't sure what to think about that.

We finished our meal, which Mick insisted on paying for. I went to the ladies', and when I came out, Mick was straddling the bike outside with it started, waiting for me.

"Get on behind me," he said. "You need to rest."

I made a noise of impatience at his high-handedness, but it did feel good to sit back and close my eyes against the heat. I slid my arms around his waist, trying not to enjoy the feel and scent of his body so close to mine.

Mick knew how to ride. He had us out of there and through city traffic in less time than I'd ever have been able to without getting a ticket. Soon we were streaming south and east on the 10, curving toward Tucson.

More interesting names: Toltec; Eloy; Picacho Peak, where a Civil War battle had been fought; and so on into Tucson.

This city didn't sprawl as much as Phoenix, but it still took some time to thread through traffic to the south side. We took a quiet road not far from San Xavier del Bac, an eighteenth-century Spanish mission church, the city fading behind us.

An adobe wall surrounded the complex I rode to, with a high wooden gate topped with a copper bell. I dismounted the bike in front of this and pulled the rope to ring the bell.

Mick got off with me, but I stopped him. "I don't think they'll let you in."

He looked at the small, square sign on the wall and grinned. "I'll be right out here. Yell if you need me."

"This place looks pretty safe."

"You never know."

He was right. Where my mother was concerned, it was best to be cautious.

A plainly dressed woman came in answer to the bell. She let me in, quickly shut the gate, and led me to an office. There an older woman in gray blouse and black skirt received me and introduced herself as Sister Margaret.

"Yes, she is here," Sister Margaret said. "I told her of your request, but she said she didn't recognize your name."

"She doesn't know me, but her parents have asked me to talk with her."

A bit of a lie, because I hadn't told the McGuires I was coming down here. I hadn't wanted to get their hopes up in case the woman I had found here wasn't really Amy McGuire. Sister Margaret had almost hung up on me when

I'd called, and refused to let me talk to Amy on the phone, barely agreeing to let me visit her.

"Please," I said. "They're worried."

Sister Margaret looked as though she didn't care whether Amy's parents were worried or on the moon. I knew it was part of her job to protect those who lived here, but I had no intention of riding all the way back to Magellan without an answer.

"I will speak to her," Sister Margaret said. "Wait here."

After she walked out, I sat down tiredly in a wooden chair and let the office's plainness soothe me. The only decoration on the smooth white walls was a carved wooden crucifix. Quietness pervaded the room, the small windows open to let in the air and scents of the garden and the musical sound of finches. It was warm, I was tired, and this place exuded peace.

I jumped when Sister Margaret clumped back in. "She says she'll see you. For five minutes only. I must tell you that I don't approve." She looked me up and down the same way as had my first-grade Sunday school teacher, as though she knew every sin I'd ever committed and those I would in the future.

Sister Margaret gave me a last once-over, clucked in disapproval of my tight black top and dusty motorcycle chaps, and then led me away.

We walked through the inner garden, the path taking us past vegetable beds brimming with life. Wildflowers burst out here and there, some growing in the cracks of the adobe walls. Bees and flies hummed, birds called, but above that was *silence*.

Sister Margaret took me from the garden to an orchard, the orange trees spaced in exact rows and now flowering with white, sweet-scented blossoms. A woman waited for me near a stone bench, also wearing a gray blouse and dark skirt. She was a young woman, slender but not overly thin, with pale skin, green eyes, very short blond hair, and a frightened expression.

Sister Margaret gave me a stern stare and said, "Five minutes. I'll be in my office."

"Thank you." I waited until she'd walked back through the garden; then I said, "Amy?"

"My name is no longer Amy," the young woman said. Her voice sounded stiff and stilted, as though she didn't much like to speak. "It's Barbara now."

"Why?"

Her gaze flicked away. "I thought it best."

"I mean why are you here? They all think you're dead. Your father and mother, everyone in Magellan, Nash Jones."

She bowed her head, showing me her hair cut close to her scalp, as though her head had been shaved and the hair was just now growing out. "Poor Nash. Is he all right?"

"No, he isn't. He's done nothing but brood and wonder what happened to you for a year. Same with your parents. If you could see them, it would break your heart. Or at least, I hope it would make you feel bad for being such a selfish bitch. You never even bothered to call them to tell them you were all right."

My voice rose as I spoke. I was suddenly furious with her for all the grief she'd caused, and it didn't help that she aroused the guilt in me as well. After meeting my mother, I'd taken off halfway across the country before I calmed down and called my dad. He must have been scared to death wondering what had happened to me. But at least I'd called after a week. Amy hadn't in twelve months.

Then again, I hadn't exactly rushed home every weekend to embrace my family. I'd been avoiding them for six years. I was angry at Amy, but part of my anger swung around and directed itself back at me.

I stepped toward her, right into a patch of sunlight. Amy

jerked her attention to me, and then her eyes widened, her face paled, and she scrambled back, lifting her hands.

"No. This is sacred ground. You can't touch me here."

"What are you talking about? I'm not going to hit you, mad as I am."

"This is sanctuary. You can't bring her in here."

"Bring who here? No one is with me but Mick, and he's waiting outside."

"I see her in your eyes. I see her shining out of you." Amy slammed her hands to her face and started babbling. *"Hail Mary, full of grace, the Lord is with thee . . ."*

Twenty-three

"Stop it." I grabbed Amy's shoulders and shook her. "I'm not her. I swear to you. I know who you mean, and she's not inside me."

Amy blinked at me, her eyes more gray than green. In spite of her shorn hair, she looked much like the girl in her photos, with a lovely face and a soft look. I could see why Nash had fallen for her.

"Sit down with me." I led her to the bench under the tree and patted its flat surface. The stone was cool through my jeans, soothing after the glaring heat of the road.

"When did it start?" I asked her.

Amy didn't sit down. "Who are you?"

"My name is Janet Begay. Your parents asked me to find out what happened to you. They're grieving, sick with it. They've pretty much decided you're dead."

"It's better that way. Go back and tell them that I died."

"Screw that. What happened wasn't your fault."

Amy's face twisted. "You have no idea what happened. The things she made me do."

"What things?"

"I don't want to talk about it. I don't know you, and if my mom and dad sent you, I don't want you to tell them what happened to me."

I bit back a sigh. I had to know what this was all about, but Amy wasn't just afraid, she was ashamed. She'd always been the good girl, and my mother was badness personified.

"How about if I promise not to tell them anything but that you're all right?" I asked. "They deserve to know that. What they truly deserve is for you to call them and tell them yourself."

"Don't admonish me when you can't possibly know what I've been through. The things I did . . ."

"That wasn't you."

"No," she snapped. "What you don't understand is that I *wanted* to do those things. I was evil before the demon ever came to me. It was difficult to do the right thing all the time, but people were so proud of me for being good that I had to keep on doing it, no matter what was going on inside me. I don't know if you can understand that."

I completely understood it, more than she knew. "Trust me, Amy, we're all shoved into roles that we don't fit. We either adjust or rebel. Me, I rebelled. I made my grandmother's life living hell, not that she didn't give as good as she got. You at least made your parents happy and proud."

"Which is why I can't leave here. Let them think I'm a saint or something, sacrificing my life to do good for others." Amy's expression turned wistful. "I do like the work we do here. We go to shut-ins and take them food, clean their houses, look after those who can't help themselves. I like that. I feel useful for the first time in my life."

"You helped Nash Jones. I heard he was pretty crazed when he came home from the army, but when he took up with you, he calmed down. Everyone agrees that you were good for him."

Amy looked away with a shudder. "I don't want to talk about Nash."

"I think we'd better. Was it your idea to lure him from Maya? Or hers?"

"I don't know." Amy turned back to me, angry. "Don't you understand? I can never be sure. I always thought Nash was attractive, I always liked him, but I never believed he'd look twice at someone like me. Besides, he was going out with Maya. I used to watch him whenever he came into Magellan. Sometimes I'd follow him into stores or the diner, pretending I happened to be going there too, so I could talk to him, or just watch him."

I snorted with laughter, and Amy broke off, looking offended.

"Don't be embarrassed," I said. "Nash is a gorgeous, hard-bodied man. I'm surprised he can walk anywhere without a string of women stumbling after him. It's natural for you to want to look at beautiful men. I do too. It's the mating instinct. We can't help our hormones."

"But we can. We can behave like civilized human beings and not stalk whatever person happens to strike our fancy. It's why we abhor rape—the violation of others to satisfy our own needs."

"I wasn't talking about rape."

"But I was." Amy's face was set. "What I did to Nash was as good as. I coerced him away from Maya, a woman he loved, and took him for my own. I made him have sex with me so that I could carry his baby."

"You didn't exactly force him. He and Maya were already falling apart."

"But they'd have married and made it if not for me."

"Possibly, but you can't be sure. I know that my mother

can't manifest in people for very long. I take it that there were periods when you didn't know what you were doing?"

"Hours at a time. Sometimes an entire day, though never longer. I'd come to myself out in the desert, not realizing I'd walked there. But I'd be dressed, wearing sweats and carrying water, as though I'd decided to go hiking."

I nodded. "She had you take her back to the vortexes. She can get her spirit through the cracks, but she can't manifest fully. So she grabs the nearest woman, usually one young and pretty, and does what she pleases. She hasn't possessed any men as far as I know. I wonder if that's because she can't or because she doesn't want to."

Amy stared at me with wide eyes. "What are you talking about? I was possessed by a demon. A devil, from hell."

"More or less. She's a goddess from Beneath. It's not really hell; it's another world, but she's trapped there, she and the other gods and goddesses who were considered too evil to emerge. She got sealed in by gods like Coyote with the help of the dragons. Other, weaker things got out— they became the skinwalkers and what we call demons and evil spirits. She can manipulate the skinwalkers who live around the vortexes when she wants to."

Amy listened with her mouth open. "You're crazier than I am."

"No, just more experienced. These evil things are real, Amy."

She looked away again. "The devil tested me with a demon, as the Lord allowed him to with Job. Except I failed."

"It wasn't your fault."

Amy moved restlessly. "Yes, it was. The demon wasn't in me all the time. I'd go home when I came to my senses, and there would be Nash, sleeping in my bed, and I'd be so proud of myself and happy that he belonged to me. Even if the demon had to seduce him for me, Nash was all mine. I told myself that I'd take care of him far better than Maya ever could. But if I'd loved Nash—truly loved him—I'd have let him go. I'd have been horrified at what I'd done and told him to stay away from me. Instead I let him kiss me and sleep with me, and I planned to marry him and have his baby. I wanted to prove that Amy McGuire could get the best-looking man in the county and have the perfect life with him. I'd use the demon to make Nash fall in love with me if that's what it took." She stopped pacing. "Now look at me and tell me that I'm still a good person."

I'd met girls at college who'd ruthlessly hunted handsome, rich, successful men, intending to marry them for their money, and those girls hadn't needed demons to help them. But I didn't think Amy wanted to be placated.

I hiked my boot up on the bench and wrapped my leg around my knee. We must have looked odd together, me in my tight jeans and low-cut shirt, she in her plain blouse and skirt that was just shy of being a nun's habit. But I shared something with this young woman that most people wouldn't understand.

"What happened to the baby?" I asked in a gentle voice.

Amy's eyes filled with pain. "I lost it. I was four months."

"Did you go to a hospital? I couldn't find any records . . ."

"I'd come down here to talk to the sisters about joining them. They weren't going to let me. I wasn't Catholic, and there's a process of study and prayer—and besides, the things I'd done with Nash, especially outside of marriage. I had the miscarriage here. They brought in a doctor and agreed to keep it quiet. I've been working here to pay them back ever since. The demon child must have known it was in a holy place and couldn't fight."

I didn't dispute her, although I believed Amy simply hadn't been strong enough to carry a child filled with my mother's power.

"So the day you left Magellan, you were coming down here to scope out the place?"

She nodded. "Sister Margaret gave me the appointment that day, and I feared I wouldn't have another chance. I didn't want anyone to see me leave—I thought that if the convent rejected me, I could come back home and no one would be the wiser. If they had accepted me, I would have called. But when I had the miscarriage, I got scared. I didn't want to have anything to do with Magellan or anyone in it, ever again."

"No one saw you leave. You didn't take your own car."

"I'd bought an old car from a couple in Winslow a week before and hid it south of town. I walked through the desert to it that morning and drove away."

A private cash purchase would leave no record, an old car wouldn't cost much, and she could have stashed away the cash for it little by little, so we wouldn't have seen large withdrawals on her bank records. A police chief's daughter would think of things like that.

She could have easily hidden the car in a juniper- and mesquite-lined wash south of Magellan—there were so many of them, and that road wasn't well traveled. Amy had planned with care, making certain no one would see her or stop her. Knowing Nash, if he'd had any inkling what she'd planned to do, he'd have done everything shy of padlocking her into her own house, and I wasn't so sure he'd have stopped at that.

"Maybe you did do the right thing leaving," I said. "Getting far away from the vortexes was a good plan. If you do want to stay here and do good works, who am I to say you're wrong? But tell your parents. It's killing them."

Amy nodded, tears in her eyes. "You see? I'm selfish, like you say. I was so afraid of what had happened to me, so afraid that my family would make me come home again, that I didn't think about what they were going through. They have each other and they're strong. I thought they'd be all right."

"Well, they're not." I thought of Mrs. McGuire and the dead look in her eyes. "Call them. It's your life—you can choose to stay here and grow vegetables and take food to shut-ins if that makes you happy. But tell them."

"It does make me happy." Her look turned defiant. "And I'm not faking my desire to join the sisters. I've always been devout, and coming here was the logical choice. I'm working through the study and have already converted to Catholicism. God will look after me, and in return, I will serve Him."

"Good." This place was peaceful, I had to admit. It was tempting to stay in this silence—pulling weeds in a garden or praying and meditating sounded like a balm to the soul. But Mick waited for me outside, I had responsibilities, and it would take only one desert storm for me to destroy the peace and quiet around here. This place was sanctuary, but not for me.

"Will you promise to call your mom and dad?" I asked as I rose. "I understand if you don't want to talk to Nash or anyone else, but call your parents at least."

"Can't you just tell them I'm all right?"

"It has to come from you, Amy, and you know it."

She nodded, her eyes showing her misery. "All right. I'll call them."

I believed her, though I planned to ask Sister Margaret to make sure Amy did it. Good intentions sometimes never manifested.

I felt a huge weight lift from me as I turned away. I'd fulfilled my mission, found Amy McGuire, solved the mystery of her disappearance. I was free of the investigation now.

But when I emerged and saw Mick leaning against my bike in the shade of the bougainvillea-hung wall, I reminded myself that however much I didn't like it, I had many more things to do before I could find my own peace.

Mick drove again, and I was content to hang on behind him. I drooped with exhaustion and opened my eyes only when he pulled into the parking lot of a chain motel on the northern outskirts of Tucson.

"What are you doing?" I asked as he stopped. "We have time to make it to Magellan tonight."

"Not with me worried about you falling off every mile. We'll stay the night, have breakfast, and make a fresh start."

His plan did make sense. I was very tired, and a long snooze sounded like a good idea. I waited by the bike while Mick went in and booked rooms. He handed me a plastic key card and told me to find my room while he parked the bike.

I walked through the motel, which wrapped around a sparkling pool full of kids, until I found the room number. I let myself in, dumped my backpack on the floor, dropped the key to the beside table, and landed on my back on the bed. I was just dozing off when Mick opened the door and came in.

"You didn't bring anything for yourself," I said sleepily.

He held up a plastic bag. "Gift counter has toothbrushes, and I don't wear pajamas."

I was tired enough to smile. "Don't swim in the nude, though; I think they'll throw you out. Where's your room?"

"This is my room." He tossed the plastic bag into the bathroom and sat down on the bed.

I rose up on my elbows. "Then where's mine?"

"You're staying with me, Janet. I told you, I'm not letting you out of my sight."

"No one knows where I am."

"Amy does."

"She's an innocent in all this, and she wants to become a nun. You wouldn't trust a nun?"

"Not when the lady from Beneath is involved," Mick said. "She's tricky."

True. I wasn't in the mood to argue, and I didn't have the energy for it. I dropped back down to the mattress, reflecting that he'd at least gotten a room with two beds.

Mick stripped the boots from my feet and peeled off my socks. His strong hands felt good as he started to massage the bottoms of my feet.

"I miss you," I whispered.

"I miss you too, baby."

"It can't ever be like it was, can it?" I said. "You and me, on the road, arguing and making up. I mean, now I know that you were there because you'd been sent to kill me."

Mick rubbed his thumb deep into the arch of my foot, and I let out a sigh of pleasure. "I'd never hurt you," he said. "Never."

"No matter what?"

"No matter what."

"What if your dragons come after you?"

"Let them come." Mick leaned to me. "I'll fight them to my last breath to keep them from touching you."

"Why?" For some reason I was getting angry. "I'm just a Stormwalker, Mick, who might open vortexes and destroy your kind. Why are you so interested in me?"

Mick's body pressed mine into the mattress, his heat all over me. "Dragons aren't like humans; they don't have the same emotions—not love and hate, sadness and grief. But when I met you, I felt something, something new. I didn't want to let it go until I figured out what it was. Dragons do have one thing in common with humans. Curiosity."

"So you didn't kill me because you were curious about me?" Very flattering.

"Curious about my reaction to you." He nuzzled my

cheek. "You awakened feelings in my human form, ones I'd never experienced. Protectiveness, worry, desire." He kissed the corner of my eye. "Love."

I wanted to melt but I resisted. "You should have told me."

"I can't change what I did. But I don't regret one second of being with you, of touching you, of loving you. Exploring your body was one of the best things I had in my life. That hasn't changed."

I started to warm. "We could get pretty crazy sometimes."

Mick skimmed kisses down my throat and chest to my bared abdomen and rested his lips on my navel.

"Crazy," he whispered, and his breath burned my skin.

Twenty-four

"Mick . . ."

He kissed his way back to my breasts and nuzzled my nipple through my shirt. The point rose, and he took the bud between his teeth.

"Mick." My voice changed from admonition to a soft groan, me responding to him like an instrument to an expert musician's touch.

He licked my throat and nipped it. My hips rose to meet his, his hardness moving between my legs.

"Let's ride to Las Vegas," he said. "Better still, New York. Just you and me. I'll take you out on the town. We'll get a limo, and I'll buy you anything you want."

"Now?"

"We'll check out of here, go to the airport. Fly out tonight. We can eat breakfast in Manhattan."

"What about my hotel?"

"Sell it. Even with the damage you can make a profit on it."

"You know I can't leave, Mick."

"Why not? You found Amy. You did your job, and now it's done."

"My mother is still out there. Who knows how many other women she's killed trying to make a child-slave? I can't let her keep trying, keep killing."

"You can't fight her." Mick regarded me with grim seriousness. "She's a god. You have part of her in you, yes, but you're human. You can't beat her one-on-one, even with your storm powers. Even I can't fight her, not if she fully manifests. You'll be much safer if we get you away from the vortexes. Please let me take you."

I pushed him just hard enough so that I could slide to a sitting position against the headboard. "No, Mick. I've been running too long. It's time for me to face what I am and what I'm meant to do."

"What do you think you're meant to do?"

"Stop her."

"Even if you can't?"

I touched his face. "I'll find a way."

"Janet, what *I'm* meant to do is stop you from being used by her, by any means necessary." He kissed my chest where the shirt bared it. "That's why I want you away from here. If you open the vortex and let her out, if she doesn't kill you, the dragons will."

I ran my fingers through his hair. He felt so human, his hair so warm, his skin firm over muscle. But I'd seen him with wings and scales, tail and talons, fire blossoming from his mouth. It was easy for me to accept my friend Jamison as a Changer. I'd seen him shift, and somehow, he seemed the same to me whether in human or mountain lion form. But the connection between dragon and Mick was more difficult to understand.

"Is this any means necessary?" I asked him. "Seducing me?"

He hesitated just long enough to let me know I was right. I should have been angry, and deep down inside somewhere, I was. But I was also afraid, and lonely, and Mick was here with me, protecting me like he always had.

Tomorrow I was going back to Magellan, with or without Mick. Tonight, we were alone in this motel room. I wasn't used to city sounds and felt hemmed in when I was in a big town, but this room was a little hideaway. Mine and Mick's.

I pushed Mick onto his back and climbed on top of him, kissing him as I skimmed off my shirt. He cupped my waist with his hands, his pupils widening as I unhooked my bra and let it fall.

"You are so beautiful," Mick whispered. He moved his hands beneath my breasts, his thumbs touching the aroused nipples.

I touched him as he touched me, tracing the tattoos on his arms, the jagged lines of the twin dragons. When I'd first met Mick, I'd so admired his tattoos I'd wanted some to match. A dragon on the small of my back maybe, or one nestled on my hip. But for some reason the tattoos wouldn't take. I'd spend a painful hour while the artist worked, and then the next morning, the indentation would be gone, my skin smooth and healed. I didn't understand it, and neither did Mick, but I'd given up. Another uniqueness that was me, I suppose.

Mick ran his fingers over my bare skin, dipping beneath the waistband of my jeans. He unbuttoned them and pushed them down my hips, and his large hands rested on my buttocks, fingers warming between my legs. I rubbed against him, he still with his clothes on, my jeans bunching until they came all the way off.

He rolled me over onto my back, pressing me into the hard mattress, pinning my wrists over my head. His mouth met mine, then again, and again. I rose to him, my restrained hands not allowing me to reach for him, but that didn't mean I couldn't touch him with my entire body.

Mick gave me a wicked smile and teased me with licks and kisses. His arousal teased me through his jeans, my naked cleft burning for him. He moved down my body, licking, kissing, until he pressed his mouth over my opening and used his tongue until I reached screaming climax.

His clothes came off then, revealing muscles sculpted in light and shadow. Mick liked to take me in unconventional positions: me on my hands and knees; him lying on his back with me leaning back against him; me straddling him on a chair. But tonight he lay full length on top of me, face-to-face, kissing my lips while he slid himself inside me.

Gods, if I could stay in this magical and drab motel room forever, in our bubble of isolation, I'd die happy. I loved this man, and the thought that I might lose him made tears run down my cheeks even as he licked the shell of my ear and groaned his climax.

I woke hours later. Mick slept facedown beside me under the light of a single lamp, his arms wrapped around a pillow. I watched his back rise and fall with his breath, traced the gleam of sweat along his bare hip.

We'd thrown off the covers in our sleep, the room hot despite the air conditioner blowing under the window. The curtains rippled, but the cold air barely reached the bed.

Whatever magic had stuffed Mick into this human body knew what it was doing. I watched the play of light on Mick's muscles as he breathed, skimmed my gaze over his tight back.

Someone tapped on the door. "Janet Begay?" a soft voice called. "Are you there? I need to talk to you."

I was up and in my jeans, snatching my shirt, when a strong hand closed around my wrist.

"No." Mick's eyes were solid black.

"It's Amy. She sounds upset."

"It's not Amy. I can smell it."

"It?" My heart started to race, and I pulled on my shirt.

"Get your stuff. We'll go out the back window."

I saw a bulk move near the door as the AC fluttered the window curtains. Too big to be Amy.

"Skinwalker?" I whispered. "But they don't like public places."

"Tell *it* that."

Mick had dressed and lifted my backpack, and he quietly slid open the back window. The drop was about six feet down to the parking lot, but I landed without mishap, followed by Mick, who hurried with me to where he'd parked my bike.

"He didn't kill Amy, did he?" I asked as we mounted, Mick in front.

"If he had, he'd have taken her form instead of just imitating her voice. But it means someone knows you found Amy."

"Oh gods."

"They want you, sweetie, not her, but they're not getting you as long as I'm around. Hang on."

He stomped on the starter and screamed the bike out into the street. I gripped his waist for dear life as we ran a red light to zoom onto the freeway ramp. I heard a frustrated scream behind us that died into nothing; then we were riding north into the cool desert night.

I knew Amy had made good on her promise to call her parents, because they arrived at the hotel the next morning as I stumbled around, groggy and exhausted. The skinwalker that had found us in Tucson hadn't pursued us here, which was fine with me. Maybe its purpose simply had been to drive us back to Magellan. If so, it had succeeded.

I couldn't have looked good, my hair still wet from my shower, my shoulders slumped, but Maude McGuire hauled me into her arms and gave me a hard hug.

"Thank you." Her face was wet with tears. "You worked a miracle."

It hadn't been a miracle, or even magic. "The biggest clue was Amy asking Father Matthews what had made him decide to become a priest," I told her.

A harmless question, except I had already suspected Amy of having been scared out of her mind, thinking she was possessed, and hoping that God had the answer. The grunt work had been phone calls to every convent in the state. I'd crossed most off my list and was about to work on the ones in New Mexico and California, when I'd found her in Tucson.

"We're driving down to see her," Maude told me.

I wondered if Nash would be visiting Amy as well, but I didn't ask.

The chief didn't hug me, but he thanked me quietly. His eyes said everything else. The McGuires left, and I turned back to the sounds of work on the hotel, which seemed louder now that I had a splitting headache.

With the amazing speed of small-town gossip, everyone had heard that Amy McGuire was alive and well. No one got the story exactly right—I heard everything from speculation that she was in seclusion in Mexico to the rumor that she'd started her own religious sect in California. I didn't correct anyone. I was the hero of the day, uncovering what the police chief and sheriff couldn't, never mind the special investigators from the state.

Maya Medina didn't join in the relief that Amy was alive and well, but she did look less unhappy.

"I told you she was a selfish bitch," she said to me when we found ourselves alone in the kitchen.

"Yeah, selfish to give up her whole life to help shut-ins."

"You know what I mean. She loves God so much that she couldn't call her parents? Or her fiancé? A convent's a good place for her. I hope I never see her again."

"I don't think she'll be back anytime soon." I gave Maya a speculative look. "If you don't like Magellan, Maya, have you thought about moving away? Leaving town, finding a better job somewhere else?"

"No." The answer was quick. "My family is here." So was Nash, but she'd never admit that she stayed for him.

I worried about Maya. My mother's modus was to look for young women to inhabit, and Maya already had a relationship with Nash, albeit a strained one. Of course, Maya had dark hair and my mother seemed to prefer blondes. I wondered if my mother was trying to reflect what she looked like Beneath or simply liked being a blonde.

I started losing sleep wondering how to get every light-haired woman out of Magellan. Tourists would soon be arriving by the busload, and I imagined there would be young blond women sprinkled through them. What could I do?

The McGuires went to Tucson to see Amy and returned changed people. I'd never seen them so happy. Maude McGuire told me that Nash refused to visit Amy or even to talk to her. He was furious, and I couldn't really blame him. Amy had, in effect, used him and dumped him.

I didn't want to talk to Nash either, but I'd invited him over so I could get Coyote to tell me what he was. Because no one I talked to had seen Coyote lately and I didn't know his cell phone number, I stood on the railroad bed every morning and night calling for the annoying trickster god. I'd seen him the morning I'd gone to Tucson, but I'd been too groggy and embarrassed by my ménage dream to remember to ask him. But as much as I shouted for him,

Coyote never answered or appeared. The crow would perch on top of the juniper and watch me, and I swear she looked amused at my lack of success.

The magic mirror didn't know where Coyote was either. Jamison and family, who were good friends with him, hadn't seen him in days.

I'd told Nash to show up on Friday, and Friday night he actually stopped by, but Mick and I were out looking for Coyote, so Nash departed again, not bothering to wait for us.

Coyote did eventually come to me, but in another dream.

We were both naked, standing on a rise in the desert east of town. The deep wash of Chevelon Creek cut to our right, and the moon bathed us in white light.

"It figures," I said. "Any dream instigated by you will have me naked in it, right? Does everything with you have to involve sex?"

"No fun if it doesn't." Coyote looked me up and down and grinned. "Nice rack, Janet."

I folded my arms, hiding my breasts. "What do you want?"

"You're the one who's been looking for me."

"You don't make it easy. Where've you been?"

Coyote shrugged. "Around. The time is coming."

"What time?"

"The time when you decide who you are. What you are."

"I already know. I'm a Stormwalker with a hell goddess for a mother."

"That's not what I mean. You have come to a fork in the road, and only you can choose which direction to take."

"Very sage," I said. "I can get that advice from a fortune cookie."

Coyote laughed, loud and long. "Gods, I'd love to bed you, Janet. It would be glorious."

"Resist the urge. Will you show up?"

Another shrug. "If you think it's important."

"I do."

"Then I'll be there. I wouldn't miss your coming out for the world."

On Wednesday, inspectors from the county came to look over the repaired damage to the plumbing and electricity and make sure everything was up to code. It was agony watching the man drift around with his clipboard, examining things, testing with his little devices, checking boxes on his form.

Finally he told me that not only had everything passed but that I'd employed one hell of a talented electrician, and who was he?

"*She* is Maya Medina," I said.

"A woman?" He turned around like he wanted to go back over the wiring again.

"I'll tell her you complimented her work." I reached for the clipboard and signed off on the sheet. "Thank you very much."

Passing the inspection meant I could close up the walls and paint again. I doubted I'd be able to open the place until the end of June or beginning of July now, but I could still get some of the tourists this season. Plus those passing through would note the hotel and hopefully tell their friends or return themselves next year. The extra time would also give me a chance to get the Web site up and running. I could start taking reservations now.

The thrill that went through me surprised me. I'd never before contemplated being a businesswoman, thinking I'd be an unwanted drifter my entire life. Now I was worried about Web sites, paint, and advance reservations.

That afternoon I interviewed employees for the hotel, a couple of maids, cooks, and a bartender. I'd have to hire a manager to keep track of all the employees and someone to worry about the endless forms—taxes, liquor license, food permits, and other things I'd never known existed. Hoteliers lived a complicated life.

By six that evening I was tired. I sent everyone home and started making sandwiches. I'd rescheduled with Nash for tonight, and Coyote had promised me in my dream to be here. The least I could do was feed them. I also felt another storm coming, and I hoped I could get through the deal with Nash before it struck. A glance outside showed white stacks of thunderheads to the south and west, another line to the north. The setting May sun made them glow from within.

Coyote hadn't arrived yet, and Mick had disappeared again. It might be just me and Nash. Or me by myself. Men were notoriously unreliable. Excepting, of course, my father, who lived by such an unvaried day-to-day routine that you knew where he was at any given time of the day or night. He was comfortably predictable.

The men I'd surrounded myself with were not predictable at all. I'd never had girlfriends, not close ones anyway, and my female cousins my age barely could bring themselves to speak to me. I'd always connected better with men for some reason, as with Jamison and Mick. In a weird way, my only female friend in Magellan was Maya.

I changed my mind about that, however, when Maya walked into the kitchen and pointed a pistol at me.

Twenty-five

"Would you like roast beef or ham?" I asked her.

Maya's eyes snapped black anger over the nine-millimeter. She'd dressed for the occasion in a tight blue dress and matching pumps, as though she planned to go out on the town. Maybe she wanted to look good for the magistrate after killing me.

"Don't you believe I've come to shoot you?" she demanded. "I'd shoot you in a heartbeat."

"I think you'd do it if you were angry enough. But there's a big storm building, and it makes me able to do this." I tapped the power of wind to jerk the pistol from her grip and send it flying. The gun clattered to the floor and I winced, expecting it to go off and shoot me in the foot.

Nothing so dire happened. Maya stared at me in terror. "You freak."

"Sit down and have a sandwich." I pushed the plate across the counter. "The building inspector from Flat Mesa complimented your work today. Said you were . . . Let's see, what was it? 'One hell of a talented electrician.'"

Maya opened her mouth in surprise, and then her bravado evaporated and she sank onto a stool at the kitchen counter. She contemplated the sandwiches and picked up a ham and cheese. "Nash hasn't talked to me since you found Amy. Why couldn't you leave it alone?"

I shrugged. "Now that you know what happened, each of you can stop worrying that the other killed Amy and get on with your lives. You and Nash need to shack up for a couple of days and get it out of your systems."

"Nash wouldn't. Not with me." Maya glumly chewed her sandwich. "You're staying in Magellan, aren't you?"

"I like it here."

"I thought this hotel thing was just a cover for looking for Amy. That you'd leave town as soon as you figured something out, or gave up."

"Nope." I gave her a cheerful look. "We open in July. Want to be my on-call electrician? It's an old building; I'm sure I'll have plenty of problems."

"I want you to go away."

"Is that why you came tonight?"

"No, I wanted to see your blood."

I leaned my elbows on the counter. "I understand. I'm used to being everyone's scapegoat. You can't beat up Nash or beat sense into him, so you try to shoot me. I get it."

Maya finished one half of her sandwich. She sighed. "You really are a bitch, Janet."

"So people tell me. Next time, just bring tequila."

Maya reached for the second half of her sandwich, her mouth softening into a near smile. I brought her a beer and popped the top off. She reached for that too, with a little nod of thanks.

"Are you going somewhere tonight?" I asked her. "I mean besides here to shoot me."

"I was going to meet some friends in Flat Mesa. But someone told me you'd invited Nash over tonight. I have to wonder why."

"I have my own boyfriend. I don't need yours."

Maya made a show of glancing around the kitchen. "I don't see Mick anywhere. Is he hiding in the freezer, waiting to pop out?"

Mick was so unpredictable, he might be. "He's supposed to be here," I said in irritation. And Coyote. Where were they?

"So why is Nash coming over?" Maya persisted.

She watched me closely. Remembering the kiss I'd shared with Nash, my face grew warm with guilt. "I told you, Maya. I wouldn't have Nash if you wrapped him in a bow and gave him to me."

"Thank God for that," a dry voice said.

Both of us jumped. Nash leaned against the door frame, looking out of place in his civilian clothes—jeans and a button-down shirt and boots.

I should have felt him come in through the wards, especially with a storm dancing around the darkening desert. But no, he'd walked in right through my protective spells without me realizing it. I wondered how much he'd heard.

Maya was obviously wondering the same thing. Nash's cold gray gaze went to Maya in her tight dress, then to me.

"What is this?" he asked.

"Two women eating sandwiches and talking about men," I said without blinking. "Would you like roast beef or ham?"

"I meant what is *that*?" He pointed to the semiautomatic lying on the floor.

Maya and I eyed each other, and I shrugged. "Someone must have left it there."

Nash retrieved it, unloaded it, and laid the pistol and its

magazine on the counter. "This had damn well better be registered."

"It's mine," Maya snapped. "And it is."

Nash's gaze flicked to her in surprise. "Since when do you carry a gun?"

"Maya was showing it to me, and I dropped it," I said.

Nash's mouth hardened. He didn't believe me for a minute, but he let it go. "What did you want to see me about, Begay?"

I shoved the plate of sandwiches at him, but he ignored them. "I want you to meet someone who promised he'd be here, but he hasn't shown up yet."

"I should go." Maya slid off her stool. She didn't reach for the gun or look at Nash.

"No," I said sharply. "Stay."

Maya frowned at me, not happy, but she sat back down again. She did look beautiful tonight, the blue dress complementing her dusky skin, black hair, and coffee-colored eyes. If Nash would turn his head and really look at her, he might notice, the idiot.

I heard voices in the lobby, male voices, both rumbling and gravelly. "About frigging time."

Coyote and Mick entered the kitchen through the lobby. I blinked at Coyote, realizing that in all my encounters with him, I'd never seen him in clothes. He'd braided his black hair into a long ponytail, and he wore jeans, a button-down shirt like Nash's, a big turquoise belt buckle, and cowboy boots. Maya glanced at him without surprise.

"Oh, hey, Coyote. I haven't seen you around for a while."

"Been busy," Coyote said. "Mmm, roast beef. Don't have any wild rabbit, do you?"

"Fresh out," I answered. Mick came around the counter to me, kissed the top of my head, and helped himself to a sandwich.

"You and Maya know each other?" I asked Coyote.

Maya answered. "He used to hang out in the town square, talking to the tourists. Everyone calls him Coyote. I've never heard his real name."

"Coyote's fine, ma'am."

Nash was giving him a chill eye. "You don't seem to have a place of residence here, or in Flat Mesa."

"I'm not homeless, Sheriff." Coyote grinned. "Me, I have plenty of homes. Did you drive your SUV tonight? Ever clean the pee off the tires?"

Nash scowled and snatched a sandwich. "Is that story all over town?"

"I didn't say a word," I said in a mild voice. I caught Coyote's eye. "So what do you think?"

"Mmm, not as good as your grandmother's fry bread, but not bad."

"I meant about Nash." He knew that; he was just being a pain in the ass.

Coyote swallowed, then grinned at me again. "I think he's a null."

Mick made a look like *Interesting*, but I had no idea what Coyote meant. "What's a null?"

"It means there's nothing there. He's like a black hole. Nothing and something at the same time. Like he doesn't really exist."

"What the hell are you talking about?" Nash dropped his second sandwich back to the plate. "I exist. I've lived in Flat Mesa all my life, I was in the army, I served in Iraq, and I'm the sheriff of Hopi County."

Thunder rumbled, the electricity in the atmosphere tingling on my skin.

Coyote looked Nash over. Nash was a big man, but Coyote was bigger, standing half a head taller. "When Janet poured every bit of storm magic into you, you didn't even flinch," Coyote said. "Not even when she kissed you. That should have been the kiss of death."

Maya's beer bottle fell from her hand and shattered on the tiles. Mick calmly bent to clean it up, but Maya remained stiff on the chair, her fury almost knocking me over. I wondered if she'd shove Nash aside and go for the gun.

Nash went red. "I don't know what happened that night. I didn't feel anything."

"You absorbed her magic and stayed upright, that's what happened," Coyote said. "If she'd thwacked me with that kind of power, even I'd go down. Janet also told me you broke a protection spell like it was powder."

"And Mick's light spell," I said. "The little ball bearing you took from me. I saw it spark, and I thought it malfunctioned. But Mick felt it go off. I bet anything you set the thing off without knowing it and sucked down the spell."

Nash looked at me, Mick, and Coyote as we eyed him speculatively. "You are all insane." He turned away, saw Maya, and scowled again. "Where are you going dressed like that? You look like jailbait."

I wouldn't have blamed Maya if she'd decked him. *I* wanted to deck him.

"Fuck you, Nash," she said. "I go where I want to."

A vein started throbbing in Nash's neck. I saw firsthand what Fremont meant about Maya being able to rile him up. Nash looked ready to explode. "Who are you going to meet?" he demanded.

"None of your damned business."

"It is my damned business. I'm not letting you go to Flat Mesa looking like a working girl for one of my deputies to arrest."

"Who says you get to *let* me do anything at all?"

"Are they always like this?" Mick asked me, putting the broken pieces of beer bottle in the garbage.

"Fighting or fucking," I said under my breath.

"I heard that," Maya shouted.

"Children." Coyote held up his hands. "Kill each other later. Right now, I want to know about Nash. How'd you get to be a null? Were you born that way, or did something strange happen to you in the Middle East?"

"Like a building falling on you," I suggested. "Or maybe you survived the collapse because your magic canceled out the danger."

Nash got off the stool. "Janet, you're crazy. I don't go in for your Navajo woo-woo shit. I told you."

"*I'm* not Navajo." Mick's quiet voice cut through the room. "You might want to move, Maya."

Coyote grinned and stepped out of the way. Maya took one look at Mick's face and vacated her stool in a hurry.

"No," I groaned. "Mick, don't you dare. I just got everything fixed in here . . ."

Coyote jerked me out of the way as Mick's eyes burned black. The man I loved raised his hands and let fly a stream of molten fire.

Nash didn't have time to duck or run. The full blast of fire, hotter than a flamethrower's, hit him. Maya screamed as Nash's body went up in flames, engulfed in a white-hot inferno.

Maya ran at Nash and shoved him to the floor, trying to beat out the fire. The flames burned her instead, and she screamed again.

The fire flared up, and imploded. The flames dove straight into Nash's torso, and then as suddenly as they'd appeared, they vanished.

Nash sat up, breathing hard. Maya cradled her right arm, her pretty dress streaked with black. Nash's clothes weren't even singed.

Maya was crying, tears tracking down her soot-streaked

face. Nash tried to get her to let him look at her arm, and I knelt on her other side. "You should take her to the ER."

"I'm fine," Maya snarled. "It barely touched me."

"You're not fine," Nash said. "We're going."

"Let me see." Coyote bent over the group and lightly touched Maya's arm. She flinched in pain, then her eyes widened as the blistered, red skin *un*blistered, fading to smooth, creamy brown.

I unfolded to my feet. Mick stood on the other side of the counter, big hands resting on it, the only one of us unperturbed. "Sorry," I told him.

He'd pinpointed the fire so accurately that not a spark had touched my new appliances and repaired walls. I remembered how, when he'd been a dragon, he'd sent a focused burst of fire that had fried the skinwalker with pinpoint precision.

Mick nodded, accepting my apology. "Everyone all right?"

Nash stood up fast, facing Mick. "What the hell did you do?"

"Hit you with dragon fire, enough to melt you. And you didn't feel it, did you?"

"Dragon fire. Right."

Coyote looked amused. "Nash Jones, the notorious Unbeliever. You should be nothing but charred remains. Not even enough left for a barbeque."

"He absorbed it," Mick said. Nash's angry glare didn't faze Mick; he studied Nash as though he thought Nash an interesting insect. "He didn't deflect the fire and didn't turn it back to me. He absorbed every molecule and rendered it null."

"A walking magic void," Coyote said. "Could be very useful."

"Useful how?" I asked.

"We could stand him in front of the vortex while you open it. He could suck all the vortex energy into him and negate it. End of worry about those Beneath."

I stared at him in disbelief. "We can't be sure he doesn't have a limit. That much energy might kill him."

"Maybe. But those Beneath would be finished. Worth the sacrifice of one human being."

"*No*," I said.

Coyote cocked his head to study me, then he burst out laughing. "I love you, Janet. If you'd stood there calmly and said, 'You're right, let's sacrifice him,' I'd have been sorely disappointed and probably would have had to kill you. But you're not your mother. You care, even for a man you want to deck."

"Please stop reading my mind."

"I don't have to. I can read your face."

"Stop talking about me like I'm not in the room," Nash snapped. "I don't understand any of this."

"Neither do we," Coyote said. "You, Nash Jones, are an enigma. I've never met a null before."

Maya struggled up from the floor. Her hair hung in tangles, and her dress was ripped, but she faced Coyote with her head high, eyes snapping. "Leave him alone. All right, so magic is real. I felt my arm heal, and it hurt like hell, if you care. But that doesn't mean you can bombard him when he doesn't understand what's going on. You aren't going to use Nash for anything."

Nash put his hands on her shoulders. "Maya, why don't you go home?"

Maya jerked to face him. "Don't be condescending to me, you son of a bitch. I'm only saying what's right."

I saw the pulse beating in Nash's neck again, his growing anger on top of confusion. I did the best thing I possibly could for him. I grabbed Mick's hand and told him and Coyote that I needed to talk to them out front.

I closed the kitchen door behind us as Nash's and Maya's voices rose. The saloon outside was peaceful in comparison, a haven from anger.

"What is it, baby?" Mick asked me. His warm voice sent shivers down my spine, the answering storm magic rising inside me.

"Nothing," I said. "I want them to be alone so they'll fight it out."

Coyote laughed at me. "I like the way you think, Begay. I'm out of here. Have things to do and places to go before morning. Be careful." His voice dropped to serious tones. "Things are dangerous, and your time is coming."

He swung around and walked out, his boots grating on the tile floor.

"I wish he wouldn't do that," I said. "Cryptic is one thing, but he's just spooky."

"I agree with him. I'm still not sure I understand why you wanted to come back here, now that you found Amy."

"I have to stop her, Mick. She's dangerous, and I'm the only one who's been able to get away from her—as far as I know."

"And what makes you think you can fight her?"

I ran my hands up the insides of Mick's arms. "I have you."

His kiss breathed new life into me. I'd been avoiding him since we'd returned from Tucson, and we'd retreated somewhat into the shells we'd worn before. I'd buried myself in details of the hotel, and he did whatever it was he did when he wasn't here protecting me.

But I'd realized on our trip to Tucson how much I needed him. Whatever Mick's motive for manipulating our first meeting, whatever his motive for protecting me, he'd done more than simply keep me alive. He'd showed me how to *live*.

Mick had allowed me to become more than Janet the

misunderstood, misfit child, or Janet the woman running away from her terrifying origins. Being with Mick had been more than about sex, more than about riding together. Mick had given me life itself.

I wound my arms around his neck, and opened my mouth for his kiss. My braless breasts ached, the nipples tingling where my shirt rubbed them.

Mick lifted me and set me on the bar. I wrapped my legs around him, letting us contact, groin to groin, through our clothes. He moved his hands under my shirt, cupping my breasts.

The magic mirror drew a shuddering breath. "Oh, sweethearts, normally I'd die before I interrupted this *stimulating* little scene, but . . ."

"What?" I asked it in irritation.

The mirror's voice dropped to a whisper. "She's here!"

Mick whipped around, but there was nothing behind him. Outside the window, emptiness filled the dark parking lot, with the glow of the Crossroads Bar beyond it. Behind that, on the western horizon, forks of lightning fingered the earth.

From the kitchen, I heard a clear, light voice. "Nash?"

Mick and I looked at each other again, Mick's eyes holding knowledge and fear. We nodded in silent agreement, then he released me, and we did what we needed to do.

Twenty-six

Amy McGuire stood inside the back door of the kitchen, the screen rattling in the wind. She wore the same plain blouse and skirt I'd seen her in down in Tucson, and the fluorescent light glinted on her close-cropped hair.

Nash and Maya had been locked in an embrace, Maya against the counter in a position almost as erotic as the one Mick had put me in. Maya was a vibrant contrast to Amy, all color and brightness, while Amy was a pale ghost. Only Amy's eyes held any color, irises burning bright green.

"Nash?" Amy repeated, looking from Nash to Maya. "I don't understand."

"There's nothing to understand," Maya said. "You went to find God. I stayed with Nash."

Amy gave Maya a glower of vast annoyance. "You are the Whore of Babylon, Maya Medina. Look at you, dressed to seduce. I'm surprised you didn't come riding in on the Beast."

"The Beast." Mick's smile was more intimidating than I'd ever seen it, his eyes darkening to midnight black. "That would be me."

"Ah, so *that's* what you are."

Nash broke in. "Amy, what are you doing here?"

Amy flicked her green gaze back to Nash. "I came to see you. To explain what I'd done and why." She moved nearer. "To touch you again. To taste what we had. And I find you here with this *slut*. May God forgive you." She laughed. "Because I won't."

"What is wrong with you?" Maya asked. "You think you can waltz back here like nothing ever happened? You deserted him without so much as saying good-bye. Did you desert the nuns too? What did they ever do to you?"

Amy smiled, and I recognized the smile. "They gave me teeth," she said.

Before Nash could move, Amy had gone for a knife, the big, long chef's knife I'd been using to slice tomatoes for the sandwiches. I grabbed the pistol that was still on the counter and jammed the magazine into it.

Nash remained frozen and so did Mick. Only Maya knew I wasn't joking and dove for the floor. Amy rushed at Maya, knife raised, and I shot Amy, three slugs, straight into her shoulder.

Amy went down, eyes glazing, blood rushing out of her to pool on my newly cleaned ceramic tile floor. Maya rolled away from her, gasping.

Nash rounded on me, gray eyes lit with fires of wrath. He had the pistol out of my hand and me slammed facedown into the counter before Mick could move to stop him.

"What the hell did you do?" Nash screamed at me.

"It's not her," I shouted into the counter.

Nash yanked my hands behind my back, and I felt the cold steel of handcuffs. "You have the *fucking* right to remain silent. Anything you say I'll make damned sure is used against you . . ."

He went on, but I had bigger things to worry about. My mother would desert Amy's body now that she was down, which left the question—where would she go?

"Mick, get Maya out of here!"

Mick was hustling Maya out before I finished the command, figuring out the problem the same time I did.

"Don't you go anywhere. Call an ambulance!" Nash shouted. "I'm hauling you to jail, Janet Begay, and I'm going to make damn sure you never see the light of day again."

"Nash . . ."

"Shut up!" He grabbed towels and pressed them to Amy's shoulder, Amy's face pale and drained. I heard Mick's bike starting up, the loud throbbing dying into the distance.

Amy blinked in confusion, her eyes clear and sane but filled with pain. "Nash?"

My heart hammered. My mother had left her, but damn it, where was she?

Sirens erupted into the night air, help racing toward the hotel from Magellan. The storms converged as well, the two from the south and the west meeting that of the north. Chill wind cut across the desert, followed by a shower of hail.

When the paramedic team burst into the kitchen, one of them the woman who'd patched me up after the wreck on the highway, Nash dragged me out through the saloon, past the groaning mirror, and out the front door, not caring how much I tripped and stumbled on the way. When we reached the sheriff's SUV, Nash slammed me into the backseat, locking me inside.

He opened the driver's door, grabbed his radio, and started

talking. He was going to lock me in jail and toss away the key, probably giving his deputies orders not to feed me either. This was the thanks I got for saving Maya's life.

Lightning forked into the wash beyond the railroad bed, the air crackling. I laughed as the power surged through me. Electricity sparkled through the handcuffs, and I pulled them apart as though they were made of butter.

Ah, this is perfect.

Cold knifed through me. Well, there wasn't much doubt where my mother's spirit had gone. She'd always said she wanted to get chummy with her daughter.

My body was icy with fear, the fear growing as I watched myself hook fingers around the grill that separated front from back seats and with one tug loosen it. I let it go, making it look as though it was still fastened in place so Nash wouldn't notice.

I waited while Nash went to help the paramedics, lounging with my feet up and yawning in boredom. I watched Amy being carried on a stretcher from the hotel to an ambulance. Chief McGuire and his wife had come, Maude McGuire leaning against her upright husband while McGuire spoke to Nash. No doubt he was telling them the whole story. They'd never understand what I'd done—that I had to hurt Amy to save her life as well as Maya's. I wondered if they'd ever speak to me again.

They don't matter, you know. They're ants, crawling on the earth. Are you upset if one ant gets hurt?

"I am, actually," I said out loud. Proving I could still use my mouth to talk made me feel a little better.

Janet, the compassionate. You can't bleed for every living creature, my dear. There will never be enough time for that.

"I can bleed for some of them."

Of course you can, darling. Where is that Nash? I need him.

"Leave him alone."

Do you not understand how powerful he is? He can resist the strongest magic of this earth. Think what someone with both his power and mine could do. He can help break us out from Beneath and resist those who try to stop us— like the dragons. You saw what happened when that dragon you keep as a slut poured fire into Nash. Nothing. The dragons will bow before me now. And you.

Gods help me, she was right. Nash could resist my magic and Mick's, my strongest lightning and Mick's hottest fire. If Nash could be commanded by those Beneath, nothing could stop them.

Nash got into the SUV, slamming the door. He didn't look at me or acknowledge my presence, but I felt rage boiling from him. He started the truck and roared off onto the dark highway, leaving the other vehicles behind.

Halfway to Flat Mesa, where the road dipped to accommodate a winding wash, my mother said, *Now.*

Unable to stop her, I ripped the grill from between the seats and laced one arm around Nash's throat.

Nash was strong, fast, and well trained. He had me hauled over the seat with his elbow in my neck before I could think. I grabbed the steering wheel and yanked it, feeling the SUV careen off the road and out onto the rocks. We hit the bank of the dry wash and plunged straight into it.

In silence, Nash fought me off and reached for his radio. I fried it with one zap of lightning magic and, for good measure, fried his cell phone as well.

We make a good team.

"We don't make any team, bitch."

"What the hell are you talking about?" Nash was on me, his breath hot on my face. "And why are your eyes green?"

"Nash, just run," I urged.

He had my shoulders pressed to the seat. *Oh, nice. He's making it easy.*

Lightning flashed overhead, and the boom of thunder split my ears. The truck lit up brighter than day, showing Nash's eyes clear like diamonds.

My magic wouldn't work on him—that was a slight comfort. Nash, of course, could strangle the life out of me if he needed to. He'd be safe, and my mother would have to dissipate, since his null magic probably wouldn't let her possess him. She'd have to limp, somehow, to a crack in the earth to seep Beneath. I'd be dead, of course, but the world would be safe for another day.

I wasn't in the mood for self-sacrifice. I fought Nash as he pinned me.

With a sudden burst of strength I rolled Nash over on the seat, grunting with the effort of it. Then I was on top of *him*. He was a trained fighter and struggled hard, but he was no match for my doubled physical strength.

I broke his belt, ripped open his pants, and dragged them and his underwear down his thighs. Nash fought me like crazy. His cock sprang out, and I closed my hand around it, stroking until it hardened. Nash was gone on adrenaline, fear, and fury, but his body still responded to both my touch and the pheromones from my storm magic.

"Janet, damn you . . ." Nash jabbed his thumbs at my throat, trying to cut off my air, but I batted his hands aside.

"Don't *fight* me, you idiot—get away from me!" I shouted. Then my voice changed, and my mother said through my lips, "We'll make a fine baby together, and you'll be a consort in my kingdom. You'll have everything, even that Hispanic whore as your slave, if you want her."

"Jesus H. Fucking Christ, what is wrong with you?"

Nash was a fighter. He wouldn't go down easily, which I guess was the point. I laughed with my mother's voice and cried Janet's tears.

"Stop me," I whispered.

The door behind me was ripped from its hinges, and the storm came pouring in. Freezing hail pounded on my back, and a lightning bolt struck a tree not twenty feet away.

A rock-hard arm wrapped around my waist and ripped me from Nash. Nash sat up, pale in the dome light that somehow still worked. He was breathing fast, his penis deflating quickly against his abdomen.

Mick's strength squeezed the breath out of me as he turned me directly into the hail. "Let her go!"

"No, Dragon," my lips said. "She's my daughter. I love her, and you can't have her."

I realized that Mick had me positioned so that he could quickly snap my neck.

"Don't make me do it," he rasped. Tears streamed down his face and mingled with the rain. "Please, don't."

"Poor Dragon," my mother said through my mouth. "This is what you were sent to do, wasn't it? To kill her so I couldn't use her. But, foolish Dragon, you fell in love. And now you must make a sacrifice. You should have killed her all those years ago and been done with it."

Lightning strikes multiplied until the sky was almost constantly white. Mick's eyes had gone black, his dragon tattoos writhing like live things.

"Mick, I love you," I shouted. "If you have to, stop her."

"Oh, no you don't," my mouth said. I jerked my head up to gaze into the heart of the storm, and I called it to me.

The storm was huge. As it descended on me I sucked every bit of its essence into my body.

I'd never handled anything so gigantic before. I became living lightning. I had my mother's strength inside me, and even as I knew her strength would eventually kill me, as it had my biological mother and Harold Yazzie's lover and Sherry Beaumont, I reveled in every second of it.

Nash had sprung out of the truck, gun in hand. I didn't

bother to throw anything at him, not knowing how much he could suck down until it had an effect on him. Instead, I tried to destroy Mick.

Mick roared as the storm magic poured into him. He'd taken a lot from me before, but never in the heart of the storm, when I was at my strongest. He'd always drawn off the remainder of my magics, not the whole, living stream, and never with the impact of my mother's Beneath magic mixed with it.

Nash pointed the gun at my head, the flares of the electricity around me bouncing off him. "Let her go, Mick."

A bullet to my brain probably wouldn't stop me. I was swimming with so much magic that it would probably animate my body for as long as it took. *Nice try, Sheriff.*

Mick whipped me away from the gun. His body chilled as it began to swell and grow. Nash jumped back, and Mick spread enormous dragon wings and lifted himself—and me—off the ground.

My stomach dropped as we rose abruptly, straight into the apex of the storm.

Mick fought the wind. His dragon fire flamed out, clearing a path through the chunks of ice pouring from the clouds.

I kept drawing the lightning into me, sending it surging into his body. I don't know why my mother wanted to do that—if Mick dropped me, it could kill me.

More fire shot from Mick's mouth as he struggled to gain height. I didn't know where he'd try to take me, and I wondered whether it would be to whatever volcano had created him. Drown the magic from Beneath in the magic of the earth's bones—that was a good idea. However, that would mean flinging me into molten lava, which would be a pretty final solution.

My mother realized this too. Together we sucked lightning into my body, she laughing maniacally. Mick roared in pain and dipped toward the ground.

I felt a suction down there, a faint, swirling light that rose to meet the black clouds. A vortex, the one between the small hills, where I'd found the animal bones.

Open it, she whispered to me. *Then we'll be safe.*

I'm not letting you win.

We'll retreat there. Let the dragon go.

Oh, sure, you'd never lie to me.

You are my key. Open the vortex, Janet.

"Screw you," I screamed out loud.

Mick bellowed in reply, though I don't know if he heard or understood me. My mother threw all the swirling hail, wind, and lightning at Mick.

Open it, or I kill the dragon.

Damn it. I believed wholeheartedly that she'd kill him, but if I opened the vortex and let her fully manifest, he'd die anyway, and so would Maya and Fremont and Jamison and Naomi and the rest of the friends I'd made since arriving in Magellan. This was my place now, and I wanted to protect it.

I thought I now understood why, the night I'd stood near this vortex when we'd fought the skinwalkers, my mother hadn't simply possessed me, thrust me into the keyhole, and turned me. That night I hadn't had a storm. Now this intense storm and the Beneath magic made a perfect mixture—my mother drawing on the mystical energy of Beneath, me drawing on the wild magic of the earth. That was why she'd sent the Nightwalker to drag me to her on a stormy night, why she'd sent the skinwalker to waylay me during another storm.

It took both magics to open the vortex. My mother needed me, Janet, and my unique heritage. She couldn't open the vortex by herself, nor could I open it without her.

She needed a child with Beneath magic that she could tap, but also one with strong earth magic. In this moment, above and Beneath tied together and could rip a hole in the fabric of the universe.

The vortex flared, and a crack spread from it to follow the little arroyo that snaked from it. Twists of electricity swallowed Mick's body, and his dragon voice echoed across the plateau as he faltered. He plummeted downward.

Jump, my mother screamed in my head.

Right. We were at least a hundred feet up.

Mick rolled, one wing folding up under him. He was weakening, tail lashing as he fell down and down. His right wing swept out and uprooted a line of trees, branches and roots crashing into me as I huddled inside his dragon claw against his chest.

At the last minute, my mother took charge and pushed me free of Mick. We plummeted through the gnarled body of a juniper hugging the side of the arroyo, then fell to hard ground. I rolled as soon as I hit, doing everything to survive the fall.

Mick wouldn't survive it. His wings dragged uselessly against the ground, legs limp as he fell. A fork of lightning hit the crack in the ground and it widened with a groaning sound. Mick fell inside the widening wash and disappeared into the light.

"Mick!" I screamed. Torrents of rain beat on my face. My hair and clothes were plastered to my body and the wind threatened to lift me from my feet.

A big coyote bounded toward me, snarling. I took off running toward the hole that had swallowed up the man I loved. My mother had vanished, leaving me alone, weak, and wanting to vomit. I was screaming and crying, unaware of doing either.

Debris swirled around Coyote and he became a tall,

naked man. His snide, good-humored self was gone, and Coyote the warrior god stood in his place.

"No!" he shouted.

"Get out of my way!"

He lifted his hand. He'd kill me, and Mick would die, falling through the cracks to whatever lay Beneath. I knew my mother would tear him apart.

"Let him go, Janet," Coyote said sternly.

"Screw you!"

I gathered the storm magic and shot it at him. Coyote leapt out of the way faster than I could contact him, and the tree I'd fallen through exploded with light.

The crow burst from it in a flutter of black feathers, cawing in rage. The bird circled me once, fighting the wind.

As it flapped frantically for safety, a line of winged creatures appeared against the sky. The next lightning flash glinted off the scales of five huge dragons, wings beating as they flew toward me.

Dragons coming to do what Mick couldn't and what Coyote didn't want to. They were going to kill me. I saw Nash struggling toward me, gun in hand—to stop me or help me, I couldn't be sure.

One of the dragons swooped, and unbelievably, the crow flung herself between it and me. The dragon sent a fire stream straight at the crow, but Coyote threw a nimbus of blue light around the crow's body, deflecting the flame harmlessly into the night.

I used the distraction to sprint for the edge of the wash. Water spilled through it, the torrents of rain making the dry creeks flow. In the desert, water didn't sink into the hard ground—it ran along the path of least resistance to collect in rivulets and washes, canyons and rivers. Anything in its path, the water simply took with it.

Like me. My boot heel slipped on the muddy bank, and

I slid on my backside into the deep arroyo. I scrambled to my feet and ran through the water toward the glowing vortex.

Fire rained around me, and I heard Coyote shout, "Janet, no!"

I took a running leap and jumped feet first into the crack. I was falling, falling, I heard a resounding *snick*, and then all was silent.

Twenty-seven

Beneath was nothing like what I'd expected. I stood on damp loam in a wood of towering trees, humidity surrounding me like a heavy cloak. The patches of sky I could see were leaden gray, though the rain had abruptly ceased.

I couldn't identify the trees—they were huge, the foliage beginning many yards above my head, the leaves almost fernlike. Flowers as big as my hands brightened the branches with scarlet and primrose. The forest's floor was covered with decaying leaves and flower petals, but there was no scrub, no undergrowth. Likely enough light didn't filter down to sustain plant life on the sodden floor.

Primeval, that was a good adjective. If a dinosaur had come blundering through, I wouldn't have been surprised.

The trees stretched in all directions, no paths, no break, no sign of a clearing anywhere I looked. It made me claustrophobic—I'd grown up under soaring skies, with visibility for many miles, nothing blocking the view.

The air under the trees didn't move. It was heavy, wet, and warm. Suffocating.

I shivered, despite the heat, and put my hands into my pockets. I yanked them out again with a grimace, my jeans still soaked from the rainstorm.

The land of Beneath was dull, hot monotony, and all was silent. Very silent. No birds or insects. A faint breeze moved the trees far, far above me, but other than that, nothing.

Logic told me that this landscape was wrong—plants depended on insects and birds to spread pollen so they could propagate. Didn't they? But then, this was Beneath. The rules might be different.

Somewhere in the dense clouds high above was the slit that led to the world I had left. The *snick* I'd heard was likely the vortex snapping shut behind me. I had no clue whether I could reach it again, or whether I could open the vortex from this side or not.

I closed my eyes against a cold wash of panic. I couldn't lose my nerve, not now. I'd come down here to find Mick. I had the magic of Beneath in me as well as that of the earth above. I wouldn't be helpless here.

I pretended to believe that as I started walking. I had no clue where to go. All directions looked the same. I moved around clumps of dirt and fallen branches, discovering the hard way that there was, in fact, some undergrowth hidden by the dead foliage. Fungi spread everywhere, a white variety that seemed to glow. Trailing ivy also carpeted the ground, threatening to trip me at every step.

After fifteen minutes of walking, everything still looked the same. I didn't think I was going in circles; there was just so much of this forest flowing toward every point of the compass, on and on in endless tedium.

I knew from school science classes that the desert where I'd grown up had once been primeval forest, a very wet place until geologic events had drained lakes and changed the weather. Somehow, I preferred the new, drier look. I was panting in the heavy air, nauseated by the smell of rotting vegetation.

I'd lost track of how long I walked—more trees, more vines, more decaying leaves and flowers, more mushrooms—when I saw something out of place. Ahead of me, partially hidden by a tree trunk, a pale shape moved against the monotone of the woods.

I hurried toward it, not caring whether I'd found a demon or one of the nastier gods of Beneath. Even if it tried to kill me, at least I'd have someone to talk to.

I rounded the tree. A naked man sat with his back against the trunk, his legs folded to his chest, brawny arms around his knees. His head was tilted back against the tree, his eyes closed, black curly hair hanging in torrents. Something seemed wrong about him, and it struck me after a few heart-pounding moments that his arms were now bare of tattoos.

"Mick?"

He opened his eyes and looked at me. Dark brows drew together over very blue eyes as he regarded me without fear but without recognition either.

"Mick, it's Janet." My heart sank as I crouched next to him. "Are you all right?"

"I seem to be whole," he said, still not recognizing me. "But I don't know where I am."

His familiar voice made me want to fling my arms around him and bury my face in his shoulder. I'd grown used to Mick protecting me, even when I didn't like it. Even when he drove me insane, I'd felt cared for, safe. The way he looked at me now, I realized that, in this place, it was my job to protect *him*.

"This is Beneath," I said. "You fell down here during the storm." I started to touch him, then curled my fingers into my palm. "I'm so sorry. I didn't mean to hurt you. She made me."

"I don't remember."

"Do you remember me?" I asked.

Mick looked me up and down again. "I don't know." A faint smile touched his mouth. "Do I remember having sex with you? Or do I just want to remember that?"

I exhaled and let myself put my hand on his bare knee. "You do remember that. It was fantastic, every time."

"Good." He slanted me a smile through his hanging hair. "I'd like to remember more."

Even here, he could make my skin heat. "I'm not sure how to get us out of here, but I'll try. I have some magic tied to this place, but I have a feeling that you don't."

I ran my fingers down Mick's arms where his dragon tattoos used to be. His skin bore no sign he'd ever had them, the flesh smooth, whole, unmarked.

His eyes darkened. "You keep that up, and I'll be happy to create new memories with you right now."

I smiled, trying to bolster my spirits. "I'd rather do it back home, with you being *you* again. You're a creature of the earth; you don't belong here."

"I didn't think I did." Mick glanced at the surrounding trees. "I hope not. Gods, this place is boring."

I agreed. "No wonder the ones who got left Beneath are trying to get out."

We looked around some more, neither of us voicing the thought *How do* we *get out?* I had an idea, but I wasn't certain it would work. At least, I thought it might work on me, but Mick would be trapped if I left him behind.

He lied to you, a voice whispered in my brain. It wasn't my mother's voice—this time it was my own. *He hid the truth from you for years. What loyalty do you have to him?*

I willed the words to silence. I cared about Mick enough to not leave him here, no matter what was between us.

Mick tensed as he gazed into the distance. "There's something alive over there."

I followed his line of sight. I saw nothing at first, but after a few moments I spotted a shadow flitting from tree to tree, never stilling long enough to be identified.

Mick unfolded to his feet, the harmony of his raw-muscled body a joy to look at. He might have lost his dragonness, he might be confused and without his memories, but Mick was still a beautiful man. I'd have had to be dead not to notice him, and even then I might come back as a ghost just to watch him.

Mick reached for a fallen branch and tested its weight. Without having to tell me to stay behind him, he started softly toward the creature.

With no storm handy, I felt powerless, uncertain of what kind of magic I could wield in this place. Storms were of the earth, like Mick was—I knew in my gut I couldn't use that magic here. But I had the Beneath power in me as well, the power I'd used to open the vortex. What I didn't know was whether my Beneath magic was strong here, or whether I wouldn't have enough to crush a gnat.

The shadow resolved into a huge creature that bellowed at Mick and charged. Mick met it with his makeshift club, grunting as branch connected with flesh.

The thing reminded me of a skinwalker—tall and broad, hard-muscled and fast, giant hands with claws, yellow eyes. However, skinwalkers had hideous faces and equally hideous BO, and this one bore the face of an angel with no odor I could detect.

Mick fought hard, but he was limited to his human strength, his fire magic gone. I swore I heard Mick's rapid heartbeat thudding in my own ears, felt his anger and growing worry. I picked up a sturdy branch and sailed in to help him.

The creature lunged at Mick, picked him up by the throat, and squeezed. Mick thrashed, dropping his club to dig at the fingers cutting into his windpipe.

I screamed and beat on the thing with my branch, but I

might as well have hit an alligator with a twig. Mick's face turned purple, his eyes bulging as he fought to breathe.

"Leave him alone." I whacked the creature's back with my stick. "Drop him and die, asshole."

The monster let go of Mick. Mick fell to the ground and folded up, coughing.

The creature swung around, and I backed up a step. The thing was twice my size, and my only weapon was a dead branch.

Then, before my astonished eyes, the monster crumpled to the ground. He exhaled with a little sigh, his eyes fixed, and he lay still. Mick and I stared, dumbfounded, as the dead body dissipated into dust.

"What the hell?" I whispered.

"What did you do?" Mick raked his hair back from his face, his voice harsh with fear and anger.

"Nothing." I flung away the branch as though it burned me. "I didn't do anything."

"You said 'drop him and die,' and it dropped me and died."

"Did I?" I'd yelled words, not too worried about being coherent.

"Say something else."

"Like what?"

He pointed. "Tell that vine to move out of your way."

"You've got to be kidding me." I looked at the vine in question, a scraggly tangle on the forest floor. I felt like an idiot giving orders to a plant, but I said, "Move aside, you."

A gust of wind swirled around the vine, uprooted it, and tossed it away. I gaped, heart pounding.

"Looks like you have magic here," Mick said. "Amazing magic. If we get into an argument, please don't accuse me of having a small penis."

I couldn't laugh. "I don't know how I did that. I shouldn't have been able to."

"Maybe it's this place. It took all my powers but gave you more."

I reached for him, and my chest felt hollow as Mick flinched from me. "I'm scared," I said.

"I am too."

Mick was never afraid. He laughed at danger—literally; I'd seen him do it.

I folded my arms and didn't try to touch him again. I was afraid to say anything as well. What if my words accidentally magicked Mick somewhere or made his arms fall off or something?

By the look on Mick's face, similar thoughts were occurring to him. "Have you ever seen a being like that?" he asked me.

I shrugged. "He looked like a skinwalker, but a clean, pretty one."

"Skinwalkers should be foul, smell of death."

"In our world," I said. "But here? Maybe this is what they really look like, and what we see above are shadows of what they used to be. Coyote appears to us as a coyote and a man, but who knows what he looked like when he lived down here?"

"Coyote." Mick grasped the word. "I've heard of him. I know him. I remember what his magic feels like."

"Is that good?"

Mick's muscles rippled as he shrugged. "How can I know?"

I wanted to touch him. More than that, I wanted to hold him. I wanted to make love to him, right here in the mud, to feel his warmth around me, to hear him tell me how much he loved me.

"Mick, I wish—"

He clapped his hand over my mouth. "Don't. Don't wish, don't command, don't say anything until we figure out what kind of damage you can do."

Damage. He meant to him. Gods, he was afraid of me.

His eyes were pure blue, his hand firm across my lips. I
touched my tongue to his palm, liking the warm sensation
that started in my breasts and between my legs. His skin
prickled with goose bumps, as though need pulsed through
him too.

"Janet," he murmured. "I don't think . . ."

"I don't want to think at all." I rose on tiptoes and kissed
his lips.

Mick's arms came around me, the adrenaline rush of the
fight transferring to his kiss. He held me hard against him,
mouth opening mine, hand sliding to my breast. I curled
my fingers around his neck, trying to draw his warmth into
me. I needed him, wanted him, craved him.

"Mick, please, let's . . ."

Mick abruptly broke the kiss. I looked up at him, worried that I'd hurt him, but he wasn't looking at me.

He jerked his hands from me, and I spun around to face
whatever he'd seen behind me.

A woman stepped from the shadow of the trees, a woman
I'd never seen before. And yet I knew her.

She had blond hair, shimmering gold, even though little
sunlight penetrated the leafy canopy to touch anything. Her
hair tumbled all the way to her delicate, bare feet. She had
milk white skin—pasty white, in fact—eyes disproportion-
ately large for her face. I couldn't tell what color they were
at this distance. Her iridescent gown shimmered like her
hair. She was the shimmer queen.

I realized now why my mother liked to inhabit blond
women. Both Amy and Sherry Beaumont looked a little
like her, as had the woman I'd met at the diner. Same color-
ing, same slender build, same softness. She'd been trying
for a woman with looks as close to hers as possible.

As she neared me, I saw that her eyes were a dark, intense green like that of the leaves on the trees around us.

"Janet." Her voice was a whisper of silk, a strain of music too beautiful to be understood. "My daughter. At last, you have come to me."

She closed the final measure of space between us and brushed my face with her fingertips. Her touch nearly froze my blood. She was ice-cold, no warmth anywhere.

"I have so longed to touch you," she said. "How horrible it was that I could only connect to you through another's flesh."

I clenched my jaw to keep my teeth from chattering. "It's only through another's flesh that I was born at all."

"That is true. Think how heartbreaking it was for me to leave you behind, to not be able to hold you, comfort you, even touch you. My child, and I had to abandon you to others."

"You didn't abandon me." I was angry, very angry, but so cold I couldn't move. "You killed the woman who gave birth to me."

"The female vessel was weak. She was stronger than the others, able to carry you to term, but still too weak in the end."

"That 'vessel' was my mother," I snapped.

"No, child. She bore you, but I gave rise to you. She was a surrogate, nothing more."

"There were other surrogates. Amy. Sherry Beaumont. The woman who seduced Harold Yazzie. I'm sure the list goes on."

"But in all the centuries, there was only you." My mother brushed a light finger across my lips. "You with your powerful storm magic. You are very, very special, daughter."

If I didn't like her touching me, Mick certainly didn't. He was at my side, growling a warning, ready to do battle.

I think I realized in that moment how much I loved him. He was helpless here, and he knew it, and still he wanted to protect me.

"How sweet," my mother said to me. "Will you give him to me as a present?"

"Leave Mick alone."

"No, darling. I won't. This *thing* is nowhere near good enough for you." She gave Mick a look that was nearly identical to the one my grandmother had given him upon meeting him. I'd have found that comical if I hadn't been so terrified.

"You belong to me now, Janet," my mother said. "You will love *me*, not this monster."

"Mick has been far more loving to me than you ever were."

My mother looked hurt. "I didn't have a chance, darling. I can't exist above except through other shells—you know that. The dirty little town where your father raised you was too far away and too protected for me to come to you. Thankfully you escaped it in the end."

"I didn't escape." But hadn't I regarded leaving home as an escape? Fleeing the cage my aunts, cousins, and grandmother had placed around me?

"Your grandmother was a fool and kept you for herself," my mother said. "But now you are with me."

I took a step back. "If you wanted to be with me so much, why didn't you just take over my body the first time you met me? You jumped into me readily enough tonight."

"Because I didn't want to weaken you, love, and my power would have strained you. I wanted you to stay strong for me. Tonight, all I needed from you was for you to take me to the vortex and open it. I knew you'd dive down here after your dragon if I made him fall in. And you did."

"Fine. You've got me. Let Mick go."

"No, darling." My mother leaned toward me but didn't touch me again. "Kill him for me."

I ground my teeth, fighting fear. Not of her, but of the fact that I *could* kill Mick with a word, and she knew that. I felt Mick tense next to me, knowing it too. "I would never hurt him."

My mother gave me a pitying look. "Dear heart, I wasn't talking to you." She looked behind Mick and smiled a chilling smile.

Twenty-eight

"Janet," Mick said, very softly.

I swung around. A horde of skinwalkers—the Beneath version of them—had formed an arc behind us. They didn't carry weapons, but they didn't need to; they could rip Mick to pieces with their bare hands.

Leading them was a *thing*. I didn't know what it was supposed to be. It had the body of a man, one taller and bigger than Mick, but its head was a cross between that of a bull and a wolf. Long muzzle, pointed teeth, horns, round, blazing eyes.

"What the hell is *that*?" I managed.

"This is my consort," my mother said. "You will like him." She smiled at the monstrosity. "Kill him for me, love."

The minotaur-like thing charged, the skinwalkers right behind him. Mick balled his fists and faced the onslaught. I saw in Mick's face that he knew he was going to die, that he was fully prepared to die, but that he was happy he could go out fighting.

"Come on, let's tangle," he shouted at the monster. He laughed, his blue eyes flashing with the wickedness I loved. "This could be fun."

"No!" I screamed. "No, Mick. *Go!*"

I grabbed Mick around the waist and shoved him as I shouted. Mick's feet left the ground, and he gave me a startled, then a horrified, look. He reached for me, his mouth forming my name, and then he vanished. My hands closed on nothing, and Mick was gone.

I whirled, my grappling hands reaching for my mother. "Where is he? What did you do?"

Behind me the monster and the skinwalkers stopped their charge, their halt kicking mud that spattered the backs of my legs. My mother smiled and shook her head.

"I did nothing. You sent him away, dear. He is wherever you told him to go."

Icy panic hit me. Where the hell had I shoved him? Back to the desert of above? To the realms of the dragons? Or to some world worse than this one? I tried to picture the exact thought I'd had when I'd yelled the word, "Go!" but I had no idea.

"You're making me do this."

"No, child. You did it yourself. You have great power here. You will fit in nicely."

"No." I wanted to cry, but my eyes and throat were too dry. "I belong with my father, in the lands of the Diné."

"You have made yourself believe that. But what do you have there? A family who is deeply suspicious of you, an outside world that herded your people onto reservations as though they were cattle. You weren't human to them, just animals to be penned up and starved, shot if you put a foot wrong. They did it so they could take everything you had for themselves, no other reason. Why should you go back to a world like that? When you can stay here, and be strong, and thrive?"

"Here?" I looked at the enclosing woods, the heavy sky I could barely see, the skinwalkers with beautiful faces. I thought of the land around Many Farms, the stark beauty of its measureless vistas, the scorching blue sky that faded to crimson and gold at dusk. My recent ancestors had been penned up as my mother claimed, but Navajo had lived on that land for centuries, and it was in my bones.

I wanted to be back there so much I could taste it. I wanted to see my father walking in from the fields, his fists stuffed into his jacket pockets, his head bowed as he moved along, careful not to step on stray insects or lizards in his path. I wanted to see my grandmother chopping vegetables for the stew, frowning at me for some wrong or other she was certain I'd done. I missed them with an ache as big as a cavern.

"What is here that I could possibly want?" I asked my mother.

"This woods is not the only place. Take my hands."

I stared at her outstretched fingers in suspicion. "Why?"

"I will show you my true home. But it's a long journey."

I continued to look at her hands, beautifully shaped, so pale they might have been made of moonlight. Impatiently, she grabbed my much browner and mud-coated fingers, her touch ice-cold.

The woods spun around me, faster and faster until I snapped my eyes closed. Before I could decide to be sick, the world stopped, and I opened my eyes again.

The woods were gone. We stood in a garden perched on top of a rocky hill, with a green meadow studded with flowers flowing away from our feet. A fountain bubbled beside us, water falling over natural rock to splash in a wind-carved sandstone bowl. Bright fuchsia hung along the rocks beside honeysuckle and light blue flowers I didn't recognize. The air was deliciously cool and scented with sweetness.

"Is this real?" I asked. "Or illusion?"

"My, you are distrustful, Janet. Had I raised you, you would delight in this place and your powers. But you've been tainted by that awful woman you call your grandmother."

"She isn't awful." I'd grown up resenting Grandmother, but in retrospect I could see many reasons for the things my grandmother had done. She'd feared what I might become, feared *for* me and tried to protect me.

"She brainwashed you," my mother said. "Taught you to hate me."

"She didn't, actually." I sat on the lip of the fountain, mostly to see if it was real. I felt cold stone through my jeans and a spray of water on my skin. "She tried to teach me to fear and hate you, which of course made me romanticize you. My grandmother never met you, but she saw you in me and feared what might happen if I gave in to you." I nodded. "Rightly so."

"Ah, but when you join me, my love, you'll understand."

"And what did you mean when you said that *thing* was your consort?" I asked. "You don't have sex with it, do you?" I thought of the minotaur's snout with its jutting teeth and shuddered.

My mother's answering smile gave me the creeps. "He is most pleasing. He has many brothers, if you would like one for yourself."

"Ick. No. And I mean that with all the offense it implies."

"Yet you sleep with a dragon."

"Not while he's a dragon."

"You can have Mick back, you know. I will teach you how to call him to you, how to bind him and make him do whatever you wish. He will exist for you, for your pleasure, and do everything you command. You can't tell me you wouldn't like that."

Having Mick as my love slave? Of course I wouldn't mind that. But my mother didn't understand that I wouldn't want Mick coming to me because I forced him to, loathing me every time he touched me. But by the look on her face, the words "free will" weren't in my mother's vocabulary.

"And the others," she went on. "The human who absorbs magic—Nash—he will be a powerful ally, and he's lovely to sleep with. Such strength. Even Coyote could be useful. He chose to bind himself to the earth and abandon his Beneath magic, so he'll be helpless when we pull him down here. He will do anything we want." She wet her lips. "We could share him."

I wasn't so sure Coyote would be helpless—knowing Coyote, he'd hedge his bets to retain power wherever he went. But I didn't argue. I saw no point.

My mother touched my head, and my mind flooded with images I couldn't stop. Erotic images like those in my dreams: Mick and Nash touching and licking me; Coyote behind me with his hands cupping my naked breasts. All three men making love to me, taking my pleasure to heights it had never seen.

I jerked away. "Stop that."

"You see what it is you want, deep in your heart. You can make it reality."

I knew then that she'd never understand me. She confused sex with love and caring, physical pleasure with deep emotion. "I don't want to make that reality."

"You do, you know. You just don't want to admit it." My mother reached for me again, but this time she put her hands on my elbows and pulled me to my feet.

"I know this is difficult for you, dear," she said, sounding like a mother genuinely concerned for her child. "But you will understand in time. Here, in my realm, you are as powerful as you were meant to be. Together you and I can be more powerful still. You'll have the power of the gods, Janet. Nothing will be able to stop you."

I looked into her green eyes and saw pure ambition but also desperation and the need to be accepted.

The temptation to take what she offered—to embrace the magic I could have here, to not be shunned for what I was—was great.

Altruistic thoughts tumbled through my head as well, tempting me as much. If I agreed to join her, I might be powerful enough to stop her from breaking through the vortexes and wreaking havoc above. It would be worth the sacrifice of my earthbound life if I could keep her down here, to make sure she never hurt anyone again.

What did I have to lose above, anyway? Few friends, a family who didn't respect me, a dragon-man who'd admitted that his purpose in coming to me had been to kill me. I'd spent my life trying to please everyone, to prove to them that I was worth something. Even with my beloved photography, I only sold what other people were willing to buy, what made *them* happy, not me.

In this place, I would be accepted without question, the daughter of a goddess, able to command hordes of skinwalkers—hell, I could command the vines and the trees. Everything. I could do anything I wanted, have anything I liked.

All I had to do was stay here with her.

"If I go back above," I said slowly, "the magic I have here won't follow, will it?"

"Not in the same way as it is here. But you are a unique being, Janet, able to exist as you truly are both on earth and Beneath." She smiled. "But when we leave together, when we break free of my prison and my magic joins with yours, there will be no one to stop us. Nothing we can't do."

I stuck my thumbs in my belt loops, a teenage habit my grandmother had abhorred. "Yes, I could enjoy that heady power. How wonderful to be able to punish everyone who ever hurt me."

My mother's green eyes glowed. "Yes. Now you understand."

"But I think you don't understand me."

She looked puzzled. But I suddenly understood what Coyote had been trying to explain to me with his cryptic hints. I had not been able to choose the path that led me here—I hadn't asked to be born of a goddess and inherit Stormwalker powers through my father. I hadn't asked to be the strange by-product of a powerful bitch queen and a quiet human, hadn't asked for the amalgam of magic that tore me up inside.

Now my path forked, and Coyote's words from my dream came back to me: *Only you can choose which direction to take.*

I could remain with my mother and embrace my own goddess-like power, or I could return and be a slightly crazed Navajo Stormwalker, struggling to finish a hotel, pay my bills, make new friends. An all-powerful goddess from Beneath like my mother, or a creature of the earth like my grandmother, like my father, like Mick. My life, my path, my choice.

My mother watched me with narrowed eyes, as though she knew the thoughts that spun inside my brain. She leaned to me, her beauty dimming for a fleeting moment into something gray and hideous.

"My darling, if you reject me, if you leave me, I'll make certain your precious dragon is tortured for eternity and that your so-called father and grandmother die horrible deaths."

We were the same height and faced each other eye to

eye. Her beauty returned almost instantly, but I'd glimpsed the monster inside her.

"You don't know where I sent Mick," I said. "Maybe I do."

"You don't, my dear. You said so yourself."

I smiled, brazening it out. "You don't know much about kids, do you? Growing up is a constant struggle between adoring your parents and wanting to push them away. You want their approval and you want to be your own person at the same time. During this complicated process, a few lies get told."

Her brow puckered. "You are grown-up, Janet, in the manner of earth children. When I found you, you were an adult."

I contrived to look wise. "Sometimes, though, the growing up process stretches into the adult years, especially when you're as confused as I was. But then you get over it." I stepped closer to her and spoke in a hard voice. "Mother dearest, I gave up wanting to please you years ago."

She gave me a hurt look. "But I never gave up wanting to please you."

"You should," I said. "Because you never will."

"Why are you being so cruel to me?"

"To show you what it feels like. My magic is very strong here—you've let me discover that. Here I flick my fingers, say a word, and get what I want."

"Is there something wrong with that? Embrace it, my dear. Understand that you can have *anything* you've ever dreamed of."

"Except real love," I said. "Peace of mind. Knowing what's true."

"Don't be stupid. You can have all the love you want. No one will be able to help adoring you."

She meant sex again and pleasing born of fear. I thought

of my father, with his warm eyes, loving me hard at sacrifice to himself. I thought of my grandmother and her constant scolding but her understanding of why I needed to be fiercely protected. I thought of Mick, who'd defied his own kind to keep me alive. Life would have been so much easier for him if he'd simply killed me when he first met me. But he'd loved me and protected me instead.

"What you offer is not enough," I said softly.

Again her beauty flickered. "You are mad, Janet. It's perfectly adequate."

"Coyote told me I'd have to choose, so now I'm choosing. I will never forgive you for trying to kill my father and my grandmother. And Mick. I'll never forgive you for killing Sherry Beaumont and causing such grief. I won't forgive you for driving Amy McGuire half out of her mind and messing up the lives of her parents, Nash, and even a woman who hated her. I'll never forgive you for the sorrow you caused a Navajo man I'd never even met. I choose the earth above, and the earth magic that makes me insane and all the people who are pretty sure I'm crazy because of it. I choose that path, because I never, *ever* want to be like you."

My mother flinched during my speech, but when I finished, she smiled. "Too late, my darling. You are exactly like me."

"I know that if I let myself, I could be. But I don't have to be. And so I make the choice."

Emotion swam in her enormous eyes—surprise, hurt, anger. The anger rose and burned until her eyes were black with it.

"No, daughter. You had the *illusion* of choice, and you made the wrong one."

Wind rose as she spoke, chilled droplets from the fountain sweeping over me like a freezing curtain. The grasses, flowers, and little trees in the meadow bent as sudden black clouds blotted out the sky. Lightning forked across the valley, bringing with it the smell of fire.

"Above, you walk with the storms," my mother said. "But here in my realm, *I* command them."

Thunderheads welled up in the sky with purple black ferocity. Fingers of tornadoes reached from flat-bottomed clouds, dust and debris exploding where the funnels touched the earth.

I held up my hand to the storm. "Stop."

It ignored me.

I stared at the clouds in sheer, watery terror. Never since I'd been a child had I been afraid of a storm. I'd feared what I could do with its power, yes, but I never worried about what it would do to *me*.

Rocks exploded as lightning struck a boulder. Shards of rock rained on me, slicing into my skin. I knew with certainty that if the next bolt hit me, it would splinter me like glass.

Heart pounding, I pointed to the rock I'd been sitting on. "Grow."

The rock trembled for a few seconds before it burst upward. Pebbles shot out like bullets and slashed red across my mother's face.

So she could bleed, I thought abstractedly. I wondered if she could also die.

"Cease," my mother shouted at the rock. It went obediently still. "What do you hope to do, Janet?"

I didn't know. Confuse her, panic her, scare her? Distract her long enough for me to flee?

She gave me a pitying look and swept her arm toward the garden. The pretty fuchsia and honeysuckle burst out of their beds and shot toward me. I beat at them to no avail as they closed leafy fingers around my flesh. I tried to run, but trees' roots thrust from the ground and wrapped around my ankles. Lightning bolts struck with wretched speed. I felt hollow and helpless with no weapon, nothing to fight with.

I lunged at my mother. I couldn't fight the vines that cut my skin, and I couldn't fight the storm that whipped my hair and clothes, but maybe I could fight her. She still bled where the rocks had cut her.

Rain pounded in my face, and my fingers slipped as I grabbed for her throat. My mother's stare was disdainful, but finally I managed to fasten my hands around her neck, and I started to squeeze.

Her eyes widened. She grabbed my wrists in a crushing grip, her strength immense. I twisted away, letting her go, but I'd learned something. I could hurt her, possibly kill her. Goddess or no, down here her body obeyed the same laws of physiology that mine did.

My mother flicked her fingers and more vines spewed toward me. I dove to the ground and rolled away, but they rose around me, ready to pin me, to bury me alive.

My mouth was dry with terror as I fought. My mother might have bleated that she loved me and needed me, but once I proved I wouldn't capitulate, she had no more use for me. She'd kill me and find another woman above to serve as her vessel, trying again to make another Janet, this one more malleable. She'd been trying for centuries, and she'd keep on trying. My little rebellion would slow her only a little.

I had to get away, or I'd die here, painfully. She'd crush me into oblivion and make me scream all the way. She'd kill me and not care.

I kicked and twisted until I managed to get to my feet. I leapt to the top of a boulder, but the vines kept coming. Wind threatened to throw me to the ground again, and the rain beat on me with ferocity.

I jammed my hand into my pocket and dug out the broken piece of mirror I'd shoved into it before I'd run into the kitchen to stop Amy. The mirror's surface was dark, but when lightning lit it I saw that it didn't reflect me or this place. I saw desert, thin lightning flickers, a smaller storm. I was looking above, outside the vortex.

"Mick!" I screamed into it. "I need you."

I waited for several sickening heartbeats while another lightning strike sent me tumbling from the boulder. I landed on my butt, and the earth itself rose to wrap muddy fingers around me.

When the mirror lit with red-hot fire, I laughed with joy. I wrenched myself free of the mud fingers and clenched my hand around the mirror shard, welcoming the pain as it cut into my palm.

I lifted my bleeding fist and shouted, "Up!"

I started to rise. The wind buffeted me and the lightning slammed toward me, but I picked up speed and punched my way into the dense clouds. Below me, my mother stood like a white flame in the middle of the meadow, her eyes gleaming black, her red mouth open.

I couldn't fight her, couldn't control what she controlled, but I could command myself, and I could stop her. She lifted her arms, screaming something, and the storm dove at me.

"Up," I shouted again. I rocketed through the clouds, the magic mirror, made from sands of the earth above, instinctively returning home.

Twenty-nine

The magic mirror's strong pull nearly yanked my arm from its socket, but I didn't care. I flew upward at sickening speed, away from the landscape trying its best to kill me.

I wasn't certain of the physics of the barrier between one world and the next, but I shot above clouds of Beneath, and then everything went black as I flew into a void of freezing darkness.

Red fire broke the blackness with a suddenness that made me scream. I started to fall, to where I didn't know, until something grabbed me and jerked me upward again.

I kicked and fought, but whatever held me clamped like iron. I realized after a terrified instant that I was in the grasp of a dragon's talon. Remembering the winged formation that had filled the sky before I'd jumped into the vortex, I prayed to any god who would listen that the dragon was Mick.

Wind pounded at me, then hard rain. Lightning flared, trying again to wrap itself around me. Except this time, the lightning wasn't trying to kill me. It burned through me and made me sick, and my skin tingled like crazy. But the pain was familiar. I laughed out loud and raised my face to the storm.

"Mick!" I shouted. "Please tell me that's you."

The dragon screamed in response. I didn't speak dragon, but the sinful gleam in his eye as he twisted his head to look at me told me that my lover had come to my rescue. My heart wanted to break. Mick was all right.

He swooped, streaming at a dangerous speed toward the desert floor. I smelled dust and rain, the desert heat turning steamy, but it felt nothing like the cloying humidity of the forests Beneath.

The dragon set me on the ground. My knees buckled when I felt my feet on solid earth, but I forced myself to stand. This wasn't over. Light glowed from the arroyo I'd burst from, and I sensed the Beneath storm reaching up to this one.

Mick shot into the air again, the downdraft from his dragon wings like hot wind. A large coyote sprinted to my side, and under the next lightning flare, he rose to his man shape.

I shouted to him. "Help me close it!"

Coyote put his hands on his hips and regarded me with dark eyes that had seen so much. "You know that if you seal that, you can never go back."

"Fine by me."

"You sure, Janet? You're a goddess there. Here, you're just a Stormwalker. A good one, but nothing more. Weak flesh. Beneath, you can be all-powerful."

"Screw that. I like my weak flesh."

"Are you sure you won't regret it?"

"Are you going to help me or stand there and lecture me? Why would you want to keep it open, anyway?"

"I don't. I'm just seeing if I need to kill you."

"I'll kill *you* if you don't shut up and help me."

Coyote burst out laughing. "That's my girl."

A dark shape detached itself from the shadows beyond the wash, a drenched and dirty Nash who looked mad at me as usual. "What are you two doing, having a chat? Things are coming out of there."

White light burst through the crack, solidifying as it rose, resolving into a face of terrible beauty. My mother was emerging, along with a crawling mass of skinwalkers. She grew, rising into the night, becoming bigger by the second.

I reached for the lightning, and it came to my hands with pinpoint precision. I'd never been able to draw it so quickly, so elegantly. With control I'd never known I had, I directed the lightning at my mother and to the crack in the earth.

The white light around my mother shot toward me like a deadly arrow. Nash leapt at me, knocking me aside. The lightning dispersed, I fell heavily to the mud, and Nash took the full power of Beneath straight into his body.

Nash clenched his fists, throwing back his head, his jaw hard with agony. The magic poured into him, faster and faster. Nothing came out of his body; he absorbed every molecule, just as he had the little shards of the protection spell I'd tried on him, just as he had with Mick's fire.

Mick swooped above me, his wings outstretched like a glider. He dove for the wash's edge, his mouth opening wide.

The blast of dragon fire flowed through the wash like lava, melting everything in its path. My mother screamed, but she kept growing, reaching Beneath to enhance her power.

Mick's fire wasn't enough. I shook off Coyote and grabbed the storm again. The familiar bite of it filled my body; the power made me stretched and warm—and I knew I could control it. The two magics that had always warred inside me swirled together like yin and yang, and I suddenly knew exactly how to mesh them.

I stretched out my hands and lightning burst from them in a focused stream, meeting Mick's fire and joining it. We poured our magic into the crack, the melding of Mick's fire with my white lightning warming me like an embrace.

The earth shook, rocks shattered, and then the banks of the wash began to collapse in on themselves. My mother shrieked. As the vortex closed, its swirling energy started pulling her back inside, like a giant drain that had just been cleared.

The Beneath light still poured into Nash, his body deflecting it from Mick and me. Coyote, his animal's body surrounded by a blue glow, simply watched.

My mother's form started to crumple, breaking apart and falling into the crack in the earth like rubble from an avalanche. My mother reached for me, her face twisted in hatred, and then the white light plummeted back Beneath, taking my mother with it. The banks of the wash fell, the wash itself becoming a line of tumbled trees, mud, and boulders.

The suction of the vortex faded, and abruptly, as though someone had thrown a switch, the hum of it ceased. The white light winked out and Nash staggered back.

Hail poured down, lightning crackling along the ridgeline. I was shaking all over, my magics breaking down into disparate parts again, which meant my hangover rushed at me with the speed of a Mack truck. The shard of magic mirror fell from my grip and hit the gravel at my feet.

"Oh, sugar," I heard it say. "That was *something*."

Mick flew high, turned on one wing, and landed a little way from us. As soon as his dragon feet touched down, he morphed into the tall human I knew so well. I ran for him, which turned into stumbling and blundering, tripping on clumps of grass and thistles. The hail became rain, then slackened to a gentle shower. The lightning gave one last, determined strike before it rumbled away.

My body didn't calm. Electricity crawled through me, coupled with the Beneath power, again wanting to tear me apart. Gone was the easy, painless magic I'd wielded Beneath, even the controlled storm magic with which I'd sealed the vortex. Back was the horrific, bone-aching, head-pounding insanity that usually greeted me.

"Mick," I panted.

Mick caught me in arms that were once again covered with the black tattoos. I'd never been so happy to see body art in my life.

He kissed me. The kiss told me he loved me, no matter that I was an insane, out-of-control Stormwalker with mommy issues. However much he'd feared me Beneath, he'd protected me, had been ready to die for me. I rose into the kiss, wishing Coyote and Nash far away so I could make love to Mick right here in the rain.

Coyote came to us, human once more. He'd not helped us seal the vortex, but I could tell he was satisfied with what I'd done. If I'd failed, or tried to join my mother, I have no doubt he'd have killed me and killed me quickly. Gods didn't have the internal dilemmas of human beings.

"Heads up, kids," he said.

Then I remembered. The dragons.

They were there all right, hovering in formation over the dark desert, well away from the vortexes. They'd waited, not bothering to lend a hand, or a wing, to see whether I succeeded or failed.

"What the hell?" Nash demanded of Mick. He was drenched and splattered with mud, but other than that he looked pretty good for a man who'd just absorbed a ton of Beneath magic. He wasn't even breathing hard. "There are more of you?"

The dragons flew toward us, five of them, three black like Mick, two fiery red. I didn't have to guess at their intention. I was about to become dragon toast, a little pile of ash that someone could put in a museum case and label "Janet Begay."

Mick took about ten running steps, spread his arms, and launched himself into the sky. He turned to dragon as he rose and flew to meet the others. Dragon bellows shattered the air. They circled one another, growling and roaring, bodies moving in sinuous streaks. Tongues of flames burst into the darkness. I had the feeling that we were going to be hearing reports of unidentified flying objects from here to Gallup. That is, if we lived that long.

Mick came hurtling back at me, five dragons on his tail. Coyote grabbed Nash and yanked him out of the way, but I remained, transfixed, eyes wide.

I expected Mick to change when he landed, but instead he whipped his dragon body around me, enclosing me in a wall of black scales, his hide rising higher than my head. His scales were unexpectedly warm, smooth as silk, as the dragon held me in a protective embrace. A *tight*, protective embrace.

The five dragons attacked. Claws out, fire raining, they dove for me and Mick. Mick answered them with a roar and a shot of flame. The dragons broke apart. I couldn't see all of what they did, but I heard them surrounding us, Mick bellowing while they screeched back.

I expected the dragons to incinerate both me and Mick at any moment, but after a long time of dragons screaming at one another, the five backed away. I felt a rush of wind from their wings, and then their shrieks faded into the distance and were gone. A rumble of thunder sounded from far away, and moonlight broke through a tear in the clouds.

"Aw, ain't that sweet?" I heard Coyote say.

"Sweet?" I shouted from behind Mick's wall of scales. "I thought I was dead. I didn't hear you trying to talk them out of it."

"I didn't have to," Coyote called back. "He told them you were his mate."

"What?" I pushed at Mick, but it was like trying to move a mountain.

"Dragons don't mess with each other's mates," Coyote answered. "It's a law or something. Dragons take laws very seriously."

Nash would approve of them, then. I pushed at Mick again. "Mick, let me go. You're suffocating me."

Instantly Mick's dragon body flowed apart, and I drew a breath of relief. He lowered his head, tilting it so he could regard me with one unblinking black eye.

I put my hands on my hips. "Mate?"

Mick's dragon body shrank rapidly, Mick morphing until he became the human I knew so well. The dragon tattoos slithered into place around his arms, black eyes gleaming in the moonlight.

"Sorry, sweetheart." He didn't look one bit sorry. "It was the only way. The dragons will leave you alone now."

"What about you?" Coyote asked, his eyes shrewd. "Will they leave you alone?"

Mick gave Coyote an evasive look I didn't like. "Who the hell knows? But Janet is safe." He came to me again, his body slick with rain. "You all right, baby?"

"Squished, muddy, scared, hurting, and the storm magic is making me crazy. Otherwise, fine."

Mick slid his hands down my back. "Need me to draw it off?"

"Please." I needed him. Desperately.

He smiled, the same old Mick smile. Electricity crackled out of me and crawled across his body, huge doses of

storm power and Beneath power all mixed up. I'd handled
a lot tonight, more than I ever had before.

"No," I said, trying to break away. "It's too much. I'll
hurt you."

Mick kept his hands firmly on my hips. "Jones, come
here and help me."

"Help you what?" Nash asked, but Coyote laughed.

"Come on, Sheriff," Coyote said. "I'll show you."

Nash came to us uncertainly, but Coyote told him to
embrace me from behind. Nash slid his arms around my
waist, muttering something under his breath. I felt his hard
chest on my back, his thighs against mine, and his arousal,
though I knew he didn't want to be aroused, pressing my
buttocks.

Mick lowered his mouth to mine, his lips warm and
powerful.

Another pair of arms slid around my waist as Coyote
pressed against my right thigh. I remembered my erotic
dreams about the four of us together, and Coyote, who always seemed to know what I was thinking, laughed softly
in my ear.

I let my lightning flow into Mick through his mouth,
into Nash and Coyote through my body. Nash absorbed my
magic without a sound, as though he barely felt it, which
made me realize just how powerful he must be. He'd taken
the brunt of magic from Beneath and never said a word,
not to mention the storm magic I'd thrown at him when my
mother tried to make me rape him in the police SUV. All of
that, and he didn't even look tired.

I let go of those thoughts and concentrated on kissing
Mick. I laced my hands behind his neck, pulled him down
to me. I loved this man, this dragon, who raced to my rescue, who'd driven away the dragons and saved me one more
time.

Having the two other men surrounding me with their warmth was strange but not bad. I felt cozy between them, so safe. Had my dreams been a prophecy? Or wishful thinking?

Mick cupped my face and drew back a little. I moaned. "No, don't stop."

He grinned. "Sounds like you're feeling better."

"Aw, too bad." Coyote's teeth grazed my earlobe, his hot breath tickling.

"Back off," Mick growled. "She's mine."

"Yeah, so you said to the dragons."

Nash removed his hold and stepped away abruptly. Coyote chuckled and gave my behind a pat. "You're a babe, Janet."

I started to wind my arms around Mick's neck again, ready for him to take me home. He'd carry me back to the hotel, undress me, and wash me, then we'd fall together onto the bed.

Instead, someone wrenched first my right wrist, then my left, behind me, and I felt the unmistakable chill of handcuffs against my flesh. "Oh, you've got to be kidding me."

"I'll warn you again, Begay. You have the right to remain silent . . ."

"Nash," I said. "I really, really hate you."

Thirty

I woke the next morning, rolled over, fell out of bed, and landed on a hard, cement floor.

My eyes popped open. Instead of my comfortable little bedroom at my hotel, I found a jail cell, one I recognized. I closed my eyes again and groaned. Damn Nash.

Lopez came to get me not long later, after I'd tried to scrub my face in the paltry stream of water and use the rather disgusting toilet. He gave me coffee, which I tried not to heave up again, and took me to an interview room.

Not long later, Nash Jones faced me across a cold table, a folder open in front of him. Once again, he was clean, shaved, and neatly dressed, while I looked and felt like hell.

"Haven't we done this before?" I asked him.

"This won't take long. I need a statement from you."

"I state that I hate all sheriffs named Nash Jones."

"Very funny." Nash touched the paper in the folder with

a clean finger. He must scrub under his fingernails every hour, they looked so pristine. "I witnessed you committing assault with a deadly weapon against Amy McGuire. Amy will live, but that doesn't exonerate you."

Amy was in the hospital, Lopez had told me when he'd brought me coffee. She was weak but expected to make a full recovery. Her parents were with her, confused by what I'd done, but glad that their daughter would be all right.

"Amy went after Maya with a knife, if you remember," I said. "She would have killed Maya, and Amy might have died too. My mother was controlling her; she could have made Amy turn the knife on herself. I'm sorry Amy got hurt, but I really had no choice."

Nash glanced at the report again, and when he looked up, his expression had changed to that of a man facing something new and uncomfortable. "Three weeks ago, I would have said you were talking pure bullshit."

"And now?"

"Now I don't know what to think."

We sat in silence for a few moments, then I asked in a quiet voice, "Has Amy asked to see you?"

Nash sighed and raked a hand through his hair. "No. McGuire says she wants to go back to the convent."

"I'm sorry." I was sorry; Nash could be a pain in the ass, but he hadn't deserved my mother pretty much wrecking his life.

"So that's that," he said. He looked resigned, but I could see in his eyes what this last year had cost him.

"What about Maya?" I asked. "You and Maya, I mean."

His cold look returned. "None of your business." Personal revelations over. Nash shut the folder with his usual brusqueness. "I'm charging you with illegally discharging a firearm and with destruction to a police vehicle. I'm letting the bigger charge of assault go because Amy did attack

Maya, and you were trying to stop her. I've also decided to overlook your assault on me, because Mick has convinced me you were not in control of your actions at the time."

A nice way of saying, *possessed by a crazy goddess who tried to have sex with the sheriff so she could make a messed-up demon child with him.* "Believe me, I never would have touched you if I could have helped it," I said.

"I'll be watching to make sure you turn up on your court date. If the judge is reasonable, you'll probably only get community service."

I brought my fists together and leaned my head on them. "You're such a softie, Jones."

"I witnessed the shooting; I can't let you off completely. I'm not the kind of sheriff who gives favoritism to my friends."

I raised my head, regarded him with aching eyes. "Are we friends? Aw, that's sweet."

Nash rose, picking up his folder. "Get out of here, Janet. Go home, clean up, and show up on your court date."

"You're all heart, Sheriff."

He said nothing, only walked out the door, taking his folder. He left the door open, and I lost no time obeying his order to get the hell out of there.

A month or so after my overnight at the jail, the hotel was almost finished, the electricity and plumbing working, the new bar varnished and ready. The magic mirror was sulking a little because I hadn't yet found anyone to fix it, but I cut it some slack, because the little shard of silicon had saved my life.

Jamison brought me his gift of sculpture for the lobby, a coyote of beautiful black stone he set on a pillar at the bottom of the stairs. Above it I hung a framed photo I'd shot of the moonrise my father and I liked to watch over the mountain near Many Farms. I'd captured the blue twilight, the red of the cliffs, and the disk of moon sailing into place.

"There's one mystery you haven't solved," Jamison said to me as he stood back and admired the setting.

"What mystery is that?"

Maya was helping Fremont hang more of my photos, and I sensed them listening. Technically their jobs with me were finished, but they'd taken to dropping by to see how things were going. They'd chat, help out, have a beer with me. By tacit agreement, Maya and I steered clear of tequila.

"How Sherry Beaumont came to be stashed in your basement," Jamison said.

Mick looked up from behind the lobby counter, his blue eyes meeting mine. Mick had been sticking around lately, no unexplained trips. The dragons hadn't swooped down to fry him, or me either, but I remembered the look he'd given Coyote when he'd said he wasn't sure what the dragons would do to him. I still didn't like that.

"Fremont," I said. "It was you, wasn't it?"

Fremont dropped his hammer, the clatter echoing through the lobby. "What are you talking about?"

"You found Sherry dead in the desert and worried that people would think you killed her," I said. "So you brought her into a building you thought would never be used again. She could be hidden behind the basement wall until she crumbled to dust."

Fremont's mouth hung open. Mick leaned on his elbows, listening. A casual observer might think him relaxed, but I knew he could vault over the counter and grab Fremont the instant he thought he needed to.

"I told you," Fremont stammered. "I thought Sherry had gone home. I never saw her again."

"I bet it scared you, stumbling across her body while you went for your usual walk."

"I swear to you, Janet, I never touched her. I never knew she was dead."

"Would you swear that to Chief McGuire? Or Sheriff Jones?"

"Dios mío." Maya didn't drop her hammer; she threw it. It skittered across the floor until it hit the reception counter. "Leave Fremont alone. He doesn't know anything about it. *I* put Sherry Beaumont in the basement."

"I know," I said softly.

"Then why the hell were you going on at Fremont about it? Just when I think maybe you aren't a bitch—"

"To get you to admit it," I interrupted. "You found her, and you thought Nash killed her."

"Yes." Maya gave me a look of defiance. "I thought he'd had one of his episodes. Maybe he thought she was Amy and killed her for running away from him. Or maybe he just didn't know what he was doing. He wouldn't have killed her on purpose."

Mick cut in. "But she had no signs of violence on her. Why did you think she'd been killed?"

"How could I know? I'm not police or a doctor. Even if there was no obvious sign, if her body was found, Nash would be suspected. Look how fast everyone suspected him when Amy disappeared. He'd be arrested and sent to prison—or to a psychiatric ward. I'd never see him again." Maya's voice was thick with tears.

"And here was my hotel, empty and derelict," I finished. "No wonder you hated me when I moved in."

"I hated you for dredging up things that should have been left alone," Maya said. "But I had to come work for you. I had to be the one to find her. That way, if my fingerprints were still on the panels, no one would think it strange, because I had to pull them off to get to the wiring." She folded her arms. "What will you do now, run to Nash and tell him?"

"No, I think you should tell him yourself."

Maya scowled, but I could tell that she realized she'd have to. "Have I mentioned lately how much I hate you?"

"Only every couple of days. Maybe we'll get community service together. Nothing so bonding as working side by side in a soup kitchen."

"Oh, please."

I grinned at her. Maya didn't smile back, but our friendship had moved forward in these last few weeks. By inches, maybe, but the very best friendships take time.

I did get sentenced to community service, and so did Maya. As Jones predicted, the judge decided that I'd acted because I'd feared for the lives of my friends.

Amy wasn't charged at all, because I convinced Nash that what Amy had done that night wasn't her fault. Besides, the McGuires didn't need any more grief. Nash agreed to keep Amy's part in all this quiet, and she went back to Tucson when she recovered. Even Maya didn't argue about that.

The judge was a little more severe on Maya, because she'd covered up a death and caused trauma to Sherry Beaumont's family. I thought maybe John Beaumont would sue her, but Fremont had filed a complaint against him for threatening us with a gun, and the man was persuaded to go home and be quiet.

I never had learned the identity of the crow that still hung around my parking lot. She showed up with a hunk of tail feathers missing after the big battle with my mother but otherwise looked none the worse for wear.

I had grave suspicions, though, and walked up to her one day as she sat in the twisted juniper tree. "Tell Dad I love him," I said. "I appreciate you looking out for me, but he needs taking care of more than I do."

The crow bent her head and took on the annoyed expression my grandmother reserved especially for me. I stared right back without blinking. Giving me another look of annoyance, she launched into the sky and floated away north.

I watched her go, wondering if she'd return. But she'd be home in Many Farms anytime I wanted to talk to her. I had the feeling the relationship between myself and my grandmother was going to become complex, though perhaps not in a bad way.

Maya and I did work in a soup kitchen together, and we got the joy of cleaning the entire shelter together too. But every night, I got to go home to Mick.

On a moonlit night in early July, I lay in his arms, reveling in the beauty and the silence. The hotel would open the next morning, and the silence would be gone.

Mick kissed my neck, sensing I was awake. "Can't sleep?"

"Thinking of the future."

"I'm thinking five minutes into the future." He grinned. "Wondering whether we need to reinforce those Tantric spells we did a while ago."

I smiled, releasing my thoughts. "That might not be a bad idea." I didn't move to put it into practice. Not yet. "We haven't talked about this mate thing. You've been avoiding the subject."

Mick kissed the tip of my nose. "I claimed you as mate in the dragon way. It doesn't mean anything in human terms, but to dragons, the bond is sacrosanct. It means they'll leave you alone."

"But you said you didn't know what they'd do to you."

"They're angry at me, true." Mick brushed my hair back from my face with a soft touch. "They won't let it go. I know that."

I felt chilled and moved closer to him. "It would be nice if they realized we were on the same side. I could use their help in case my mother finds another way out. She isn't dead, just sealed in."

"I know. And I know I'll have to face the dragons sooner or later. But not right now."

"No," I agreed. I ran my hands down his arms, tracing the dragon tattoos. "Not just now."

"Right now, we need to work on those spells." Mick smiled down at me, his black curls straggling across his face. "Can't let the hotel go unprotected if it's going to open tomorrow, can we?"

"No. Definitely not."

"Now, how did that go?" Mick nuzzled me. "Mmm, it's all coming back to me."

I wrapped my arms around him and pulled him down to me. There were things we needed to talk about, things we needed to take care of, but for now, I let it all go. I opened myself to him and let Mick make love to me in his usual wicked ways.

Far out over the empty desert, the wild, laughing yips of a coyote drifted on the night.

Turn the page for
a special preview of the next book
by Allyson James

Firewalker

Coming November 2010
from Berkley Sensation!

One

I knew she was a Changer the minute she walked into my little hotel. *Wolf*, I thought from her gray white eyes, but her human features were Native American. Her dark skin and black hair made her incongruous eyes all the more terrifying. So did the fact that she was shifting even as she raced across the lobby, grabbed me by the shirt front, and slammed me against the polished reception counter.

I looked up into the face of a nightmare. Half-changed, her nose and mouth elongated into that of a wolf's, fangs coated with saliva jutting from bloodred gums.

I had no defenses. There wasn't a cloud in the sky, no storm to channel to fight her. The wards in my walls functioned to keep evil beings like skinwalkers and Nightwalkers from entering the hotel, but Changers weren't inherently evil, just arrogant. Except that when provoked, they tended to attack first, ask questions of the shredded corpse later.

I brought up my fist to slam her jaw, but she shook off

the punch and hung on to me. I couldn't scream for Mick, because Mick had vanished into the night three weeks ago, and even the magic mirror didn't know where he was.

There was no one was in the hotel but myself and my new manager, Cassandra, in her neat turquoise business suit, her blond hair in a sleek bun. The tourists were out or not yet checked in, the saloon closed. It was just us girls: a crazed Changer, a powerless Stormwalker, and a witch who stared across the reception desk in shock.

"Janet Begay," the wolf-woman said, her voice clotted with the change.

"Who wants to know?" I tried to kick her off, but she held on to me, claws poised to tear out my throat.

On the other side of the desk Cassandra crossed her arms, placed her palms on her shoulders, and started to chant. An inky cloud snaked out of her mouth, shot across the counter, and wrapped around the Changer. The Changer snarled. She shoved away from me and leapt over the counter at Cassandra.

Cassandra went down with the wolf-woman on top of her, the two grappling in a tangle of raw silk and black leather. I charged behind the counter and grabbed the Changer by the hair, her sleek black braid giving me something to grip. I pulled, but she was damn strong. She had Cassandra's head in her hands, ready to beat her skull on the Saltillo tile.

I grabbed a talisman from my pocket, clenched it in my hand, and screamed, "Stop!"

The Changer halted in midslam. Cassandra's head fell from her slack grip and bumped to the floor.

I waved the talisman—a bundle of rosemary bound with wire and onyx—in the Changer's face and said in a hard voice, "Obey."

The Changer straightened up, fangs and claws receding,

her face becoming human again. Her eyes remained gray, the fury in them electric.

Cassandra rose beside her in the same rigid compulsion and fixed me with a frustrated stare.

Oops. But I couldn't release Cassandra without also releasing the Changer. Mick and I had made this spell for emergencies, such as a horde of skinwalkers attacking. It was a blanket spell that wouldn't stop the attackers entirely but might at least slow them down until help arrived.

"In there," I said, panting, pointing at my little office behind reception. "Go in. Sit down."

The Changer marched inside, still growling softly. Cassandra followed her like a robot.

The Changer and Cassandra sat next to each other on my new sofa, both women radiating fury. They looked odd together, the sophisticated hotel manager, only a little disheveled in spite of the fight, and the Changer in black leather pants and jacket. Both struggled to break the spell, bodies swaying a little as they willed their muscles to obey. But the talisman held both dragon magic and Stormwalker magic, a potent combination, so they'd have to put up with it.

"Who are you?" I asked the Changer.

"Pamela Grant."

"Cassandra Bryson."

"What are you doing here?"

Cassandra started telling me about whatever job she'd been doing before the Changer attacked, but Pamela said, "I was sent."

"Who sent you? To do what?"

They both started talking at once. I tuned out Cassandra and focused on Pamela. "I have a message for you, Stormwalker."

"Is that all? Then why did you attack me?"

While Cassandra protested that she had no intention of

attacking me, Pamela said, "I had to, to pass on the message. Then this Wiccan bitch tried to paralyze me."

"What the hell is this message? You couldn't just tell me?"

For answer, Pamela pulled out a short-bladed knife. My eyes widened, and I shook the talisman. "Stop! Obey!"

Cassandra went rigid. Pamela came at me, her eyes fixed, as though she listened to a voice more distant than mine. I realized as she jumped me that she was under another compulsion spell, one strong enough to cancel out mine. That couldn't be good.

I fought. Cassandra remained seated, eyes fixed in agony. Pamela pinned me to the desk with her strong body and extended my left arm across the top of it.

"Cassandra, get her off me!" I shouted.

Cassandra sprang to her feet but fell back as though an invisible hand had shoved her. At the same time I smelled a bit of sulfur, hot wind, fire—the scents of dragon magic.

I stared at Pamela in shock as she nicked my palm with her knife. She flipped my hand over and squeezed a puddle of my blood onto a pristine piece of Crossroads Hotel notepaper. Dipping my forefinger in the blood, she forced me to write the words, *Help me.*

As soon as we'd formed the last "e" in "me," Pamela went limp, and her eyes rolled back in her head. I lowered her slumped body to the floor, my palm stinging where she'd cut it. As the compulsion spell released her, the Changer woman drew a peaceful breath.

I straightened up. My veins burned like fire, and my temples started pounding as the compulsion spell latched onto me. I understood now why Pamela hadn't simply relayed the message verbally or at least reached for something as conventional as a pen. She'd needed to transfer the spell through my blood.

Help me. The words screamed at me from the paper

and brought my own fears boiling to the surface. I'd been worried sick about Mick, even though I'd told myself he'd simply gone off to do whatever dragon thing he needed to do. Mick came and went as he pleased—he always had—although lately he'd been nice about telling me where he was going.

Pamela's message meant that Mick was in trouble. Trapped. Ill. Maybe dying. If Mick was begging for *my* help, he was in deep shit, indeed.

My head turned of its own accord, and my gaze moved out the window to the west, where the distant mound of the San Francisco peaks, the traditional boundary of the Navajo lands, lay in misty silhouette.

The spell made me want to race out of the hotel, leap on my Harley, and ride off toward the mountains, now, now, *now*. But Mick would want me to be smart. I needed supplies, I needed to plan, and I'd need help. The fact that the spell let me calm myself and think this through meant that I was right.

I forced my gaze back to Cassandra, who was still sitting stiffly on the sofa. I lifted the talisman, broke it, and said, "Be free."

Cassandra leapt to her feet, face dark with rage, and kicked the inert Changer in the buttocks with her Blahnik heel. "That's for calling me a bitch."

Pamela opened her eyes. The white in them had faded to human brown, and though she retained the arrogant scorn of the Changer, she no longer looked terrifying.

She pushed herself into a sitting position and smoothed back hair that had fallen from her braid. "Hey, doesn't mean I wouldn't want to sleep with you."

Cassandra flushed and folded her arms, but she didn't look as offended as she could have.

"She was under a spell," I said tightly. "And now it's gone. Right?"

The Changer woman rubbed the back of her neck. "Finally. Your boyfriend is damn strong."

"Can you give me more specific directions than 'head west'?"

Pamela shook her head. "I was on the northwest side of Death Valley when your dragon man's spell grabbed me. But there must be a memory cloud spell on the place, because I don't remember exactly where. I was doing some hunting, minding my own business, and the next thing I know, I'm digging my way through a tunnel and talking to a dragon. He couldn't talk back; he just invaded me with that damned spell. Bastard."

"When was this?" I asked.

"Middle of last night. Then I rode straight here."

"Mick was alone? No other dragons around?"

"One was enough. I'd never seen a dragon before, never believed they existed." Her eyes flickered to gray and back to brown again. "Imagine my surprise."

That was Changer for "It scared the shit out of me." Changers didn't like to admit fear. Fear meant weakness, submission, and they took dominance-submission roles very seriously.

Pamela pulled herself to her feet with lithe grace. She was tall for a Native American, but most Changers were tall. She towered a good foot over me. "Compulsion spells make me hungry. Is there anything to eat in this gods-forsaken town?"

"The saloon's closed until five," I said while I stared again at the clear blue of the western sky. "But there's a diner in Magellan. Two miles south."

"It'll have to do. Come with me, Wiccan?"

Cassandra gave her a withering glance. "In your dreams, wolf-girl."

Pamela gave her a half smile, shrugged, and sauntered out of the office. Cassandra followed close behind, her spiked heels on the lobby tiles a staccato contrast to the thud of Pamela's motorcycle boots. Through the window, I watched the Changer woman walk out of the hotel, mount her bike, and ride off toward Magellan.

Once she was gone, Cassandra returned to my office and shut the door. She looked none the worse for wear for the fight, except for a faint bruise on her lower lip and one strand of fair hair fallen from her bun.

"What are you going to do, Janet?" she asked. "You can't charge off looking for Mick on the word of a Changer."

"It's not just her word." I pressed my fingers to my temples where the spell throbbed mercilessly. "I have to go. I have no choice. Mick must be desperate, or he wouldn't have sent her."

"Don't go alone."

Cassandra's eyes were light blue, beautiful in her pale face. She was from Los Angeles, where she'd held a prominent position in a luxury hotel chain. Why she'd wanted to move out to the middle of nowhere to help run my hotel I had no idea, but I never asked. She was good with the tourists, knew the hotel business, and she put up with my magic mirror. I didn't want to lose her by asking awkward questions.

"I won't be going alone," I said. "Can you keep things together here?"

"Of course."

Of course she would. Cassandra ran this place better than I ever could.

"Keep an eye on the Changer," I said.

Cassandra gave me an odd smile. "Oh, I will." She turned and walked out of the office, smoothing her hair as she went.

I flopped into the chair behind my desk and put my head in my hands. I ached all over, would ache until the spell took me to Mick.

I glanced at the framed photo of my father that rested on the desk, a slim Navajo in a formal velvet shirt, his hair neatly braided. I'd taken the picture on my last visit to Many Farms, and he'd insisting on dressing up for it. My father didn't believe in candid shots. His wise eyes held no advice, only quiet confidence that I'd know what to do.

I did know what to do. Or rather, whom to turn to. I hadn't seen Coyote, who would have been the most help, in a long time, not even in my dreams, and I had no idea how to summon him. Jamison Kee, a mountain lion Changer, was the man in Magellan I trusted the most, but he had a wife and stepdaughter to take care of, and I couldn't bring myself to put him in danger.

That left the one man I *didn't* trust, but he was powerful as all get-out. I didn't understand his power, and neither did Mick, which was saying something. If I could convince him to help, I knew I'd have a potent ally.

I pulled the phone toward me and punched in the number of the sheriff's office in Flat Mesa. The deputy at the desk put me straight through, surprisingly. I'd been all set to sweet-talk Deputy Lopez, but he said, "Sure thing, Janet." The phone made a couple of clicks, and then the sheriff's voice sounded in my ear.

"Jones," he said. Dark, biting, laconic.

"Hey, Nash. It's Janet."

There was a long silence.

"Fuck," Nash Jones said clearly, and he hung up on me.

Penguin Group (USA) Online

What will you be reading tomorrow?

Patricia Cornwell, Nora Roberts, Catherine Coulter,
Ken Follett, John Sandford, Clive Cussler,
Tom Clancy, Laurell K. Hamilton, Charlaine Harris,
J. R. Ward, W.E.B. Griffin, William Gibson,
Robin Cook, Brian Jacques, Stephen King,
Dean Koontz, Eric Jerome Dickey, Terry McMillan,
Sue Monk Kidd, Amy Tan, Jayne Ann Krentz,
Daniel Silva, Kate Jacobs...

You'll find them all at
penguin.com

*Read excerpts and newsletters,
find tour schedules and reading group guides,
and enter contests.*

Subscribe to Penguin Group (USA) newsletters
and get an exclusive inside look
at exciting new titles and the authors you love
long before everyone else does.

PENGUIN GROUP (USA)
penguin.com